JULIEN PULLED DULCIE INTO HIS ARMS.

It seemed the most natural thing, in all his black and crazy world, to kiss her when she tipped her face toward him. A soft kiss, just the one, given with only the intention of bringing comfort.

Her lips lingered against his as he pulled away. Hard, to pull away. Every man should know so sweet a kiss, just once in his life. As close to the light as he'd ever get, kissing this woman.

"Rest, *chère*," he whispered, his mouth against the corner of her lips. Her skin was soft, and tasted like salt from her tears. "It's been a long day, no?"

"Stay with me."

He didn't hesitate. "I'm not goin' anywhere."

"Hold me."

"I'm here. Close your eyes. I'm here."

And maybe when he was gone from her life, she wouldn't have to cry anymore.

Her arms tightened around him, as if she sensed his thought, and Julien eased back against the pillows, Dulcie in his arms. For now, at least, he wasn't going anywhere at all.

MICHELLE JEROTT

absolute trouble

AVON BOOKS ◆ NEW YORK

This is a work of fiction. Names, characters, places, and incidents either are the product of the author's imagination or are used fictitiously. Any resemblance to actual events, locales, organizations, or persons, living or dead, is entirely coincidental and beyond the intent of either the author or the publisher.

AVON BOOKS, INC.
1350 Avenue of the Americas
New York, New York 10019

Copyright © 1998 by Michele Albert
Inside cover author photo by Edwin E. Proctor
Published by arrangement with the author
Visit our website at **http://www.AvonBooks.com**
Library of Congress Catalog Card Number: 98-92455
ISBN: 0-380-80102-7

First Avon Books Printing: September 1998

AVON TRADEMARK REG. U.S. PAT. OFF. AND IN OTHER COUNTRIES, MARCA REGISTRADA, HECHO EN U.S.A.

Printed in the U.S.A.

WCD   10 9 8 7 6 5 4 3 2 1

Acknowledgments

First, much gratitude to my editor, Micki Nuding, for believing in this book enough to take a chance on an unknown author. But this book couldn't have been written to begin with if not for the support I received from my family and friends. So, to all my cyber buddies—Judy Cuevas, Kelly Kilmartin, Denise Domning, Heidi Charters, and Jacque Sanders—thanks for your years of encouragement and friendship. I am especially grateful to Heidi for answering all my questions on New Orleans. Hugs and kisses to my family and my guy, Bob, for tolerating my erratic schedules and requests for emergency baby-sitting. Last, but hardly least, thanks to my son, Jerott, for putting up with a mother who was distracted and forgetful from time to time. This one's for you, Spud—we're going to Disneyland!

Chapter 1

"THE RED DRAGON is going down, Dulcie. He blew away Juan Hernandez in the Cracker tonight and this time we got us an eye-witness who'll put the Dragon away for good."

Dulcinea Quinn ignored the cool October rain beating against her. She even ignored the threatening sparks of lightning in the black sky as she stood face-to-face with Detective Bobby Halloran, her friend and onetime partner, on the pitching deck of her houseboat.

Elation rushed through her, quickening her heartbeat. "Are you sure?"

"I'm sure Hernandez won't be picking himself off the barroom floor where I left him with the medical examiner's team," Bobby said, and Dulcie heard the controlled excitement in his voice. "And I'm damn sure about my witness. He's standing right over there."

She glanced over her shoulder as the waves of

1

Lake Pontchartrain rolled the deck beneath her feet. Ropes creaked in protest as the boat strained away from the pier. Two cops, barely visible in the bleary light from her cabin, huddled on the pier by the back of the boat. A tall man in a raincoat stood apart from them.

With dawning suspicion, Dulcie looked back at Bobby. "What do you want from me?"

"I need your help. The Dragon's gonna come after that prize witness of mine, and I need him to stay with you until I can get him to a safe place."

Ten minutes ago, her only objective was to somehow squeeze forty-eight hours into each of the next few days. Now Bobby wanted her to stash away a murder witness on her boat. So much for forgetting the past and moving forward with her new life.

"You couldn't have picked a worse time for this, Bobby. And when are you going to get it through that thick skull of yours that I'm not a cop anymore?"

"You want the Red Dragon as bad as I do, Dulcie."

She met Bobby's intense, knowing gaze.

Jacob Mitsumi, the Red Dragon—nicknamed for the fire-red dragon tattooed down his back. She'd encountered the vicious drug dealer only once, but saw his violent legacy every day on the streets of New Orleans and in the newspaper headlines.

"Don't tell me you've forgotten what Mitsumi's men did to you," Bobby prodded.

Dulcie glared at him. "No more than you've forgotten."

He didn't look away. "Can my witness stay here or not?"

Rain continued to run in rivulets down her face, but she didn't wipe it away. Nor did she ask him to come inside, although the wet weather didn't do much for the ache in her back and did nothing at all to improve her mood. "Who'll pay me to babysit this guy? And don't . . . don't you *dare* say a word about my pension."

A corner of his mouth tipped up. "Do this for me, darlin', and I'll treat you to a bottle of champagne and dinner at any restaurant in town. We'll celebrate all night long. Dancing, singing, saying prayers to any deity you want. Just say yes."

Dulcie glanced back toward the pier. The witness had moved closer to the railing of her boat. Beneath the long raincoat—which she recognized as Bobby's—he wore cowboy boots. Nothing else that she could see. She frowned.

"C'mon, Dulcie," Bobby said, bringing her attention back to him. She narrowed her eyes. His smile widened. "Please?"

The wet silk of his maroon shirt adhered to his skin like cellophane, and she always did have a weakness for wide Irish grins and handsome chests. "Bobby—"

As if sensing her wavering resolve, he moved closer. "Just for a day or so. Honest. I can't trust him with anybody else right now, and knowing how much you love the Dragon, I thought you'd jump at the chance to help me out a little here.''

Dulcie took another look at the witness. Some low-life loser, if he came from the Cracker—one of the city's worst biker bars. It didn't matter. His testimony would put the Red Dragon in prison, and just imagining Mitsumi behind bars almost made her forget about the ache in her back.

"All right," she said. "He can stay a day or two—but no more than that. I have my first show in a week. Doll artists and buyers from all over the country will be there, and I can't miss it."

"Two days." He gave her a quick kiss on her forehead. "I promise."

Dulcie groaned. "Oh, God, Bobby, don't do that. You know you don't keep half your promises, and I'm in no mood for make-believe tonight."

"Retirement sure hasn't done much for your sense of humor," Bobby said, grinning, then made a beckoning motion with his hand. "Bring him up, Les."

Over Bobby's shoulder, she watched the cops approach the rail of her houseboat—not much more than a small trailer on pontoons—and recognized officers Les James and Lucille Pettijohn. Les opened the gate and swung himself onto the side deck, then turned toward the witness.

The witness, however, ignored the gate and vaulted effortlessly over the rail to the wet, shining deck. In doing so, the belt caught under his hand and the raincoat opened, revealing bare legs, a bare chest, and something that sparkled when the lightning flashed.

Dulcie straightened in alarm.

"Guess I should warn you," Bobby said over a rumble of thunder, his voice more subdued than usual. "He's a stripper."

As if her powers of deduction had been retired along with her badge. In ten years of police work, Dulcie had seen things most people couldn't begin to imagine, but she still stared at the approaching figure.

The man walked with the self-assurance of a CEO in a thousand-dollar suit, although beneath the raincoat he wore nothing but boots, a sequin bow tie, and a black G-string.

Dulcie turned and glared at Bobby, not at all pleased with his belated warning. "I hope you brought him a change of clothes. He's never going to keep a low profile in that." She jerked her thumb at the expanse of flesh exposed as the raincoat flared wider in the wind. The man made no attempt to pull it closed again. As if he dared her not to look—dared her not to react to such a shameless, aggressive display.

Bobby swore under his breath, putting himself hastily between Dulcie and his witness. "Ms. Quinn and I have a few details to discuss about your visit. Go stand up front."

Without a word, the stripper moved past Dulcie with an easy, almost insolent grace. His muscles were wet and sleek with rain, and he had the longest lashes she'd ever seen. A man had no business being born with lashes like that, especially with a face and body that raised eyebrows, blood pressure, and hopes.

"Heck of a night, huh?" she asked. She didn't know why she'd spoken to him at all, except maybe she wanted another look at his face.

He stopped, then turned.

Lightning sparked, bringing into sharp relief black hair and eyes as dark and cold as the depths of the Mississippi. Eyes that were flat. Eyes that made her think of an alligator's unblinking, predatory stare.

"Move it. Now," Bobby said, his voice sharp. "And for God's sake, tie that coat back up."

The stripper ignored Bobby. Instead, he treated Dulcie to a cursory and dismissive glance before continuing on his way along the narrow side deck to the front of her boat.

Her skin prickled against her damp jeans and cotton shirt. She took a deep, steadying breath and smelled the ever-present odors of dirty water, gasoline, and decaying fish and vegetation.

"We didn't have time to pack a suitcase." Bobby's deeper drawl was a sure indication of his anger. "I'll send one of the boys back with some clothes. For now, you're just gonna have to avert your eyes, darlin'."

Dulcie frowned, wondering why Bobby had hustled his witness away before the man had a chance to dress. She glanced at the gator-eyed Adonis. "What's his name?"

"Julien. Julien Langlois."

She sighed. "Have you talked to this guy? Gotten a story from him?"

"Sure did. On the way here."

"So what happened? What the hell was a stripper doing at the Cracker?"

Bobby ran a hand over the blond stubble of his jaw. "Hard to say," he said after a moment. "I need to check out Langlois' story further. Until I know for certain, Dulcie, I can't say anything other than there was a shoot-out at the Cracker between a couple of drug dealers, and one of them ended up with more holes in him than a sieve."

She supposed the whys and the wherefores didn't really matter. The only fact of importance to her was that Bobby had an eyewitness who could prove that Juan Hernandez, petty scum that he was, had been killed by Jacob Mitsumi, the prince of scum. "Seems a bit high-handed, bringing him here like this. Are you sure his lawyer is going to approve?"

"I'll take care of it. Les and Lucille will stay behind and keep watch over things. Keep it all proper like."

Dulcie made a derisive sound. She glanced at the pretty black officer behind her, then grinned. "Bet you didn't have to twist Lucille's arm too hard to volunteer for this one."

"Ha," said Lucille Pettijohn. "There'd have been two bodies lying on that smelly barroom floor if he hadn't let me come along."

"Which is why I'm here," Les James added,

arms crossed against his solid belly. "To make sure Lucy behaves."

Dulcie laughed. Maybe this situation wouldn't be so bad after all. It would be just for a day or two. She could handle that, and it wouldn't put her too far behind schedule. "When you send someone by with his clothes, bring food too. I don't have much. Hope he likes hot dogs."

Bobby chucked her under the chin, looking both pleased and relieved. "He'll be happy with anything you offer, or he answers to me." He glanced at both Les and Lucille, then added, "We'll pick up some groceries, and a pair of pants for pretty boy over there. In the meantime, don't let Langlois out of your sight."

"You're expecting trouble?" Dulcie asked.

Of course he was. Unease niggled at the back of her mind. This was no small risk she was taking, letting this stripper stay with her. But the hope that Mitsumi might finally get what he deserved overrode her fears.

"Darlin', I'm always expecting trouble." Bobby's expression grew serious. "Mitsumi will do anything to keep Langlois from telling a judge and jury who killed Hernandez. But I don't need to tell you that."

He didn't. The twinge in her back reminded her every hour, every day. She glanced at Bobby's prize witness. He stood away from the front rail, watching her. His coat billowed like wings behind him and Dulcie wondered how many hours a day it took to maintain a body like that. Realizing she was staring, she turned away, her cheeks hot.

"You know, he doesn't look very happy to be here. Tell me you really haven't dumped on me a gay stripper with a bad attitude and a price on his handsome hide."

Bobby flashed his wide smile. "Langlois says he's clean and straight. No drugs, booze, boys, or girls. He's a businessman. Charges more'n a couple hundred bucks an hour to strut his stuff. Can you believe that? I got into the wrong line of business, maybe. What do you think?" He swiveled his hips experimentally.

"I think you better get off my boat, Halloran." Dulcie couldn't help smiling back. With his usual adroitness, he'd avoided her allusion to possible danger. She must be more exhausted with these late hours than she thought, because at the moment, it seemed perfectly reasonable to hide away a half-naked murder witness on her boat. "And bring that man his pants before he starts charging me by the hour. My pension doesn't cover much more than his G-string."

Bobby gave a shout of laughter. "Dulcie, I do miss you, darlin'."

Another stab of pain hit her, this one nowhere near her back. "I miss the old job, too. So what are you waiting for?" she demanded, before either embarrassed themselves with a show of emotion. Bobby already wore an odd expression on his face, one she couldn't quite make out. She punched him in the arm. "Go catch some bad guys. Les, Lucille and I can handle Monsieur Langlois."

"Me and Monsieur Langlois are gonna set down a few rules first. Hey!" Bobby shouted. "Get over here."

The man walked forward as lightning flashed again. It amazed her, how he moved as though fully clothed. The boat's light, weak and yellow, played along his shifting, fluid muscles. Sleek. Beautiful.

She imagined him on a stage in a dark bar, the air smoky and smelling of beer and wine. Women calling for him, reaching to touch him. Slipping money inside that thin elastic band.

She was beginning to understand why a woman might do such a thing.

"That is one prime piece of male animal," Lucille whispered from behind Dulcie. "Just want to take a bite out of him, don't you?"

Dulcie heard the unmistakable noise of smacking lips. But before she could answer, Julien Langlois stepped in front of her. Near enough for her to see that the drooping sequin bow tie was red and black; close enough to watch the raindrops bead and roll down the smooth, oiled skin of his chest.

God, he was tall. At least three inches more than her own six feet. If he'd heard Lucille's crude comment, he gave no indication of it.

"Langlois," Bobby said, in a deceptively pleasant drawl. "I'm leaving you with Dulcie Quinn, who's a very good friend of mine. You do just as she says and don't give her any of the trouble you've been giving me. Got that?"

Langlois nodded once.

"Good. Now get inside the cabin back there and

stay out of sight,'' Bobby ordered. He grabbed his witness by the jacket collar and shoved him forward.

Langlois stumbled. He steadied himself, turned, and stared at Bobby, Les, and Lucille, then finally Dulcie herself. In the sudden silence rain pattered against wood and water, gently melodic, as the boat rocked on the waves.

And Dulcie, in that brief moment, saw a man who wasn't afraid for his life, who didn't look in need of any protection at all.

''You better get inside,'' she murmured, breaking the tension, and motioned to the cabin door. She glanced at Bobby as the stripper walked past. ''Was that necessary?''

Bobby eyed her. ''What?''

''Shoving him like that. He's your witness, and you *are* supposed to be one of the good guys.''

Even in the darkness, she saw his skin darken. The curse of fair-skinned Irish ancestors, that deep red flush. ''He hasn't exactly been cooperative,'' Bobby answered at last.

Dulcie waited, but when it became apparent that was all the explanation she'd get, she sighed. ''So what do you want me to do?''

''Take the boat out until I get back with the groceries and his clothes.''

Take the boat out? Getting the bulky houseboat on the lake wasn't as easy as paddling a pirogue around, and he knew that. Again, Dulcie waited for an explanation. Again, she didn't get one. ''Okay . . .

I'll chug around the shoreline. Be here by midnight.''

Bobby wiped his wet sleeve across his face and let out his breath. "Don't let him out of your sight."

The repeated warnings and angry tension between Bobby and his witness roused her suspicions. She frowned, watching as a shadow passed behind the window curtains of her cabin. "We're on a lake, Bobby. Where can he go?"

Bobby shrugged, but the expression on his face was uneasy. "Something don't smell right in Denmark, darlin'."

She recalled the cold eyes, the aggressive stride of those long, bare legs. No fear. No fear at all. "I'll keep Langlois in the cabin and your people can stay in the front room. Lucille, honey, you haven't forgotten how to steer my boat, have you?"

Lucille snapped her mint gum. "Not at all. How come I can't sit in there and play bodyguard while you steer this old bucket? I'm the one with a gun."

Bobby snorted, and Dulcie, moving along the side deck back toward the cabin, couldn't help but smile. "That's what I'm afraid of. God knows what you'd do to that poor boy if you had him at gunpoint." She turned the knob on the door. "An hour, Bobby. Be on time for once."

If Bobby answered at all, his words were lost in a rich rumble of thunder and the sound of the door slamming shut behind her.

*   *   *

Once inside the cabin, Dulcie noticed her 'guest' had made himself at home.

It was a small room, meant for one person or maybe an amorous couple, and it didn't help that the disorganized chaos of her craft lay scattered across every available flat surface. Dolls in all shapes and sizes, in various stages of assembly. Eyeless and hairless heads, bodiless limbs, dimpled baby dolls and exquisitely dressed historical mannequins no higher than the palm of her hand.

Her longtime passion: doll-making. One that had prevented her from going crazy during those interminable weeks in the hospital bed, and that even now kept her from thinking about the pain in her back and all she'd lost. But the past had suddenly intruded this night. Memories and anger came sweeping back; all because of this stranger, whose presence filled every square inch of her cabin.

A stripper. Oh, grand. Inwardly, she cursed Bobby Halloran's devious, unscrupulous hide. He'd known she wouldn't say no, not even to a man like this.

Langlois had thrown the wet raincoat aside and lounged on her bed in his G-string. Her artist's eye saw a bacchanalian figure in brooding fleshy pigments, fit to adorn the ceiling of milady's bedchamber, but her woman's eye simply saw a man fit for milady's bed.

Annoyed with herself for even imagining such a thing, Dulcie moved into the cabin. Country music drifted softly through the room as she walked past the bed with its silent occupant. She turned the lamp on her workbench higher, killing the intimate mood.

"You cold?" The belligerent tone in her voice wasn't intentional, but he didn't seem to notice. He shook his head.

Since he didn't labor under any burden of shyness, she permitted herself a further, appreciative look at the body on blatant display. Her gaze followed the faint line of dark hair down his flat belly, to where it disappeared beneath the satiny Spandex pouch that barely concealed some rather impressive male proportions. Again, she imagined what it would be like to slip a twenty-dollar bill inside that elastic band; what her fingers would encounter . . .

Dulcie looked back up at his face and met his eyes. "Don't you find those string things uncomfortable?" He shook his head again. For some reason, his persistent silence irritated her. "Do you speak English, or are you just mute?"

"All of me is in workin' order."

He had a voice to match the rest of him. Male and primal and beautiful, colored with an Acadian accent.

A moment before he lowered those long lashes, she thought she saw a spark of anger. Her own temper flared, tinged with embarrassment from ogling him with the finesse of a fourteen-year-old— even though there was an awful lot of bare male lying on her bed, and she was only human.

"If you should have a sudden attack of good manners, there's a blanket in the cupboard above your head."

"Nervous, *chère*?" Langlois didn't give her a chance to answer, coming to his feet with a lazy grace that put her on guard at once. He smiled, but it didn't reach his eyes. "You want I just take it off?"

Dulcie banished the image taking shape in her mind, and gave him what she hoped was a disapproving look. "Whatever floats your boat. I've seen it all before."

She eased her way toward the outside door, but Langlois got there first, blocking the way.

His dark gaze flicked to the double-size bed, with its faded plaid comforter, then back to her. "Cozy."

Her muscles tensed. "Glad you think so. You're sleeping on the floor." Godamighty, she'd met the man only five minutes ago and already itched to slap his face. So much for humble gratitude.

He laughed; a deep, fluid sound. "Don' star witnesses rate better?"

"You rate: the cops kept that comic-book-hero chest of your free of bad ol' bullet holes. You can show your gratitude by being good and doing as you're told."

She tried to move past without touching him. But he wouldn't stand aside, forcing her to brush close against him. A drop of water from his dripping hair rolled down the polished chest. He smelled of cigarette smoke, sweat and aromatic oils.

"I'm a good boy," Langlois said low into her ear as she pushed past. "I do as I'm told. What you want me to do, *chère*?"

Dulcie whirled around to blister his ears. But faced with the solid expanse of tanned flesh, a mocking face, and those cold eyes, she changed her mind and fled to the safe, if soggy, deck.

She stalked to the front of the boat, struggling to get her anger in check, and stared out across the wind-tossed waters of the lake, at the lights from other boats—luggers, houseboats, barges and cabin cruisers—blinking and twinkling like stars against the dark water and sky. In the distance she heard the loud blare of a horn, along with the ever-present purr of engines. The generator on shore hummed and crackled under the pattering of the rain.

"The look on your face tells me you and Julien have, ah, gotten acquainted."

Lucille stood beside her, arms folded across her chest. The light caught the gleam of her police badge's star and crescent emblem and the knowing sparkle in her eye. "He had Halloran ready to chew concrete within ten minutes of meeting him. Sure has a way about him, doesn't he?"

"A way that's going to get him kicked off my boat if he keeps it up," Dulcie retorted.

"Uh-huh," Lucille agreed, her mouth widening in a smile. "Got to you, didn't he?"

"A bit."

As she glared down Lucille's smirk, Dulcie recognized the truth in the woman's words. Langlois had goaded her to anger on purpose. A lot more than 'a bit,' she admitted with disgust. She didn't know why he'd want to make her angry, but she intended to find out.

Later. After she'd cooled off . . . and got under control those embarrassing urges to explore beneath that elastic band.

Chapter 2

JULIEN LANGLOIS LISTENED to the door slam behind him, then pressed his forehead against the wall, eyes squeezed shut. He counted slowly, until he trusted himself not to smash a fist through the screen.

So close.

Red Dragon had been *his*. Eye-to-eye over the black gun barrel, the Dragon had understood and smiled. Then that fool Hernandez lost his head and started shooting, the cops showed up, and everything went all to hell.

He'd been so close—point-blank. But he had hesitated, one second too long.

He wanted to howl with rage, but couldn't. *Mais non*, he must play the grateful witness—until he got the chance to escape.

To hell with them all. They couldn't guard him every second of the day. One of them would slip up, look away for a moment, and he'd be gone. Just like that.

From somewhere in the room came the strains of country music. Fiddles. Fast, furious. He needed

18

to stop it. Julien picked his way across the boxes toward the source of the sound, finding a tape player on a cluttered bench beneath a pile of pink lace. He shoved the lace aside, punched the 'off' button, and stepped back in the sudden, soothing silence.

New plans. He didn't have much time. The woman was his best bet. She'd watched him, a hungry gleam in her eyes, and he'd play that hunger ... *Dieu*, like a fiddle.

There was no other way out.

Julien looked around, assessing the small room with its bed, workspace and clutter. An inner door led to a compact kitchen area, and off to the side was a bathroom the size of a closet. Past the kitchen, separated by another door, was a sitting room furnished with tables and a single sofabed. All the windows were small, too small for him to fit through, and the doors were aligned centrally, so that when open one could see from one end of the houseboat to the other. His cage was nothing more than a camper on a barge, plugged into electrical lines on shore.

What kind of woman lived on a boat?

He walked back toward the bed, stepping over boxes full of arms, heads, and limbs. A woman like her, full of sass, playing with dolls. He hesitated by the workbench on the far side of the room, then picked up a baby doll. It looked real. Too real. He put it down.

His restless gaze fell on more boxes, piled on the floor by the workbench. The Doll Lady wasn't

much of a housekeeper. Lifting the lid of the top
box, he found strands of hair. Straight, curly,
coarse, and fine, in every color imaginable. He
gathered a handful. Doll wigs, some of which
looked as if they were made from real human hair.

With a low sound of disgust, Julien replaced the
things. A sudden, alien gleam of metal beneath the
doll hair caught his attention. He glanced over his
shoulder toward the closed door, then reached into
the box and lifted the object.

A Colt 45.

Julien smiled humorlessly. The Doll Lady liked
to play with guns, too. Big ones. She was something, with her wet red hair and long legs.

From what he could see in the cabin—no male
clothing, no pictures of boyfriends or husbands on
her nightstand—she didn't have a man around. A
lonely woman might be more gullible; give him an
edge. If nothing else, living as a stripper these past
few months had taught him the art of knowing just
how much to show and how much to hide. The
power of waiting until the right moment.

He ignored a sudden, surprising prick of guilt.

No other way out. He'd do what was necessary
to fulfill the only promise that mattered anymore.

Julien stared at the gun and the inner rage flared.
He had one chance left. Nothing and no one would
get in his way.

The grumbling in her belly contested with the
rumbling in the sky, and Dulcie gave up waiting
any longer. Bobby was late. She was hungry, and

all the food was inside. With the stripper.

Oh, she ought to be less judgmental and more tolerant. He was an *exotic dancer* . . . and a sanitation engineer was still a garbageman, elbow-deep in refuse despite the twenty-dollar-a-word title.

She remembered Bobby's earlier words. Two hundred dollars an hour, for doing nothing more than taking off a few flimsy pieces of clothing. It said something about people's priorities. As a cop, she'd seen too many people who'd messed up their priorities and far too many hungry kids whose parents spent what little money they had on drugs.

But there was nothing she could do about that, not anymore. Dulcie forced the thoughts away, along with the faint disquiet that seemed to dog her lately, and pushed away from the rail. She walked to Les, who was sitting on a deck chair and looking glum. "I'm getting a bite to eat. Want anything?"

"Hot coffee sure would be nice," he answered.

"Bobby's late."

"You know how he is."

"Yeah . . . but he's really late this time. Even for Bobby."

Les shrugged, then smoothed back his thinning brown hair. "He said to wait. Something probably came up. Go on, Dulcie. Get yourself some food. Want me to come with you? I should probably check on the . . . ah, young gentleman inside."

"Gentleman, my a—" Dulcie bit back her rude comment and sighed. "No, don't bother getting up. I'll just nuke a few hot dogs and brew some coffee.

But you could ask Lucille to try calling Bobby again.''

Les nodded, and Dulcie mentally girded her loins and sallied forth to do battle with too much muscle, skin, and machismo.

Poised just outside the cabin door, a hand on the frame above, she watched Julien Langlois walk from one end of the room to the other, unknowingly providing her with a glottis-popping view. Godamighty, it was as if one of Michelangelo's masterpieces had come down from its pedestal to prowl her boat.

His caged, restless pacing disturbed her. ''Now isn't this a puzzle,'' she said, and he stopped short at the sound of her voice. ''A few hours ago, you were right in the middle of a gun battle. For a guy who now has the power to put away one of the worst drug dealers in New Orleans, you should look a little more concerned about your lease on life.''

There was no relief or gratitude on Langlois' face as he turned on her. Only fury. Naked, raw rage.

Years of training had taught her how to react to dicey situations: never give the other guy an edge. She marched into the cabin with determined strides and said, ''I'm starved. How about you?''

''Get me off this boat.''

''That's not possible.''

''Listen up, I—''

''No,'' Dulcie interrupted. She pushed past him, then turned at the inside door to the kitchenette.

"*You* listen up. You saw Jacob Mitsumi murder a man tonight. The only chance you've got to keep on breathing is to stay right here and cooperate with the cops. I'd prefer your cooperation to be voluntary. But I'll tie you down on the bed if I have to."

He followed her into the kitchen. "Fun."

The answer came too pat; too automatically. She frowned, sharpening her attention, then leaned back against the counter.

"Could be fun," Dulcie said. "Until the circulation starts to go and your extremities turn numb." With a toss of her head, she swung around her hip-length ponytail until it lay like a rope down her side. She dropped an assessing gaze along his body, then raised it again. "That might kinda take the fun out of it, wouldn't you say?"

Shorts made the most of her legs, and while she often fretted her shoulders were wider than a woman's ought to be, she figured the stuff between looked female enough. Trim waist, a bit of breast, a butt still firm even after thirty years of fighting gravity. At about nineteen, she'd stopped wishing she were cute and petite, and learned to use what she had to her advantage. She intimidated most men.

Not Julien Langlois. He walked closer, with that menacing grace which seemed to underlie all his movements. Her heart thudded, and she suddenly understood what a hapless creature must feel as it stared into a pair of predatory eyes.

"So what's for dinner, *chère*?"

Me. "Hot dogs. No buns. I don't do buns."

His eyes looked nearly black, the pupils wide and round in the dim light. She came just to his nose and had to look up to meet his eyes. She wasn't used to that. He stood too close, but she didn't step back. Pointless. He filled the room.

"Pity," Langlois murmured. "Buns be the best part." With that, he turned and walked back into the cabin, leaving her with a nerve-wracking view of *his* buns.

Dulcie took in a lungful of air. She yanked open the microwave door with more force than necessary, but her reflection in the black glass of the door smiled back unwillingly.

"Dulcie!" Lucille shouted from somewhere up front.

"In the kitchen."

"Bobby's on the phone. He wants to talk to you."

So much for the hot dogs. She glanced through the door and into the cabin. Langlois was sitting in the corner shadows of her bed again, and if she hadn't known better, she'd have thought he wasn't wearing a stitch of clothing. She had a sudden urge to poke her finger into those thigh muscles to see if they were as hard as they looked.

She glanced down at the package of plump, red hot dogs in her hand and tossed them in the microwave. Bobby could cool his heels for a second or two. "When it beeps, take them out," she said, at the door to the cabin. "May as well make yourself useful, Langlois."

She made her way toward Lucille, who was sitting at the helm in the front room. Lucille blew a bubble with her gum as she handed over the cellular phone.

"Bobby, it's Dulcie. What's up? You're late."

"Sorry. Some trouble down here."

"What do you mean?" She looked up, meeting Lucille's dark eyes. She already didn't like the sound of this.

"Tell you later. I'm on my way. We should be there in the next fifteen minutes or so. Is Langlois giving you any trouble?"

"Oh, he's a charmer, Bobby. I'm not sure leaving him with me is such a good idea. I'm half-tempted to shoot him myself."

"I'm serious here. Is he giving you any trouble?"

"No," she answered, after a moment. "Not really, although he comes on a little . . . aggressive."

"Think you can manage him, darlin'?"

"Yes." She spoke with more conviction than she felt.

"Good. Hang tight. I'll be there soon," he said, and Dulcie put down the phone.

"So," Lucille said promptly, a look of undisguised curiosity on her face. "Is he a charmer?"

"Like a snake."

"He's hot."

Dulcie frowned. "So's hell."

"Girl, I sure wouldn't kick him outta *my* bed."

"Lucy. Julien Langlois is a police witness, not a boy-toy. Oh, all right, so he is," she amended as

Lucille started to laugh. "But that doesn't mean you have to slobber all over him. I'm going back in to finish heating up hot dogs and make coffee. Want anything?"

"Coffee's fine," Lucille said, grinning and bright-eyed. "Have fun!"

Fun. The word of the hour.

By the time she came back to the kitchen, Langlois had dumped the heated hot dogs into a dish and even made a pot of coffee. He'd found the ketchup and mustard, half a bag of potato chips, and a package of Oreo cookies. She took a deep breath as she came in, smelling freshly brewed coffee, salty hot dogs and chips, and wished to God he was wearing clothes.

"Just how I like to see a man. Barefoot and naked in the kitchen." She grinned as he turned. "Sorry. Couldn't resist."

He leaned back against the counter and crossed his arms over his chest. The sequins of the bow tie sparkled with each movement. "Got quite a mouth on you, *chère*."

She did, and knew it. It came from being tall and gawky, and long ago she'd decided if she couldn't be the belle of the ball, she'd be the wit. "Too many Bette Davis movies, I guess. Thanks for finishing this up. I just talked to Bobby—Detective Halloran. He's on his way."

"I want to talk to him."

"I'm sure he'll want to talk to you, too. Sit down and eat. I'm going to bring some coffee to Les and Lucille."

"You gonna let me on deck?"

She started from the kitchen, coffeepot in one hand, cups in the other. At his question, she turned and peered at him. "Not dressed like that."

Then, remembering she had a T-shirt which might fit him, Dulcie put the coffeepot and cups down on the counter. She motioned him back to her cabin. "I think I have a temporary solution to your problem."

"I have a problem?"

She ignored his insinuation and after he'd followed her inside, she opened the cupboard door above her bed. She rummaged through disordered piles of colorful lingerie and flannel shirts, blue jeans, Lycra leggings and even, to her embarrassment, a wadded-up navy gabardine suit. She shoved the suit aside, hoping he hadn't noticed, and found at last what she looked for. She pulled out the New Orleans Saints T-shirt and tossed it at him. He caught it, like a good wide receiver, close against his chest.

Langlois held up the shirt, turning it until the name *Halloran* was plain to see, then looked her straight in the eye. After a moment, a blush heated the skin of her face. She hadn't thought how it would look to him, that she had one of Bobby's old T-shirts stashed away in her cupboard.

But it was none of his business, and why should she care what a stripper—a stripper, for God's sake—thought of her?

"You want it or not? If you prefer to sit around here and freeze your pecs off, that's fine with me.

Just don't let the chattering of your teeth get on my nerves. Gets cold on the water at night.''

"Here I was, hopin' we'd share a little body heat.''

"Not on your life. And the water's cold too, so don't get any stupid ideas.'' He laughed and took a step toward her. Dulcie shot him a quick glare, one meant to keep him away. It didn't work. "I have a baseball bat under my bed. I mean it, Langlois.''

If anyone knew what damage a baseball bat could do to a backbone, she did.

He came close enough to stand beside her; close enough for her to feel the warmth of his bare skin. A lingering scent of some earthy oil tickled her senses, and again the mingled odors of sweat and cigarette smoke assailed her nostrils.

She moved back a step. "You smell like a cathouse.''

"How would you know?''

"None of your business. Put the shirt on, Langlois.''

She moved away and made a show of rearranging the jumble on her workbench—folding a few yards of pink lace and fingering the length of rolled velvet for Romeo and Juliet, who still lay unassembled beside it. By the time she'd turned around, he'd pulled the shirt on over his head. The yellow knit had faded to a mellow gold and the black fleur-de-lis looked patchy, but it fit him well enough. Maybe too well.

"Better, *chère?*''

Dulcie gazed at the word *Saints* emblazoned across his broad chest. The last "S" had long since worn away, and she didn't miss the irony. She might have laughed, if she weren't afraid she might spontaneously combust at any moment. She looked back up at his handsome face. The shirt hadn't toned him down one iota.

"I'll be right back," she mumbled and then left, grabbing the coffeepot and cups on her way through the kitchenette.

Chapter 3

~~~

DULCIE ESCAPED TO the front deck, angry with
herself for letting a man like Julien Langlois set
her heart racing. She was the practical, cautious
sort. Not the kind of woman to drool over a man
she'd just met. Besides, nice women avoided men
who took off their clothes for a living. While she
might have a smart mouth and a chancy temper,
she was a nice woman. Conservative, even, in her
own way.

Maybe she wore her hair long because most
other women wore theirs short, and maybe she
sometimes wore three-inch heels just to make people stare, but she still considered herself an indi-
vidualist, not a rebel. She'd never understood the
lure of the bad boy, having seen too many wasted
young lives to feel anything but frustration and anger for that sort of posturing.

Yet here she was, going all hot and nervous
around a man who had nothing more going for him
than a pretty face and a nice chest.

She took a deep breath, and smelled the promise
of more rain in the wind blowing against her face.

Just what she needed, to be stuck with a stripper on a boat barely big enough for the two of them to pass without touching.

She frowned. Her heart was still pounding. But really, this response to Langlois was explainable. It had been a while since she'd been with a man. A flower turned its face to the sun because that's what it did. A woman was attracted to a handsome man because her body was programmed to do so.

Fortunately, she had a brain to keep her body from doing something stupid.

Dulcie handed Les and Lucille their coffee, just as a pair of headlights swung around the corner of the dirt road and approached her pier. Bobby, finally.

But Les and Lucille at once put down their cups and reached for their guns. By habit, Dulcie did the same. She stopped herself in mid-motion, remembering she didn't wear a gun anymore.

An instant later, a white light slashed across the darkness. Lucille's powerful emergency lantern illuminated a familiar unmarked police car driving up to the end of the pier.

"Dammit, turn that off!" Bobby Halloran shouted from a distance.

Just as abruptly the light winked out, leaving them all momentarily blinded until their eyes adjusted to the darkness again. She listened as Bobby killed the engine. Car doors opened and slammed shut, and then came the sound of footsteps on the creaking wooden planks of the pier. Bobby had brought three other detectives with him, and Dulcie smiled when she recognized Adam Guidreau, another old friend she'd not seen in too long. She was even happier to see that Adam carried a grocery bag in each arm, along with a black gym bag slung over his shoulder.

Still wearing his damp clothes from earlier, Bobby strode to her side, with a nod for Les and Lucille. "Where's Langlois?"

"Sitting in the cabin."

"Good. Adam, bring those bags inside and keep Langlois in the cabin until I say otherwise."

No smile on his face, and his voice sounded grim. Dulcie stood straighter. "What's wrong?"

"You're not gonna like this, darlin'."

"Then say it fast."

"I need him to stay here a while."

Dulcie closed her eyes briefly. She should've known. This was the trouble he'd mentioned earlier. "Bobby, you said—"

"I know what I said. Nothing I can do about it now."

"Why?" But she knew. She recognized that edgy look in his blue eyes.

"Got us a body in a Dumpster off Dauphine Street. Dark-haired, well-built, and nearly a dead ringer for Langlois." He grimaced. "Sorry."

How fortunate he'd gone into law enforcement and not a career that required tact. "Who was he?"

"A dancer at one of the gay bars on Bourbon. I'm thinking you should take this boat of yours for a long ride. Lay low for a while."

Silence followed. A bird cried out, high on the

night wind against the wet, black sky. Dulcie stared at Bobby until finally he met her eyes.

"I'll do what I can to get Langlois to a safer place," he said. "But Mitsumi's got eyes and ears everywhere. It's gonna take time. That dead boy in the Dumpster was a warning, and I'm taking no chances on my witness floating face-down in the Big Muddy."

He stepped away with a quick look at the cabin door, and moved toward the rail by the pier. "I want Red Dragon, Dulcie. I want him bad."

Dulcie said nothing. She didn't have to. Almost absently, she massaged away a twinge of pain. Broken backs sometimes healed. Hers had. But the ache for justice—any kind of justice—never really went away.

Red Dragon lay at the heart of many broken lives. She would never forget the bat against her back; the sound of breaking bones and the agonizing pain. The months in the hospital, wondering if she would ever walk again, be of use to anyone ever again.

"I know," she said after a moment. "And I appreciate this small chance you've given me to be a part of the investigation, although we both know I shouldn't be involved."

Dulcie tried to gauge the expression on Bobby's face, but saw only the old, familiar guilt. She caught his cold hand in hers and squeezed it. "You keep sharp, Bobby, and get that tattooed bastard. Think with your head, you hear me?"

He glanced away. "I hear you."

"I'll go ahead and take the boat out to Mike's tomorrow. He won't mind if we stay there a few days; he's in Atlanta right now. Did you bring Langlois his clothes?"

"Yeah. We brought his bag back from the Cracker." He looked back up at her. "I'm real sorry about the show, Dulcie. I know how important it is for you to sell those dolls of yours. I'll do what I can to get him out of your hair, but we're short on staff. You know how that is, and when it comes to Mitsumi, I gotta be careful who I trust." His hesitation spoke more than words. She understood. "That's why I thought your boat would be better than a safe house that every cop knows about."

"It's all right," Dulcie said quietly, knowing very well there was another, underlying reason for his actions. But she would say nothing more of it. "If I miss the show in New Orleans, there's one in Nashville next month I can make. Putting Mitsumi behind bars means more to me than selling a few dolls. With Les and Lucille on hand, everything will be fine."

"He's already made a legit statement. No problem there. We just have to keep him alive long enough to have him repeat it in front of a jury."

"It's more than keeping Langlois alive, Bobby; it's keeping him from running. He wants off the boat."

He didn't look surprised. "That's too damn bad."

Dulcie frowned, thinking it was too damn bad

Bobby's entire case against Mitsumi rested on a stripper who wanted to disappear.

Bobby ran his hand over his jaw, an old habit he resorted to whenever frustrated or distracted. "Guess I better talk to my witness. Adam! Send Langlois out here."

A moment later Julien Langlois emerged on the front deck, Adam Guidreau behind him and the other two burly detectives planted firmly in front of the rail next to the pier. Julien still wore the *Saints* T-shirt and had slipped on a pair of shorts. He carried the raincoat he'd worn earlier and threw it at Bobby as he walked toward him.

"Hey, that's my lucky *Saints* shirt," Bobby said, catching the coat against his chest by reflex.

"Bobby, shut up," Dulcie muttered.

Langlois glanced at her before stepping up to Bobby, almost nose-to-nose. "I want off this boat."

"Can't let you go yet," Bobby said regretfully, a battle gleam in his eyes. "My job is to protect people like you. Like it or not, you need protecting."

"I don' need anythin' from you."

Dulcie retreated toward the rail. Bobby could deal with his witness without her help—although Langlois didn't believe in beating around the bush and Bobby was hardly famous for his beatific temperament.

"Look. I have this problem." Bobby handed the raincoat to Adam. "A dead guy kind of problem. You probably knew him—same line of business and all. He kinda even looks like you. Leastwise, he did, before somebody left his body in a Dumpster like a piece of garbage. You following me, Langlois?''

''Not my problem. You got what you need. Let me go.''

''You walk off this boat and you'll be dead in an hour,'' Bobby retorted. ''Maybe you don't care if Mitsumi is behind much of the crack cocaine and violence on the streets of this city, or about the lives he's broken. But I want that scum off the street, and you're gonna help me do it in a court of law. You're staying right here and in one piece until I bag him. After that, I don't give a damn what you do.''

During Bobby's angry tirade, Les and Lucille had come to stand on either side of Langlois, so that he was completely surrounded. Dulcie couldn't help but think the police weren't protecting Langlois' life as much as corralling him. She watched his handsome face, chilled by his lack of interest and emotion.

''You don' leave me much choice,'' Langlois said. ''I'll stay, but you got no idea what it's gonna cost you.''

''Sorry,'' Bobby retorted, with an absolute lack of sincerity. ''I know being here isn't exactly helping out your bank account, but we've issued a warrant for Mitsumi's arrest. He's laying low right now, but we'll flush him out. Then he goes to jail, you testify, and after that you're free to get on with your life.''

Langlois glanced at the two detectives standing between him and the pier, then at Les and Lucille. But he didn't look at Dulcie at all. "You can't touch a man like that and you know it. He'll be back."

"So I'll put him away again." Bobby's voice was flat. He and Langlois stared at each other.

Then Langlois raised his hands in a gesture of capitulation and stepped away. "You've convinced me. Now I'll be a good witness. Be on my best behavior."

Dulcie's suspicions snapped to full alert, even before she saw Bobby's frown. Langlois' sudden cooperation didn't feel right. This was a man with a game plan, and she would have to watch him even more closely than she'd first thought.

"What are you grinning about?" Dulcie demanded, facing Julien Langlois in the kitchenette a few moments after Bobby had left. "A little while ago, you looked about as happy as a crawfish in a boiling pot."

"Pralines."

"What?" Dulcie asked, staring as he picked up a package of candy from a grocery bag. He unwrapped the pecan and sugar confection and took a bite. Then he licked a crumb from the corner of his mouth. Slow and deliberate.

"I like pralines. That's what I'm grinnin' about. Okay by you, *chère?*"

Nice dodge. Oh, he was good. She wouldn't get any straight answers from him, any more than she had from Bobby. Which was too bad, because she wanted to know what had happened at the Cracker. She also wanted to know why Langlois was so determined to leave protective custody. He had to know the kind of danger he was in.

"You want one?" he asked when she didn't respond.

Dulcie reminded herself she didn't have to ask any questions, or try to make sense of it. She shouldn't get any more involved than she already was. All she needed to do was finish her dolls and make certain Langlois didn't jump ship. When she shook her head in answer to his question, he shrugged and ate the last bite of candy.

The sound of the engines cutting in broke the awkward silence, and Langlois reached out to brace himself against the side of the counter as the boat began to move. He looked at her. "Where we goin'?"

"We're heading out of Lake Pontchartrain for the bayou. Better hiding spots there, but it's too dark to go into the swamps tonight. I don't trust Lucille to know a tree branch from a shrimp lugger. We're getting a head start and tomorrow I'm driving. In the meantime, we may as well get you settled in."

She went back into the cabin, then poked around until she found a spare camper pillow beneath her bed and handed it to him. "Clear yourself a space on the floor." The floor wouldn't be very comfortable and it was likely to be damp. A drawback of living on a lake. "Sorry for the mess," she added.

"You live on this boat?"

"Most of the time. I have a bad back. The rhythm of the waves helps the pain. Don't know why, but it does."

In truth, she needed to get some sleep. Even the rise and fall of the waves wasn't helping the ache tonight. She found an extra blanket, a rather musty-smelling old Indian stripe affair. When she turned to hand it to him, she found that Langlois had moved to her workbench and picked up one of her porcelain baby dolls.

Dulcie frowned. Not because he was holding nearly a thousand dollars' worth of work, but because of the way he held it. He was a man used to handling infants; to supporting heavy heads on wobbly necks and cradling small, fragile bodies in his hands.

"Just like holding a real baby?" She had tried to make the doll as lifelike as she could, but she didn't have much experience with babies. Now, of course, she probably never would.

He glanced at her. "Live ones squirm more. You do good work. Is your real name Dulcie?"

For the first time since his arrival, her muscles relaxed a fraction in his presence and she managed a smile. "It's short for Dulcinea, but nobody calls me that except my father. He thought every girl should be named after a song." She shoved as many boxes as possible against the wall, so he would have enough room to stretch out on the floor. "Why he couldn't have called me Peggy Sue, I don't know. Instead he had to name me after some hooker in a musical."

"A reformed hooker," Julien corrected, with an ironic lift of one dark brow. He returned the doll to the workbench, carefully.

Dulcie straightened and stared at him in surprise. "You know *Man of La Mancha*?"

"Yeah."

"Don't tell me . . . you do a striptease to Don Quixote's 'Impossible Dream.'" A sudden vision of him, dressed as some sort of titillating knight tilting at windmills, flashed across her mind.

"Nope. I do jocks an' construction workers. Lots of the ladies like cowboys, too."

"Oh." She glanced away from that intense, watchful gaze of his.

Whatever did one talk about with a male exotic dancer? This was a little out of her usual realm of experience. The reality of sharing her space with a stripper who breathed sex appeal like most people breathed air, was beginning to sink in.

Annoying. Dismaying.

Delicious.

"I'm thinking about making more coffee and having a little of that deli lasagna Bobby brought. I'm getting tired of hot dogs." Food was safe, she decided, so long as she didn't mention buns again. "Want some lasagna?"

"Sure."

How polite he had become. No more radiating brute male auras, no more aggressive sexuality. It appeared her Cajun conundrum was rethinking his earlier hostile approach. Or else he had actually begun to cooperate.

Moving into the kitchen, she called over her shoulder, "Can I ask you a personal question?"

After a moment, he answered from the cabin. "Depends."

Since he hadn't exactly said no, Dulcie asked anyway. "Why did you become a stripper?"

"Easy money."

The answer she'd expected. The easy, pat answer. She rummaged around in the back of the cupboard, shoving aside jars and tin canisters of spices as she looked for the coffee filters. She wondered why she had three jars of cumin but no cinnamon. Then she wondered why she had any spices at all, since she didn't cook.

"I suppose there isn't much to swiveling your hips and unbuttoning your pants in front of a room full of drooling women."

Julien had followed her again into the kitchen, and seated himself at the fold-out table. He watched her. "Why do you ask?"

Dulcie dropped a filter, then bent to scoop it up again, annoyed that he'd turned her own interrogation against her. "Just curious."

Now that so much of him wasn't exposed, she found herself focusing on his face and mannerisms rather than his distracting body. She guessed he was in his early thirties, and presumably it was his years of fast living that had added interesting lines to a face that might otherwise be too pretty. Which brought her back to the main question nagging at the back of her mind.

She began putting away the groceries. As casually as possible, she asked, "What were you doing in the Cracker? Not your usual territory, I'm willing to bet."

"Had a show."

"At the Cracker?" Dulcie stared at him as he tipped the back of his chair against the wall.

"I don' ask why, *chère*, just go where I'm paid."

"You're lucky one of those biker boys didn't rip your face off. Last time I was in there, black leather and chains was the general attire, not G-strings and sequins." She paused, then asked quietly, "Did you know who was there?"

She shouldn't have asked, but intuition warned her that he wasn't telling the truth. Bobby didn't trust him, either. He wouldn't say why, but she figured it was for much the same reason: Jacob Mitsumi, Juan Hernandez, and a stripper named Julien Langlois all together in the Cracker just didn't add up. But Julien revealed nothing to clue her in on whether he was lying.

"I knew."

"So you walked half-naked into the meanest bar in the Quarter, knowing one of the most dangerous drug dealers in New Orleans was there." She shook her head and placed the carton of lasagna in the microwave. "Habits like that, my friend, will get you killed."

"Halloran put you up to these questions?"

"Bobby asked me to put you up in my houseboat for a few days. That's all." Dulcie looked away from Julien's dark eyes and began to measure out the scoops of coffee. She took a deep breath, more to settle her nerves than anything else. "I had my own reasons for saying yes. Jacob Mitsumi is a special concern of mine."

"Why's that, *chère*?" he asked, as she poured water into the coffeemaker. She admired the cool tone of his voice, although she noticed his Cajun lilt was more pronounced than usual and he'd said *dat* instead of *that*.

"A metal pin in my back and a nine-inch scar might have something to do with it," Dulcie answered, turning again to face him. She folded her arms over her chest. "Two years ago, I tangled with his men during a bust. One of them took a baseball bat to my back—shattered a few vertebrae. I was lucky to walk again, but my days in law enforcement are over."

Julien's mouth tightened and he leaned over the table. "You used to be a cop?" She nodded. After a moment he added, "Sorry . . .'bout what happened to you."

"So am I," Dulcie replied, as the microwave began beeping. "And the only reason I agreed to let you stay here is because I want that bastard in jail." She slid the carton of steaming lasagna onto the table, then raised a brow at the dubious expression on his face. "*Allons manger, mon ami.*"

He flashed a sudden, devastating smile. "*Chère*, if you an' me are together for much longer, I'm gonna have to teach you how to cook.''

Dulcie tried to ignore her thudding heart; tried telling herself this sudden dampening of her palms meant nothing. ''You cook? Oh, my. Do you do laundry, too?''

Julien quirked a brow. ''In my line of business? There's few clothes to wash, *non*?''

In spite of herself, she smiled. ''Touché, Langlois. This round goes to you.''

While he picked at the reheated lasagna, Dulcie brought more coffee and the tray of hot dogs, chips, and cookies to Les and Lucille, making sure they were comfortably settled in the front room. By the time she came back, he'd cleared away his own paper plate, napkin and plastic serving ware.

She made a pretense of ignoring him as she ate, and when she was done and had cleaned up after herself, she sat down at her workbench and began the lengthy chore of sewing buttons on the doll costumes. She needed to finish the baby dolls before she could begin on Romeo and Juliet.

Julien sat on the floor, cross-legged, looking through the few magazine and books she had lying about. She didn't imagine he'd find any of it of interest; all she had on the boat were a few Agatha Christie mysteries and a haphazard collection of craft magazines, mostly doll-related.

He seemed to have forgotten her presence, but Dulcie hadn't forgotten his. Even with her back to him, she knew exactly where he sat. It was as if her woman's radar honed in on his male heat and she felt him behind her, a solid wall of presence.

She hunched further over the doll's dress, as if doing so kept him at a safe distance.

"Need help?"

A soft movement, the faintest lingering scent of musk, and Julien leaned on the worktable beside her. She glanced sideways, seeing his long fingers, strong hands, and bare, muscular forearms.

"No."

"Sittin' around makes me crazy. Gotta be somethin' I can do."

"Can you sew, Julien?" That would shut him up and send him as far away from her as possible.

"Some. Buttons an' mending. Need buttons sewn on?"

At that, Dulcie turned to stare. Six foot three inches of raw male, offering to sew buttons on pink, frilly doll dresses. She searched the dark face, the shadows of his eyes, seeking some flicker of amusement or mockery. But all she saw, besides an understandable boredom, was genuine interest. "Are you serious?"

" 'Course I'm serious, Dulcinea."

"Don't call me that!"

He laughed, shifting closer until he brushed against her. "Suits you, *chère*. Dulcinea Quinn, all soft and hard."

She dropped her gaze, before he could see how he affected her. Godamighty, she could slam petty hoods up against the side of a car, but the sound of her name on his Cajun tongue made her feel hot and spicy, liquid and woman and weak.

"Great. A poet, too," she managed to retort,

keeping her voice cool and amused. "You cook, do laundry, sew on buttons, and spout poetry. Shame on me, for thinking you just an ornamental sort of guy."

He held out a hand and, when she still did nothing, wriggled his fingers suggestively. "It's gonna be a long few days, *chère*, an' I be needin' to keep my hands busy."

She hesitated, entertaining a hot and wicked thought of what else could keep those beautiful hands busy, then slapped the spool of thread in his palm.

His lips quirked upwards. "Needle."

She plunked the packet of needles in his palm.

"Buttons."

The button cards followed, three of them, each carrying four pink pearl buttons. Dulcie stared at his outstretched palm, momentarily baffled, and then looked up into his eyes.

"Scissors," he coaxed.

She laughed at last, unable to resist this wry teasing. "You missed your calling in life, Julien. You have hands like a surgeon."

She placed the stork-shaped embroidery scissors in his hand, her fingers lingering longer than need be on his. A brief second passed in silence before she dropped her hand to her lap, but it seemed an eternity. She couldn't look up at him, shocked at how easy it had been to touch him.

"You know what I'm supposed to do here. I lean over, close like this," he whispered, bending down so that his lips were just inches from her cheek.

"An' then I ask you to come play doctor."

Dulcie turned her head a fraction, seeing from the corner of her eye the beginning of a dark stubble on his face. She wanted to reach up and touch him there, too, and feel the contrast of smooth skin and coarser hair.

"Gotta be careful, *chère*, around bad boys like me. Say nice things like that, an' you just askin' for trouble."

Maybe she was. The insidious, horrible thought stunned her. How could she, sensible Dulcie Quinn, find a snake like Julien Langlois even remotely attractive? Obviously, she'd spent far too much time holed up in this houseboat.

"Thanks for the warning. Let me rephrase. How about if I say you've got musician's hands?"

"Better. But it won't work for me."

She felt the brush of his breath against the skin of her cheek, and for a brief moment she felt squeezed between a flare of panic and a lurch of excitement. Then he stepped back and lifted the dainty scissors, dangling it from the tip of his finger.

"You'll have to trust me with the real thing, *chère*. Musician's hands or no, I'm never gonna fit my finger inside this little hole."

Her desire fizzled, replaced by a cold lump of fear. He was asking her for shears. Long, pointed stainless steel shears that could inflict much more damage than blunted embroidery scissors.

Dulcie looked up again, meeting his dark eyes. If he were going to try and escape it might as well be now, when she was prepared for it.

She knew she'd hesitated too long when his eyes flattened, and the muscles around his nose and mouth tightened. Julien knew she distrusted him.

"Here," Dulcie said at last, handing him a pair of gleaming shears from her workbench drawer. Wordlessly, he took them from her. With his free hand, Julien reached around to the kitchenette and pulled one of the folding chairs to the workbench. He sat down, draped the tiny dresses across his thighs, and proceeded to thread the needle.

In spite of herself, Dulcie couldn't help but watch as he wet the pink thread with his tongue and inserted it through the hole of the needle with one, sure push. He looked up then, intercepting her stare, and smiled. An easy, slow smile that grooved his cheeks and wreathed his eyes in laugh lines.

"I come from a big family. My *mère*, she was busy with the farm an' my old man worked the oil rigs. Us older kids had to fend for ourselves an' take care of the little ones. I learned real quick how to cook, do my own laundry, an' sew on my own buttons."

Dulcie didn't doubt he spoke the truth about this, at least. He certainly could thread a needle and the buttons didn't give him pause at all as he popped each one off its card. She watched him a moment longer, just to be sure he knew what he was doing. But his movements were so quick and deft that she wondered if he sewed on his own buttons after overexcited females ripped them off.

With him attending to the detail work, Dulcie

concentrated on putting together Romeo and Juliet's kidskin leather bodies. The smaller the doll, the more time-consuming she found the assembly and costuming. She'd prefer to do it while anchored at a pier, not chugging along on Lake Pontchartrain under Lucille's heavyhanded steering.

But in only six days . . .

No. She had all the time in the world, now. Time for dolls, at least. Not the real thing. She looked for a moment at the baby doll Julien had picked up earlier, and felt a familiar rush of anger and sadness.

How she had wanted to have a baby. She'd always expected that one day she'd find the right guy, toss her birth control pills in the trash, and get pregnant. Take a few months off from the job, maybe work part-time. Do the Mother of the Year thing.

But that wouldn't happen, not now.

She looked away from the doll, angry that she'd allowed herself to feel self-pity again. She thought she'd gotten over this months ago. Why had the anger and discontent all come rushing back now?

Then her gaze settled reluctantly on Julien Langlois, where he straddled the chair with his muscular legs, holding pink lace and batiste in one hand while he sewed on buttons with the other.

Just what she needed in her life right now. Another good-looking, vital man to remind her that as a woman, she no longer quite measured up.

Dulcie sat straighter, and with an effort directed her energies to assembling her star-crossed lovers.

Chapter 4

Tuesday

DULCIE GLANCED OVER at her alarm clock, where glowing red numbers proclaimed it to be 4:23 A.M. She was as wide awake now as when she'd first crawled under the blankets of the bed, a little after two o'clock.

She listened to water slapping against the boat and the low, even breathing of the man sleeping on the floor beside her. Considering how quickly Julien had fallen asleep, maybe he had a clearer conscience than she thought.

Or maybe just none at all.

Despite the fact that her own conscience was reasonably clear, she couldn't sleep. She was wound too tight; half-expecting Julien to slither away to the kitchenette for a knife, or his powerful arm to suddenly snake up from the floor and grab hold of her, then force her to do whatever he wanted.

Whatever that might be.

Possibilities and scenarios ping-ponged around inside her head, an alarming number of them less than safe and sensible.

God, she really had spent too much time alone on this boat.

Lying awake like this was useless. She'd make herself a cup of tea and go sit outside on deck, where a little fresh air might help her relax. She and her houseboat full of 'guests' had a long day ahead of them. The trip to Mike's bayou cabin would take most of the morning.

With a soft sigh, Dulcie swung her legs over the side of the bed. She carefully felt her way toward the kitchenette, barely able to see in the dark, and made sure the door to the front room was closed, so not to disturb Les or Lucille. Only an occasional glimmer of moonlight pierced through the black, columned clouds of the night sky.

Somewhere in the top cabinet drawer, her junk drawer, she had a small flashlight. She slid the drawer silently out and then groped around for the flashlight. She pricked her finger on something sharp and almost swore out loud.

"Lookin' for somethin', *chère?*"

With a gasp, Dulcie whirled around. She hadn't heard him come up behind her. His closeness forced her to step back against the counter.

"No . . . yes! That's none of your business. Don't you ever sneak up behind me like that again!" She made an effort to calm herself. "I thought you were asleep."

"Not with you tossin' an' turnin'."

"I'm not used to having strange men sleep on the floor."

A flash of white shone in the darkness as he smiled.

"Glad to hear that, *chère*. Hope for me yet, no?"

"No."

First law of the street: Never let them see your fear.

The edge of the counter against her thighs hurt, but if she moved away she would be pressed intimately against his body. He knew it, too. Obviously, he'd abandoned the helpful-Boy-Scout approach and was back to aggressive male sexuality. Damn him, it worked all too well. She couldn't get a hold on her cool, practical sensibility. It was scattered, as ephemeral as morning fog.

"Julien, you're hurting me."

He pulled away a fraction. "Don' mean to."

"Let me by so I can turn on the light. If you're up, there's no reason for me to go stumbling around here in the dark."

As she sidled around him toward the light switch, Julien slapped his hand against the wall, blocking her escape. Dulcie focused her gaze on his hand for a moment, then looked up. She took a deep, silent breath. Whatever he meant to do, it was happening now.

"I have to get off this boat, *chère*. I need your help."

"We've been through this already. I can't help you."

"I'm talkin' life an' death here."

Dulcie's anger began a slow build. Enough of this kid-glove treatment. She stepped up close, meeting him eye-to-eye.

"Let me tell you a little secret: I liked being a

cop. I liked feeling that I was doing something worthwhile with my life.'' She could feel each breath he took; feel each slow, measured exhalation of warm air against her cheek. ''Red Dragon's maggots took that away from me—and more. He's going down, and I'll be damned if I'll help you get your brains blown out before your testimony can put him away.''

''An' here I was thinkin' you didn't care,'' Julien murmured.

He moved closer, trapping Dulcie between his body and the edge of the counter. She felt the bare skin of his legs on either side of her own, and the sudden, shocking press of something else she didn't dare name.

Right then and there, Dulcie knew she'd just veered off the safe, well-lit byways of the familiar into a dark alley of the unknown.

Second law of the street: Never back down.

''I *don't* care,'' she whispered, staring at the dark, shadowed face looming before her. ''Not about you. But I sure as hell care about making sure Jacob Mitsumi goes to prison. Don't mess with me, Julien.''

''I don' want to mess with you,'' he replied as his hands closed around her arms; arms rigid and tense as she gripped the counter behind her, trying to bend away from him. ''I just want to get to know you better.''

He intended to kiss her. She realized it just before he dipped his head lower and covered her mouth with his own. Offended and furious that he thought her stupid enough to fall for a ploy so crass and blatant, she kissed him back.

Hard.

Third law of the street: Meet brute force with brute force.

But Julien Langlois knew the same laws she did, and all the dirty, low-down tricks as well. He kissed like a fallen angel, coaxing and enticing and relentless. He didn't let up; didn't let her breathe. He just kissed her, slow and sure and merciless, until she began to feel faint from lack of air. Faint from the uneasy, exhilarating awareness that she liked this.

There was nothing soft about him; not his muscles, not his hands on her, not his lips or tongue. Nothing. She heard herself make a whimpering sound in the back of her throat. Not a sound of protest. Not a sound of pain.

Somehow, her hands were no longer pressing against him, pushing back. She slid her palms up his chest and over his shoulders, then closed her fingers over the muscles of his arms, knowing the intensity of her grip had to hurt him.

Without taking his mouth away, or letting her break free from his imprisoning hold, Julien slid his bare knee between her legs, forcing them apart so that he could move closer and rock his hips against hers. There was no mistaking the full erection pressing against her, aggressive and demanding. Wanting her, as a man wants a woman.

A familiar panic flared.

This couldn't happen. She didn't want intimacy,

or a man's hands on the scarred ruin of her back. She tried to pull her head away, but he brought his hands up, imprisoning her face between his palms. Kissing her, hot and wet. Tongue-to-tongue, smooth teeth and moist, mingling breath.

A dizzy desire took hold of her, making her forget her fear. Dulcie forgot to be practical, to play her defenses. Her body answered his demands, responding to the tingling pleasure of his mouth, hands, and body.

Dulcie slipped her hands beneath his T-shirt. She flattened her palms across his back, caressing the hollows and rises of his ribs and backbone, the wide triangular muscles across his shoulders. As his tongue slid into her mouth again, she sank her nails into his flesh.

Last law of the street: If you're going down, take them down with you.

She felt the change in him: the violent tremor in the hard body, the renewed intensity of the onslaught of his kiss. His urgency overpowered her. Then reason broke through the smothering desire, bringing a sharp clarity about what was happening.

In a few more minutes she'd be up on the counter and he'd be inside her. His intent was unmistakable, but this was one game she wasn't prepared to play.

With a low, angry growl, Dulcie turned away from his mouth and pushed against his chest. Julien stepped back abruptly, and she took a deep gulp of air. Then another. "You're one hell of a kisser,

Julien Langlois, I'll give you that. But I still won't let you off this boat.''

In the dim light, she watched the erratic rise and fall of the 'SAINT' and fleur-de-lis on his chest. If his response to her had been an act, he'd managed to be very convincing. "Maybe you'll give me another chance to persuade you," he said softly.

For the briefest of moments, she felt a twinge of regret for something that would never happen again. Then she shook her head. "It was a one-shot deal, Julien. But you get extra points for having the guts enough to try."

His silence followed Dulcie as she retreated to the bed again. She wriggled beneath the sheets and drew the blankets up beneath her chin. Not that she needed the blankets—her body felt hot enough to melt the mattress. In the dark, Dulcie touched her tongue to her lips. She could still taste him.

She had badly underestimated Julien Langlois. Beneath the cold eyes, the chill, and perfect shell ran something hot and dangerous.

Bobby never would've left Julien behind if he'd thought he posed a threat to her, but Bobby had been thinking only of physical, bodily harm.

Julien was a threat, all right. A threat to her long-denied hope that Jacob Mitsumi would finally get what he deserved. A threat to the ordered, carefully planned new life she'd built out of the shambles of the old.

A threat to her; the damaged woman who wasn't much of a woman anymore. Scarred, crippled for life. Unable to even have a child.

No. She had made her peace with all she'd lost. No slick, smiling stripper would destroy that fragile peace. From here on out, this game of truth and dare was over and she'd keep Julien Langlois where he belonged.

Out of sight and out of mind.

Julien let her go.

He listened to the creaking bedsprings and rustling blankets as she settled back into bed, then sat down on the cold metal chair and tried to make sense out of what he'd just done with Dulcie.

Dulcie. Damn, what kind of a name was that for a red-haired Amazon who kissed like every man's flesh and blood fantasy?

With a thumb, he circled the aching spot between his eyebrows. Not one of his better successes, that. He wasn't even sure why he'd kissed her to begin with, except maybe because it looked like she'd wanted him to. He'd only meant to talk to her; tease the hunger he saw in her eyes and maybe start her thinking with her sex and not her head, so she'd let him off this damn boat.

But his plans hadn't fallen out as intended. Instead of sweet-talking a lonely woman, he'd gone and kissed an ex-cop who wasn't fooled by his calculated charm. She'd all but laughed in his face and called his bluff.

She'd more than called his bluff. He adjusted a still-aching erection, acutely aware how his body had responded to her. Which wasn't part of the plan at all.

Nothing shy about that woman. Holding her in his arms and kissing her, all he could think about was what it would be like to take her to bed. Legs, fingernails, mouth, and tongue, and hot, tight places that would drive every thought clear out of his skull. Leave him boneless afterwards, too tired to even think.

Julien couldn't remember when desire had last touched him like this, sharp and hot, but it was far longer than he cared to admit.

He wanted to kiss her again, taste her once more. Hell, he wanted to do a whole lot more than kiss her in that cozy bed of hers. A vision flashed across his mind, of her long legs wrapped around his hips, that pretty mouth of hers speechless except for gasps and cries of pleasure, her hair spilling across those fussy, flowery sheets.

He closed his eyes, rubbing at his brows until the images and the renewed stirring in his groin went away. Sex was out of the question. Too risky. Feelings, messy emotions. Regrets and promises.

Promises.

The reminder of promises left to keep sobered him. If he did anything at all with Dulcie Quinn on that bed, it would only be to bring him closer to his objective. Right now, she stood in his way and he would not fail in finishing what he'd started. No regrets, remorse, pity, or any other feelings would dampen that one, low fire still burning within him.

He pushed away the nagging guilt and sat for a while longer in the dark kitchenette, thinking only

about what he'd do once he was free of Halloran's
"protection."

When he'd managed to gain control of his frustration and anger once again, he returned to the
cabin. Without a word—the stiff lines of Dulcie's
back warned him off—he lay down with his hands
behind his head and stared at the ceiling. He stared
at one spot while focusing on the sounds of her
breathing and movements. She finally fell asleep as
dawn began to lighten the sky, her breathing slow
and even.

Still too restless to sleep, and reluctant to do so
anyway, because he didn't want to dream, Julien
sat up and watched her.

She was a restless sleeper, kicking away the
blankets and sheets. She lay on her back, a knee
slightly raised. One arm rested on the pillow above
her head, but she curled the other across her chest,
almost in a defensive gesture. In doing so, she'd
pulled up most of her T-shirt. She had a nice belly,
trim but soft, not rock-hard like some of the women
strippers he'd come to know these past few months.

He could even see a little of her bra in the gray
light, a peek of plum-purple lace. A strong urge
took hold of him, a longing to push her shirt away
and reveal the rest of her lingerie, to see the contrast of plum-purple against the paler skin of her
breasts. He wondered if beneath her shorts she
wore underwear to match. Nothing he liked better
than a pretty woman in pretty lingerie.

With a small sigh, she shifted again, turning her
head away so that he faced a rumpled mass of long

hair. She moved her arm from above her head down across her chest, unconsciously trailing her hand over her breast before letting it rest, fingers loosely curled, at the juncture of her thighs.

All of his earlier resolve vanished. His body tightened, and damned if he hadn't broken out in a light sweat. He couldn't quite forget, as much as he wanted to, the feel of her sweet, pliant body in his arms, the crazy-hot mouth kissing him back like there was no tomorrow.

For a moment, he wondered what it would be like to pretend there was no tomorrow and let himself be swept away on a wave of desire. To lose himself in a woman's love and comfort.

To stop thinking. To forget. For just one day, to forget.

"Merde," Julien muttered under his breath. He did reach toward Dulcie then, but only to pull the covers over her lovely, sleeping body.

Chapter 5

~~

DULCIE AWOKE LATER that morning to the smell of brewing coffee, sizzling eggs and the warm, yeasty aroma of fresh bread right out of the toaster.

She stretched, yawning, then pushed the covers aside and stood. Straightening her hair and wrinkled clothes as best she could, she padded on silent feet to the kitchen door and peeped inside.

Julien stood before the stove, looking very out of place in her mint and maple kitchenette. He wore black boots, black jeans, and a black muscle shirt with the armholes open nearly down to the bottom of his rib cage. All the better to show off a fine set of biceps and corded chest muscles.

She remembered the feel of those muscles, the smooth warmth of his skin.

With an effort, Dulcie looked away. Her gaze settled on a coat, also black. It was one of those fancy Australian sorts with the cape in back. It lay draped across a folding chair, the heavy canvas glistening with moisture. Over the sound of frying eggs, she heard the rain. A gentle drizzle this morning, pattering against the wooden deck and the lake.

She leaned against the door frame, content to watch him while he thought her still asleep. Little by little, the memory of last night's aggressive kiss in the corner of the kitchenette came back to her. The vivid memory of his mouth on hers caused a sweet, sharp pang deep within. Stupid of him, to kiss her like that. More stupid of her to have kissed him back.

She was going to have to keep well clear of this man, and she was thankful for the long trip that lay ahead. Piloting the boat would keep her too busy to think about her reluctant guest, from worrying about what he might try next in his effort to get free of police protection, and wondering why he wanted that in the first place.

Dulcie watched as he flipped the eggs and, despite her better intentions, shamelessly admired his rear in the tight jeans. All in black, with his hair neatly tied back, he looked like an actor from a Hollywood adventure movie set. He certainly knew how to package himself for dramatic effect. Even without the G-string and bow tie, this man would never blend into crowds.

No wonder Bobby had pulled Julien into protective custody at once. Leaving him on the streets was akin to painting a bull's-eye on his back. Wanted: one flashy stripper with the body of a god and a smile that hit like a kick to the solar plexus.

She looked again at the wet coat and frowned. He must have been on deck, but she'd never heard him leave the cabin. "You were on deck?" she asked, her voice still rough with sleep.

"Yeah. For a bit." He didn't turn from the stove, nor did he evince any surprise that she was awake. "An' I brought coffee and breakfast to your cop friends."

She raised a brow at his unexpected answer. "How generous of you."

"I didn't want them comin' into the kitchen an' wakin' you up. Took you long enough to fall asleep last night, so I figured you needed the rest."

Julien turned then. Dulcie waited for his reaction, to see what he'd do face-to-face in the light of day with the woman he'd kissed silly in the dark.

He smiled at her, a smile that made her knees go weak. Godamighty, she didn't care if he could cook, do laundry, or sew buttons. This man was a menace to sensible womankind everywhere, and she wanted him to go away!

Very calmly, she said, "You're looking pleased with yourself this morning. If you mean to butter up Les and Lucille with hot coffee, think again— they're honest cops. And if you try kissing Lucille like you kissed me last night, she'll not only never let you off this boat, she'll ravish you."

"Meanin' you didn't?"

Pig.

Egotistical male twit.

She hadn't ravished him; he'd kissed her first. She'd responded because it was dark, he took her by surprise, and, well, it'd been a while since anybody had kissed her. She probably would have kissed Quasimodo back, given the same situation.

Right.

"I'm going to take a shower."

"Breakfast is ready. Wait to do that."

Dulcie pursed her lips. "Who said you could give the orders around here? This is my boat. If I want to take a shower, then I'll go take a shower."

"Suit y'self. But I make a mean fried egg." He scooped the eggs out of the pan and onto two plates, then added the toast. Dulcie felt her mouth water. She usually only had a cup of coffee and a donut for breakfast. When she looked up again, he was watching her. "No need to go runnin' off. I won't kiss you again."

She returned his look. "Promise?"

He broke eye contact with her, shifting his focus to a point below her face. "I never make promises, *chère*. Won't say I'm sorry for what I did, either."

She could almost feel the touch of his gaze along her breasts, her bare legs beneath the shorts. The air in the cabin was hot and stifling and humid.

Animal attraction. Chemical lust; hormones, testosterone, or pheromones; or whatever psychobabble excuse was popular this month. But her attraction to Julien was real and she didn't think it one-sided. The male sex in general baffled her, but she knew for certain his reaction to her hadn't been feigned. She'd felt tangible proof of that.

Dulcie pushed away from the door frame. "It's time you leveled with me. I'm flattered you kissed me and all, but it's not like I don't know why you did it. I want to know why you want out of police protection so bad that you're willing to die for it."

"Kissin' you wasn't so bad as that, *chère*."

He put the frying pan down and walked toward her, a half-smile playing at the corners of his mouth. She hated herself for letting him rattle her, for retreating back into the cabin. He followed, until she bumped into the unmade bed. She froze.

The scent of his cologne was earthy, rich, and expensive. His tank top looked like a silk knit, and his smooth, cool good looks made her acutely aware of her own rumpled appearance. She tried to ignore the liquid fire that caused a gentle ache between her thighs, and wanted a place to focus her eyes that wasn't his chest, mouth, or eyes.

Anything to help her shore up the poor shreds of her pride and good sense.

"I guess the shower can wait. I'll brush my teeth and be right back. Breakfast smells wonderful, Julien. Thanks," Dulcie mumbled at his sternum, then moved cautiously past him, half-afraid he'd try something and half-wishing he would. But he only watched her. This time, without a smile or a smirk.

Dulcie let the bathroom door close behind her with a soft click. She turned on the light. Only one side lit up, and she reminded herself she ought to replace the other bulb one of these days.

She stared at herself in the foggy old mirror of the medicine cabinet. God, she felt like a cat in heat. It hurt, in a strange, pleasurable way, and she wanted to growl or moan. She wanted to run her fingernails down Julien's chest and purr. But she knew she couldn't do that, any more than she could hide in the john all morning. With determined vigor, she scrubbed her face clean and brushed her teeth. After that she combed her long hair, tied it back in its usual ponytail, and then, almost as an afterthought, dabbed on lipstick and blush to add a little color.

She frowned at herself in the mirror and considered scrubbing it all off again, but just then Julien called her name, the tone of his deep, accented voice impatient.

The moment she opened the door, the smell of breakfast made her stomach growl. Julien had already seated himself at the fold-out table, straddled across a metal folding chair, and sipped his coffee as he waited for her.

In an awkward silence, she sat across from him and stared down at her plate. For a brief, ludicrous moment, her food seemed to grin up at her—two yellow eyes and a triangular toast mouth. "Looks delicious," she murmured with a nervous smile, and applied herself with great attention to eating.

The eggs *were* delicious, and she wasn't particularly fond of eggs. The toast was even better, drenched in sweet butter. She decided to ignore the cholesterol content of this unexpected treat, since it wasn't her usual fare.

"How is it?"

She didn't have to look up to see the smile on his face; she could hear it in his voice.

"Just fine."

"I like a good breakfast."

"Me, too. I usually don't have time for anything more than a donut, though."

What an incredibly fascinating chat they were having. If he started talking about the weather, she would scream or cackle, she wasn't sure which.

"Gonna storm some more," Julien said.

Dulcie's head snapped up. His expression was serious, but the faint smile lurking in his dark eyes made her wonder if he could read minds. "Looks that way."

"What's the plan for this mornin'?"

"We need to buy fuel, top off the propane and water tanks, then juice up the generator," Dulcie answered, licking butter off her fingers. "I'll probably go to Don's Stop-and-Shop, which is pretty close and secluded. As soon as we're done with that, we'll be on our way to the channel. I'll call Bobby and tell him where we're going. He might drop by to see us off."

"If he does, tell him to bring us some real food."

"We have real food, M'sieu Langlois."

He made a rude noise. "Don' pay to put garbage in a pretty body like yours."

Pretty body? Dulcie glanced down at her shapeless clothing, then back at Julien. He wore a secretive smile, as if he could see right through her clothes. "Julien, stop it."

"Just complimentin' a pretty lady."

Dulcie eyed him over her coffee cup, her gaze touching on the muscles of his chest beneath the tight tank top. Uncomfortable beneath his intense regard, she quickly said the first thing that came to mind. "Where did you put your . . . you know, other things."

A blank stare. "Other things?"

"The bow tie and G-string." A rush of heat spread along her neck and face. This was going to be one of her stupid days. She was already in rare form.

"Why? You want a private show?"

She almost spit out her coffee. "I think I've seen pretty much all you've got to offer."

Julien raised a brow along with his coffee cup. "Pretty much, *chère*, but not everythin'." He took another sip, watching her, and she finally glanced away. "You look good."

Even knowing what he was doing couldn't dampen the sudden thrill she felt. For a moment, it didn't matter that he was only trying to charm her, seduce her, confound her. A tiny part of her hoped that he meant what he said; that he found her desirable. Her, Dulcinea Quinn, with her nine-inch ugly scar and metal pin and crippled back.

The flare of pleasure faded away, replaced by something dark and doubting. He couldn't possibly understand how cruel his actions were. "Julien, don't play games with me. It won't work."

"You're talkin' nonsense." He stood, then picked up his plate and brought it to the sink. "Callin' the cards as I see them, an' they're lookin' good."

Before she knew what he was about, he'd leaned down and lightly brushed her lips with his. He tasted like chicory coffee.

"You said you wouldn't kiss me again," she murmured, when he pulled back.

"I lied."

She wasn't hungry anymore. Her chest tightened. Without a word, she pushed back from the table, leaving the rest of her breakfast untouched, and walked away from him.

Julien's first reaction was to go after her. To grab her by the arm, yank her back, and sit her down on the chair. Instead, he sat in silence and watched her hurry from the kitchenette to the front of the houseboat.

He felt like a dog. Worse than a dog.

He'd circled in on her, closer and closer, until she'd finally run. He'd come on stronger than he should have. Maybe because of last night. When he'd kissed her, solid ground had seemed to crumble away beneath his feet—a sensation Julien didn't like. He wouldn't lose control like that again.

Earlier that morning, he decided he'd be better off trying a helpful approach. Cook for her, pamper her. Make her feel like a queen. It had worked for a while, until he'd nearly forced her down on the bed. And he'd gone and kissed her again.

No more of that. Holy *hell*, no more kissing that sweet mouth. He was going to be polite enough to make himself puke; be a model witness. He couldn't afford to rouse any suspicions in Dulcie Quinn or his 'protectors.' Not now, when he still had a chance to get to Mitsumi.

Plan A had turned out to be a bad idea all the way around.

Plan B was a lot less risky, and all he had to do was sit and wait for the right moment.

He was good at waiting.

Dulcie stood on deck and watched the approaching shoreline as Lucille brought the boat closer. The buildings lining the pier were familiar and shabby, with peeling paint and erratic, flashing neon signs advertising bait, beer, and gasoline.

She was glad to be away from Julien; away from that small, cramped room. She'd have to keep very busy today. So busy she wouldn't have a spare moment to think of Julien Langlois, or raw, stolen kisses in the dark.

At a sudden, damp gust of wind, Dulcie glanced up. Judging by the look of the clouds, they were in for another squall soon.

God, was it ever going to stop raining? She glared at the gray, lumpish sky. But even her fiercest scowl wouldn't crack those clouds and coax out the sun, and she'd only get wet standing here. She backed away from the rail, into something hard and warm. Half a yelp escaped before she choked it back and turned.

Julien.

God, was it ever going to go away? This crazy, rushing heat she felt every time she came within spitting distance of the man? "I seem to keep tripping over you."

He smiled his lazy, muscle-melting smile. "Sorry, *chère*. Small boat."

"Get out of my way," she snapped, just as Lucille brought the houseboat to a bumping stop against the old tires along the pier.

Les threw a rope around a bleached, weather-worn post and the boat bumped again, this time more forcefully. Dulcie stumbled into Julien. Immediately, she tried to step away, but his hands held her still. Solicitous to the last, damn him. Last night's panic returned, but this time anger came with it.

"Don't touch me again," she said, her voice low. She pushed against him until he finally released her. "And I meant what I said, Langlois. Stay out of my way!"

He didn't move back, keeping her effectively trapped between his body and the rail. He must enjoy it, she thought, since he kept backing her up against things. His favorite trick.

"I meant to stay out of everybody's way all along," he answered, his breath warm against her cheek.

With a sudden, unpleasant jolt, Dulcie realized he could easily jump from the rail over to the pier. All he had to do was hit her and knock her aside.

With a rising fury, she met Julien's cold gaze. She challenged him; let him see in her eyes that she knew what he wanted. And that she wouldn't let him have it.

"You really do want to get off this boat, don't you? Too bad—because I'm not going to let you."

She watched his eyes change: glittering, black, and flat. He made a move away from her. Not enough of one to define his intent, but she didn't wait. She leaped against him, wrapping her arms around his neck in a stranglehold, and her legs around his hips. He stumbled back with a grunt of surprise as she shouted, "Les!"

Les was at her side in an instant, his gun half-drawn. "Jeez-louise, what the hell is going on here? Dulcie, get off him, for chrissake!"

She brought her legs down, suddenly feeling a little foolish, and as she unwound her arms from Julien's neck, he nipped her with his teeth. Right on her breast.

She slapped him. So hard that she jarred a lock of his long hair from its tie and left a livid imprint of her hand on the side of his face.

Julien only smiled—a cold, leering smile. Furious, Dulcie almost told Les to get Julien off her boat; that she'd had it with this man's attitude. But she stopped herself: that would give Julien what he wanted.

He was good. So good, damn him, and she'd reacted just the way he wished. Dulcie stared at him. Julien had backed away, but kept his attention focused on her face.

Les shoved the gun back in its holster and put himself between them. "What's going on here?"

"I think M'sieu Langlois is overanxious to get to shore. You'd better escort him back to the cabin."

"Why would you want to go and stir up all kinds

of trouble like that?'' Les asked Julien in his soft, reasonable voice. Les James rarely shouted or blustered, and used the same tone of voice with foulmouthed, frenzied delinquents that he used when ordering a hamburger off a menu. "Come on back with me. I don't want to have to use any force to restrain you, and you don't want to go make a fool of yourself."

Julien's whole body stiffened. "Get your hands off me!"

Les didn't even blink, but Dulcie saw how he took a step back. Enough room so that, if it came to it, he could duck a blow and launch one in return.

"Julien, you go with Les right now or I'm telling Lucille to head to the middle of Lake Pontchartrain. I mean it."

Without a word, Julien turned on the heel of one polished black boot and stalked back into the cabin, Les close behind him. Dulcie let out her pent-up breath in a long sigh. At the sound of another set of footsteps, she glanced over to see Lucille jogging her way.

"What was that all about?"

"He was going to bolt."

Lucille sent an incredulous look at Dulcie, then snapped her gum. "That's not what it looked like to me."

Dulcie felt her face warm. "He was going to jump."

"Why? He's as good as dead on the streets."

"If I'd given him the chance, he'd have

jumped.'' She stared down at the dark water and a plastic beverage lid bouncing on the waves, no longer quite so sure that was what he'd intended at all, and feeling a little guilty. After a moment's silence, she said, ''I asked Julien what he was doing at the Cracker.''

Lucille blew a bubble, then snapped the gum three times in rapid succession, like gunfire. ''What'd he say?''

''That he was the entertainment.'' She had to smile at Lucille's wolfish grin. ''So I asked him if G-strings and sequins were all the rage with bikers these days.''

''And then what did he say?'' Lucille prompted, warming to the game.

''Never did get an answer out of him.'' She glanced at the other woman, and finally asked the question that had been bothering her since the prior night. ''Do you think he's lying?''

''Julien? I don't know. Why do you ask?''

''Lucy, you know the Cracker; it's a biker bar. And since when does the Red Dragon entertain good-looking Cajuns with chiseled muscles?''

Lucille laughed softly. ''You figure he works for the Red Dragon?''

''Not unless Mitsumi's changed his style. Our Dragon is an elusive creature of shadows and darkness. Flashy strippers are a bit too . . . memorable.''

''Maybe Julien's just a junkie. Maybe he was there to buy.''

''Bobby said he's clean and it looks that way to me.'' Dulcie smiled ruefully at the other woman's worried expression. "And he's no hustler, either. All those female Quinn instincts are telling me he's as straight as they come. At least where sex is concerned."

"Glad your instincts are telling you something right." Lucille grinned, then fired off another round of her gum. "Okay. So our boy was at the Cracker dressed to get his butt kicked. Who cares why? He saw Mitsumi kill Hernandez. Once Bobby hauls Mitsumi in, all Langlois has to do is tell the jury what he saw. The law'll take care of everything else. You get your justice too, hon."

Dulcie shrugged her shoulders restlessly. "Guess you're right. What's important is getting Mitsumi off the streets and into prison. Nothing else matters."

But that wasn't quite true. Understanding why Julien Langlois wanted out of police protection mattered a great deal. He'd tried charm first, and when that failed had turned to force. As she'd just witnessed.

Why?

She stood straight, her mind made up. "I'm going to have a talk with Julien. You called Bobby, right? He knows we're waiting here?"

Lucille nodded. "He and Adam are finishing up some paperwork. Said they'd be here as soon as they could get away."

"Good enough. Listen, if Julien gives me any reason to suspect he's going to bolt, we're skipping Mike's place and parking in the middle of Lake Pontchartrain. Out of gas."

"You're taking this pretty serious."

Dulcie smiled faintly. "I may not be on the payroll anymore, but that doesn't mean I've stopped thinking like a cop. I want to put Mitsumi out of business. If I have to, I'll stretch the limits of the law to make sure Julien testifies. Whether he wants to or not."

"Well, if you get tired of the view in the cabin, my offer still stands. I'd be happy to play bodyguard. It's not fair that you get to jump on him and I don't."

Dulcie grinned, even as her cheeks warmed. "If Bobby isn't here in forty minutes, call him again. One of these days, that man has got to realize the rest of the world doesn't run on Bobby Standard Time."

She waved Lucille off, then walked back inside the boat. Even though Les and Julien were playing a companionable game of cards at the kitchenette table, she wasn't fooled that everything was right as rain. "Les, I want to talk to Julien. Alone."

The two men exchanged glances, then Les stood, adjusting his belt and gun holster. "Think the two of you can talk without drawing any blood?"

Silence. Finally, Dulcie muttered "Yes" and Julien gave an abbreviated nod.

"Good." Les cleared his throat. "We can finish the game later."

"Yeah," Julien said, watching Dulcie from beneath those ridiculously long lashes.

She waited until the door closed behind Les with a loud click before she spoke. "You were going to hit me and then jump to the pier, weren't you?''

Julien gathered the cards together before tapping them into a neat rectangle. ''You already made up your mind about me. Nothin' I say is gonna change that.''

He was dancing around her questions. Smooth, mocking; keeping the truth just out of her reach. ''Julien, I asked you why—''

''It's my business.''

''And it's my business now too, isn't it? Maybe I can help.''

He laughed, shuffling the cards in his nimble fingers. ''Cops are no help.''

''I'm not a cop.''

'' 'Scuse me if I don' buy into that. Once a cop, always a cop.''

''You do understand how much danger you're in, don't you?'' Dulcie persisted in the face of his lunatic resistance.

He dealt out the cards in a game of solitaire, then turned up the first card. The king of hearts. ''I can take care of myself.''

''You promised Bobby you'd stay on the boat.''

''*Chère*, I told you. I never make promises.''

She rubbed her breast, remembering his other offense. It didn't hurt, really. He hadn't nipped very hard. Just enough to startle her. ''You bit me,'' she said, in an accusatory tone as she glared at him.

''If you're real nice to me, I'll do it again.''

''Julien—''

''An' you slapped me,'' he interrupted. ''You like it rough?''

Her blood pressure was beginning to hit crisis level, which was precisely what he wanted, but she wouldn't give him the satisfaction of losing her temper again.

Dulcie lowered her gaze and watched his fingers turning over the cards. "The eight goes on the nine," she said calmly. "Julien, why do you want out of police protection? This isn't a game. Look at what happened to your buddy Hernandez. For God's sake, Mitsumi will kill you!"

"I'm only gonna tell you this once: leave it be. Halloran can't keep me caged here for much longer, anyway. Soon he's gonna have to let me go."

She looked back up at his face. "And then what?"

His lashes rose a fraction, revealing a hostile, black stare. "Then you can forget all about me an' get back to your nice tidy life an' your little dolls."

Chapter 6

JULIEN DEALT OUT another hand of solitaire, covertly watching Dulcie. Her pretty face was pale with anger. Or maybe frustration. He had that effect on people lately.

It made him mad, that she thought him capable of hitting a woman. Damn, he'd sunk to some pretty low depths all right, but not as low as that.

He twirled one of the cards between his fingers. Pissing her off had helped lessen some of his own anger, but not all of it. Admittedly, he'd toyed with the idea of jumping, but it hadn't even occurred to him until she'd thrown it at him like a challenge.

He'd come out on deck to apologize for being such a bastard, but once again, everything got turned inside out. Not only didn't he apologize, but he'd backed that warm, soft body of hers against the rail. Worse, when she'd gone and jumped on him, nearly pressing her breasts into his mouth, he'd done what any red-blooded, frustrated man would do.

Or so he told himself.

Dulcie Quinn had the ramrod attitude of a Marine drill sergeant, and nothing he could say or do would persuade her to let him off the boat. Making her mad didn't work. Kissing her didn't soften her up. Even his pathetic attempt at being a model witness was failing, although that was more his fault than hers.

The woman was as crazy as he was, jumping on him like that. God knows what they'd end up doing to each other if he didn't get off this boat soon.

Julien flipped over a card and stared at the three of diamonds. Then he looked up. She was watching him, and the intense frown on her face gave him pause.

Now, he told himself. *Apologize* . . . But he wasn't sure himself why he wanted so badly to touch her, or get a rise out of her. That unplanned kiss had stirred something he'd thought long gone, and that was the real reason behind much of his anger.

Several seconds passed as they stared at each other in silence. Then a shout outside broke the tension, and Dulcie looked away. "Bobby finally made it here," she murmured.

Ah, hell. The day had started out bad and now it was getting worse. As if on cue, Halloran thumped the door wide and walked in.

He gave Julien a cool nod, then glanced at Dulcie. "Adam's waiting on deck with pictures of his new baby boy. Remember to act all impressed and make a lot of approving noises. I need to talk to Langlois alone."

Dulcie came to her feet, hands in the pockets of

her shorts. Julien gathered the cards together, shuffled them, and dealt another game of solitaire.

"Fine. But I want to talk to you, Robert Michael Halloran, so don't you go sneaking off when you're done here."

Halloran nodded. Then she walked out the door, shutting it quietly behind her. Julien listened for the sound of her retreating footsteps, but heard nothing. Either she was real quiet on her feet, or she was listening outside. He almost smiled, remembering again how she'd leaped at him. Knowing that woman, she had her ear pressed up against the door.

"I don' suppose you're here to tell me you've got the Dragon locked up," Julien said, flipping over another card. A red six. Good. He needed one, and it looked like he just might win this hand.

Then a fist slammed down on the small table, scattering his cards.

Julien looked up.

"Good," Halloran said. "Reckon I got your attention now."

Julien didn't answer.

Halloran, who was wearing a striped shirt in orange and purple, pulled out a folding chair. He sat, fished a small notepad and pen from his pocket, and then leaned over the table, blue eyes unfriendly. "I don't suppose you want to revise your story for me."

"What story?" Julien asked, easing back in his chair. He folded his hands over his shirt and laced his fingers together. Tightly. Otherwise, he might be too tempted to grab the man by his loud shirt and slam him back against the wall. He regretted the need to be nice to cops. This cop in particular.

That Saints shirt of Halloran's in Dulcie's cabin sure didn't help matters, either.

"Langlois, I haven't had more than three hours of sleep, and you might say my patience is on the thin side." Halloran tapped his fingers against the chrome surface of the table. "So I'm only gonna ask this once. Is there anything about last night you sorta forgot to tell me?"

Julien glanced toward the door—the door Dulcie was probably still standing at, listening. But if Halloran wanted to pretend she wasn't there, he'd play along. "I told you everythin' that mattered. I was hired to dance. Somethin' went bad. A man got killed."

"Who hired you to dance?"

Julien hesitated. If Halloran was asking this question again, it signaled trouble and he'd best answer with care. "I already told you that, too. Chloe Mitsumi hired me."

"You sure? I talked with Chloe. She says she didn't hire any stripper."

"Chloe never talks to cops, so why would she talk to you?"

Halloran leaned further over the table. "Maybe she thinks I'm cute. Try again."

"For the last time, Halloran, I was at the Cracker to dance and give Jacob Mitsumi's sister a good time. Business is all it was." Under Halloran's unwavering stare, he began gathering the scattered cards. "A party for Chloe. She's a little wild, but you know what she's like."

"The bartender says you had a gun."

Julien looked up from his cards and smiled. "I took Hernandez's gun off him. So I could shoot back at the bad guys shootin' at me. You here to arrest me for taking off my clothes, or tryin' to protect myself?"

"Are you protecting someone else? Chloe, maybe? Is she your girlfriend? But no, that's not it, is it?"

Cold. Fingers of cold, creeping up along his spine. Julien stared at Halloran, noticing for the first time the confidence in the other man's eyes. "If this is an interrogation, I want a lawyer."

"It's not an interrogation. Yet," Bobby added. "I've got an idea about what you were doing at the Cracker, Langlois. Don't know why yet, but I'll figure it out."

Fingers of ice, closing hard around his gut. After a moment, Julien smiled again. "You have no idea what I was doin' there. Nothin' at all, but a cop's overactive imagination."

"That must be why I'm sitting here wondering if I need to protect my suspect from my witness."

After a moment, Julien looked away and shuffled the cards. Slowly. Deliberately.

Only a few days; it was all he needed. Julien tapped the cards back into a neat rectangle, thinking fast. "I don' know what you're gettin' at, but I'm cooperatin' with you. I'm here. I gave a statement. I'll even stay right where I am, for the next five days. Then I'm outta here. I got a life, Halloran. You can't keep me here. You know it.''

Halloran sat back, putting away his notepad. "Bet you'd play a mean game of poker, Langlois. Five days it is—unless I figure out before then what you were really gonna do with that gun in your hand. In the meantime, you promise not to give my people or Dulcie any more trouble?''

Julien smiled. "I don' make promises.''

"Doesn't surprise me much," Halloran said, pushing himself to his feet. He started for the door, then stopped short, as if he'd suddenly remembered something. Julien's guts knotted again. "Oh, yeah. Before I forget: let me give you a piece of advice. Dulcie is a special woman, and I'd take it real personal if anything were to happen to her. So see to it that you don't hurt her. We clear on this, Langlois?''

"I hear you," Julien answered. If he'd had any doubts that this man had an intimate relationship with Dulcie Quinn, past or present, the look in those blue eyes settled the matter. Julien experienced a startling, intense flare of jealousy.

He wasn't sure which bothered him more: that his Amazon had slept with Halloran, or that he could feel jealous over a woman he barely knew . . . until he'd kissed her clear to her soul.

Anger, rash and goading, made him say, "Didn't exactly notice your initials carved on her bedpost.''

To Halloran's credit, he kept his temper leashed. Anger flared on his face and his body stiffened, but he maintained control. "Remember what I said.''

*   *   *

Dulcie had backed away quickly at the sound of footsteps approaching the door, as Bobby said, "Doesn't surprise me much." Not wanting either of them to know she'd overheard the conversation, she quickly sought out Adam Guidreau. She found him standing at the front of the boat showing a handful of pictures to Les, who was nodding his head and smiling.

"Those pictures of your new boy, Adam?" Dulcie called out, and hurried to the young detective's side. "Let me see. Oh, isn't he sweet?"

She didn't really see the baby, beyond that he looked like most new babies, a rather lumpy little thing with no hair. But Adam beamed proudly and assured her he was already a hardy little guy.

Dulcie, like Les, nodded and smiled. But she was thinking about Julien, and the conversation she'd just overheard. Julien had had a gun. And he was involved with the beautiful, notorious Chloe Mitsumi.

Oh, God. Dulcie took a deep breath. Instead of answering questions, her eavesdropping had only added to them.

Adam was still going on about his kid when Bobby came out on deck. Dulcie took a quick measure of his temper by the look on his face. His mobile mouth was set in a tight line, and his eyes were shooting blue fire. It had been a long while since she had seen him so angry.

"You wanted to talk to me?" he snapped.

Dulcie shook her head. "It'll wait. I can tell Julien didn't leave you in the best of moods. I know the feeling.''

He glared at her. "I told him not to give you any lip and no more stupid stunts like trying to jump off the boat. He promised he'd stay and behave himself for five days.''

Promised? Oh, Bobby, Bobby . . .

"Sounds good to me," Dulcie said. She hesitated, then added, "Is there anything else you want to tell me?''

Bobby had already turned and walked away, but he stopped at her question and looked over his shoulder. His eyes were hooded. She knew that look too, and it reminded her with a jolt that she was no longer a cop. No longer part of that privileged circle. "Nothing I can think of, darlin'. Why?''

I need to protect my suspect from my witness.

The loud clothes, good ol' boy drawl, and sunny good looks had never fooled her. Bobby Halloran was sharp. If he had a reason to suspect his witness wasn't playing it straight, it was probably a reasonable one.

"Just instinct, Bobby," she retorted, unable to keep her resentment at bay. "Remember I still have it.''

"Good for you. And remember I ain't deaf. Whatever you heard through that door, you go ahead and forget it.''

She felt the heat beneath her skin, but refused to apologize. He'd involved her in this investigation, for better or worse, and he wasn't pulling out on her now. There was a piece of Red Dragon with her name on it, and she was going to have it.

"We'll be heading out to Mike's soon."

"Keep me posted. I'll tell Les and Lucy I want regular reports by phone."

"Bobby!" she called, as he vaulted over to the pier. He turned.

"Yeah?"

"Remember what I said yesterday. Stay alert. Take care of yourself."

He gave her a thumbs-up. "Don't let Langlois give you any trouble."

She smiled, although it was forced. "You know me. I never let anybody give me any trouble."

After making certain all the main doors were open, so she had a clear view down the middle of the houseboat, Dulcie took the helm and began the long, slow journey from Lake Pontchartrain to Bayou Terre aux Boeufs.

The trip took most of the morning, since her houseboat chugged along at a leisurely pace. There was plenty of opportunity to enjoy the scenery, as the mist-covered shorelines of early morning gave way to a haunting vista of gray water matching a gray sky. The sun didn't break through the thick, quilted clouds.

Fog swirled above the dark water and through the gray-green trees draped with tendrils of Spanish moss. It was beautiful. Stark and eerie and beautiful. She'd always loved the bayou—the graceful herons, and even the alligators slicing silently through dark, still water as they stalked their prey.

Speaking of gators, she'd better keep an eye on Julien. Out on the wide front deck, he was teaching Les and Lucille how to play *bourré*. With easy charm, he brushed aside Lucille's suggestion to play strip poker, saying he was here to enjoy himself, not do any work. Dulcie smiled herself as Lucille's laughter nearly drowned out the sound of the engines. For a moment, she pictured Julien in a white plantation hat, a red brocade vest, and an old-fashioned coat with tails. He'd have made a grand riverboat gambler.

Sitting apart from the others, Dulcie thought again of the conversation she'd overheard. On the surface Julien's story sounded plausible enough, but if Chloe claimed she never hired a stripper and Julien said she did, then somebody was lying.

I need to protect my suspect from my witness.

She mulled over Bobby's words, frowning, while the deck beneath her feet rolled and Julien Langlois laughed as he cleaned house with another hand of *bourré*.

Bobby had all but accused Julien of setting up Mitsumi. She wondered what other evidence he'd turned up to make him suspicious.

By habit, she reviewed the facts at hand. Looming large was Julien's insistence on leaving police protection. She might understand fear, even frustration, but not the sort of anger she'd sensed. Then there were his efforts to either charm her or anger her into letting him off the boat, as well as the one attempt in which he might have slugged her in the jaw and jumped to the pier.

Since assault was a crime, Julien presumably had a strong reason for almost crossing the line between blameless bystander and lawbreaker.

Had Julien gone to the Cracker to strip off his clothes for Chloe Mitsumi and then betray her brother to Juan Hernandez?

It was possible. Then again, maybe Bobby simply wanted to make certain his witness wasn't up to any funny business which might nullify his testimony and set Mitsumi free on a technicality.

Now, that made perfect sense.

Dulcie stared at Julien as he expertly fanned the deck of cards. One other question nagged at the back of her mind. Why had he agreed to remain in police protection for five days? Why not ten or twenty?

Julien suddenly looked up, meeting her gaze. He smiled, leaving her cold despite the warm October afternoon.

Never judge a book by its cover.

In Julien's case there hadn't been much of a cover at all, and that was the problem. She'd reacted to him just as he'd wanted.

He hadn't wanted her to look beyond tanned, oiled skin and toned muscles. He hadn't wanted her to see anything more than a flashy stripper living life in the fast lane, who assumed that easy charm and a lazy smile was a sure ticket to wherever he wanted to go.

Now she suspected there was much more to Julien Langlois than a body to die for and a killer grin.

What a poor choice of words, she thought, and shivered.

Chapter 7

"HAVE YOU LOCATED Langlois yet?"

"No, Mr. Mitsumi. Not yet."

Jacob Mitsumi adjusted the antique toy train engine on its track, then stepped back and looked at the man standing by the door. Greg was a bull of a man. Bulging thighs filled his denim jeans and a pair of mountainous shoulders strained the seams of his faded chambray shirt. Loyal. Obedient. Just smart enough to be trusted, and stupid enough not to question orders.

"We don't think the cops have him after all," Greg added. He stood in a wide-legged stance, hands clasped respectfully before him. "Stan said there's been a cop staked out at Langlois' apartment since yesterday morning."

"What did the bartender at the Cracker say?"

"Not much. He saw Langlois leave, but he doesn't know if it was with the cops. He says the cops have been asking him a lot of questions. Me and Stan, we think Langlois is hiding out. He

91

hasn't been to any of his clubs, and it looks like the cops are watching out for him there too."

"What's the word on the streets?"

Greg shifted slightly. "Halloran's in charge of this one. He's sitting tight on it. Not much information is leaking out."

Mitsumi nodded. He looked around the old warehouse he was temporarily living in until his situation settled down. He usually came here only for relaxation. It was his favorite place: an entire floor of one old building devoted entirely to his hobby of model trains. Old, new. Expensive or common, it didn't matter. He'd built the track and the terrain with his own hands, just as he'd built a life for himself and his sister out of broken homes and poverty.

He liked to build things, and the trains gave him a powerful sense of control and serenity. He needed both just now. His rivals, lesser men, sought to destroy what he was building in this city. The law wished to control his needs and desires, and his sister—his weak sister—grieved him deeply. He mourned for the perfect child she had been, the treasure of his desperate years long gone.

"It's my latest treasure," Mitsumi said, lifting the antique engine off its track again. The red paint was chipped and much of the glass in the windows was missing, but he could see the potential in the old toy. He'd fix it, make it perform perfectly. "Isn't she a beauty?"

"Sure is, Mr. Mitsumi."

He put the engine down, then walked to the far

end of the room to where he had a 1954 Lionel Surfliner running a circuit through a replica of an East Coast mountain village. Greg followed silently.

"You're keeping a close eye on my sister?"

"Yes, Mr. Mitsumi."

"I'm not happy she talked to a cop."

"Wasn't her fault, sir. He followed her into the bathroom."

"But I'm not happy with Chloe. If she wasn't such a slut, none of this would have happened. Watch her. Desperate men will use her to get to me. We know that now. She shames me."

Again, the big man shifted on his feet, obviously uncomfortable. "She's not a bad kid, Mr. Mitsumi. We'll take care of her, keep her out of trouble. And we'll find Langlois."

"Just remember, he's mine. If you find him, you are not to touch him. Only keep me informed of his activities."

This order plainly didn't sit well with his bodyguard, but Greg was too loyal to question orders. "Yes, Mr. Mitsumi."

"This man has challenged my honor. I will deal with him myself."

"Yes, sir. I understand."

"Good," Mitsumi said. "Killing that other stripper was an error, but I have seen to it that it will not happen again."

Greg, understanding, dropped his gaze to his shoes.

Smiling, Mitsumi walked around to the other

side of the miniature village and activated a switch. A second train jerked into motion, very near the other. "Watch this," he ordered.

Obediently the other man came closer, pale eyes intent on the two separate trains winding around buildings, lakes, trees, and over the top of plaster mountains, then through them. Mitsumi adjusted the speed on one. The trains continued on their separate course, but the faster train was coming closer and closer to the slower one.

Realizing what would happen, Greg straightened and said, "They're going to crash."

"Inevitable," Mitsumi agreed. "Separate circles, the course unaltered. Day after day after day, all factors the same. Until something changes. Something we cannot predict. Despite ourselves, we cannot stop what will be."

A moment later, the two trains collided and Jacob Mitsumi laughed softly.

"Am I not wise?"

"Yes, Mr. Mitsumi."

He felt wise. He felt powerful, in control. He was the Red Dragon, a creature of ancient and mystical power, and in a few days he would avenge the insult to his honor and that of his sister. He would enjoy it.

No one challenged the Red Dragon and lived.

Chapter 8

DULCIE NEVER TIRED of the beauty she found in Bayou Terre aux Boeufs, or the peaceful solitude of the old cabin which sat at the end of a warped, weather-worn pier, in the embrace of a small inlet. The cabin itself was almost completely hidden by a circle of trees. Spanish moss, like tattered mantles, trailed from the branches. As the afternoon sun tried to break through the gray clouds above, she decided city life was overrated.

Seated beside her were Les, Lucille, and Julien, all lounging in deck chairs. If not for the fact that Les and Lucille were still wearing their blues, no one would have thought anything out of the ordinary at seeing a group of people taking their ease on the deck of a boat.

She was feeling particularly complacent because she had a very full stomach.

Somehow, Julien had found the ingredients to make a spicy jambalaya for lunch. Once she looked a little closer, she recognized hot dogs disguised as sausage, but gave him extra points for originality. He'd also made fresh coffee, a salad, and rice pudding.

"I'm in love," Lucille declared, stuffing her face.

Dulcie smiled back, licking creamy rice pudding from the back of her plastic spoon. "You'll love him a little less when you see the dishes." Lucille grimaced. "There's probably a mess from one end of my kitchen to the other. Am I right, Julien?"

"Maybe." He sprawled in a deck chair, his boots crossed at his ankles and his hands behind his head. The wind blew his long hair back and Dulcie's stomach did one of those strange lurches she was beginning to recognize, and even predict.

Julien had been polite and helpful since they'd left Lake Pontchartrain. He didn't back her into any more corners, try to kiss her, or make her mad. She would've believed he'd decided to cooperate with the police, if it hadn't been for all those times she caught him watching her with those dark, hooded eyes. Looks that told her something was going on beneath that suspiciously helpful exterior.

"It's very good," Les added, diplomatic as ever. "Where did you learn to cook like this?"

"Here and there," Julien said.

"He has a big family," Dulcie volunteered, since he was being evasive. She doubted modesty had anything to do with it. She'd never met anyone as shameless as Julien Langlois.

"How big?" Les asked politely.

Julien hesitated. Dulcie looked up just as he answered, "Ten kids."

"Whoa," said Lucille. "I like kids, but one or two would do just fine."

"Good Catholics." Dulcie scraped away the last of the pudding from the coffee cup, which had been pressed into duty as a bowl.

"What I want to know, Julien, is what's for dinner?" Les patted his round belly with satisfaction. If the route to Lucille's approval was by way of her libido, the key to Les's good graces was predictably through his stomach. Julien was a smashing success with both his 'jailers.'

"I was thinkin' redfish," Julien answered. He glanced over at Dulcie, where she still sat sucking on her spoon and debating whether she should ask for seconds. "Got any fishing gear on board?"

"I think so."

"Looks like good fishin' here. Les can catch us a couple redfish and you an' I can clean those dishes."

"You cooked," Dulcie reminded him pointedly. Whenever possible, she still avoided being alone with Julien, despite his improved behavior. She couldn't quite shake the feeling that she was a mouse sharing a cage with a great, hungry cat. "Lucille can help me."

"Me?" Lucille sputtered. "Uh-uh. No way. I'd rather put worms on hooks than do dishes. Besides, I'm on duty."

Julien pushed himself out of the deck chair. "That's it, then." He collected the dishes with an expertise that had Dulcie wondering if he'd waited tables between taking off his clothes. She caught Lucille watching Julien's rear, and repressed her sudden urge to shake the woman until her teeth rattled. "C'mon, Dulcie. We got work to do."

With a sigh, Dulcie pushed herself out of her own deck chair. "In a minute. I'll get the fishing stuff."

She finally found the gear stashed in a storage compartment on the rear deck. Four fishing poles and a tackle box with a mishmash jumble of lures, line, and shriveled 'live' bait. "There you go," she said, handing the mess over to Les and Lucille.

"I'm beginning to like this bodyguard business," Lucille said, cranking a reel tighter. "Beats driving around city streets in a squad car. And the scenery's real nice, too." She grinned at Dulcie.

"That," Dulcie said, heading toward the front room, "is one fish you'll never land."

Lucille laughed and Les gave a snort of amusement. "I don't want to exactly land him, hon. I'll settle for just playing him on a lure for a bit."

"Lucille, for shame! You're a police officer. You're supposed to be morally upstanding."

Lucille, whose mind was perpetually in the gutter, howled with laughter. With a long-suffering groan, Dulcie pushed the screen door open, then went inside to wash dishes and keep Julien Langlois at a safe distance.

Julien surveyed the kitchenette. He'd made a mess all right. Dulcie wouldn't be happy. He'd done as much damage control as possible while the others talked and laughed on deck but hadn't made near enough progress by the time she breezed into the room.

God, she was a fine-looking woman. He'd watched her in the hazy light as they ate lunch, with her auburn hair a bright spot of color against the gray sky and swamp. He'd half-answered all Les's questions, fielded Lucille's exuberant innuendoes, and never completely taken his gaze from Dulcie.

She'd avoided him since the morning she'd slapped him. While Julien figured he'd deserved that slap, he wasn't used to women avoiding him, not like that. But now and then, he'd catch her gray-green eyes watching him, a frown puckering her brows, before she'd look away. Almost as if she were waiting for something.

"Oh, my God."

Those gray-green eyes were wide with shock as she surveyed the shambles of her kitchenette. Julien self-consciously rubbed at his jaw—he needed a shave, he realized—and tried his best lady-killer smile. "Sorry, *chère*."

"What a mess. You *are* a pig, Langlois!"

"Am not," he said amiably, maneuvering around her body to dump paper plates and plastic utensils in the garbage can. "I do everythin' with passion. Even cookin'. You're lookin' at artistic passion, not a mess."

"Interesting excuse. Can't say I've heard that one before."

She stiffened when his chest brushed against her shoulder, but she didn't pull away. He hadn't meant to do anything more than clean up, but finding himself with his Amazon shot his better intentions all to hell. *Merde*, maybe he'd meant all along to get her alone.

"I'll scrub. You dry," he said, drawing back toward the sink. He needed to get himself under control. This instant, powerful response to Dulcinea Quinn caused him a stab of unease. He didn't want to react to her. He couldn't.

There was only blackness inside him, ever since the day he'd stood above a grave and let dirt trickle through his fingers, fine dust settling on the polished silver casket, pebbles thudding off its lid.

Yet whenever he was around Dulcie, something of an old spark returned, which wasn't good. He couldn't let her close. There was too much to lose if she found out the truth.

"Mind if I put some music on?"

The question startled him from his thoughts and Julien looked up. He met her measuring gaze. He did mind, but said, "Not at all."

Silently, he listened to her rummage through a box of tapes on her workbench and then she made a small sound of satisfaction. By the time she joined him again at the sink, the easy, twangy voice of Garth Brooks spilled from the cabin.

"Garth okay?" she asked as he filled the small sink with warm water.

"Fine."

"You like country?"

Dieu, fiddles and steel guitars, harmonicas and boot-stomping beats. Everything lost to him. He looked down at the sink. "I like pretty much any music. Don' you know us *Cadiens* are born with music in our blood?''

He plunged his hands into the soapy water as she said, ''I'll put some zydeco on next, maybe a little bluesy blues. I've got everything from Nine Inch Nails to Gregorian chants. Depends on my mood.''

''And you're in a Garth Brooks mood?''

She looked away when he caught her watching him. ''Yeah.''

''Good. Don' think I can manage singin' monks today.''

Nothing monklike about what he was feeling right now. It was small comfort that Dulcie appeared equally uneasy with this attraction between them. He applied his muscles to the dried egg on the pan, aware that his leg brushed against hers. She moved away a little, trying not to be obvious about it.

Silence. Les and Lucille laughing on deck. The sound of steel wool scratching on cast iron. Her slow, even breathing.

The music. The beautiful, living music . . .

''I really appreciate your cooking like this, Julien.''

Taking a deep breath, Julien handed her the heavy pan. Her fingers closed over his. The pan was slippery with water, so he held on longer than need be, wanting to make sure she had a firm grip before letting it go. Or so he told himself. ''Least I can do, seein' as how I put a damper on your doll show plans.''

He grabbed the next pan from the stove while she toweled that one dry.

''I suppose we put a damper on a few of yours, too.''

A fraction of a second passed before he trusted himself to glance at her. But she had focused her attention on the pan, scratching off a nonexistent piece of debris from its surface.

''Nothin' I can't pick up when I get off this boat,'' he said evenly.

She met his gaze then. Over the sound of Garth singing about burning bridges, Julien looked into her eyes and, with a jolt, saw suspicion.

Heat roared through his body. Sweat beaded on his forehead, his upper lip. He turned his attention back to the pan in his hands.

She knew.

He pushed back the fear. She couldn't. Not the whole truth. She had guessed that his relentless attempts to charm her were intended to gain her cooperation; he hadn't been at all subtle about it. But she couldn't know about the rest. Not even Halloran had guessed. Yet. Just his luck, to tangle with the sharpest homicide cop on the New Orleans police force.

He had four days. Four days to keep Dulcie guessing; four days to hope Halloran was too busy chasing down Mitsumi to dig up old bones. Four days to keep himself alive, and then it wouldn't matter anymore.

Julien couldn't do anything about Halloran, but he knew one sure way to distract the ex-cop standing beside him, watching him with growing suspicion in her eyes.

No. Let go of the music and the feeling. Let go of what he hungered for. He silently counted. Oblivious to the music, the sound of footsteps on the deck, or the steady breathing of the woman beside him, he counted until he'd buried the need again.

"Julien?" She was talking to him. He felt a gentle poke in his arm and looked up. "Are you okay? Kinda spaced on me there."

"Tired, is all. This cloak an' dagger crap must be catchin' up with me." He finished with the pan in his hands, then handed it over. This time, when her hands closed over his, he brushed his thumb against the inside of her palm. A slow rhythm, unmistakable in its intent.

She blinked once but didn't move. After a moment, he took the pan from her and put it aside. When he tugged a little, she came to him without protest or hesitation. He slipped his wet hands around to her back, then lowered his mouth to hers. Before he touched her lips in a gentle kiss, her eyes closed.

She tasted faintly of vanilla. He pulled her closer, pressing her breasts against his chest, her hips against his own. She responded sweetly. So sweetly. Her arms twining about his neck, pulling him down to her mouth, meeting the growing intensity of his kiss with her own.

White heat, this woman in his arms. Her mouth opened beneath his, against the insistent pressure of his tongue. With a low groan deep in his throat,

Julien dropped his hands to her firm rear in those red shorts. He cupped her roundness, urging her hips closer to his, against the erection that strained toward her, no matter how he tried to will it away; no matter how he tried to deaden himself against his need for her.

He began easing the T-shirt from her shorts, then went still as she yanked at his tank top. She ran her hands up along the skin of his back, then her fingernails closed over the muscles of his shoulder.

Smack-bang, she kicked his control clear out the door.

With a quick, sure movement, he turned her against the counter and coaxed her legs apart with his knee. She arched her hips against him, enticing and begging without words.

"*Dieu*," he muttered, breaking away from her lips to draw in a deep, ragged breath. He brought a hand up to cup her breast, and in a heated flash remembered a peek of plum-purple lace. He bent, kissing the side of her breast, wanting to fill his hands with soft roundness and kiss her skin through the lace.

Then, without warning, she pushed him forcefully back.

"That mouth of yours is something," Dulcie said, breathing harshly, her breasts rising and falling beneath the white knit of her shirt. "All of you is something," she added, her eyes wide and pupils dark and round. "Make no mistake, Julien, there's nothing I'd like better than to go to bed with you. But as much as I want to feel you inside me . . ."

She trailed off, as if struggling to admit this truth. "It's just not going to happen."

Julien couldn't move. Growing anger, confusion, and a raging lust held him still and silent where he stood. He stared at her, uncomprehending. Her body said she wanted him, yet she pushed him away. Dammit, everything she said and did tortured him with images of them joined together.

He wanted to be with her . . . and he didn't want to be with her. She was making him crazy, either way.

"You're only doing this to get what you want," Dulcie continued softly, so that her voice did not carry. "You may tempt me, Julien, but I won't let you off this boat, or go to bed with you. It wouldn't be right, and I know the difference between right and wrong. Unlike you."

She walked away from him without a backward glance, leaving him hurting and angry and, for the first time in many months, ashamed.

Dulcie told Les and Lucille that Julien had decided to do the dishes himself. She tried to keep the sharpness from her voice, but could tell by the looks they exchanged that she hadn't been successful. She was too upset to care, and retreated without a word of explanation to the helm.

She sat there, alone and uncommunicative, while Les caught three redfish and a speckled trout and Lucille fussed around at Mike's old cabin, trying to make it habitable enough for her and Les to sleep in. Julien didn't come back on deck, but she hadn't expected him to show his face anytime soon.

Why did he keep this up? She'd told him, all along, that she wouldn't help him escape police protection or let him off her boat. That she wasn't fooled by his smooth charm, even if she wasn't immune to it.

So why hadn't he abandoned his attempts at seduction?

It scared her. She had never felt such a powerful, irrational attraction to a man before, and sometimes she didn't want to push him away. She wanted to pull instead.

She never should have trusted herself to be alone with Julien. This latest near-disaster was more her fault than his.

Why did she turn into mindless female putty at one touch, one kiss, from a dark, handsome Cajun with mystery in his eyes? Because she was lonely— as much as she hated to admit it.

Although she sat long enough worrying about it, Dulcie still hadn't found a reasonable solution to her dilemma by the time she saw the familiar unmarked car drive up beside Mike's cabin.

Bobby got out of the mud-splattered car and Adam Guidreau followed. The two burly detectives from the other night climbed out of their own car, which they'd parked right behind Bobby's.

"Wonder what's up," Lucille said from behind.

"You didn't know Bobby was coming here?" Dulcie asked, glancing over her shoulder. Les leaned further over the rail, frowning.

"No," Lucille answered, as Bobby began walking toward the pier. "He didn't say anything when I talked to him an hour ago."

"Guess we'll find out soon enough," Dulcie said, and a sudden dread pressed down upon her. She watched Bobby exchange a few brief words with the two big detectives. Then they went to stand on the cabin's porch, which drooped into a smiling line between the supporting stilts. Bobby crossed the pier, and jumped to the side deck.

"Hey, Dulcie."

"Bobby, we weren't expecting you."

"I know. Where's Langlois?"

"In the cabin."

"Adam, get him," Bobby ordered. "I want to see all of you in Mike's place. Now."

No smile, and he was dressed sedately—except for the purple tie—in a light gray shirt and pleated black chino pants. He even carried a briefcase. Her feeling of dread intensified.

Without a word, Dulcie brushed past Bobby and climbed over to the pier. Her footsteps pounded against the wooden planking, joined by the others' as they followed. She nodded at each of the Bruiser Boys, then entered the little cabin.

Smelling like an old earthen cellar, it looked much as it had the last time she'd visited, except that Lucille had tidied it some. Its single room contained only a card table, three folding chairs, and a cot. There was no plumbing or electricity. It was strictly a place to stay when hunting and fishing, just one notch up from sleeping on the ground.

Dulcie pulled out a chair, sat down, and waited

for the others to file in. Julien, Bobby, and Adam came in last. She saw how Julien's glance rested briefly on her face before he looked away.

"Sit down," Bobby said. The brusque tone of his voice didn't bode well. Julien shook his head, refusing the chair. Lucille sat instead. Everyone else remained standing.

Bobby slammed his briefcase down on the table, the explosive sound echoing in the quiet of the room. Dulcie glanced at Julien, but he was busy making patterns in the dusty floor with the toe of one black boot and didn't meet her look.

"What's going on?" Dulcie asked, turning back to Bobby as he opened the briefcase. He pulled out a folder, then tossed it on the table. Dulcie caught it before it slid off the edge, and raised her eyebrows at Bobby.

"Take a look. It'll answer your question."

Silently, Dulcie picked up the folder. It was thin for a case file, and marked by a coffee stain on one edge. Then she saw the name on the label. With a gasp, she shot a look at Julien. He watched her, his eyes dark and glittering in the low light of the room. "Marcel Langlois," she said.

At her soft words, Julien lowered his lashes, turned sharply on his heel and walked to the window.

"Adam found this while doing a background check on my prize witness here. Go on. Look. I figure you deserve to know the truth."

Dulcie looked from Julien back to Bobby again, teeth worrying her lower lip. She opened the folder, seeing a photo of a sullen-eyed teenaged boy with dark hair. A baby. He was no more than a baby. She lifted the photo and found another beneath. She closed her eyes against what it revealed.

"Kid showed up dead about six months ago. Caught in cross fire. We blamed it on gang warfare." In the silence, Bobby's voice sounded even and dispassionate. "He was sixteen, had a few brushes with the law, and he was a junkie. The pathology report says he had enough crack in him the night he died that he probably never even knew what hit him."

Dulcie couldn't look at Julien, where he leaned against the wall by the window, hands in the pocket of his jeans and staring out across the gray swamp. After taking a deep, calming breath, she thumbed through the file, her fingers hesitant.

There wasn't much. Typed forms, scribbled reports, and heartbreaking photos were all that remained of a young life that had come to a violent end. She knew the answer to her question before she found it on the last page, spelled out in blue ink on yellow lined paper. "Julien's brother."

She heard Lucille let out a small sigh and Bobby spoke again, his voice quiet. "The case is still open. No convictions. The witnesses who'd cooperate pointed fingers at Red Dragon's people. But there wasn't enough evidence to arrest anyone. Not even a motive for pumpin' a sixteen-year-old kid full of bullets, beyond that Dealer A muscled in on Dealer B's territory and Dealer B got even—no matter who might've been in the way."

Silence followed again, heavy and ripe with speculation. Dulcie carefully placed the coffee-stained file back onto the table. She still couldn't look at Julien. "Oh, God," she whispered.

More silence, finally broken by the sound of Bobby's footsteps as he moved back from the table. "Game's up, Langlois." There was no note of victory in his voice; only weariness.

I need to protect my suspect from my witness.

It all fell into place. The desperation to get out of police protection. The lack of fear.

Chloe Mitsumi had never hired Julien to dance at the Cracker the night Hernandez died.

Julien had gone there to kill Jacob Mitsumi.

Dulcie lifted her gaze to Julien. He still hadn't turned from the window, and she tried to swallow past the lump in her throat.

Bobby was speaking again. "You must've known it would only take me a couple of days to make the connection. Right?" More silence. "Hey, I asked you a question, Langlois." At Julien's short nod, Bobby ran a hand through his hair, then rubbed at his brow. His voice was bitter. "Thought so. We try so hard to be obliging."

"Get to the point, Halloran," Julien said at last.

"The point is, I can let you go. Right now. But I'll be on you every second of the day. You won't even be able to take a piss without me knowing about it. Go after Red Dragon yourself, and I'll haul your butt in jail for attempted murder. You'll be safe enough there, I reckon. So go on—leave. Give me a chance to lock you up. Legal-like."

Dulcie briefly closed her eyes as Bobby put her fear into words. But, oh, a sixteen-year-old! She should've been angry over Julien's deceptions. Instead, she felt only a deep, hollow grief—for a boy shot to death on a street corner, probably just for being there, and for that dead boy's brother, who had finally turned from the window. In the dark room, he was all blackness and shadows.

"I could refuse to testify."

"You won't, if you know what's good for you. You know, I've talked with Chloe. She admits to an 'acquaintance,' but swears she never hired you to dance at the Cracker, and she's willing to testify to that in court. The initial crime scene report says Hernandez's gun was found under his body. The only other gun we found at the scene was reported stolen four months ago. Things don't look so good for you, Langlois. I don't know exactly what went down at the Cracker, but I bet you had a whole lot more to do with it than a jury's gonna like."

"I didn't kill Hernandez."

"Your word against Mitsumi's," Bobby retorted, a note of frustration sharpening his voice. "Even the bartender had hit the floor by the time the shooting started. You were my only witness, dammit, and now I find out you meant to kill Mitsumi. Couldn't wait for the police to do their job; you had to go take the law into your own hands. For Marcel, who was sixteen and a junkie and died in a drive-by shooting. You were taking care of him, weren't you? Not very good care of him, I guess, but—"

They had no warning. Before anyone could move to stop him, Julien had Bobby on his back across the table, fingers tight around his neck. Bobby's face began to turn a dark, mottled red. "One more word an' I break your neck," Julien said softly.

"Let . . . go," Bobby gasped, grasping at the fingers around his neck. But when the two big detectives moved toward Julien with grim intent, Bobby gave an abbreviated shake of his head.

"Julien," Dulcie said, her own fingers digging into the tense, rock-hard muscles of his arm. "Let him go."

Julien tightened his fingers in a final warning before he let go of Bobby's neck and stepped back.

Bobby sat up, readjusted his tie, and smoothed back his hair. He coughed. "Don't like cops much, do you, Langlois?"

"Can't say I do."

The tension in the room was thick, dangerous. Les and Lucille were on their feet, hands on their guns. Adam had moved behind Julien, and the two Bruiser Boys—O'Donnell and Martindale—radiated a need to hurt something. Dulcie's own muscles were so tight she thought she would shatter if anyone touched her.

"Deal with it," Bobby said, after clearing his throat again. "Kids are murdered every day. Sometimes the killers go to jail, sometimes not. I don't like it any more than you do, but help me put Red Dragon away and you'll do right by your brother. I understand what you did, even if I don't agree with it, and you gotta know any other cop would just haul you into lockup right now. But I'm giving you a chance, man. Don't throw it away."

"Not enough, Halloran. It'll never be enough!"

Julien and Bobby faced off against each other in the dimness of the bare room. Two men with the same objective; one working from within the law, the other without. Bobby's way was the right one, but because her own assailants were never convicted, Dulcie could understand Julien's anger. Sometimes the law didn't punish the bad guys, it just tucked them away for a spell and returned them to the streets meaner than ever.

"Langlois, I'm real sorry about what happened to your brother. But you gotta let me do my job. You'll get yourself killed if you go after Mitsumi yourself. Give the law a chance."

Julien's answer was to turn away. "I already did."

For a moment, there was no sound in the room. "Then I reckon we understand each other," Bobby said coldly. "What are you gonna do?"

Julien returned to the window, seemingly oblivious to Adam and the Bruiser Boys hovering around him. "Already told you. I gave you five days to get Mitsumi. Now you got four."

Bobby exhaled loudly. "Adam, take him outside."

"You arrestin' me?"

"Not yet. But jump ship, and I promise I'll have you in jail so fast your head'll spin. Think of what I've been saying to you. Dulcie, I want you to come back with me. This changes everything. I don't feel right, leaving him with you. Even with Les and Lucille on hand.''

"I'm staying.''

"Dulcie—''

No. No way. After what she'd just learned, Bobby would have to drag her away kicking and screaming. "You let me see this through to the finish. I'm still part of the team, Bobby. I want my piece of Red Dragon.'' She delivered her coup de grâce. "You owe me.''

Adam had brought Julien to the door, his hand firm on Julien's arm. Dulcie took a sharp breath, watching Bobby and Julien staring each other down. Like a couple of mean junkyard dogs. It sickened her, the violence barely held in check beneath muscle and skin, silk and civility.

"Hurt her, Langlois, and there isn't a rock you can hide under where I won't find you. Remember that. Get him out of here.''

After Adam and the Bruiser Boys hauled Julien back to the houseboat, Bobby turned on Dulcie, Les, and Lucille. "I don't like it,'' he snapped.

"Is he dangerous?'' Dulcie shot back.

"He was gonna kill a man, for chrissake!''

"Red Dragon is still breathing, isn't he? Do *you* think Julien's dangerous?''

"No,'' Bobby admitted with a short, exasperated shrug. "Except maybe to himself. Man's got a damn death wish.''

"You ran a background check on him, right?'' Lucille demanded.

"Yeah. Adam turned up nothing. Until six months ago Langlois didn't even have a parking violation to his name. Just a construction worker who liked the night life. In the past few months, he's been rounded up a few times in drug sweeps and an occasional raid on the clubs he danced at. Always came away clean. No drug use, no prostitution. Just a dancer."

Les glanced at Dulcie, then said, "Langlois hasn't been any trouble, except for the one incident. Knowing what we do now, we can keep a closer eye on him. We should head back to Lake Pontchartrain. He can't get into much trouble there. Here, he can always run off into the bayou. And he's been through hard times. Some understanding might help straighten him out."

Dulcie made up her mind in that moment. *Game's up*, Bobby had said, but she didn't think so. The players and rules had changed, that was all. She stood. "Give me those four days, Bobby. We've both lost something to Mitsumi. Maybe he'll listen to me in a way he won't listen to you. Let me at least try."

"Not here," Bobby said at last. It was a capitulation. As close as she was likely to get. The look in his blue eyes told her he hated the idea. Bobby didn't trust Julien Langlois.

Dulcie didn't, either. But Quinn instinct whispered that this crackling attraction between her and Julien just might be strong enough to burn through all the anger and the lies.

"We'll drop anchor in the middle of the lake and

stay put," she said. "I promise I'll holler at the first sign of trouble."

"She did, the other day," Les pointed out, helpful as ever.

Dulcie watched Bobby struggle with his common sense and the desire to make sure his tarnished witness survived long enough to put Jacob Mitsumi in prison. Common sense lost out. It usually did, with Bobby Halloran. She knew her man.

"I want regular phone contact. You report in every hour on the hour. Got that?" Bobby demanded, jabbing his finger at her for emphasis.

"Got it," Dulcie said, repressing the urge to sigh with relief.

"Lord, I must be outta my mind," Bobby muttered.

But he'd agreed, and as soon as the realization settled in, Dulcie wondered what the hell she'd just done.

And why she cared so much for the future of a man who'd lied to her, tried to use her, and who she wanted to slap half the time.

Chapter 9

BY THE TIME Dulcie headed back to the houseboat, her confidence had given way to unease, and now she tried to isolate and understand her fear.

What was she afraid of?

Julien, for one. He wasn't the man she'd thought he was, and his ability to keep so much turbulence hidden beneath a smooth surface left her cold. She'd known next to nothing about him before; now, she knew even less. Except that he'd lost a young brother to Red Dragon's thugs, who cruised the streets and alleys looking for any excuse to hurt and kill. She'd seen that truth in heart-wrenching black and white.

Was he a stripper, or had he only used his looks and body as a disguise to descend to the dark underworld of crime and drugs? Hide in plain sight; simple, but perfect. It would even explain the acquaintance with Chloe Mitsumi, whose fondness for male strippers and male prostitutes was well known. An unexpected pang of jealousy shot through Dulcie at the thought of what that "acquaintance" implied.

More than anything, she was afraid of what she'd risk when she confronted Julien and tried to show him how wrong he was to abandon his belief in the law. Instinctively, she knew this would be no neat, well-mannered discussion between two opposing forces. Things would get complicated. Messy. She was going to get emotionally involved—as if she weren't already!—and she was going to care about the outcome. A lot.

God, she hoped she didn't screw this up, too.

She found herself standing at the closed door to her cabin. Taking a deep, steadying breath, she opened it and walked in. Julien lay on her bed, arms behind his head and ankles crossed. He'd removed his boots and she saw that even his socks were black.

Everything about him, outwardly, was so black and cold. But beneath that ran something she could only begin to guess at . . . and it wasn't cold or dead.

As Dulcie watched him, an odd ache tightened her chest. "I'm sorry," she said at length. He knew she stood there, but didn't acknowledge her presence. "About Marcel."

He didn't respond. He didn't move.

"Bobby might come across as hard, but he cares. It's just how he handles it. Drives you crazy, all that death and violence, if you don't harden to it. I know."

"A dead stranger in a body bag ain't the same, not until it's one of your own."

"No. I'm sorry," she repeated, not knowing

what else to say. She came further into the cabin, then closed the door behind her. "Want to talk about it?"

"No." The tone of his voice told her he meant it.

"I just want to do something."

"You done enough. Leave me the hell alone."

So. He'd shucked his charm at last, like a snake shedding its skin. She preferred his anger and rejection to the boy-toy poses and electric smiles. It was progress. Of a sort.

"Fine. I'll work on the dolls. Let me know if there's anything I can do."

"I don't want your goddamn pity!"

Dulcie froze. She'd half-expected such a reaction, but his words still hurt. She forced herself to move again, to affect a calmness she didn't feel. "You're not getting it, any more than I'd want it for myself. I know what happened to me is minor in comparison to your brother's death, but I lost more than a job when Red Dragon's men broke my back. I probably lost any chance to have children."

She said the last part in a near whisper, sitting down at the workbench. She pushed away the dressed baby doll and picked up Juliet, staring at the doll's serene face without really seeing it. "Red Dragon killed my babies, too. It doesn't hurt any less that I never gave birth or raised them first."

She didn't expect an answer, and didn't get one. She let out her breath in a nearly silent sigh. Then, with her back to Julien, she proceeded to attach Juliet's head to her kidskin body. After that was done, she transferred her attention to Romeo. Arms on the body, next the legs. Finally, the head. A pretty boy. Young, with eyes that seemed to foresee tragedy.

Dulcie focused on the dolls, hardly noticing how little the houseboat rocked on the calm waters of the inlet. Tomorrow they'd start back to Lake Pontchartrain. But tonight there would be quiet and peace, the smell of deep water and cloudy skies. The smell of timeless earth.

Julien made no sound behind her. She didn't know if he was asleep or awake, and wouldn't turn to look. He had to make the first move. She couldn't help him; not until he took that first step away from the edge himself.

She forced herself to think only of the dolls.

Juliet's dress had twenty pattern pieces, including the bodice, wide skirt, and slashed sleeves. The velvet was buttery-soft beneath her scissors as she made each precise cut, along scooping armholes and over pointed darts. Deep crimson velvet, the color of kings, queens, and these star-crossed lovers, she always thought. The color of old blood.

Gold tissue would puff through the slashed sleeves of crimson velvet, and she'd need to sew on each tiny pearl by hand over the sleeves and bodice. The only ornament to Juliet's long braid would be an embroidered cap.

It would take all night to put the costume together. She ignored the pain in her back as she bent over the workbench, intent only upon finishing the gown.

She had no idea how much time had passed, her arm rising and falling with each careful stitch, before she felt the light touch of Julien's hand on her shoulder. She didn't turn or acknowledge him, any more than he had earlier. The slight pressure of his fingers turned to a gentle massage, as he silently worked out the stiffness from her muscles. She finally put the needle and thread down over the velvet gown and sat still, her eyes closed, and let him ease the aches away.

"Sorry," he said.

She didn't know for what. He could have been sorry for the little tragedy she'd confessed hours ago, or his harsh words. It might have been for his brother, or the ugly violence in the world. Maybe all of it.

Nor did she know where the tears came from. They welled up from a place so deep inside her that she couldn't stop them. Tears for herself, for her little babies that might never be born. Tears for a boy shot to death. Tears for Julien, standing so close to the edge of blackness that he could no longer see how lost he was, much less the way to return.

She didn't even protest when Julien pulled her up from the bench and wrapped her in his arms. She cried like a child against his black silk shirt, holding on to him as if he could keep her from falling over some dark, unseen edge as well.

Dulcie would *not* let him go. She would not let him fall. She held tight to Julien as he murmured nonsense words of comfort in her ear, smoothing back her hair from her wet face.

She would not let the Dragon have him, too.

Julien held Dulcie close, ignoring the tears that made a sopping mess of his shirt. It didn't matter. All that mattered was to soothe her hurt, the hurt he'd unknowingly caused her. He'd never imagined so much pain buried behind her sass, and he hadn't thought of her as another victim of Red Dragon, because she was alive. Unlike Marcel.

Her warm tears dampened his shirt, and he envied her ability to let loose the hurt. He'd never cried. Not when he had stood beside Marcel's body and seen the damage the bullets had done to his baby brother. Not at the funeral, when his mother had collapsed from grief and his father had turned away from him without a word, his stiff back in that old suit damning Julien more than curses ever could. Not even sitting in his apartment afterwards, folding away Marcel's clothes, picking up the odds and ends of his brother's life. All the things Julien had never really noticed, except to tell Marcel to pick them the hell up off the floor so he wouldn't trip on them when he came home from work at night.

He'd learned at his old man's knee that grown men didn't ever cry. He wished he could.

"Shush now, *chère*," he murmured into Dulcie's hair, feeling the tremors in her tensed body. Her warm body that was all woman, all kindness. So full of comfort, and even while he ached to take her to bed, he wanted to hold her close and chase away her tears. Make her laugh. Make her mad. Anything but this.

"It's not fair," she said miserably. "I should've had kids, and your brother should've had a chance to grow up."

There was nothing to say to that, so he remained silent.

She sniffled, lifting her face. "I've ruined your shirt."

"*N'importe*, Dulcie. Don' matter. It's just a shirt."

She took a ragged breath and he felt the shudder of her exhalation beneath his hands, where they rested against her back. "I don't know why I'm crying like this . . . God, I'm such an idiot sometimes."

"Not true, an' you know it. It's no one's fault."

Fault. What a world of hurt in that one word. His fault Marcel had died. His fault he hadn't seen the danger until it was too late. His fault that while he was out looking for his brother, his brother was dying, with only strangers at his side.

He'd trusted the police to find Marcel's killers, but they hadn't shown any interest in pursuing the murder of a drug addict with a record of petty crimes. He'd come away from each visit to the police department feeling dirty. The looks he'd encountered told him that they, like Halloran, thought he was responsible for letting a sixteen-year-old go bad in the first place.

And it *was* his fault. He should have found a

way to stop the trouble. He had failed Marcel, and he sure as hell didn't need surly cops telling him where he'd gone wrong. No fancy detectives either. All he'd wanted was justice, and the law wouldn't, couldn't, deliver.

But he almost had.

If the cops hadn't come, the Red Dragon would be dead, Marcel's murder avenged, and then maybe his mother could stop her crying and his old man would speak to him again.

"Here, here, *chère*—you're gonna make y'self sick, goin' on like that. Sit down. Let me make you some tea. Leave those dolls be, now." He forced her down on the bed, still sniffling, and handed her a tissue from the box on the floor. "I'll put on a tape. You'd like that?"

Dulcie only nodded. *Bon Dieu*, she looked so lost and sad. He wanted his Amazon back. The Amazon was tougher, she rolled with the punches. But not Dulcie. Dulcinea.

He left her with the box of tissues in her lap and heated up the water on the little gas stove. While he waited, he searched through her box of tapes. She hadn't exaggerated about her wide taste in music. He found what he was looking for, and snapped the cassette into place.

The smooth, polyphonic chant filled the cabin with its celestial, timeless harmonies. As her rigid body began to soften, Julien knew he'd made the right choice—even if the beauty of the music tore at him, making emotions he'd tried so hard to bury bleed again.

The music begged for peace, but he poked the angry thing inside him until it coiled and twisted and hated again.

He brought her the tea, which she only sipped at twice before putting it aside. She sat close against him, an occasional tremor rippling through her body, until finally he gave in to her silent plea and pulled her into his arms again.

It seemed the most natural thing, in all his black and crazy world, to kiss her when she tipped her face toward him. A soft kiss, just the one, given with only the intention of bringing comfort.

Her lips lingered against his as he pulled away. Hard, to pull away. Every man should know so sweet a kiss, just once in his life. As close to the light as he'd ever get, kissing this woman.

"Rest, *chère*," he whispered, his mouth against the corner of her lips. Her skin was soft, and tasted like salt from her tears. "It's been a long day, no?"

"Stay with me."

He didn't hesitate. "I'm not goin' anywhere."

"Hold me."

"I'm here. Close your eyes. I'm here."

And maybe when he was gone from her life, she wouldn't have to cry anymore.

Her arms tightened around him, as if she sensed his thought, and Julien eased himself back against the pillows of the bed, Dulcie in his arms. For now, at least, he wasn't going anywhere at all.

Chapter 10

~

DULCIE AWOKE WITH a jolt, gulping for air as she scrambled to sit in the bed.

Something was wrong.

It was black in the cabin. Night had fallen, with only a sliver of cold, white moonlight to cut through the thick darkness.

Where was Julien, and God, how long had she been sleeping? She swung her legs over the bed and hurried out to the side deck. The cool, wet wind made her shiver, and she wrapped her arms tight around herself. The boat was still tied to the pier. Insects creaked, frogs croaked, and in the distance she heard the shrill, eerie cry of a hawk.

"Well, if it isn't Sleeping Beauty. Glad to see you decided to rejoin the land of the living."

Dulcie turned to see Lucille walking across the deck toward her. Despite the light words, Lucille wasn't smiling. "How long was I sleeping?"

"A few hours. You holding up okay? We're a little worried about you, hon . . . I almost called Bobby."

"Don't. Don't do that," Dulcie said instantly,

her voice angry. Lucille blinked in surprise, then Dulcie added, more calmly, "I'm okay. Really."

Lucille grated on her nerves now and again, but when it came down to it, she had a soft and generous heart. More than once in the past, they'd cried in their beers over men. In the blanketing darkness, with only the faint light of the moon to illuminate their faces, Dulcie decided it wasn't necessary to pretend everything was wonderful.

"This whole thing with Mitsumi brings back bad memories. And worse," she admitted quietly. "I guess I haven't worked through it all as well as I thought." But before Lucille could reply, Dulcie changed the subject to a more immediate concern. "Where's my Cajun?"

Lucille could take a hint, especially when it was a broad stroke. "Sitting over there and getting drunk."

Dulcie looked to where Lucille motioned. Julien leaned on the rail along the back deck, half-hidden in the shadows, and seemed absorbed by the black water lapping against the boat. A bottle sat on the deck beside him. He wasn't wearing a shirt.

"Getting drunk on what?"

"Said he found a bottle of wine in the kitchen."

Dulcie frowned, thinking about the gun she had hidden at the bottom of her doll wig box. "He's pretty free about rifling through my stuff."

"You like him, don't you?" Lucille asked abruptly. "I see how you look at him."

"I'd have to be dead not to notice the man."

"That's not exactly what I asked, Miz Quinn."

Dulcie looked away from Julien and focused instead on Mike's place across the pier, on the weak light spilling out from its narrow windows and Les sitting outside the door, apparently dozing. Dark threads of Spanish moss danced in the breeze. The hawk cried out again.

"How can you like someone you don't know?" Dulcie replied. Beneath a bastion of bare skin, sex, and mystery, Julien was impenetrable to her. "On the surface, he's shown me pretty much all he's got, but I can't tell you anything about the man himself. Not what's hidden inside."

"You said you'd help him."

"I can give him a piece of my mind. I can try, in four days, to show him he has the legal power to put Mitsumi in prison. But I can't make his decisions for him. He has to do that himself."

"The man's got cause to want Mitsumi dead."

"I have revenge fantasies, too." Dulcie's voice was sharper than she meant it to be. "But I don't go out and act on them. Julien has the chance to do it right, Lucy, but he won't. That makes him no better than Mitsumi, when you get right down to it."

"Except he hasn't killed anyone yet," Lucille pointed out. "It's not too late."

Dulcie glanced toward Julien. He still stood with his back to them. "Maybe," she said. "How much has he had to drink?"

"No idea. I keep checking on him, to make sure he hasn't passed out."

"Or decided to swim off." But even as she

spoke, Dulcie knew he wouldn't run. Not now, with Bobby's threat hanging over him. Or at least not for another four days. She frowned. Three days, now, not four. "I think I'll go take back my bottle of wine."

Lucille's teeth flashed in the darkness as she smiled. "Go get him, Dulcie. Nobody else plays for keeps like you do, girl."

Dulcie watched Lucille walk back to Mike's cabin, then she squared her shoulders and made her way toward the unyielding expanse of Julien's broad, bare back.

Why oh why couldn't he be wearing a shirt?

Her footsteps were quiet and he was unaware of her presence, not even looking back as he bent to retrieve the wine bottle. Murky light rendered the angles of muscle and bone in sharp relief, black against gray. His curving spine was a shadowy valley, the rounder surfaces of his muscles pale until they blended into fluid seams of sinew.

She hesitated when he lifted his arm. He took a swig of wine, and her gaze lingered on the arching biceps and strong muscles of his neck, which rolled like waves as he swallowed.

Hot hunger coursed through her, and she dared to imagine what it would be like to hold him in her arms, to run her palms freely along the hard belly, over the symmetrical planes of his back and wide shoulders. Imagined how it would feel to make love with him in her bed, as the water swelled and crested beneath them.

Dulcie took a deep breath. She was no better

than those women who grabbed at him when he danced, making catcalls and crude gestures. She was out of her mind to think she could influence this man. Producing orderly thoughts within twenty feet of Julien Langlois was a lost cause. She'd best return to the cabin, before she made a complete fool of herself.

Perhaps an inner sense, or a shifting shadow or sound alerted him, for Julien turned from the railing as she took a soft step away. Across the deck, and the milky smudge of the moon reflected against its wood, his gaze met hers. She didn't move or breathe. For a long, agonizing moment, Julien stood still and silent. Then he lifted the bottle to his mouth and took another deep swallow.

Dulcie was trapped. Stubborn pride wouldn't let her retreat to the cabin, but every sense in her body warned against going anywhere near him.

"You missed dinner," he said.

"Why didn't you wake me up?"

He shrugged his bare shoulders. "I put a plate in the fridge. When you want, heat it up."

"I can't believe I slept through one of your passionate cooking episodes."

Julien watched her, then took another long drink. "Didn't cook. I found a fire hearth outside the cabin and grilled instead."

Turning a fraction from the rail, he kept her directly in his line of vision. She couldn't look away. She supposed she could talk about how she'd cried all over his shirt, but the timbre of their relationship had changed since she'd learned about Marcel's death. She hadn't been honest with Lucille. She liked Julien; liked him much more than she should.

"Are you really a stripper?"

He didn't blink at the sudden change of subject. Nor did he smile, as she expected, and brush it off. He just took another drink, then wiped his mouth on the back of his hand. "Really am."

"Oh." So much for her disguise theory.

"Done a lot of things, *chère*. Worked oil rigs and construction. Even played in a band—I'm pretty good with a fiddle. But I never stuck with anythin' long. Don' mistake me for one of the good guys."

Dulcie didn't quite believe that. Her instincts told her otherwise. She stepped closer. Close enough to see his eyes gleam in the moonlight, the curl of a nostril and the rich curve of his upper lip. Praxiteles would have killed to sculpt a mouth like that.

"What happened with your brother?"

Julien turned and stared down into the black water. "Marcel left home to live with me, because I was the only one who could handle him. He was a good kid, most of the time. Never had a lick of common sense, though. Lookin' for *bon vivant* . . . the good life. He was in deep before I even knew somethin' was wrong. Lost him, is all. One night, he just never came home."

His voice was cool and dispassionate, as if he referred to a lost dog and not a sixteen-year-old kid.

"Killing the Dragon won't bring him back, Julien."

"I know."

She would try and reason with him. Keep her temper in check. Be patient, for once. "You're fighting a hydra. Knock one Mitsumi out of the game and others like him will only take his place. You can't win."

"Neither can the cops."

"Maybe. But they have the law behind them. You don't."

Julien didn't argue or take up the challenge. He just shrugged again and took another long swig. She reached for the bottle. He pulled it away and she overbalanced, twisting her back. At her involuntary grimace of pain, he put out a hand to steady her, his eyes watchful.

"Back hurt?"

At his touch, she took a step back. The ache wasn't bad tonight, but it provided a good excuse as any for moving away from him. "Comes and goes."

He gave the bottle a sloshing shake. His eyes, on her, were darkly intense. "Might help, *non?*"

Dulcie wrapped her arms around herself, suddenly feeling exposed. Endangered. She didn't want those watchful eyes to see how fast and uneven each breath came, how her nipples pressed against the thin fabric of her T-shirt. She shook her head at his half-mocking offer. "Booze isn't the answer either, Julien."

"Not lookin' for answers."

"So what are you looking for?"

Julien leaned back over the rail. "*N'importe.*

Let's talk about somethin' else—maybe this place. It's somethin' to see at night, the bayou. All black and white.''

Outmaneuvered again. He'd just told her to shut up and leave him alone, but with a peculiar sort of courtesy.

"It's not all black and white. Not if you look closely enough. Shades of gray, sepia, and green.''

"You never let up, do you?"

His accent came heavy tonight, along with a liberal sprinkling of Cajun French. Dulcie wondered how much wine he'd consumed. She took the last step to his side and leaned against the rail. She tried to see his expression, but the breeze blew strands of hair across his face.

"I'm not very good at giving up, even when the odds are against me. I don't want to see you make any mistakes, Julien. That's all.''

He leaned further over the rail, the powerful muscles of his arms bunching. "Why should you care?'' He looked up, one dark brow raised. "Like you said, you just want your piece of Red Dragon an' I'm the means to an end. Why pretend you give a damn about me?''

Dulcie stared at him, startled to have her own words thrown back at her like this. Then she glanced away.

It was the truth, but his bitter response angered her, even discomforted her. She wasn't the one in the wrong here. He had the legal power to put Jacob Mitsumi in prison, and he rejected it. Power she would have given almost anything to have. A power, she admitted to herself, she wanted to direct for him if at all possible, and whether or not she had the right to do so.

She did care for Julien, although she'd never admit as much. It would give him power over her, and she was certain he wouldn't hesitate to use it against her.

Since she couldn't find a safe answer, Dulcie said nothing. She shivered. Godamighty, he did that to her, made her hot and cold all at once.

He put the bottle down and turned to face her, his eyes shadowed. "*Que c'est beau.*"

She shivered again, uncontrollably, then looked away from his unswerving regard to the inky depths of the bayou. She knew enough French to make sense of what he'd said—and to know what he really meant. "Beautiful it may be, but swamps are full of snakes. I hate snakes."

"C'mon now, *chère*. Not all snakes."

"*All* of them," she retorted fiercely.

"Some snakes ain't so bad, I hear tell." His voice had low, suggestive humor washing through the deep tones.

She blinked, then sucked in her breath with a whistle. "Julien!" she hissed. After a moment, she laughed as her muscles relaxed a fraction. He did that to her, too—made her laugh, so that she let down her guard. Oh, he was good at getting past all her defenses. "That one's as old as the hills, you know."

"So's this," he whispered and, before she had any warning at all, he covered her lips with his.

He tasted of wine; a dark, heavy wine. His lips were warm and soft, an insistent pressure against her mouth. Sparking the fire; fanning the flame waiting just beneath her controlled surface. She tried to push him away. "Julien!"

"I want to kiss you. No games, *chère.*"

"Les and—"

"Let 'em look," he murmured against the corner of her mouth. "*Ferme ta bouche* . . . Shut up an' kiss me, Dulcinea Quinn."

So she did.

With the small part of her still capable of reason, Dulcie blamed her weakness on that bare chest of his. On the prehistoric rhythm of creaking bugs and croaking frogs. On the smell of old wood and deep water, of rot and life and a pall of rain. On the mysterious alchemy of man and woman.

She took Julien's face between the palms of her hands, and kissed him back without caring if Les or Lucille noticed, without thinking where it might lead. She felt the rasp of his beard beneath her mouth and fingers; his hot, uneven breath against her ear. She moved her hands down his chest, marveling at how his body could be soft and hard at once. She slipped her hands around his waist and up his back, and his own fingers moved beneath her T-shirt, sliding along her spine.

Along her scar.

Nobody touched that—nobody saw it.

She tried to pull away, to hide from him, but Julien held her still, hands firm on her hips. "Don' do that."

Tears welled in her eyes. She fought them back with a defensive anger. "It's ugly," she whispered. "I hate it!"

"It's just a scar, an' it's part of who you are. If you're gonna tell me how to live with mine, you'd best learn to live with yours first."

Dulcie stared at him, at the shadowed eyes and still, handsome face; a face so like his dead brother's. How could she have forgotten what had brought Julien out here to get drunk in the first place? In what muddled depths of her mind had she believed that kisses or lovemaking could help either of them? When she pushed away from Julien again, he dropped his hands to his sides.

But right or wrong, she wanted Julien. In three days he would leave, and there was little she could do to prevent it. Still, she could fight for him. The old Dulcie Quinn knew how to fight for something she believed in, wasn't afraid to take a risk and perhaps fail.

But although she could try her most persuasive reasoning, he had a good reason not to hear: one viscerally caught in a black and white photo. She had no hold on him, except for a physical attraction already deepening into something else. She had nothing to fight with, except her compassion and the strength of her belief in the goodness of life, in the power of right over wrong.

It might not be enough, but it was all she had.

Dulcie backed away. He let her go, watchful and silent. She glanced at Mike's place, but saw no one outside now. Then she went to her cabin, shut the door, and waited.

Chapter 11

HE DIDN'T WASTE any time.

Dulcie looked up when she heard the click of the door latch, and a dark shadow fell across the floor. Julien loomed above her, his face unreadable, his stance unyielding. Her heart beat fast again and her stomach gave a strange twist, but she didn't give in to the sudden leap of fear.

"I wondered if you'd come after me," she murmured.

"Got unfinished business, you an' me."

"What makes you think that's what I want?"

"Same thing makin' you think it's what I want."

Dulcie blinked, trying to follow this convoluted line of reasoning, until she realized the simple answer behind the evasion. She didn't get up from the bed, and knotted her hands into fists against the mattress. She watched the blood beating in the vein of his neck, then raised her gaze to his face and bluntly asked, "Do you want to make love to me?"

He lowered those long lashes, shielding himself from her. "*Mais oui, chère.*"

Oh, yes. There was something about French

words of love in the dark and moonlight. Heat eased through her body, like a slow-rising tide. Relentless and unstoppable. A force of nature. She took a deep, silent breath and came to her feet. No more than an inch or two separated his body from hers.

Dulcie placed the palm of her hand on Julien's chest, feeling the same rush of adrenaline as when she used to walk, gun drawn, into a dark alley. His muscles jumped, and she heard the shift in his breathing. Heat crackled all around her hand as she massaged his smooth skin.

"Life has so much to give us, Julien. The beauty of the bayou at night." Following the line of dark hair, she trailed her finger down the middle of his chest to his belly, then back up again. "This."

He had a face born for the touch of moonlight and shadows. Hollows and planes, sharp angles and softer curves. She yearned to run her fingers across the whole of him, delineating and exploring.

The corner of his mouth turned up slightly. "A good back rub's right up there with nirvana, *chère*." He brought his hands to her waist and pulled her against him. "Let's finish what we started, and you can show me all 'bout . . . this."

'Dis' was his own hands brushing the sensitive flesh below her breasts, then he turned her around before she had a chance to protest. Dulcie found herself caught between his half-clad body and the bed, her knees pressed against the mattress. She sucked in her breath when he pushed up her T-shirt, exposing the length of her back.

Without meaning to she tried to turn, but his hands held her still. She struggled to stay calm; telling herself a woman's body, even a scarred one, was no mystery or novelty to a man like Julien Langlois. He'd known hundreds of women. Thousands.

"Don' fight it, *chère*. Let me take the pain away."

Dulcie shivered at the cool air against her skin, and closed her eyes as his thumbs kneaded her tight muscles. It felt good. So good. She let out her breath on a long, airy sigh and tipped her head back on his shoulder, losing herself to the heat of his bare skin against her own and the firm, circling touch. She tried not to care that he could see the scar, or that he touched it, gliding a finger along its length.

He moved behind her and then something else pressed against the scar; something soft and warm.

He'd kissed her. There.

The magical haze spun from his fingertips vanished. Dulcie straightened with a gasp. "What are you—"

"Shush," Julien whispered. "You're beautiful, Dulcie, an' that makes it beautiful, too."

He bent to kiss her again on the small of her back, sliding his hands from the base of her spine around to her belly, then upwards. When he stood, she leaned back against his warm body. All thoughts of protest vanished when he touched her breasts through the soft lace and skimmed her nipples with his palms. She moaned softly as he pulled her T-shirt higher, exposing her to his hands and gaze. Then a new ache replaced the old; a warm and pleasant ache that took root in her heart and bloomed at her womb.

She didn't want to fight the fear anymore, and she didn't want to be careful. She wanted to make love with Julien Langlois and leap into it with eyes and arms wide open, no matter how it all might end.

"*Très belle, chère,*" Julien whispered, then bent to kiss the curve of her arched neck. "Put your arms around me. I want to feel you. Let me take away all the pain."

And take away my pain.

Dead. Numb. For so long, nothing inside him but cold anger.

Dulcie made the rivers of his blood run warm again, and that hard and icy thing inside him cracked. She made him want to dig his fingers in the black grave dirt and resurrect the part of him he'd buried with his brother.

"I want to feel." He said it against the skin of her throat, to make it real. "I want to feel you."

Dieu, he wanted to look forward to each new day when he opened his eyes in the morning. He wanted to go to sleep at night without fearing the nightmares. He wanted to feel clean; to love a woman and be young again and new.

He wanted to feel anything but the hate and the guilt.

Dulcie turned in his arms, molding herself

against him. Julien pulled the fabric tie from her ponytail, loosing hair and a faint scent of roses. White heat, wrapped in auburn silk. His body tightened in reaction and he lowered his head.

Her mouth opened beneath his, in a hot, wet kiss full of questing tongues and erratic breathing.

She engulfed him, and Julien let her fill his senses and his hands. Let her fill the cold, hungry places inside him, and he wouldn't think about the consequences.

He popped open the snap of her shorts and eased the zipper down. Her hands curled around his hips, the tips of her fingers resting beneath the waistband of his jeans. The pressure of her nails was driving him wild already, but then she trailed her fingers back to his belly and unfastened the snap of his jeans. Resting her hand on his erection, where it swelled against the fly, she slowly rubbed her open palm against him. His body jerked in response.

Smack-bang, she'd gone and kicked his control clear out the door. Again.

He flicked his tongue against her full bottom lip, then pulled away just far enough to get a firm grip on her hips. "I already got my shirt off. Your turn."

With a single, sinuous movement Dulcie pulled the shirt over her head, leaving her standing in a lace bra and shorts. His gaze roamed her body, admiring both her firm muscles and rounder curves. He tugged at her shorts, then watched as they slipped down around her ankles before she nudged them aside.

She wore the plum-colored lace bra he'd fanta-sized about before, and a matching floral pair of high-cut underwear that made her legs go on and on. He wanted those legs wrapped around him.

"Your turn," she whispered and slowly un-zipped his pants.

Julien might've spent the last six months taking off his clothes for money, but wanted none of those games now. He stripped off his jeans and in ten seconds flat stood before her wearing only a pair of briefs.

"Plain old white underwear," Dulcie said with a smile, running the palms of her hand over the fabric covering his rear. "I was expecting some-thing more risqué. Bells or whistles, maybe."

He lifted the curtain of her hair with both hands, spreading it wide before letting it fall, one gossa-mer strand at a time, through his fingers. "Yours is real nice. I want to take it off."

"So what's stopping you?"

He kissed her again, pulling her close so that he could feel the crisp lace against his chest. He moved his hips against her, hard and aggressive, and she made a soft, yielding sound deep in her throat. He unhooked her bra, still tangling his tongue with hers, then slipped the shoulder straps down, one at a time, until her bare breasts pressed against him.

He wanted to go slow. To savor this feeling of waking from a dream; of coming alive beneath her mouth and hands. He broke away from the kiss, taking in her heavy-lidded eyes, her mouth open and lips wet from his kiss, the rapid rise and fall of her breasts. Beautiful breasts, creamy pale and tipped with pink. "*Ça c'est bon.*"

"What does that mean?"

He felt the progress of her lips from his jaw to his collarbone, his nerve ends snapping and leaping at each touch, each swirl of her warm, wet tongue. "It's so good, *chère*. So good."

"*Ça c'est bon,*" she whispered, then slipped her hands inside his underwear.

He groaned, pushing himself against her warm, stroking hands. "Makin' me crazy. I want you so bad I can't think."

"Good." The word was little more than a tickle of breath against his ear.

He closed his eyes, fighting for control. If she didn't stop touching him, this would all be over much too soon. He tightened his fingers on her shoulders. "Go slow."

She wriggled a little, and he nearly lost his battle when her nipples brushed against his chest. "No. Julien, I don't want to go slow."

Of course not. This was the woman who'd jumped him and held him in a headlock. Making love to her would near beat him to the ground, and he couldn't wait to get inside her and give her his best shot.

When Julien trusted himself to open his eyes again and look at her, he found she'd peeled off her panties and was completely nude.

"That does it," he muttered. He pressed against

her shoulders until she sank, without hesitation, to the bed.

For a moment he stood still, simply looking at her—the long hair spilled against the floral sheets, the pale skin and lithe body. She was even more beautiful than he'd imagined that first night, when he'd lain awake on the floor and watched her sleep. He shucked his underwear, and the hunger in her eyes, the way her gaze lingered on the erection straining toward her, made him ache. He came to the bed and lowered himself over her warm, welcoming body. Her arms closed around his neck as she kissed him, demanding and fierce.

He settled between her thighs with a low groan, kissing her breasts, her belly. He couldn't go slow, even if he'd still wanted to. He took her mouth in his as her fingernails drove into the flesh of his hips, pulling him close as she raised her body in a silent plea.

Julien pushed within her. Hot, wet. Tight. He took a quick breath, muscles shaking with the effort to control his response. *Dieu*, he'd made her angry, he'd made her cry. Now he wanted to please her. It became important, to offer her all the pleasure he was capable of giving.

He counted, mouthing numbers against a tangle of dark red hair, then slowly let the sensations take hold of him again. Each erratic puff of her breath against his shoulder. Her breasts brushing his chest. Himself in her, moving slowly. Her nails digging into his skin each time he withdrew, a soft ''Oh'' at each deep thrust. He focused on that, her grasping fingers and the soft cries from her open mouth, until her nails began to dig deeper and her cries came faster, louder.

He moved his arms to the pillow, capturing her restless head between his forearms. He kissed her again, his tongue moving in and out of her mouth to the flow of their joining until he felt her body go rigid beneath him and then the tremors wash through her, one after the other.

He let go his control then, smothering her cries and his in a rough, devouring kiss. Moving fast and hard, he gave himself over to her hot, enveloping body, her sweetness and softness. A distant part of him heard the hoarse words he repeated over and over again, knowing she couldn't understand the Cajun French. He didn't want to let the pleasure go, or ever come back down from its rising crest.

Then the climax slammed every last thought out of his skull and there was nothing but wave upon wave of pleasure so intense he expected to die right there in her arms.

In the aftermath of their lovemaking, Dulcie lay still and quiet and let the pieces of herself settle back in place. She kept her eyes closed, feeling boneless and languid beneath the weight of Julien's sweat-slick body. She listened to his rapid gulps for air, each breath pressing their bodies closer together. Her legs, still around him, were shaking. She couldn't summon enough energy to care.

Outside, she heard the lapping of the water and the discordant chorus of croaking frogs. Low laughter, from a distance. The real world, encroaching.

She held Julien close, unwilling to separate and end what they had just shared. She didn't even want to think. In silence, she stroked his back. Long, lingering touches up and down the muscles, the curving spine.

He made a low sound of male contentment against her throat. She smiled and opened her eyes to a view of his shoulder and a disheveled mane of black hair. "That was very nice," she murmured. "The *bon* thing that you said."

The shoulder by her nose quaked with his silent laughter. She frowned when he slid from inside her, but he eased the emptiness with another kiss. Her lips felt swollen and tender, like the rest of her, and she was glad for the softer touch. "*Ça c'est bon.* I'll keep sayin' it until you remember."

"I'm counting on it." She slid her hands down his back to his buttocks. His face was just inches from her own, dark and shadowed and partially hidden by the fall of his hair. Dulcie felt a strange prickling of sadness, reminded of how easily he'd kept so much of himself hidden from her. "You make me very happy to be a woman," she said, her voice soft and wistful.

He smiled, then kissed her breast. Fresh desire rippled through her body. "Pleasure's all mine, *chère.*"

Her prickling of sadness deepened to unease . . . Dear God, what had she just done here? Then his warm mouth closed over her breast, his tongue gently teasing the nipple into a taut peak.

Taking a deep, shuddering breath, Dulcie tangled her fingers helplessly in his hair. "What are you doing?"

"Loving you right," he replied and moved to her other breast. "Slow and easy."

Julien was giving her no time for regret or doubt, and she ached to have him inside her again, almost to the point of pain. She hadn't known what to expect; what sort of lovemaking a male exotic dancer might consider normal. She'd been prepared for sexual athletics, even sex games. But he'd loved her deep and hard, to the brink of mindless, incoherent pleasure. Now she wanted a slow and gentle touch, which he seemed to understand. Maybe he wanted it, too.

He was careful and patient, focusing on the pleasure; on coaxing each fine, sharp sensation from her until she couldn't stand it any longer. She caressed him in return, wanting to make it last this time. To draw the ecstasy out for as long as they both could bear it.

When they lay tangled once again in limbs, hair, and wrinkled sheets, Julien shifted to his side and pulled her back against him. He wrapped his arms around her waist, tightly, as if he didn't want to let her go.

"Do that again, an' it'll kill me," he said, kissing her shoulder.

Dulcie sighed, snuggling deeper into his arms. "Better me than Red Dragon."

As soon as she spoke, she knew it was a mistake. His body behind her stiffened. For a long moment, he said nothing and there was no sound but the wind and water, and creatures moving in the blackness of the night.

"Tryin' to teach me a lesson?" he said with deceptive softness, lips against the skin of her shoulder. "Did I pass the test? An 'A' for effort, at least?"

She tried to turn and face him, but he held her too tightly. The pressure against her rib cage began to hurt. "Don't," she said, her voice hardly above a whisper. "Please."

"Halloran put you up to this, too? How do I compare to him, anyway?"

All the beauty of what they'd shared vanished at his sneering words.

Ashamed and vulnerable, feeling far too exposed, Dulcie's temper flared. She jabbed him with her elbow, heard his grunt of pain. She twisted around and sat up, not caring what she must look like with her hair wild around her, the moist strands sticking to her body. She could smell him on her; smell the scent of their mating in the close confines of the cabin.

She couldn't face him, or even meet his gaze. "Get out."

"No." His fingers closed over her arms.

When Dulcie looked up, she saw the anger hardening his features. "What Bobby and I had is none of your business," she said, her voice low. "I don't owe you any explanations."

Julien narrowed his eyes. Then he pushed himself off the bed with a curse and walked away. Since there wasn't anywhere for him to go, he finally stopped, his back to her. He clenched his fists tight together. "Yeah . . . an' just so we're clear on this, I don' care if you slept with the whole damn police force."

For a moment, her breath caught. Then she inhaled again, slow and even.

He was angry . . . jealous!

Without thinking, Dulcie swung her legs over the edge of the bed and went to him. She slipped her arms around his waist, then pressed against his bare back. His muscles went rigid.

She needed to know if she meant more to him than an all-too-willing outlet for his passion or anger; needed to know if maybe he was as lonely for a gentle touch as she. Deception came so easy to him that she couldn't simply ask. She had to watch his hands, his eyes. Listen to what he didn't say.

"It was good sex, Julien. Best I've ever had. I expected something a little more kinky from a guy like you, though." Encouraged by his continued silence, she went on. "Did Chloe know you were screwing her just so you could kill her brother?"

"You never let up, do you? Not even . . . To hell with you!"

She held him, letting him think the worst of her. In his anger, she might just find the truth. He could have broken free of her grasp if he'd wanted to, but he didn't try.

"Were you sleeping with Chloe?" A coldness

settled over her as she waited for his answer.

"What do you care?" he asked, his voice rough.

With a sort of hazy surprise, she realized she was jealous, too. "Like you care that Bobby and I were lovers."

Dulcie was so close that her lashes brushed against his skin when she closed her eyes. Loosening the grip of her fingers around his waist, she trailed her fingers down and he made a half-choked sound. "It was really good sex, Julien." She kept up her stroking. His breathing altered. Quickened. "Think how much better we could be. We can have this, night after night. But if you go after the Dragon, it's all gone."

His groan sounded in the darkness of the cabin and she pressed a kiss against his ear. "This. Night after night. Dead men can't feel this. No more loving. No more going deep in a woman." She broke off, swallowing, then wet her dry lips with her tongue. "In prison, there's nothing left but the memory. You can't touch a memory." She closed her fingers over his hardening penis. "And a memory can't touch you."

He moved so fast she had no warning. His arm snaked around, grabbing her from behind and twisting until her weakened back flared with pain. She yelped and let him go, only to find herself imprisoned between his hot body and the cold smoothness of the wall.

"Some damn game, is that all it was to you?" he demanded, in a deep, savage whisper.

She licked her lips again, staring at his angry

face before her. "No," she answered truthfully. "It's no game."

It never had been. While she still had no answer, she had found a crack, his raw place where she could slither within him and irritate and goad. An irritation needed to be soothed, after all. She meant to fight for him. She would make him listen; make him see how wrong he was to turn away from life, from the power he had within his grasp.

"Were you sleeping with Chloe?"

"What difference does it make if I was?" he whispered, pressing himself full against her. Dulcie had never known she could feel both sorrow and lust all at once, but she did. It hurt.

"Women in love like to know they're the only one," she said, looking him straight in the eye.

Julien released her and stepped back, his movement strangely awkward. For a long time, neither spoke. Then his lashes lowered, shuttering his eyes. He turned and walked away.

"I started playing the strip scene six months ago so I could get close to Chloe, an' get to her brother through her. I wasn't sleeping with her. Let it be, Dulcie. I done what I had to." He sat back down on the rumpled bed, watching her. She met the intensity of his gaze without faltering. "You'd say anythin' to get me to testify."

She didn't pretend to misunderstand his accusation. "Maybe I mean it."

He rubbed his palms over his face, a gesture of such weariness that she wanted to go to him and hold him close. She'd spoken before really thinking, but her impulsive words had been truth.

The previous, angry tension between them had faded; replaced by a different tension. Edgy. Brittle. She took a step closer. "Julien? What would you think, if I meant it?"

His mouth was set in a tight line. "I think maybe you're outta your pretty little head. Too bad we spend so much time lyin' to each other."

Dulcie thought she most likely was out of her head, but not that either she or Julien were lying about what had just passed between them. Maybe it was only the result of beautiful lovemaking, all this warmth and care and wanting that he engendered in her. But it was no lie, and she knew he had felt it, too.

She came to sit beside him on the bed. "Were you and Marcel close?" she asked, probing at his deepest wound with the compassion of a surgeon delineating the extent of the hurt, so it could be closed and healed.

Julien leaned back against the wall, drawing one knee up. He seemed so unconcerned by his nudity. But she supposed one couldn't be shy and be a stripper . . . even if it was only a guise, after all. Her instincts had been right again. Dulcie pulled the sheet over herself, keeping her hair around her.

Julien let out his breath. "I was seventeen when Marcel was born. Changed his diapers, gave him his bottle an' sat with him when he fussed. When he fell down, I put Band-Aids on his knees, dried his tears, an' told him what my old man told me.

That he was gonna grow up to be a man, an' a man didn't never cry.''

He swallowed, the sound audible in the silence of the cabin. Then he continued, his voice eerily calm. ''And when he was sixteen I threw a handful of dirt on his coffin an' promised to kill the man who'd killed him.''

''Oh, Julien. I'm sorry. So sorry.''

Silence. How poor, how useless, those words sounded, even to herself.

''I need a shower,'' he said, coming abruptly to his feet.

He left her sitting alone. After a moment, the light came on in the tiny bathroom. She blinked against the brightness, dim as it was, but didn't move. She wouldn't let herself think. Later, maybe. But not now.

It hurt too much.

Chapter 12

~

JULIEN STOOD IN the small shower stall. He didn't
know how long he'd been there, staring at the white
porcelain faucet, when he heard Dulcie come into
the room. His first thought, as the lock clicked behind her, was that he just wanted to be left alone.
The fire of his anger, the fire that had sustained
him through all the darkness of the past months,
had burned to ashes, leaving in its wake only a
weary need to shut himself away.

"I want a shower, too," Dulcie said, pulling the
shower door open and stepping in beside him.

She didn't give up, his Amazon. Went right for
the jugular, every time. He tried not looking at the
pale roundness of her pretty rear and breasts peek-
ing through the long tumble of her hair. Tried not
to smell the soft musky scent of her, the faint per-
fume of roses in her hair. More than anything, he
tried not to remember how he had felt, with her
and inside her.

It had been so right. Like coming home, after
wandering too far without any direction or desti-
nation. Peace.

"What are you doin'?" he asked, moving back as far from her as he could, reminding himself he had rejected peace of mind months ago.

"What does it look like? This isn't the Hyatt, Julien. The tanks only hold so much warm water. We have to conserve it." She turned the faucet and a sluggish, lukewarm spray trickled down their bodies. She splashed him with water, then ducked her head under the nozzle.

He watched her hair darken; her upturned face and wet, half-open mouth. His body, his tired body, began to respond. "Why're you doin' this?"

Her eyes opened, wide and dark in the low light. "Soap doesn't work very well on dry skin," she answered lightly, then wetted a sponge and squeezed water over his shoulders, chest, and finally his hair.

The shower stall wasn't meant for more than one person. Julien couldn't move away from her slick, wet body. Even if he'd really wanted to.

"You know that's not what I meant, *chère*."

Dulcie didn't answer, dousing him instead with another spongeful of water before turning off the faucet. Then, dispensing a circle of shampoo in her hand, she reached up and began to wash his hair. He watched her breasts bounce with each vigorous movement. With brisk efficiency, she squeezed the excess lather out of his hair and the thick, white foam fell in plops at their feet.

Damn, she even had pretty toes.

"Wash my hair, Julien?"

He brought his gaze back up, from toes to ankles

and long legs, stopping for a moment at the damp curls at the apex of her thighs before moving upwards again over the hips he'd grasped, the breasts he'd kissed. The mouth that had breathed out soft, frantic "Ohs."

He was going to touch her again. No point in resisting, not anymore. She'd cracked through, and he wanted her. Not just now, but tomorrow. And tomorrow's tomorrow. For however many tomorrows he had left.

Taking the shampoo bottle, Julien dumped a portion in his hand and washed her hair. Not easy, since she had a lot of it. He gathered all the ends together on the top of her head, then stroked his fingers through the slippery soap and thick hair. Her arms slid around his waist, and he felt her mouth and tongue at his chest, teasing his nipple.

His fingers stopped. "Don' do that."

"Don't you like it?"

She couldn't mistake the press of his growing erection against her body. "What do you think?"

He moved his fingers again, circling and massaging her scalp. He let his fingers stray, tracing the line of her jaw, the full lips. The shape of her ear. The arch of a brow, and curve of her nose.

"Why are you angry with me?"

Damn good question. He reached behind her to turn the faucet on, then let the warm trickle of water rinse away the shampoo. He helped her with her hair, lifting the sodden mass away from her body, baring her completely. When he let her hair go, he slid his hands down over her shoulders to her breasts, brushing her nipples with his fingers. Along the length of his body pressed to hers, she shuddered.

"I'm not angry," he said at last.

God, she felt fine. His lips found hers, under the running water. What she roused in him wasn't anger. Not at all. Anger didn't make his heart pound, his guts knot.

Desire did, and fear. Fear that if he let these unexpected, powerful feelings for her take hold of him, he couldn't do what still needed doing. The single, relentless goal he'd worked toward since Marcel's death was lost; taken away when Hernandez lost his nerve and died, and the cops had interfered. For these past few days, he'd foundered without purpose, lost and empty.

Now this woman had somehow slipped into that inner emptiness, wanting to show him a new direction and purpose, but Julien turned from it. Mitsumi had to die. Nothing would change his mind, not the beautiful breasts he cupped in his hands. Not her tongue tracing the line of his opening lips. Not the place within her, where his body was already demanding entrance. Not even the twist of frustration and shame that made him doubt himself. Made him break another promise.

Tomorrow he'd think about making plans again. Now, this moment, he just wanted to bury himself in Dulcie's hot, delicious body and forget.

The liquid soap was in the shower caddy behind her, and Julien squeezed out a generous portion. "How 'bout we scrub each other clean?" he murmured, slathering the soap across her belly, over her breasts and arms and shoulders. He rubbed the soap into a foaming lather, circling and skimming her skin, then teased her breasts until she sagged back against the shower wall, eyes closed and head tipped back. She made no protest when he nudged her legs apart and knelt.

More soap. Feet, ankles, shins, and knees. She had strong legs; the sort that came from regular exercise. Her muscles were trembling a little, her skin prickling with gooseflesh under the soap. He lathered her thighs, working upward as she made soft, gasping noises, her fingers digging into the skin of his shoulders.

"Clean everywhere," he said, kissing a spot on her thigh clear of soap. She moaned when he slid a finger inside her, then whispered his name. A gentle stroking of his thumb brought her to orgasm within moments and only his own body, surging upwards, kept her from sinking to her knees.

He held her close, lightly touching the smooth scar on her back. She seemed not to notice, and it pleased him.

"Oh, God, Julien," he heard her whisper against his ear, her voice catching. "I love you . . . I love you."

Julien went still, then continued with his gentle caressing, as if he hadn't heard her.

I love you.

She'd say anything—do anything—to make sure he testified against Jacob Mitsumi. But even with that bitter understanding, he couldn't keep his hands off her.

He turned on the water again, to wash away the lather. More kissing followed, feather-soft and weak on her part. Then it was Julien's turn to be tortured by hands that stroked and teased every bit of his body. She washed his back first, then his chest and belly. The moment she went down to her knees he slapped his hands against the shower wall for support, and not a second too soon.

She had a mouth to reduce a man to jelly, and he was rock hard and shooting toward a peak sooner than he ever thought possible.

"No," he muttered, pulling her up against him, all slippery and wet. "In you."

He maneuvered her up against the wall of the shower stall, bringing her legs tightly around his waist as he slid inside her body once again.

Dieu, three times in as many hours. A first. She wasn't like any other woman he'd ever known: not his ex-wife; not the breezy, hard-living women he'd used to chase away the loneliness; not the women who reached for him—those faceless women whose cheeks he'd kissed as they slipped their money beneath the waistband of his G-string.

I love you.

She didn't love him. Love was something that grew between two people over time, and time was the one thing he didn't have. Love was a low and steady warmth, not coercion or mindless sex against a shower wall. Love was truth and honesty, and there was none of that between them.

Julien knew she didn't want love from him, but he gave her what she craved. Against the wall, slow and deep, he gave her what she wanted. What he needed.

It couldn't be love.

Chapter 13

~

Thursday

HOLDING A WARM cup of chicory coffee close against her chest, Dulcie stepped out her cabin door onto the deck. Early morning rays of sun streaked through trailing clouds, the deep red-gold light shimmering brightly on the still water. She took a deep breath. Beneath the pervasive scent of the swamp, the day smelled fresh and new.

The soft tones of a harmonica had roused her early. She'd awakened to pillows that still smelled of rosehip shampoo and Julien. She'd lain quiet in the half-light, taking inventory of tender muscles and heavy limbs, when the harmonica's notes had filtered through her haze, followed by the smell of fresh coffee. She had smiled, knowing Julien was already awake.

She picked out a broomstick-pleated skirt in a rosy gauze and a pretty, fitted ivory T-shirt, then dressed to the music. She recognized the melody as a Cajun love song, "Pauline." A melancholy piece. She'd heard a band play it once, at Mulate's restaurant.

She stopped at the front deck when she saw the morning musician. Julien had let her think him a slick stripper, a street tough, but Dulcie knew he was none of these things. At the moment, he was a man with no past she knew of, and one whose future she might not share beyond the week's end. He was simply Julien, a puzzle to unravel; a mystery to reveal, layer beneath layer.

She padded across the deck in her bare feet to Julien's side, then leaned back against the wall and watched him. He sat on the deck with a cup of steaming coffee beside him, and played to an appreciative audience of Les, Lucille, herself, and a gull. The big gray bird perched on the far rail, its head cocked to one side as if listening.

Les smiled and raised his coffee to her in a greeting. "My days on the clock should all begin this way," he said softly. "He's good."

Dulcie wasn't an expert on either harmonicas or Cajun music, but the liquid harmony wrapped around her, layer upon layer of high and low, sharps and flats. The song was eerily discordant, yet beautiful. She felt herself swaying to the melody. "He's full of surprises."

Without stopping, Julien glanced up at her. A flash of his dark eyes and the slow, mingling slide of notes brought to mind all that had passed between them during the night. Heat rose beneath her skin.

Dulcie looked away, flustered, and saw Lucille hiding a smile behind her coffee cup. But Les wore a troubled look, and Bobby wouldn't be pleased about this new development either. She toyed briefly with the idea of asking them not to say anything, but decided against it. They had a job to do, and would do what they felt was right. Just as she had done last night.

She still wouldn't let herself look too closely at why she'd gone to bed with a man who'd coldly plotted murder for six months. What had seemed so right and reasonable in the darkness was a little more muddled in the light of day.

But what hadn't changed in this clear, fresh morning were her feelings for Julien. Once again, the entire timbre of their relationship had changed. It was less adversarial.

They were lovers now.

Julien finished the music on a flourish of notes, then put the harmonica aside. "Mornin'," he said, his voice warm and intimate and meant only for her.

"Good morning," she whispered, smiling down at him through the steam of her coffee.

Les cleared his throat. "That was nice, Julien. You're pretty good."

Julien shrugged. He wore a pair of sweatpants cut off at mid-thigh for shorts, and a gray T-shirt with a faded Nike logo in red. Somehow he managed to look as crisp as a *GQ* cover, even in old clothes. "I'm better on a fiddle. Learned it from the old ones, back home."

"Where did you get the harmonica?"

"Leave it to Dulcie to ask the practical questions," Lucille murmured.

"In my gym bag," Julien said.

Dulcie took a quick sip of the hot coffee. She ached for him, her emotions all tangled together. Desire, compassion, desperation. A sudden, volatile love for this man who made her laugh and cry, and feel to the depths of her heart. It was dark and intense. Irrational.

Real.

"When you lovebirds are done making eyes at each other," Lucille said with a grin, "we better get going back to Lake Pontchartrain."

Julien pushed himself to his feet. He glanced at Les, then at Dulcie. "I want to stay here."

The gull gave its piercing cry, then flapped heavily away. Dulcie watched it perch on the cabin's sloping roof. "I made an agreement with Bobby. I said we'd go to Lake Pontchartrain."

"I want to stay. I won't run off."

"Promise?" she demanded, looking Julien straight in the eye.

He rubbed at his freshly shaven jaw, not looking away, then said, "Somethin' like that."

Of course he wouldn't promise, but she believed him anyway. He would stay with her. For the next few days. After that, it was anybody's guess what he'd do.

Les shifted from one foot to the other, frowning. "Wait a minute, Dulcie. Halloran was specific in his orders. Lucy and I have a job to do here. We go back to Lake Pontchartrain."

"We stay. I'll handle Bobby."

*　　*　　*

Twenty minutes and one shouted phone conversation later, Dulcie switched on the houseboat engine, then motioned for Les to untie the rope from the pier and push the boat away with a pole. Maneuvering the bulky houseboat back into the waterway of the Terre Aux Boeufs bayou took everyone's concentration for a while. Once they were puttering down the wide, flat river toward the fishing village of Delacroix, Les sat out back and continued the onerous task of organizing the tackle box, and Lucille headed for the shower.

Dulcie perched on the chair at the boat's helm, and watched Julien put away the poles and wind the ropes into a tidy, circular pile on the deck. Then he turned, caught her gaze, and made his way toward her.

"How'd the talk with Halloran go?"

She rubbed her ear. "Short but hardly sweet. He wasn't happy."

"You tell him?"

"What?"

"About you an' me."

The question surprised her, and left her feeling uncomfortable. "What's there to say?"

"Are you gonna tell him?" Julien leaned against the dashboard beside her, arms folded over his chest. His faded gray T-shirt was too short, or the cutoffs rode too low on his hips, giving her a peek of flat, tanned belly with a light dusting of dark hair. The soft fleece didn't disguise much more than the black satin G-string, either.

The gas gauge snagged her attention as she

looked away. "It doesn't matter. He'll hear about it from Les, I'm sure."

"Is that why you're runnin' off?"

Yes, she almost said. *It's what I do best; run away and hide.* "I'm not running anywhere, Julien; we're going to Delacroix for a few . . . necessities."

"Like what?"

"Aren't you full of questions. I liked you better with a harmonica in your mouth."

"You're mighty cranky this mornin', *chère*."

"In case you've forgotten, I didn't have much sleep last night." Memory rushed over her: gasping, grasping, and darkness, sweat and straining and the sweetest kisses. Discomforted, she shifted on the stool. "If you really must know, we need gas."

Had he been standing so close before? She squelched the shiver, and wondered how she could have ever thought those dark eyes cold. Heat rose beneath her skin at his unwavering regard. They were going to end up in bed again, no doubt about it. "And coffee, chocolate, and condoms. What more could a woman need?" Her self-conscious glare defied him to poke fun or say something smart.

One side of Julien's mouth tipped up in a wry smile. "She needs a man to make her coffee and feed her chocolate." He moved behind her, his body brushing against her. "Why condoms, Dulcie? You said you can't have kids."

"There's reasons for condoms beyond birth control." They'd been careless last night; more careless than he realized, but she couldn't admit that to him.

His hands settled on her shoulders, massaging and kneading the stiffness away. His body kept her hidden from Les's view at the back of the houseboat and, as his hands strayed lower, she understood why.

"More than anythin', a woman needs a man to make her feel good," Julien murmured. "Love her long into the night."

Despite his tingling touch, the seductive words, her bitterness swelled. "If only for the next night or two. Then he's gone."

His fingers hesitated for a fraction of a second before he brought his hands back up and massaged her shoulders. "I never made any promises, *chère*." His voice was low, with a note of frustration or anger. She held the steering wheel so tightly that her knuckles were white. "You knew how it would be. I can't stay."

She wouldn't turn to look at him. "You can't, or won't?"

"What difference does it make?"

"A lot. To me."

He dropped his hands from her shoulders, then eased down onto the vinyl upholstered chair beside her. "I can't."

Their gazes met and locked, and in his dark eyes she saw her own anger mirrored. "You're just going to walk away in a few days, as if nothing happened between us? As if last night was nothing more momentous than—''

''Than what, *chère*? You said yourself it was only good sex.''

''I told you I loved you.''

''You didn't mean it.'' His face showed nothing, but he'd focused on some distant point beyond her shoulder.

Dulcie bristled. She'd exposed a great deal more to him last night than her body, and it hurt that he could brush her words off so easily. ''You're telling me how I feel?''

''In the heat of the moment, women say things they don' always mean. Maybe you loved what I was doin' to you, but that's different from lovin' me.'' After a moment, when she still didn't respond, he looked back at her and added, ''Any man can give you what I did last night, *chère*. Stick to guys like Halloran. They're what you need. Not me.''

Her anger began to build, but she made an effort to keep it in check because of the weary lines on his face. ''Bobby and me . . . it wasn't what you think. We got drunk together one night and ended up in bed. I was depressed because I'd had to leave the force, and Bobby was feeling guilty because he'd cleared my team to go into the building.''

She stared out over the flat river, the violence of that night clear and sharp in her memory. ''It was my bad luck to get between a baseball bat and a creep anxious to get away, but Bobby doesn't see it that way. The affair, if you can call it that, lasted only a couple of months and we fought a lot."

"You didn't have to tell me that."

"I know, but I wanted to. If you think about it, you'll understand why Bobby brought you here to me in the first place."

He said nothing to that. He didn't have to.

"And what about you?" she asked after a moment. "How many women have told you they love you in the heat of the moment?" She turned her attention from the river to Julien, wanting to know and yet afraid of his answer.

"Not as many as you're imaginin', *chère*."

"Just once, I wish you'd be straight with me."

He didn't look away from her challenging stare. "My wife, for one. She loved showing off her nice-lookin' Cajun to her friends. She loved what we did in bed. She hated the nights I was gone, hated my musician friends, my family, and the farm. She was in love with the idea of marryin' a Cajun fiddle player, but sure'n hell didn't love the reality."

A wife. Before she could stop herself, Dulcie looked for a ring on the finger of his left hand. There wasn't one. She raised her eyes to his unsmiling face. "Are you still married?"

"Married Alana when I was twenty-five, divorced her at twenty-six. My *mère*, she didn't talk to me for months after that. In my family, see, promises are supposed to be kept. They didn't approve of Alana, my family, but we'd taken vows."

"How old are you?" She felt foolish for asking. It was the sort of thing she should've known about him before they'd had sex, not after.

"Thirty-three."

"Where is your family from?"

"Heart of Lafayette Parish. Can't get any more Catholic than us Langlois."

They were dancing around the issue of the feelings between them, but she didn't press for more answers. It was enough to know he came from rural Cajun stock, considered himself a musician, had married a groupie, and that his divorce had left him bitter and at odds with his strict, Catholic family. The reality was a far cry from the posing boy-toy she'd first met only a few nights past.

It came to her then—a sudden, chill understanding. She saw it; heard it in her mind. Mother Langlois telling her scapegrace son to take care of the young Marcel. Julien giving his promise.

And another promise was broken.

She shifted her attention to the river, watchful for shoals, floating debris, or other boats. But stretching out before them was flat, grassy swampland dribbling its way to the Gulf of Mexico. After taking a deep breath, she looked back to Julien. He watched her from his seemingly casual sprawl on the chair. "It must have been hard on your family. What happened to Marcel."

Down went those lashes. "*Mais* yeah."

"And on you," she continued gently. "You must have blamed yourself."

"Somethin' like that."

"I told you this last night, before we made love." She said the word deliberately, but he wouldn't raise his lashes. "Killing Mitsumi won't bring Marcel back. The best thing you can do for your brother is to cooperate with the police.''

''The police can't even catch Mitsumi. Halloran won't find the Dragon. He's too good.''

''He's an arrogant bastard who thinks he's above the law,'' Dulcie snapped. ''He'll make a mistake. The murder charge, even if reduced, is enough to bring his other crimes crashing down around his head. By the time the jury is done with him, he'll have a dozen life sentences.''

Julien shifted in the chair, moving forward to dangle his hands loosely between his knees and stare at his bare toes. ''An' in the meantime, I'm supposed to hide away like a damn coward an' wait for the cops to catch him.''

''Something like that,'' Dulcie retorted.

He snapped his head up, and she took the full force of the anger in his black eyes. ''An' one ex-cop gets to see the man she hates go down. You're real convincin', *chère*. I might almost believe you really do care.''

It couldn't have hurt more if he'd struck her a physical blow, and it was all she could do to rein in her temper. The solution to his problem was so obvious: convict Mitsumi and send him to prison. Yet again, Julien rejected it. A wary, suspicious part of her wondered why, even now, he turned from the law.

Dulcie clamped her hands down hard on the steering wheel. ''Yeah, I hate him. I've seen a dozen Marcels, you know. I hurt for every one of them, because there was nothing I could do to make up for the choices they'd made.''

''I don' need this,'' he muttered, pushing himself abruptly from the chair.

Her temper snapped.

''*His* choices, Julien. Not yours!'' Her shout brought him short, his back turned to her. ''You didn't give Marcel drugs, or make him hang out with the wrong bunch of kids. And I bet you told him drugs were bad and that you didn't like his friends. I bet you did everything you could, short of chaining him in his room, but in the end it wasn't enough, was it? If a sixteen-year-old kid is hell-bent on going down, it's damn hard to stop him. Blame yourself if you want, but don't pretend that everything you've done here was for Marcel. You want to kill Mitsumi for no better reason than I went to bed with Bobby—stupid, blind self-pity!''

Julien turned on her, pale beneath his tan. ''You got no right,'' he said, his voice a tight, hard whisper. ''No right to interfere!''

''I do now.''

''The hell you do!'' he snarled. ''Go ahead an' dress it up in high-soundin' words, like you're some goddamn Joan of Arc, but what you wanted all along was for me to scratch an itch. Tell me you didn't go to bed with me because you were feelin' sorry for yourself. Go ahead!''

The world narrowed to contain only the two of them, leaving Dulcie to face Julien's dark, furious eyes.

And her guilt. Her sorrow and her lust. Her love and pitiful arrogance that she could have ever thought to fix this man's problems. Sharp emotions, coiling all together like a nest full of snakes inside her. Hurting. She blinked back the tears, hating that they'd come at all.

"Maybe . . . I've been a little lonely," she murmured, her stubborn pride keeping her from looking away. "But I care, Julien. Everything I said last night . . . Everything," she repeated in a whisper, "is true."

After a moment, as a traitorous tear slipped down her cheek, the tight muscles of Julien's shoulders visibly loosened. He took a deep breath, exhaling with puffed cheeks, and then briefly squeezed his eyes shut.

"Dulcie," he said, "I'm sorry for what I just said. But he was my brother. He was my responsibility. I failed him, an' now he's dead. You got no right to tell me how to grieve."

"Murder is a poor monument to the love you had for him, Julien," she whispered, wiping away the tear. "Whether you want to hear me say it or not."

They stared at each other for a moment longer, then Julien stalked off. Dulcie returned her attention to the river, and listened to the angry pounding of his bare feet as he left her. Alone.

Chapter 14

~~

DULCIE CONSIDERED DELACROIX a charming fishing village, although some tourists would think it poor and bleak, with its run-down stilt houses and old shrimp luggers lining the piers—End of the World Marina, the locals called it. The bridge crossing the river didn't look safe enough to walk over, much less drive, and the road ended against the marsh and water, as if its builders had suddenly realized they'd fall into the Gulf of Mexico if they went an inch further. The terrain was flat except for an occasional tree soaring like a lone, watchful sentinel. A far cry from the metropolitan bustle of New Orleans. It might as well have been another planet.

She cut the engines and let the houseboat drift toward a pier by a bait and tackle shop and gas station. Once again, Les took care of securing the ropes. He'd changed into a less conspicuous outfit, with a denim jacket hiding the bulge of the gun stuffed into the back of his pants. Lucille wore a long Loyola University T-shirt over a pair of leggings, which also effectively disguised her gun.

"I'll take care of fueling up the boat," Les said, fixing a stern brown gaze on Dulcie. "Lucy goes with you and Julien. You stay with her at all times."

"Nobody is going to try and pick off Julien down here." Dulcie frowned, hoping Les wasn't about to give her another unsolicited lecture on responsibility and common sense.

"But we're not concerned about somebody shooting Julien, remember? We're concerned about *Julien* running off and shooting someone."

"He's not going anywhere."

"And how can you be so sure?" Les asked mildly.

Because he's waiting for something, she wanted to say. But didn't. "Just because. I need to buy coffee, and I'm dying for a candy bar. Maybe I'll take a walk. Julien and I need a little time alone, without you and Lucille hovering over our shoulders."

"I don't want you out of my sight or Lucille's, or we go back to Lake Pontchartrain. I mean it."

Dulcie tightened her lips, repressing the urge to argue with him again. He did mean it, which translated into no privacy for her and Julien. Unfortunate, since they needed to talk.

"I'm going to get Julien," she said, not bothering to hide her vexation. "If I don't come out in fifteen minutes, you can keep the tackle box, Lucy can have my boat, and make sure they don't bury me in panty hose, okay? I can't imagine going through eternity in those damn things."

Les laughed. She could tell he didn't want to, but a smile tugged reluctantly at his mouth and the laughter sprang loose. "You're a piece of work, Dulcie Quinn."

"And don't you forget it," she said, with more bravado than she felt. Turning from Les, she marched to the cabin door and pushed it open without knocking.

Julien sat on the bed, playing his usual game of solitaire. He looked up when she came in, and Dulcie saw anger lingering in the tight lines around his mouth and nose. Lucille was standing in the doorway to the kitchen. At Dulcie's sharp jerk of her head, the other woman retreated without a word and shut the door quietly behind her.

"Are you coming into Delacroix?" When he didn't answer, she came closer. His long fingers flipped over a card. "Or are you going to sulk in here all day?"

"Don' push it, *chère.*"

"Get your good-looking butt out that door. Now. You can be mad at me all you want, but we're going to talk about it like two civilized adults."

"Who the hell said I was civilized?"

Dulcie stepped even closer, deliberately touching her body against his. "You're as tame as I want you to be. Get up. I need you to help me decide on Hershey's milk chocolate or a Snickers bar. And if I should go for Colombian, or a French roast."

He slapped the cards down and looked up. She'd left her shopping list incomplete, but she saw by his narrowed eyes that he remembered what the last item was.

Again, he moved too quickly for her to avoid his strong grip. Dulcie found herself yanked down, half on his lap and half on the bed over a scattered deck of cards. "You want 'em ribbed or plain?" he muttered, his hand effortlessly finding its way beneath her skirt.

"Stop that!" She knocked his hand away, annoyed that he was using sex to avoid talking with her. Then she grew annoyed with herself, because it was her fault. She'd been the first one to use sex in the place of honesty, and now she was paying for that deceit.

He smiled then, slow and lazy.

Oh, that smile! She went soft at it and when he brought his hand back, she didn't push it away. "Julien, we have to—"

"I asked you a question, *chère*."

Dulcie sighed. "I don't . . . um, have a preference, really."

His mouth dipped dangerously close. "You're sure an easy woman to please."

She didn't have time to reply, even if she could have formulated some snappy comeback, before he kissed her. She could still feel his anger in that hard, relentless kiss. He left her gasping for air, and when he released her, she was too light-headed to argue, and wasn't sure why she'd been arguing with him to begin with. He nibbled at her shoulder, making her tingle.

"Maybe we could get the glow-in-the-dark

kind," she murmured. "Although I suppose where it's going, that won't really matter."

Julien burst out laughing; a deep, rolling belly laugh, straight from the heart. A sound she'd not heard before. "I don' know any woman who can make me angry, crazy with lust, and laughin' out loud like you, *chère*, one right after the other. There's nobody like you."

There was an oddly wistful note to his voice, and the laughter faded from his eyes. Silence followed, and a sudden awareness of his body against hers, the soft fleece against the back of her thighs, his one hand on her hip, the other at her back. His mouth, close to her own. She touched his face, then leaned forward to kiss him.

After a moment, Julien pulled back. He continued to slide his finger up and down her scar until, slowly, she relaxed at the touch. "Why do we always fight?" he murmured. "Especially since we get on so well in other ways."

Because after the sex, the problems would still be there. She almost said it out loud, but didn't. It was much easier to hide behind a kiss, to retreat with a caress. Surrender beneath the sheets.

He locked her against his chest, and again there was nothing gentle, nothing light, about his mouth on hers. He shifted her completely to his lap so that she straddled him, a leg on either side of his hips, her breasts pressed against his shirt. He grew more aroused as their kiss deepened, but when he started pushing up the back of her shirt, Dulcie broke away.

"None of that." She didn't move when Julien loosened his hold on her and added, with real regret, "We have to get going. Lucille is waiting."

"Any chance you an' me can steal a few hours together without the guard dogs?"

"No," she sighed.

He managed a forced smile. "Gonna be a long day."

Dulcie slid off his lap, and glanced down as she came to her feet. "Oh, my," she whispered. Then, her voice stronger, "You'd better change into something else. Those shorts are just one shade shy of indecent."

Julien didn't bother to glance down at himself, but then he was likely quite aware of his state. He pushed himself off the bed, then reached for his gym bag. After kicking aside the cutoffs, he pulled out the black jeans. A shame, to cover such a nice rear, but at least she wouldn't have to fight off every female in Delacroix between the ages of sixteen and ninety-six.

"Happy?" he asked, as he zipped the fly and snapped it shut.

"No," she answered, with a loud exhalation. "But now you won't cause any riots among the natives. I'd hate to tell Bobby we lost his prize witness to a crazed horde of females." She watched as he pulled his hair back and secured it with a rubber band he'd retrieved from the pocket of his jeans. "What were you and Lucy talking about?"

"Nothin' much."

"Julien."

He raised a brow. "Really. She was askin' about my music."

"Oh." She chewed on the inside of her cheek. "You know, I don't know much about you at all."

"Nope. An' I don' know much about you."

"We kind of put the cart before the horse, didn't we? I mean, what we did last night and only now getting to know each other . . . Oh, hell," she finished on a frustrated mutter. "I never was any good at this stuff."

After a moment, he crossed the short distance between them and circled her waist with his arms. "Since we got to keep our hands to ourselves all day, we have time to talk. If you want."

"I'd like that. We can talk about Marcel, too. Maybe," she added, as his body stiffened. The effort it took for him to relax his muscles also registered against the length of her body.

"Maybe," Julien said quietly, then reached out and touched the side of her cheek.

To say they turned a few heads in Delacroix wasn't true. Everybody stared. Dulcie might blame all the attention on him, but Julien knew both women caused equal degrees of speculation. They were an odd sight, to be sure. One six-foot-tall woman with long red hair, one petite black woman in a huge T-shirt, and himself. One lucky bastard, those looks told him.

Dogs barked, fisherman stopped their work to watch, children playing in the streets came to investigate, and shopkeepers along the riverfront poked their heads out doors. Old men sitting on weathered benches nodded at them, polite but watchful.

"Where's the closest grocery store?" Dulcie asked one old man, whose dark face was nothing but wrinkles, stiff white bristles, and a pair of rheumy black eyes.

The old man jerked a thumb to the left. "Down a ways. Next to the bar."

"Thanks."

"Lead on, *chère*," Julien said and followed her long-legged, purposeful stride. Lucille had to hustle to keep up. He grinned down at the smaller woman. "Where did you get that shirt? Looks like it's gonna drown you, *'tite*."

"It's Halloran's."

Julien stared. "You got to be kiddin'. Is it some sort of territorial thing with him, giving his shirts to all his women?"

"I ain't his woman," Lucille retorted.

Julien saw that Dulcie had already moved too far ahead to hear the conversation. "But Dulcie was?"

He felt only a little guilty for prying about her relationship with Halloran behind her back. He had to know if it was as dead as she made it sound.

Lucille shot him a shrewd glance, snapping her gum several times before answering. "They go back a long way. Dulcie's brother Sean was on the force, and Bobby, Sean, and Dulcie were real tight. After Sean transferred to Baton Rouge, Bobby and Dulcie stayed friends. And that was all they were, except for a few months after she got out of the hospital.''

''Who broke it off?''

''Dulcie did.''

''Why?''

''That's something you'll have to ask her. I already said too much.'' She grinned. ''You like Dulcie.''

Thwarted, his answer came a bit surly. ''When I don' want to gag her, sure I like her.''

By this time, Dulcie had noticed she'd lost them. She stopped and waited for them, hands on her hips. Lucille gave an exuberant wave. ''You walk too fast,'' she hollered. Then, more quietly to Julien, ''She's a good woman. All heart. You could do worse.''

Not sure if he should be alarmed at Lucille's matchmaking—or his own too transparent motives—he said nothing. But they'd caught up with Dulcie by then and he couldn't have answered, even if he'd known what to say.

''This is going to take all day if you two don't hurry up,'' Dulcie complained.

''We have all day,'' Lucille pointed out.

''That doesn't mean we have to take it.'' Dulcie glanced toward a charter fishing boat, and in doing so noticed the blatant stare of a young fisherman. She blushed and fidgeted, as if she were unused to such appreciative interest.

Julien found it hard to believe she couldn't see her own dramatic looks, or that the way she carried herself drew the attention of anything male. Himself included. The morning sunlight provided a tantalizing glimpse of her long legs through the sheer material of her skirt. No doubt every fisherman along the wharf was enjoying the same view.

In a sudden protective and possessive reflex, Julien stepped behind her and blocked further randy speculation.

"What are you doing?" Dulcie demanded, glaring at him over her shoulder.

"Keeping the sun behind me. That skirt doesn't leave much to the imagination, an' you're probably leavin' a trail of hard-ons all along the wharf."

"Oh my God," Dulcie whispered, her eyes widening with dismay.

"I like the view myself, but I don' like sharin' it," Julien said with a teasing grin. It surprised him, a little, that he meant it. In just a few short days, this woman had managed to get under his skin in ways he couldn't ignore. In ways that were pleasant and fine, and in ways that weren't.

"With you hovering over her like some big ol' bull, I think they'll get the message she's taken," Lucille said dryly. "Shall we move along here?"

They set off again, and Julien stayed close to Dulcie. At first she resisted his protective efforts, complaining that she was a big girl and could handle herself. But after a few more stares and one whistle, which made Julien glare, she moved in front of him. Walking so close together caused an occasional tangle of feet, and they were laughing by the time they arrived at the grocery store—which was nothing more than a run-down shack advertising a lunch counter, gas, bait, food, and a bathroom "cleaned every day," as slanted writing boasted on sun-faded cardboard.

"I'll wait out here by the door. Grab a bag of M&M's for me, would you?" Lucille asked. "And if they carry anything besides fishing and girlie magazines, I'd appreciate something to read."

"Is that all?" Dulcie asked from the doorway, and Julien grinned at how she arched her eyebrow.

"Grab anything six foot tall, single, and good-looking."

"We'll keep an eye out," Julien said with a laugh, then captured Dulcie's hand and pulled her into the store. He nodded a greeting at the heavyset older woman behind the counter.

"Can I help you folks?" she called out, in a deep, rich voice that he bet could belt out a spiritual and give him goose bumps to hear it.

"We're here to pick up a few things, thank you," Dulcie said with a smile.

"Just holler if you need me." The woman's gaze was frankly appraising and Julien decided, in view of Dulcie's bashfulness a few moments ago, there was at least one item on her shopping list he should pick up himself. Once Dulcie wandered off down a narrow, overcrowded aisle, Julien dredged up his best lady-killer grin and sauntered toward the counter.

"Mornin'," he said. "Weather's clearin' up some."

"Sure is," the woman replied, bright-eyed. "What can I do for you?"

"My woman an' me, we're spendin' some time together, an' I forgot to pack a few necessities. Lookin' for some rubbers."

The clerk didn't bat an eyelash at his request, but she was salt-of-the-earth people, his kind of people, not some blushing teen-ager working in a city drugstore. She grinned, then reached beneath the ancient cash register to haul out a dilapidated cardboard box. "Take your pick, hon, or you just want 'em all?"

He laughed, which brought Dulcie's head poking up above a row of boxes. "Don' I wish," he murmured, and quickly selected several boxes of serviceable-looking condoms.

"Julien, what are you doing?"

"Shoppin,' " he answered, and this time the woman laughed with him. "Don' worry, *chère*. Get your coffee and chocolate. I took care of everythin' else." He saw her head disappear again, and grinned to himself. She was probably having fits behind the cereal boxes. "Be right back," he said to the clerk, then went in search of his woman.

His woman.

Julien liked the thought of it, which had the effect of making his smile fade. She had him thinking of futures and tomorrows. She had him questioning his plan, the rightness and wrongness of it. She had him wanting peace of mind, and damned if she hadn't been the reason he'd played the music again.

Dieu, he'd made a mess of this. What should've been nothing more than a few days spent sitting on a boat and waiting for Saturday night had become much more complicated than he liked.

But it was too late to back off now.

He found Dulcie in the narrow aisle, still pink-cheeked, and slipped behind her, taking hold of her hips. "You're blushin'," he whispered into her ear.

"I'm thirty years old. You think I'd be able to deal with this in a more mature fashion, but all I can think is how that woman will look at us and know what we'll be doing!"

"I'd like nothin' better, an' right now. You make me crazy, you know that?" He gave in to the need to touch her, sliding his hands higher, briefly brushing her breasts. He bent his head and kissed the side of her cheek. "Crazy for lovin' you, that's what I am."

Her eyes widened at his words; words that had come rolling off his tongue before he'd known it. Instead of feeling all wrong, the words felt all right.

He didn't stop to think it over, and didn't care who might be watching. He wanted to kiss her; kiss this woman who made him laugh, who made him so angry he wanted to smash his fist through a wall, who stirred his desires to a mindless haze. It made him feel alive again, just being with her.

Pulling her close, he kissed her soft, mobile mouth. If he'd meant to curb his desire, it didn't work. Julien wondered if Lucille could be bribed to let him take Dulcie out to some quiet, secluded part of the swamp and make love to her for hours under the blue-gray bowl of the sky. Two days wasn't long enough. He had so little time left with her.

The realization made him pull back, and guilt took hold of him. He wouldn't hurt any more people who cared for him, or those whom he cared for. Never again.

Stupid, stupid! He'd already hurt her, even if she didn't know it yet. A few days ago it hadn't mattered, but it did now. While his plans hadn't changed, Dulcie no longer had a place in them, and even if one of those bullets he planned to pump into Jacob Mitsumi was for her suffering, she didn't need to know about it.

He had no damn business being with her at all.

Julien dropped his hands away, avoiding her questioning gaze. "I better go wait outside." Before Dulcie could speak or even protest, he turned and walked away. He nodded at the grinning clerk, then joined Lucille sitting outside the door. Lucille had attracted a crowd of four little boys, and one of them had a puppy.

Little boys and puppies.

"Hey," he said, getting the word around the sudden tightness in his throat. "That's a nice dog, him. What's his name?"

Julien's abrupt departure left Dulcie angry and hurt, and not a little afraid. She didn't understand what she'd done, if anything, to make him withdraw from her as he had.

Pasting a mechanical smile on her face, she went through the motions of making small talk with the clerk who checked out her grocery items. She kept her eyes averted from the condoms, which suddenly seemed to loom bigger than the Andes. He'd bought them, then pushed her away. She didn't know what to think anymore, nor what to expect or hope for.

"Hello? You in there?"

Dulcie suddenly realized the clerk was speaking to her, and she made an effort to pay attention. "I'm sorry. Did you say something?"

The woman misinterpreted her dazed response. "Never mind, sweetie. You just have fun now, y'hear?"

"Yes. Thank you." She was relieved to get away from the clerk and the knowing look in her dark eyes, but not at all pleased to immediately encounter Julien's broad back the moment she pushed through the screen door.

As Julien turned, Dulcie pulled the grocery bag close against her as if it were a shield. She couldn't meet his eyes. Dropping her gaze, she saw that he held something in his hands. It moved. "What is that?"

Julien opened his hands wider. All at once, a fluff ball tried to wiggle its tail and climb out of Julien's hands, but managed to do nothing more than yip in excited distress. "A present."

"For who?"

"You." He brought the squirming puppy close to his face and the little pink tongue darted out.

"I don't believe this. Take it back."

His smile vanished. "I'm not bringin' it back."

"Hey," Lucille broke in, frowning.

Dulcie whirled, unable to control her sudden

spurt of anger and fear. "I will not have that animal on my boat!" she shouted and all but ran back toward her houseboat. With each step, she forced back the tears of panic. She would not break down in front of Les, Lucille, and all of Delacroix.

She didn't know if Julien followed or not, and the shrimp luggers and stilt houses passed by in a numb blur as she focused only on her houseboat and Les's heavyset figure standing on the pier. By the time she got to the boat her arms ached from clutching the bag so tightly. As Les opened his mouth, she took a deep breath and said, "I'm upset. Leave me alone."

"Jeez-louise," he muttered from behind, but didn't try to stop her.

She swept through the kitchenette, slamming the door, and was yanking cartons out of the grocery bag when she felt a hand on her shoulder. She looked back to see Julien, with that tiny puppy, behind her. "Don't touch me!"

"What the hell's the matter with you?"

"What the hell's the matter with *you?*" she shot back. "An animal is a responsibility, Julien. It means you've got to be there to teach it not to pee all over the floor. Means you've got to be there to feed it, walk it, and throw it a bone of affection now and again. Who'll take care of the poor little mutt if you can't?"

He dropped his lashes in classic Julien avoidance mode, and stroked the puppy's head. "I meant to give him to you."

Dulcie knew why he'd taken the puppy. Idiot

man. "Oh, no. It's yours. I'm not taking it. I won't."

"A dog's a good idea. I worry 'bout you, *chère*, all alone on this boat."

"I will *not* take the dog. You damn coward," she ground out, tears brimming in her eyes. He raised his lashes then. "I don't want your lies, Julien, and I don't want your guilt offerings."

"I don' know what you're talkin' about."

But he did. Everything about him—his expression, his body—was tense and taut.

Now she understood why he'd withdrawn from her at the store. "I'm getting too close, aren't I? It's okay to have sex with me, but when I dared care about you, then you pushed me away." She took a deep, steadying breath. "That's why you got me this dog: something to remember you by. Something to keep me from being lonely, because you won't be around."

He said nothing. He didn't have to. She'd spoken the truth and they both knew it.

"Well, I'm not having it." She jabbed him in the chest with her finger. "I'm not taking this mutt. It's yours. You want to keep it from ending up in some pound and slotted for euthanasia, then you better rethink a few things." She looked for a moment at the sweet creature, with its wide eyes, pug nose, and licking tongue. She hardened herself against all those soft emotions threatening to overwhelm her. "Going after Mitsumi is wrong. Why the hell can't you see that?"

She turned away from him, away from the

whimpering puppy she'd frightened with her shouts. She slammed the coffee can on the table, and the puppy yelped.

In an instant, as understanding crystallized, all her anger vanished. She turned back to him. "Who are you trying to fool, Julien? You don't want to punish Jacob Mitsumi."

Julien stood still before her, a wary look in his eyes, but he'd taken a step back.

"The one you want to punish is yourself. The one you want to suffer . . . it's yourself. Not Mitsumi. You!"

Chapter 15

JULIEN STOOD IN silence. At first, he felt only shock. Shock at her anger, at her accusation. Then his own anger began to build. And something else besides the anger. "You're wrong."

"Am I?" Her gray-green eyes were hard, and glittered when she moved. He realized after a moment that it was because she was crying.

The puppy made a distressed whimper and Julien loosened his grip. It wouldn't take much to crush fragile ribs. "Let it be, Dulcie. Leave it alone." He took a step toward the door.

"Or what? You'll turn tail like you did the last time? Every time I bring up Marcel, you run off. What are you afraid of, if not the truth?"

Her angry challenge brought him up short. "I said leave it alone!"

"I can't," she answered, the line of her mouth tight. "Part of me might wish I could turn my back and let you do what you think is right. Part of me wishes Bobby and every cop in New Orleans could turn their back. But you can't kill Jacob Mitsumi. It's wrong."

"After what he did to you, you can tell me—"

"Mitsumi never touched me. Mitsumi never sold your brother drugs, and he sure didn't pull the trigger of the gun that killed him. The Red Dragon is nothing but an excuse," she said with soft force. "An excuse you can use to punish yourself."

She didn't have his nightmares. She hadn't lost a brother. She couldn't ever understand. "Mitsumi deserves to die."

"Maybe he does. But there's nothing to be done about it, except convict him and his associates and send them to prison. It's a small victory, but it's all Marcel will ever have."

Julien turned back toward the door. A couple of steps and he could walk away. Stop listening. Sever the invisible tie pulling him back from his promise. She'd called him a coward—maybe he was. He'd failed at so much already, why not this as well?

Looking down, he met the wide eyes of the puppy. Trusting and eager, like those of a child. He squeezed his own eyes shut, but nothing ever kept the bitter memory away.

"When I came home from work that night, there was a message on the answerin' machine," he said after a moment, stroking the puppy's head. "Marcel wanted me to pick him up. He was so high I could hardly understand a word he said."

In the following silence, he waited for Dulcie to say something. When she didn't speak, he continued. "He was always talkin' crazy. We'd argue, then the next day he'd promise to do better an' I'd feel bad for losin' my temper. Marcel had been doin' better. I thought we were gettin' over the problems. So when he called, high again, I was too angry to go after him. Let the fool find his own way back, I thought. I figured it was time he learned the consequences of his actions.''

Julien opened his eyes. ''He never came back.'' The puppy was drifting to sleep under his soft, steady petting. Turning, he looked at Dulcie. She sat on the counter, watching him. ''By midnight I knew somethin' was wrong an' went after him. He wasn't at any of his usual hangouts. Nobody had seen him. Thinkin' maybe he'd made it home, I headed back. But he wasn't there. Then I called the cops.''

Dulcie remained silent, holding her hands clasped tightly in her lap.

''From there, it all went bad. Hours in the hospital, then with the police. Callin' home to break the news, makin' arrangements for the funeral. Did it all myself. My *mère*, she didn't take it too well. My old man hasn't spoken to me since. You can't tell me I've no right to make sure justice is done.''

''That's not what I said, Julien,'' Dulcie answered, her voice quiet. ''What I want you to understand is that sending the Dragon to prison *is* justice. It won't make you feel better. It isn't fair, or severe enough. But it's justice.''

Justice.

Walking along a dark street on a rainy night. The cemetery, the grave still an unhealed wound in the soft grass. Touching the stone, tracing the

*name. Tonight, he had said, tonight I slay dragons
for you.*

"I made a promise," Julien said, remembering
that night. The night Hernandez died. The night the
Dragon had almost fallen. The night Dulcie had
come into his life. "I won' break it."

She shifted on the counter. "A promise to a dead
boy."

"A boy I raised since he was a baby!" He heard
his own voice, tight with anger. "I was supposed
to be takin' care of him, an' I loved Marcel, Dulcie
. . . right up to the end, I never stopped lovin'
him."

"I know that, Julien."

He walked to the door.

"Where are you going?"

"I want to be alone," he said, then shut the door
quietly behind him.

Julien headed for the back of the houseboat and
sat on the deck, the sleeping puppy on his lap. He'd
expected Dulcie to take it, and now he didn't know
what the hell he was going to do with it.

He needed to think, but the memories he'd kept
locked inside for so many months surfaced with
relentless force. Not all of them were bitter, though.
He'd been living in the cold and darkness for so
long he'd forgotten all the good times, all the
things that made life worth living.

Everything Marcel would never know.

The drug problem had been bad, but together
they could have beaten it. There was always that
chance, in the distance. No chance with a half-

dozen bullets, though. Everything gone, in a split second. No matter how much he'd loved his brother, no matter how much he missed Marcel or how great his guilt or anger, none of it was enough to reverse death.

Violent, brutal death. On a concrete sidewalk beside some dirty alley. Julien could only hope there hadn't been much pain, and that his brother hadn't lived long enough to know fear, to know that no family or even a friend was with him in the end.

He stared out at the stark beauty of the swamp, trying to remember only the good times, like teaching Marcel to spit through his front teeth, to fish and ride a horse. He remembered the pride on his young brother's face when he'd learned to ride a two-wheeler, his astonishment when he finally got an A in math, his red-faced embarrassment the first time a girl tried to kiss him. He remembered Christmas mornings and chaos on the farm, his *mère's* home-baked bread filling the house with a heavy, yeasty aroma, and how his old man smelled of sweat and petroleum.

He tried to remember only the good, but somehow the ugly images always rose above. What the bullets had done to Marcel's body. The pasty-white face in the coffin that didn't look real, the pile of blood-stiff clothes the ER staff had cut from his body. That last, slurred message on the answering machine he'd ignored.

Here, amid the blue-gray sky and vast expanse of the swamp, he couldn't hide from his mistakes. His whole life, he'd let his family down. Never fitting in at home, but tired of being the *gui-gui*, the redneck country bumpkin. Heading out and living wild in New Orleans, his *mère* disapproving and his old man tight-lipped. The marriage with Alana that had been nothing but anger and sex. Taking Marcel in and promising to take care of him. Working hard the whole week long, in hot sun and dirt, living for the nights he played the music, making people smile and dance and forget their cares.

The emptiness of the swamp before him offered no comfort, no forgiveness.

Julien shifted his attention toward the snoozing bundle in his lap, watching the rapid rise and fall of its rib cage, how it curled in on itself. Maybe Dulcie would change her mind. Women liked little baby things. He didn't think she'd really toss it overboard into the river. As Lucille had said, Dulcie was all heart. All soft heart.

He didn't know what else to do, but take things one day at a time. The puppy needed a bed, so he'd have to find a box as well as something to eat. He'd try to make Dulcie understand he couldn't stay, no matter what happened Saturday night, because he wasn't the kind of man she needed.

He brooded, wondering what had put Halloran and Dulcie at odds. The cop wasn't exactly cool toward Dulcie. Julien could see it, even if she appeared not to. Halloran was a man with a future, and a steady paycheck to support a family.

Not a fiddle player who spent his nights in honky-tonks and seedy blues clubs beneath a swirling pall of cigarette smoke, hardly taking home a dime when the lights went down. Not a man who'd already failed dismally at marriage and even worse at raising a kid. Not a man who'd stripped off his clothes for the past six months and never once felt a speck of shame. No reason to feel anything, because he was only a piece of meat on display before a blur of anonymous faces. Easier to deal with women that way, when he couldn't tell color of their hair or skin, if they were young or old, pretty or plain.

Much easier to leave it all behind, when they didn't have names or faces. Or long red hair and green eyes that saw beneath his very skin.

Scooping the puppy back into his hands, Julien stood and made his way back to the cabin.

Dulcie was still in the kitchenette and looked up as he walked in, her face calm. A cool one, his Amazon.

"I thought you wanted to be alone."

Hard and sharp, too. An itch demanding to be scratched. An ache whispering to be soothed. "I don' want to be alone anymore," he said, too tired to pretend otherwise.

She returned to her busywork, rattling around in drawers and cupboards. Finally, she turned to face him and he saw the lingering sheen of tears on her cheeks, the faint redness in her eyes. "Sit down, Julien. I'll make some coffee."

"I want to keep the dog."

"Fine. But he's yours, not mine. Remember that."

"He's kinda cute, for a mutt."

"Julien. Don't."

"I need a box for a bed," he pressed, wondering if that metal pin in her back contributed to her ramrod attitude. He liked her better when she was soft and wanted his kisses. But he liked the Amazon, too. He liked near everything about Dulcie Quinn, which was a shame.

"I've got extra boxes by my workbench. Towels, too. I'm afraid I didn't pick up any puppy chow at the store." She crossed her arms over her chest, which pushed her breasts against the low scoop neck of her ivory T-shirt. His temperature jacked up a notch or two at that.

God, she had felt so good last night, and it had felt so right for him, being with her. "I was thinkin'," he said, abruptly.

He expected her to say something all smart and sassy, but instead she said, "About what?"

"About everythin' Marcel is gonna miss, all the good things in life he'll never know." His gaze lingered on her face for a moment, touching on the wide eyes, the soft mouth, then moving lower to her breasts swelling above the thin cotton.

Taking a deep breath, Julien smelled the dense, heavy scent of the bayou mingled with engine exhaust. Boat engines hummed low, men talked and laughed. Simple and fine. A better place on earth than the bayous didn't exist, this he felt for certain. He looked at Dulcie. "With some things, you don' get a second chance."

Her expression grew troubled. "No. With some things, you don't."

They stood in awkward silence, a hundred things unsaid but simmering between them, before Dulcie lifted a plastic bag. "I bought pecans. You said you like pralines, and I have the sugar and everything else you need. Thought maybe we could make some. The pecans didn't come shelled, though. Not much of a selection in the store."

"I'd like that, *chère*. I'll go take care of the dog—get him settled in a bed. I'll make sure he behaves an' won' get into any of your doll things."

"Thanks," she said, and smiled a little.

Dulcie watched him leave, then sank back against the counter. She raised a hand to brush away the hair from her face and stared at her hand, which was shaking worse than a drunk with DTs. Drug busts and domestic abuse situations had never left her as scared as she was now.

She'd glimpsed the anger; his blind, hard determination; but she'd never imagined the extent of Julien's grief. She'd almost cried as he'd tonelessly described his brother's last night. He had left so much unsaid, but she could imagine the hell he'd gone through. His loneliness touched a chord deep within her. Marcel might have died without someone to hold his hand and tell him everything would be all right, but his brother had been left to deal with the aftermath alone. Not even his family had stepped forward to take him in hand. Perhaps they had tried and he'd turned away.

I don' want to be alone anymore.

Solitude could be a strength in the right situation, but it also cut one off from those who could listen, who could be around when their help was needed. She was offering him a helping hand, and her heart and care with it. If only he would meet her halfway.

Julien didn't take long in settling his new dog, and by the time he returned Dulcie had herself under better control. He stood in the door between the cabin and kitchenette, thumbs hooked in his belt loops. He didn't move forward, as if he feared to cross a threshold. Lord, he had reason to hesitate, she thought with regret. They fought more than they talked.

Finally, he came to her side. "Got a nut-cracker?"

"Oh, rats. No. I forgot about that."

"Hammer?"

She had no idea. Some women were perfectly organized and could find even the smallest toothpick in their house, but she wasn't one of them. She opened her junk drawer to see what might be lurking in its jumble. Screwdrivers—all Phillips—and several wrenches, the flashlight she had looked for the night Julien had kissed her. How could a body throw off so much heat, she wondered, and moved a little away from him. She shut the drawer. "No hammer."

He looked faintly perplexed by the lack, but his eyes were unfocused. As if he were somewhere else. Somewhere far away.

She didn't like that unfocused look. "Oh, wait,"

she said, remembering the big chunk of granite she kept on her workbench, to hold down pattern tissue paper on windy days. "I have something that will work just as well."

Dulcie hurried into the cabin, carefully stepping over the box with the dozing puppy, then poked around the piles of fabric, doll parts, and boxes on her bench. She located the rock under a remnant of gold tissue. On her way back, she stepped over the puppy again, then hesitated. With a glance toward the door, to make certain Julien wasn't watching, she bent down and stroked the tiny head. The puppy snuffled in its sleep, curling tighter. The poor thing felt cold. She flipped the edge of the towel over its body, then went back into the kitchenette.

"Here," she said, holding up the chunk of granite. She pulled out her oldest cutting board and handed it, along with the rock, to Julien. "That ought to do the trick."

Julien cleared a place on the counter and opened the bag of pecans. He eyed the rock for a moment. Taking a pecan from the bag, he placed it precisely in the center of the board. Then he raised the rock and brought it down with a focused force that smashed the shell open.

Dulcie jumped at the loud, sharp crack. She imagined it might sound a little ominous to anyone outside. She cast a quick glance toward the screen door and decided she'd better go reassure Les and Lucille that nothing was wrong.

Les met her at the door and Lucille was clambering over the railing to the deck.

"It's all right," Dulcie said quietly, holding up her hands. She stepped a small distance from the kitchen. "I bought some pecans to make pralines, but I don't have a nutcracker. Julien is using a rock to crack open the shells."

Les exhaled noisily. "Jeez-louise! Scared the daylights out of me. The way you two fight, I figured one of you was killing the other."

Dulcie frowned with annoyance. "Really, Les. I holler a lot, but violence isn't my mode of communication."

"Maybe it's not yours, but who knows about him," Les retorted.

Another resounding crack sounded from the kitchenette. She winced at the sound and stepped closer to Les. "You know better than that. Nothing is wrong. Now please, take the boat back to Mike's and leave Julien and me alone."

"I called Halloran," Les said, frowning. "Lucy and I have a job to do, whether you like it or not, and I'm not too happy about the way things are going here."

"Isn't that too damn bad," Dulcie retorted, glaring at both Les' stubborn face and Lucille, who looked hesitant and unsure as she glanced back between Les, Dulcie, and the cabin. "Since I'm not on the police payroll anymore, I don't have to listen to either you or Bobby. Your job ends at my bedroom door."

Les James was a good man, probably the most

practical and unflappable human being she'd ever known, but sometimes he was as stubborn and contrary as a mule. "You're going to end up hurting yourself over this," he said. "Julien agreed to stay only until Saturday. He's going to leave you, Dulcie."

"I know." Deep inside, she knew Julien would leave in two days. But he might come back.

Crack!

Les shot a look toward the kitchenette, then sighed. "You're making a mistake."

"So let me make it. God knows I've made plenty of them. All you have to worry about is driving the boat to Mike's."

Before Les could protest further, Dulcie ducked back into the kitchenette. She shut the door just as Julien brought down the rock. Even though she was prepared for it, she still flinched as pieces of pecan shell shot out, skittering across the floor. She watched as he took another nut and smashed it into useless bits, shell and meat both.

A cold fear immobilized her. His every motion was precise and deliberate. One pecan. In the center of the board. The granite rock raised high, then slammed down with punishing force. Another shattered piece of shell fell to the floor.

Julien reached for the next pecan.

She moved forward then, and touched his arm. He went still. "Hey," she said, softly. "Easy does it, big guy."

He said nothing, and deliberately turned his face away. He placed the smooth, brown nut dead center in the remains of the others. Dulcie tightened her fingers on his forearm.

He pulled free of her grip, then brought the rock down so hard that he cracked the cutting board and rattled the dishes and silverware in the cupboards.

In the following silence, he brushed aside the pulverized pecan with slow, delicate movements. It wasn't until Dulcie looked away from his hands that she saw his shoulders shaking.

Instinct took over. She stepped behind him and wrapped her arms tightly around his chest. With her cheek pressed against his back, she could feel each ragged breath as he struggled to keep his grief inside.

"Please. Let it go." Remembering what he'd said the night before, she whispered, "It's all right. Marcel deserves your tears. Cry, Julien. No one will ever know but me."

Dulcie closed her eyes. She wouldn't watch, didn't want to see his tears, as he finally let go. It was hard to feel the uneven rise and fall of his ribs, the jerk of his muscles, the uncontrollable tremors. It hurt listening to the sounds of a man weeping, trying to keep the unaccustomed sounds muffled inside. She squeezed her arms around him, not knowing what else to do.

She held him until the worst of it was over, slowly loosening her grip, rubbing his chest, murmuring words of comfort. She felt the change in his muscles as the rigidity began to ease. He shifted, and Dulcie opened her eyes when he turned and took her in his arms.

The embrace hurt, hard and unyielding. Her face was caught so tightly against his neck that she could hardly breathe. But she didn't let him go, and after a moment began pressing kisses against his warm skin, above the pulsing artery of his neck.

More tension ebbed from his body and his grip became less hurtful, less binding. He slid his hands lower, past her hips to her bottom. She continued to kiss his neck, his earlobe, the stubbled skin of his jaw. He moved his head, bringing his mouth closer, and they connected.

A raw connection. Instinctual, animal. No thought beyond tactile impressions, taste and smell. Sensations melding all together at once. The salty taste of his sorrow. Harsh breathing, and the softest whisper against her ear, "*Ma douce aime, ma jolie fille . . . Trop tard. Trop tard.*"

The knit of his shirt beneath her fingers was soft as butter, full of heat; a second skin stretched across the moving and sliding bands of muscle and sinew beneath. He smelled like fresh air and wind, like Julien.

Only when the edge of the counter cut against the back of her thighs did she realize they'd switched positions. His fingers gathered bunches of her skirt, drawing it further up along her leg, a little at a time, while his mouth slanted across hers and his tongue made a wet, hot circuit over mouth and teeth.

Sliding her hands beneath his shirt, Dulcie trailed her fingers upwards until she had a grip on the hard shoulders, and pulled him as close as possible. He had the fingers of one hand beneath the elastic of her panties, kneading her buttocks, moving down ever so slowly. Dulcie let her legs spread wider as his fingers drew closer to the throbbing ache.

She gasped when he touched her, then he lowered his mouth to kiss her arching neck. "Not here," she managed to whisper.

Julien pulled back, breathing heavily. He said nothing, but grabbed her hand and yanked her into the cabin. He locked the door leading to the kitchenette, while Dulcie locked the outside door to the deck. "Careful of the puppy," she said.

Maneuvering around the box with its tiny occupant, they fell backward onto the bed. Julien moved over her at once, his hands impatient, his mouth rough. He was silent, but his knee nudging her legs apart spoke loudly enough. What he wanted, she wasn't sure she could give, but she would try. He was demanding, needful. Fighting against himself, against a bestial blackness that wanted to keep him fast beneath its claws.

Her fingers closed tightly over his shoulders at his abrupt entry. Then, as he began moving deep within, her body relaxed and the discomfort eased. She slid her fingers to his neck, his long hair, gently caressing. His face was buried in the harbor of her neck, so she kissed his hair, murmuring more words of love, nonsense, and comfort.

She gave Julien all she had, and he took it without a word. His shuddering climax left her unfulfilled, beyond the quiet pleasure of holding him, feeling him within her, and the fierce gentleness she experienced at her power over something so wholly male, so dark and adamantine as Julien Langlois.

Dulcie knew they hadn't made love as much as they'd battled something dark and violent, leaving behind an imperfect peace. She continued to play with his hair, focusing on the weight of his body against hers, the sounds of his breathing as it slowed, his presence lingering yet in her body.

Time passed, a few minutes or many, before he moved. He propped himself on his elbows and gazed down into her face, his expression regretful and shamed. "Sorry," he sighed.

She kissed him. "Nothing to be sorry about, Julien."

"Yeah, there is. All that trouble to buy condoms an' I didn't even—" He paused, then swallowed. "I wasn't thinkin'. Bad enough I was so rough with you, but to forget somethin' like that again. If . . . are you sure you can't get pregnant?"

Chapter 16

~

PREGNANT.

Guilt rolled over her, leaving her cold. Dulcie hadn't wanted to acknowledge the possibility, or look too closely at her reasons for denying it. But now his blunt question forced her to admit what she knew was the truth.

"I never said I couldn't get pregnant, Julien," she said at last, her voice unsteady. She couldn't meet his eyes.

His answer was slow in coming. "So exactly what did you mean?"

He pulled away from her, leaving her chilled and alone. "I don't know," she whispered.

Silence. Then, "Does this pin in your back have somethin' to do with it?"

"No . . . Well, yes."

Julien took her jaw in his hand and forced her to look at him. "I'm not followin' you, Dulcie."

"I can't carry a baby to full term."

"Why?"

He kept his fingers to her jaw, so she couldn't avoid his intense, dark eyes. "My back is weak," she whispered. "The extra weight . . . it would be too much."

Julien stared down at her for a long moment, then his brows slowly drew together in a frown. "What does that have to do with it? It's the uterine muscles holdin' a baby, not back muscles. I've been around enough pregnant women to know that much. Did a doctor tell you that you couldn't have a baby?"

"No, but—"

"*Bon Dieu*," Julien muttered, rolling over. "You have a bad back that hurts like a bitch some days, so you just up an' decided you can't have kids?"

"That's not true . . . It was a severe injury, Julien. I had several reconstructive operations. Months of physical therapy."

"Which has nothin' to do with havin' a baby."

Again, silence hung between them.

She pushed away from him, with a rush of hurt anger that he could reduce her fears to nothing more than a backache. Bobby, who'd wanted to marry her, hadn't understood either. When she'd refused him, citing her inability to have children, Bobby had accused her of hiding behind a lie rather than having the courage to take a risk. So she'd kicked him out, and for three months not a single word had passed between them.

Scooting into a corner of the wall, as far from him as she could get, Dulcie pulled a sheet over her and then smoothed it down with a shaking hand. Tears threatened, and she fought them back;

fought them back along with the cold fear that overwhelmed her whenever she thought of being pregnant—and losing her baby.

"They beat me," she said, in an oddly conversational tone. "Besides a broken back, I had damage to my fallopian tubes and an ovary. The doctors were concerned. How could I trust them to tell me the truth? My whole life had turned upside down. I'd lost my job, and I had this ugly scar. Instead of telling me I couldn't have a baby, they said I might have difficulty carrying a baby to term without complications. They were trying to be kind."

"Never met a doctor who didn't give bad news when they had to. Dulcie, I sure hope this isn't another game you're playin'."

"A *game*?" She jerked up her head, brushing away the sudden tears with the back of her hand. "I wanted to have a family, Julien. I wanted to have children—how can you even suggest such a thing? You'll never carry a baby inside you, feel it move, and know you could lose it. You don't have to be afraid to tell people you're pregnant, because then you might have to tell them the baby died and then they'd give you those pitying looks again. Poor Dulcie Quinn," she said, mimicking a sorrowful tone. "Isn't it a shame about poor Dulcie, and I hear she picked out the paint for the nursery—"

She stopped abruptly, as Julien's hand closed over her own.

"Don' go there, Dulcie." After a moment, with a gentle squeeze, he released her hand, then covered his eyes with his arm. "But I want you to be straight with me here. I need to know if there's a chance you could be pregnant."

Through her fear, she managed to say, "I suppose there is a chance, yes."

He sighed. After a moment he said, in a weary voice, "For a woman who demands truth, you spend a lot of time lyin' to yourself."

Lying? Her body stiffened with anger, overrunning her fear.

He was wrong. All along, he had been the one to lie and hide the truth. She had been honest.

"You're accusing *me* of dishonesty? I wasn't the one who plotted for six months to kill a man, or who used poor Chloe to do it. You were rude. You tried to kiss your way off my boat. You—"

"Yeah . . . An' who turned the tables on who, *chère*." He hadn't lowered his arm, and she watched his Adam's apple shift as he swallowed. "You wanted a man in your bed, an' you got one. You wanted stud service, an' looks like you got that too."

"That's not true! Besides, I didn't exactly hear you protesting. And don't forget how you tried to dump some poor mutt on me so I wouldn't get all weepy when you . . . when you leave me on Saturday?" Somehow, the self-defensive accusation had turned into a question.

He dropped his arm and rolled over on his elbow to face her, his eyes watchful. "I *am* leavin'."

She couldn't find an answer to that, so she only nodded. To show him she understood; show him how reasonable and mature she could be about it. How honest.

He sighed again, this time loudly. "I did follow you into the kitchen that night with every intention of kissin' you, an' I wanted the dog so you wouldn't be alone. I do worry about you, stayin' on this boat by y'self."

He reached over and traced the line of her jaw. Another damn tear slipped down her cheek and he caught it, then rubbed it between the pads of his thumb and finger. "It's not that I don' hear what you're sayin' to me about Mitsumi. But I got to work this out in my own way. Truth is, Dulcie, half the time I feel I've gone too far to come back. Just ain't worth the effort."

At his admission, all her anger, all her outrage, faded away.

"I think you're worth the effort," she said quietly.

He looked at her for a long while, his expression almost surprised, then he glanced away. He yanked his pants up and snapped them closed. "I sure would like to believe you, but it don' change the fact that I'm not the sort of man you need around." Reluctantly, he returned his gaze to her. "Maybe you should rethink things with Halloran. I hate the man's guts, but he seems decent enough."

She stared at him. They'd just made love, and he sat there matter-of-factly telling her she should be with another man. "That's the stupidest thing I have ever heard! Bobby and I were a mistake. He's hot-tempered and the most irresponsible man I've ever met—''

"Dulcie, what you got is a weakness for irresponsible men an' a habit of believin' what you want to, despite the facts.''

She opened her mouth to argue, but the words wouldn't come. Not this time. The old excuses, the old defenses, deserted her in the face of his quiet accusation.

Julien was right. She hadn't been honest with him—or herself—and he had every right to be upset.

There was, after all, a reason why she'd disregarded safe sex with him.

Maybe, deep down, she wanted to get pregnant; to have a hold on Julien, any hold at all. Maybe she wanted him to stay so badly she was willing to risk a pregnancy now, where she hadn't before. Maybe, just maybe, she wasn't so sure about those differences between right and wrong. Was lying wrong, if by doing so you managed to help someone? Was it all right to play games and manipulate someone's emotions, if everything turned out for the best in the end?

No. It wasn't all right, and Julien had seen her weakness more clearly than she had. In the beginning, her interest in Julien had been rooted in lust and her own wish to see Jacob Mitsumi get what he deserved. But at the moment, she didn't care if a hundred Jacob Mitsumis were loose on the streets. She only wanted Julien to stay with her.

She met his gaze. He still looked angry, with the

tight lines around his mouth and nose, his eyes shuttered. But his touch along her breasts, her stomach, was gentle.

"What would you do if I were pregnant?"

His touch had grown bolder, his fingers roaming wider and lower. "I sure as hell don' know. Shush," he said, when she opened her mouth to question him further. "No talkin'. We'll just end up fightin'. I may not believe every word that comes out of your pretty mouth, *chère*, but your body . . . your body talks true to me. We understand this. For a few hours, a few days, let your body show me how much you love me."

She wanted skin to skin, sliding and slippery, hot friction and pulsing union. But she wanted something beyond it, too. It saddened her, this possibility that she and Julien might never have a chance to share anything more than a physical passion.

Still, she had two days left, and she sensed uncertainty in him, a wavering of purpose. His anger no longer felt so lethal, so cold. He'd cried in her arms. Cold-blooded killers didn't have tears.

So they communicated best in bed. One had to start somewhere. She was falling in love with Julien, and she wouldn't let him go. She wanted more than sex, good as it was, but she wasn't afraid to take risks anymore.

When Julien tongued her nipple through her T-shirt and bra, all her thoughts scattered. Before she could react, he'd captured her hands and lifted them over her head, pressing them into the soft pillows. She didn't want to think anymore. She wanted to chase away the shadows and the doubts, drown in the forgetfulness Julien gave her. The troubles would still be there afterwards, but their lovemaking helped make the hurt, the problems they faced, more bearable. If for no other reason than they faced them together.

Wanting more of his mouth on her hypersensitive skin, she arched her back. Low, wordless sounds came from her throat and her fingers clenched and grasped where he held them imprisoned above her head.

He moved to her other breast, and only the weight of his body kept her from rising off the bed. Beneath the wet knit, her nipple hardened with the cold and with the shooting sensations his tongue and lips were rousing.

"Let go of my hands," she pleaded.

He did so at once, and they made short work of her T-shirt. His followed. He slipped off her skirt, then she lost her panties, kicked off feverishly after he'd yanked them down to her ankles. She tried to unsnap his jeans, but he wouldn't let her.

"Julien!"

"Patience, *chère*. I'll show you what I know about feelin' good, and you can teach me even more."

She tried again to get to his fly. His hands blocked her. "I want you inside me, Julien. Please. Don't be such a—"

He stopped her words with a hard kiss and proceeded to unhook the front of her bra. First he eased the straps off her shoulders, then dropped the delicate bit of lace over the side of the bed. She was left with no cover but her long hair.

Julien's hands were rough-soft against her skin as he traced the mounded contours of her breast and the erect nipple. His finger dipped lower to the damp, aching place between her thighs and reduced her to inarticulate moans. Slowly he coaxed her knees up, spreading her legs further apart, until he settled between them. Dulcie closed her eyes as Julien ran his fingers up and down the length of her legs, from her ankle to her calf, then to her knee, which he kissed. He continued to kiss her skin, following the upward stroking of his fingers. Higher, higher, until his hands were tight on her hips and his mouth was on her, hot and wet.

She bit her lip to keep from screaming, her hands clenching the sheet. Her knees were shaking, but his hands held them steady as he teased her with his tongue until the climax rocked through her, convulsive and pure as white light.

Afterward, when he eased back and pulled her against him in an embrace, the first thought to penetrate her numb haze of pleasure was that he was still dressed. His half-clad body on her naked skin sent tiny shivers through her limbs. Smooth flesh, rough denim, the rasp of his zipper against her thigh. She felt a vague sense of unfairness.

"Take those pants off."

His handsome mouth curved in a slow smile. "Anticipation," he said, pushing himself back from her.

"What are you doing?" she demanded, but he

didn't answer. Instead, he left the bed and walked to her workbench. "Julien!"

"Anticipation," he repeated and began rifling through her tape box.

"I'm going to kill you if you don't get back here right this instant and finish what you started!" Godamighty, she was lying naked and aching in her bed, while he whistled between his teeth and tried to find mood music! He'd pay for this.

"Aha," Julien muttered. He snapped up several cassette tapes, grabbed the tape player from her bed, and brought it, cord and all, down to the floor by the bed. He grinned. "In case you get loud."

Dulcie was not amused. "You're dead, mister."

"You have no sense of adventure," Julien retorted, as the music began to play. More Garth Brooks. "Nope," he said, dissatisfied. "Not the one I want."

She pulled the sheets over herself in a huff while he fast-forwarded the tape. Maybe a piece of pecan shell had imbedded in his brain and that was why he was suddenly acting like an idiot. But when the familiar refrain of "Shameless" belted out in the cabin, she understood and began to laugh. "You can't be serious."

"Sure am," he said, with that slow, lazy grin that grooved his cheeks and wreathed his dark eyes in laugh lines.

How quickly he could hide all that inner pain away again, she thought with a pang. Maybe one day it would be gone for real. Maybe one day he would learn to forgive himself for his brother's death.

"You're gettin' a damn fine deal, *chère*," he said, stepping away so that he was just out of reach. "I'll play bad boy to your good girl any day. Sit back an' let me show you what a shameless sonofabitch I really am."

He began a striptease, for her eyes only.

It was all an act, but a particularly effective one, and a shiver did a sliding shimmy down her backbone. Oh, he was good. Shameless didn't even approach the thoughts she entertained as he moved his body before her. Either he'd done a routine to this music before, or he had an instinctive affinity for how to move with the music, and when to bump and grind to the beat.

He pirouetted with the grace of a ballet dancer—which startled her—then flicked open the snap of his jeans. Her mouth went dry, and she suddenly hated the thought of other women watching him do this. Envy surged through her as she wondered what else Julien might have done with the infamous Chloe Mitsumi for two hundred dollars an hour.

He was hers, and like hell was she going to ever share that body with another woman. Or a room full of women!

Oh, my. The sight of his fingers outlining his penis beneath the denim rapidly caused her temperature to approach a meltdown point. On an upward swell of music, Julien unzipped his pants partway and she experienced that familiar, breathless sensation.

He didn't remove his pants, but instead touched himself in all the places she wanted to touch, beneath fabric and along bared skin. In her mind, she felt the crisp hair; the smooth, warm skin. She remembered the contours of the muscles and bones, the silken length of his dark hair. His taste. His smell.

"Damn you, Julien," she muttered, smiling. He was driving her crazy, but she was enjoying his wicked teasing far too much to ask him to stop.

He drew her torture out to the very end of the song, as her muscles grew more taut. She sat at the edge of her bed like a cat poised to pounce. With a practiced curl of his hips, he slipped his jeans down and still managed to move to the music, standing on one foot at a time as he removed his pants. The evidence in his white briefs revealed he was enjoying himself immensely.

"Let me," she whispered, as his fingers slipped below the elastic waistband of his briefs.

"Against the rules, *chère*. You can look, but you can't touch."

She boldly stepped up to him. "To hell with the rules." Her hands dipped beneath the elastic to cup his marvelous, tight rear. "You ever do this in front of another woman again and I'll hurt you."

He looked intrigued, rocking his hips against hers as the song faded away. "Didn't peg you as the pathologically jealous sort."

Dulcie smiled. "I find myself acting strangely, where you're concerned. Time to do things my way."

Up went a brow. "Depends on what you've got in mind."

She make a tsk-tsk sound. "You have no sense of adventure, Julien."

His shout of laughter warmed her. It was a beautiful thing to hear. "Okay, you got me," he said, amused. "Where do you want me?"

It was Dulcie's turn to arch a brow. "Well, let's review all the options." She tapped a finger against her bottom lip. "The bed. Or . . . the bed. Or . . . " She grinned. "The bed."

"Just what I like. A woman with style an' imagination," Julien murmured. He lay down on the bed, hands behind his head, and watched her with an expectant gleam in his eyes.

"There's no room in my head for imagination right now." She let herself indulge in a single, long look at the long, lean body lying in her bed. Yes, oh, yes, there were definite advantages to being female.

She sat beside him and drew one fingernail down the center of his chest. He jerked at the first touch, giving lie to his seemingly casual sprawl. Down, down her fingernail trailed, finally hooking the waistband of his briefs and pulling them down one breath-catching inch at a time.

Yes, there was something to this whole anticipation business. Delayed gratification. She could get to like it. And there he lay, just waiting to do some gratification with her.

"Julien, I have to admit," she said quietly, earnestly, "I could get used to waking up to you every morning."

Some of the laughter faded from his dark eyes, and he reached up to touch her. Gently. A brush of fingers along her cheek, her jaw. Across her lips. He said nothing, speaking to her instead with his body, his touch, and the look in his eyes. He wasn't quite as uninvolved as he'd like, she realized. Maybe he was a little on the way to falling in love with her, too.

She took a deep breath, determined to make the most of the time she had with him, and teasingly pulled his briefs the rest of the way off, with lingering touches down the long, smooth muscles of his legs. Then she straddled his hips in one quick movement, bringing a grunt of surprise from him.

"Scratch what I said about no imagination," he murmured.

"I don't intend to try out every position in the *Kama Sutra* in one afternoon," she said, reaching for one of the condom packets under the pillow. "Me and you, face-to-face, that's what I like best."

"Gonna put out the hound after the fox already made off with all the chickens?"

She blinked, not understanding at first. Then she gave him an indignant glare. "I'm not sure I like being classified with a bunch of squawking chickens, Julien."

His hands, on her hips, urged her to move on him. "I was thinkin' you're the fox."

Dulcie smiled, but it faded as she stared down

at him. Maybe there was something he could give her after all, if she asked.

A chance.

She was thirty years old. This might be her only opportunity, and if he left her, if he never came back, she might at least have something to remember him by. A little one with black hair and eyes, just like his.

"I want a baby, Julien," she whispered. "I want yours."

His eyes darkened and his entire body went taut beneath hers. "Dulcie, you don' understand what you're askin'."

"I'll risk it," she said, then kissed him, deeply. The most erotic, sensual kiss of which she was capable. "If you give me nothing else, Julien, give me this."

"You just can't ask a man to—"

She kissed him again. Longer this time, rubbing her hips against his until his skin, beneath her grasping hands, grew damp with sweat.

"Dulcie, I can't—"

"Please," she whispered. "Here's honesty, Julien . . . I want a part of you, if I can't have all of you."

He swore, low and crude, and took the packet out of her hand. He tossed it to the floor, then wrapped her hair around his hand and pulled her face close enough to kiss her. A surprisingly soft, gentle kiss. Vaguely, Dulcie was aware of his other hand groping around the floor, then the radio came on. Dark, bluesy sounds. Thick, throbbing saxophones and wailing trumpets; the pounding chords of a piano.

She moved above him, taking him inside her a little at a time. Julien's eyes closed. He arched his neck, and his lips cracked open with a low, growling groan of pleasure.

Godamighty, it was wonderful, this hard invasion filling her body. Julien, breathing between his teeth. Julien, moving his hips against her, his hands gripping like talons.

The pressure built, enrapturing her within its vortex of power, but she kept her eyes open, focused on Julien's face. She wanted to watch him when it happened.

Soon. It wouldn't be long. He arched his back, eyes shut and lips drawn back from his teeth in a rictus of pleasure, then he gasped her name. "Dulcie, come with me. Now . . . now!"

It was all she needed. She closed her fingers over his shoulders as he lunged upwards, meeting her frantic downward movements. Even as her own climax washed over her, she watched him, seeing the power she held over him in each spasm of his body, his heaving chest, and the sheen of sweat on his face.

Then he opened his eyes as his body gave one last, shuddering tremor, and she didn't look away. For a long moment, they were still and silent. The saxophone had given way to the thready, sliding notes of a clarinet and a woman with a rasping voice singing about love. Dulcie wanted to tell Julien about her own love, but words would shatter the fragile, vulnerable moment they'd just shared. In his eyes, those expressive and unshuttered dark eyes, she saw tenderness and a powerful need.

"Come here," Julien said quietly, and pulled her into his arms. He held her tightly for a long while, in silence, and Dulcie focused on the peaceful profile of his face.

He might not know it yet, but from their loneliness they'd found the strength of comfort and understanding. Out of hate, they had created love—or something very, very close. Given time, it would take root and grow.

He would walk away from her when Saturday night came. But he'd come back. She knew it. She believed in the power of life, in the triumph of right over wrong.

She believed in Julien.

Julien brushed Dulcie's hair as she sat at her workbench. He drew the brush through the long, auburn strands and felt the silk of her warm hair in his hands, the water push against the deck beneath his feet.

He ought to be comatose, after everything they'd done these past few hours, but he was wide awake, his body thrumming like the strings of a piano after the last violent chord had been struck.

"Boy, am I hungry," Dulcie announced.

Julien smiled, working at a tangle. Her head moved back against his bare belly at every tug. A quick glance at the alarm clock on the floor showed it was well into the afternoon, and they'd last eaten nearly six hours ago. Which alone might account for his shaky hands. "You want me to cook?"

She sighed. "Would you? I'd eat a ten-gallon pot of your rice pudding right about now."

"Feelin' okay?"

"Mmmm," she said, a low, throaty growl.

"A sound to warm any man's heart, *chère*." He tossed the brush down on the workbench. When he kissed her shoulder, she jumped. Her muscles were tight. How that was possible, he couldn't imagine, since only stubborn male pride kept him on his feet. Sitting down on the bed sounded real good about now, but instead he kneaded her shoulders. "I'll fix us a meal. Don' expect anythin' that requires thought or energy," he added. "Toast and jelly is all I'm likely to manage."

Dulcie rested her head against his belly.

"No rice pudding?"

"Not right now, *chère*." Her soft hair tickled him, and his damn fool body just didn't seem to know when to call it quits.

"We should check on the puppy."

Julien grunted. He'd shoved the yipping, tail-thumping critter outside earlier. "Yeah."

"I suppose we should get dressed."

"Les and Lucille would probably appreciate the effort."

Dulcie blushed, and he thought she looked beyond pretty when she went pink in the cheeks like that. "I hope they didn't come on the boat."

"Can't say I'd have cared if they did," Julien admitted, dropping her panties into her lap. "You have fine taste in lingerie, *chère*. Noticed it that first night, watching you sleep. You wore a dark purple bra, and I worked myself into quite a state wonderin' about your underwear.''

''You didn't!''

''Did so.''

''Pig.''

He grinned as he pulled on his underwear. ''Wasn't me squealin' a little while ago.'' She whacked him, a solid slap against his chest. ''Ow! That hurt.''

''Good.'' She stood, then shimmied into her T-shirt and wiggled into her underwear.

Julien couldn't keep his hands to himself. He pulled her against him, then kissed her resoundingly on the lips.

She was something, his Amazon. His woman. *Mais* yeah, here was a good reason to be home every day by five o'clock. Maybe he'd made some mistakes in his past, but he deserved a shot at happiness. He could be a good husband. He could settle down and make himself belong, make himself grasp life by the horns and ride it through all the bumps, the spills, the wild exhilaration. He and Dulcie together, making a red-haired little hellion daughter who'd turn him gray by the time she reached sixteen.

Hell, since he already had a dog, why not a wife and baby too? Why shouldn't he take a great big piece of that all-American dream for himself?

A darker thought niggled at the back of his mind,

but he ignored it, and the anger that had coiled in him for so many months lay dormant.

Then he heard the rapid, heavy thud of footsteps on deck, coming straight for the cabin, followed by a furious pounding on the door that rattled the glass in the windows.

"Dulcie! Dammit, you open this door right now before I kick it in!"

It was Halloran, and the sound of that angry voice triggered the coiling thing inside Julien. Irrational, sharp, and primitive; fury roused, shook itself off, and reared its hateful head.

Chapter 17

"I DON' THINK he took the news about us real well," Julien said mildly.

Fighting down a sudden panic, Dulcie grabbed for her skirt and yanked it on. "Julien, don't you start on him!" She threw his pants at him. "Get dressed!"

The pounding came again. "Dulcie!"

"Hold on!" Without looking back to make sure Julien was dressed, she unlocked the door and yanked it open. "Bobby—"

He shoved past her. His face was dark with anger, and sunlight made a pale nimbus of gold around his blond hair. Dulcie turned, then went still. Julien was pulling on his jeans with an insolent and maddening slowness, leaving Bobby no doubt at all about what they'd been doing behind the locked doors of her cabin.

"What are you doing here?" Dulcie demanded, even though she knew very well why he'd come hotfooting to her boat. Godamighty, he was worse than her brother Sean, prying in her life and telling her to do this and do that.

"Checkin' up on my witness. Making sure everything was just fine and dandy." Bobby's lip curled. "I see you went and made yourself right at home, Langlois."

Julien didn't answer, but he sent Halloran an arch-browed look. Reading that look correctly, Dulcie quickly put herself between the two men. She'd known Bobby would be angry, but this went way beyond what she'd expected. She grabbed his arm and pulled him back.

"You bastard," Bobby said softly, not even looking her way as he shook her loose. "I told you not to touch her."

"You told me not to hurt her," Julien corrected. "Does she look like she's hurtin'?"

Rushing heat stung beneath her skin. Dulcie knew what she must look like to Bobby, with her hastily donned clothing. It didn't help she was probably blushing like a virgin, and she wanted to kick Julien for goading Bobby's anger.

She gave them both a hard, quelling glare. "Exactly what brings you banging on my door, Bobby? You'd better have a good reason because, if you recall, I don't work under you anymore."

"Much rather work under *him*?" Bobby shot back.

Julien lunged, but Dulcie managed to keep herself between his body and Bobby's. "Stop it right now, both of you!" she snapped, shaking with anger. "I'm not some damned damsel in distress. I can fight my own battles. If you came here to tell me something, Bobby, then do it. But don't make the mistake of thinking you can tell me how to live my life!''

"Get out," Bobby ordered Julien. "I want to talk to her alone."

"Only if the lady says it's okay," Julien answered. He glanced at her. "Dulcie?"

"Go on. I'll be fine. Bobby's more bluster than bite." When Julien hesitated, she nudged him with her shoulder. "It's all right."

Julien didn't bother putting on a shirt. He walked past Bobby and deliberately brushed against him—mostly with an elbow. A male thing, she realized. *Sniff around my woman and risk losing your sniffer.* There was something rather flattering about it all, underneath her exasperation.

After Julien had slammed the door behind with a bang, as a final punctuation point to his displeasure, Dulcie turned her attention to Bobby. "Let 'er rip."

She braced herself for a furious barrage, but instead, Bobby said quietly, "What the hell have you done, Dulcie?"

She knew how to handle his loud temper, but not his quiet hurt. Self-consciously, she smoothed back the loose strands of her hair. "I thought it was rather obvious."

He wouldn't meet her eyes. "Yeah . . . Reckon you don't need to paint me any pictures. But why? Why him?"

And not me. He didn't need to say the words; she could hear them in the tone of his voice. Stunned, she looked at him in silence as she slowly realized what lay at the root of his anger. Beneath the smiles and light banter, he still felt something more than friendship for her. Oh, God . . . How much she must have hurt him, never once realizing what she'd done.

She thought for a long moment, then said, "I don't have an answer. I'm not sure there ever is one, in situations like this. Fate. Karma. Biological programming. It just happened."

He moved away from her, away from the rumpled bed. Today he wore black jeans, a turquoise shirt patterned with yellow triangles, and the Wile E. Coyote tie she'd given him for his thirtieth birthday a few years ago. Affection and sadness warred against her lingering anger. "I'm sorry," she said at length. "I didn't know. You . . . hid it well."

"Not that I've been pining away for you, darlin', but there's something to seeing that cocky, low-life bastard succeed where I didn't—"

"He's not any of those things. Except maybe cocky," she amended. "His brother's death hit him hard."

"So what lines has he been feeding you? The good man gone wrong, the misunderstood victim? Let me tell you about the *real* Julien Langlois," Bobby said.

He stepped close to Dulcie, nose-to-nose. It was an uncomfortable, intimate position and reminded her that Bobby was a handsome man; hardly a stick in the mud. Yet she thought of him only in terms of friendship. He stirred nothing in her, except for an uneasy sadness at the moment.

A few seconds passed, then Bobby stepped back from her. "He's a man who has trouble holding down a regular job. He's done farm work and oil rigs. Construction, house painting, and building roads. He's a man with no focus, Dulcie. Little better than a drifter, hanging out in bars and clubs. His friends, who he blew off six months ago, said he lived fast and partied hard. His family kicked him out years ago, and he's already gone through one wife. If he'd kept closer tabs on that brother of his—"

"I know all this," Dulcie interrupted. The cataloging of Julien's shortcomings sounded worse coming from Bobby than it had from Julien. "But you've got it wrong."

"Do I?"

"At heart, he's a musician, and musicians play in bars and clubs. Music was the focus in his life. Stop judging him by a nine-to-five rulebook, and you'll find a man who worked hard to make a living, managed to enjoy life, and made a few poor choices. If he made any mistakes with his brother, I think he's paid enough for them."

"So what's this supposed to do?" Bobby gestured toward the bed, with its tangled sheets and blankets. "Tame the bad boy? Make him repent? When you said you'd try and make him see reason, I figured you were gonna talk, not sleep with him!"

"Reasoning with him was my original intent," she retorted. Even to her own ears, she sounded sharp and defensive.

"And just what changed your mind? Got bored?

Lonely? Or did he just have a repertoire of good lines you couldn't resist?''

Dulcie balled her hands into fists and struggled against the urge to slap Bobby's face. ''I can see you're not going to be reasonable about this. I don't care what you think. My relationship with Julien is private, and I don't owe you an explanation.''

After a silence, Bobby finally said, ''I don't want to see you hurt, is all.'' His own anger had gone and again he looked unhappy, confused.

She wished she could make him understand, but he was far too upset right now to use that sharp, savvy mind of his. ''I'm a big girl, Bobby. I know the consequences of playing with fire.''

More silence. Outside, she could hear the excited yapping of the puppy.

Bobby rubbed at his eyebrows. ''We haven't nailed Mitsumi yet. I'm beginning to think he slipped out of New Orleans and is kicking up his heels in Colombia or Paraguay by now. I won't see you again until Saturday, when I come to take Langlois off your hands. Unless he's planning on sticking around?''

As far as probing went, it was less than subtle. ''No. He's leaving.''

One winged, blond brow hiked up. ''I don't get this at all.'' When she refused to elaborate or explain, he added, ''Just so we're clear on the details, then. You need to be back at your pier on Lake Pontchartrain by nine o'clock Saturday evening. I'll meet you there. I can't hold Langlois here against his will any longer. Once he steps off this boat, he relinquishes further rights to police protection. If he ends up shot to death a few hours later, it won't be my fault." After a moment, he added angrily, "I did what I could."

The puppy clamped down on the wiggling thumb, his pink mouth and tongue making a valiant effort to engulf the plaything. The tiny teeth barely pricked Julien's skin as he gently shook his hand from side to side. The puppy growled, an effective growl even, if it weren't for the fact his whole tail end was sashaying back and forth.

"Tenacious fellow."

Julien sat on the back deck overlooking the placid inlet and hunting cabin, and glanced up as Les came to stand in front of him. The older man hitched his pants up over his solid belly.

"He sure is," Julien agreed.

"Got a name for him?"

"Nope."

"Needs one. Can't keep on calling him 'puppy' or 'mutt.' "

"I haven't given it much thought."

"Looks like you could call him Blackie."

"Not too original."

"How about Rex or Prince?"

The puppy flopped over, growling, and yelped when Julien poked at its fat, round belly. "Not dignified enough, him."

Les chuckled. "I think you're right about that."

Julien was quiet for a moment as the puppy

launched an all-out attack on his fist. If he concentrated on coming up with a name, it'd keep his mind off what was going on in the cabin between Dulcie and Halloran. Jealousy warred with calm, and right now jealousy had the upper hand. "I could call him after the place where I got him. Del, maybe."

"Now, that'll work. Del's a good name for a dog. Won't embarrass yourself hollering out 'Del' at six-thirty in the morning when he's taking a dump in your neighbor's yard."

Yard. A dog needed a yard. Something else he'd overlooked. "I live in an apartment. I'll have to find somewhere else to stay. Meant to anyway. Got too many bad memories, that place."

"Maybe Dulcie'll take a shine to the little guy yet," Les said quietly.

Julien looked up and met the older man's kind, wise eyes. "You're a decent cop. An' Lucy too. Want you to know that, before I go. I appreciate all you've done for me."

Les smiled. "Glad to hear it. A thankless job, law enforcement, but I could never do anything else. I've been on the force for twenty-five years. Seen a lot in that time. Lost good friends, and spent more than a few nights staring at a blank TV screen trying to understand why things are the way they are."

The puppy had abandoned Julien's thumb. He trundled off to explore the tackle box, ears flapping, tongue lolling, and nose wiggling, intrigued by the new scents. When Del attacked the metal box with his teeth, Julien smiled faintly. "Dumb, that dog." He reached over and scratched its squirming behind.

"I'm pleased to hear you talking about plans after you leave on Saturday."

Les had gently redirected the conversation back to where he wanted it. Julien didn't bother to dodge the implied question. "I don' know what I'm gonna do after I leave her. I need to get a few things straight in my head."

"I'd rest easier knowing you were safe. Is there somewhere you can go outside of New Orleans? Family or friends?"

Julien shrugged, the question making him edgy, moody. "Family won't have anything to do with me. Things weren't too good before my brother was killed. Got a lot worse after that. Lost track of most of my friends, an' I wouldn't want to put any of them in danger. I don' think the Dragon would care who he took out along with me."

"Halloran thinks Mitsumi's hightailed it out of the country. Things got a little too hot around here, so he's slithered off to safer climes."

Julien met Les' gaze, then looked out across the gray-green bayou again. He didn't believe that any more than Les did. Or Halloran. "Maybe."

"It's a big country, Julien. You could settle anywhere, start all over again. Put the past behind you. You've been good for Dulcie," Les said, changing the subject abruptly. "We were worried about her. She'd withdrawn, spending all her time on her dolls. Not healthy, locked up inside like that. Never getting out. She seems to have taken quite a shine to you.''

Julien smiled. ''You're a nosy man, Les James.''

''Asking questions and sticking our noses into bad situations is second nature to cops.'' Les smiled back and hitched up his pants again. Which then required him to readjust the gun stuck in the back of his waistband. ''You make a nice couple. Told Lucy so just a couple minutes ago. Maybe you can look Dulcie up again, after you've done that thinking.''

This was more than Julien was willing to discuss, nor did he have any answers. The only constant was how much he wanted to stay with Dulcie.

Three days ago, what he'd wanted and needed had been crystal clear. Then the Amazon had kissed him and exploded all his careful plans: scattered six months of single-minded plotting; and made him see, and put a name to, that cold, twisting thing inside him.

''Uh-oh.''

Les' mutter yanked Julien back from his musings, and he looked up to see Dulcie walking toward him. He pushed himself to his feet, taking the puppy up with him. The puppy wasn't happy with the change of venue and barked loudly. ''Hush, you,'' Julien said.

She didn't look pleased, but as she came closer, he saw her smile. A strained smile, but all the same relief rushed through his tensed muscles. He wasn't sure what he'd been afraid of, her and Halloran alone together, but now it didn't seem to matter.

"Bobby's waiting for you inside," Dulcie said, fixing a faintly sympathetic gaze on him.

"Can I skip this?"

"I don't think so."

"You okay?"

"I'm fine," she said and smiled again, as if to reassure him. *Dieu*, did he look that wrung out? "We had a little heart-to-heart, and we understand where each other's coming from. Let me take the mutt."

"Del," Julien said. "His name is Del. He's been tryin' to eat the tackle box." He bent and picked up a napkin. Inside was a cold, half-chewed hot dog. "Must be hungry."

Dulcie took the squirming animal from him. "Eating that junk can't be healthy. We'll have to find something else for it . . . for Del to eat. Hey, Del," she cooed, as the puppy gave her nose a tenuous, experimental lick. "Be good and don't piddle on me, okay? You better hurry up. Bobby's not in a good mood."

On a sudden impulse, Julien pressed a kiss against her forehead. He caught her smile, the look in her wide, gray-green eyes. No hiding from that look. He knew what it was. He recognized it, because somehow he was falling in love with her, too. "I won't be long."

Julien already knew how many steps it took to get him from the back of the houseboat to the cabin door, but he counted anyway, since it was the one sure way he knew to keep his control. He didn't look forward to facing Halloran. The man made his fingers twitch.

He walked into the cabin and Halloran looked up from where he leaned on the workbench. There was no smile on the man's face today, and his eyes wore a familiar hostile expression.

"You wanted to see me, Halloran?"

"Past time you and me talked about what went down at the Cracker on Monday. Sit down."

Julien shook his head. "I'll stand."

"Are you going to cooperate with me, or are we going to have to do this the hard way? I'm telling you, Langlois, it's been a bad week and I'm in one helluva lousy mood."

There was no point to hiding the truth anymore. Halloran knew why he'd gone to the Cracker, and Julien was too tired to lock horns with the man. For Dulcie's sake, he'd force the anger back down where it belonged and give the man his answers. Halloran was only trying to do his job.

"Ask your questions. I'll answer them."

Halloran hauled out a small tape recorder from his shirt pocket, then sent Julien a pointed look as he turned it on. "Mind if we tape the conversation this time? My fingers are getting cramps from re-writing your eyewitness report."

Julien eyed the recorder for a moment, then shrugged. "I don' mind."

"Good. Let's start at the beginning. What were you doing at the Cracker?"

"You already figured it out. I went Dragon-huntin'."

"So what went wrong?"

"Everythin'," Julien said quietly. "Startin' with me not pullin' the trigger." He couldn't be sure, in the low light of the cabin, but Halloran's shoulders seemed to relax.

"So Hernandez did."

"Yeah." He didn't want to remember how Hernandez had twitched and convulsed as he died, or the red, slippery mess over his shirt, the floor. The wall. Sometimes Hernandez and Marcel got mixed up in his mind, and his hands would shake. Already his palms felt damp. "Damn fool. Next thing I knew, I was in the middle of a war zone."

"And Chloe Mitsumi? What part did she play?"

"None. I used her to get to her brother, plain an' simple. I've been in the New Orleans night scene long enough to know her preference for good-lookin' men, her habit of hiring private male dancers for her and her friends. All I had to do was get her attention." Which hadn't been difficult, but that was his business, not Halloran's, and he wasn't particularly proud of how he'd used that sad, haunted woman.

"Why the Cracker?"

"Hernandez arranged that. He wanted things to go down on his own turf. I didn't care. All that mattered was for Mitsumi to show up so I could kill him."

"You were working with Hernandez then?"

Julien moved toward the bed. "If you can call it that. We both shared a grudge against Jacob Mitsumi."

"And how did it come together?"

The events were not even a week past, but to Julien it seemed far longer than that. He felt as if he'd aged a century in just a few days.

"Hernandez sent Mitsumi a message sayin' he'd set up a party for Chloe, and that they needed to talk a little business, about a few dealers who were skimmin'. It was a lie, but the Dragon came. Along with a couple of his bodyguards."

"What happened?"

"Nothin', at first. I did my routine for Chloe and her pals to relax the situation, make it all look real. The plan was for me to make my move after Chloe was gone. When she was out the door, Hernandez made for the bar under the pretense of gettin' drinks, except he was supposed to cover me from there."

Julien tugged the sheets and blankets into order, then glanced over his shoulder at Halloran's expressionless face. "Lost his nerve, I guess, or maybe he just wanted the first bullet in Mitsumi to be his. Before I could stop him, Hernandez started shootin'. Mitsumi killed him, all hell broke loose, and the cops showed up. That's where you came in."

"So you had Mitsumi in your sights and you didn't kill him."

"That's right."

"Why?"

"Maybe I was rethinkin' my chances on livin' to see the next sunrise." Julien straightened, then flashed an empty smile. "Maybe I'm just a coward."

"Do you think you would have pulled the trigger?"

Julien's smile faded, then he sat on the bed. Dulcie had turned the radio down, but the strains of music still sounded loud in the silence. Halloran didn't move.

"I asked you a question, Langlois. Do you think you would have pulled that trigger?"

In a flash, the memory returned. The split second he'd had Mitsumi. Eye-to-eye. Time had stopped, his heart thudding with thick, ponderous strokes. He hadn't heard Hernandez's dying screams, the retort of the guns, or even the sound of bullets slamming into the plaster wall behind him. He'd only seen those black eyes. Soulless, amused. Challenging.

A fraction of a second was all he'd had, before he dove behind the bar to avoid the rain of bullets. The sirens had sounded almost at once. Later, he'd learned the first squad car had been only a block away and the cops had heard the shooting. In less than five minutes, all his long months of planning, of waiting, were over.

All over, and he hadn't pulled the trigger. Julien blinked and met Halloran's steady gaze. "I don' know," he said.

Halloran let out his breath, turned off the tape recorder, and then adjusted the knot of his tie. Julien stared at it. A cartoon tie. A homicide detective who wore cartoon ties and loud clothes. And underneath, a purpose of steel; relentless as a Mack truck.

"I'd just as soon use you for gator bait," Halloran muttered. "But Dulcie seems to think a lot of you, and seein' her happy is important to me. So I hope you answer my next question carefully."

Halloran had guts, Julien grudgingly granted him that, but suddenly the idea of playing the martyr and handing Dulcie over to this other man was no longer an option. If it really ever had been. "This has got nothin' to do with Dulcie."

"Yeah, it does. What are your intentions toward her, Langlois?"

"I don' know that, either."

"Wrong answer."

"It's the only one I got. I feel for her what she feels for me, an' I can tell you I'd lay down an' die for Dulcie Quinn. But that's all the answers I've got right now."

Halloran cocked a brow. "So you're staying with her? You're not leaving?"

"I've got a few things to settle first. Can't tell you more than that. By Saturday, I figure I'll have a better idea about what I need to do."

Halloran's eyes narrowed. "Just remember what I said before. You go after Mitsumi yourself and I'm gonna lock you up and swallow the key. I'll bury you so deep you'll wish you'd died."

There were a lot of times these past six months when death hadn't seemed so bad, but Julien didn't feel that way anymore. "I hear you."

"Good." Halloran moved to the door. "It ain't

my place to say this, but I'm gonna anyway. If you decide to stay with her, I won't cause any trouble."

Julien was startled. He hadn't expected that, and he looked at Halloran with more respect. It couldn't have been easy to say those words. "Thanks."

"Well. There you have it," Halloran muttered as he opened the door. "See you on Saturday at Lake Pontchartrain."

"Yeah."

At the door Halloran paused, then turned. For once, Julien saw genuine compassion on the man's face. "Hope it all works out for you, Langlois. I'd like to see everything about that brother of yours laid to rest. If we can convict his killers, if we have a chance at it after all this time, I'll do everything I can to help."

Again, surprise. No one had seemed to care before. Or maybe they had, and he'd been too stupid-blind to see it. As Halloran walked out, Julien called after him, "It's too late for Marcel. But if by testifyin' I can keep other kids from dyin' like him, I won't give you any trouble about it."

There was a ghost of a smile on Halloran's wide mouth. "I never had any doubts on that account, Langlois. You were gonna testify against Mitsumi even if I had to drag you into the courtroom myself. Glad to hear there won't be any need for that. Catch you later. And you take care of Dulcie."

"Always," Julien said without thinking. But long after Halloran had left, he stood in the doorway and reflected on that single word and what it meant.

Dulcie was talking with Lucille and Adam Guidreau, although she found herself doing less talking than glancing toward the cabin, on edge and nervous. She still expected a body to crash out the door or a head slam through a window. But it was quiet, and she couldn't decide whether that was good or bad.

Finally, she couldn't stand to listen to one more word about Adam's new son. "Adam?"

"Yeah?" He sounded slightly aggrieved at her interruption.

"What does *trop tard* mean?"

Last night, Julien had whispered to her, *Ma douce amie, ma jolie fille . . . Trop tard. Trop tard.* She understood everything but the *trop tard*, and it bothered her—she wasn't so sure she wanted to know.

Adam gave her a blank look, then frowned. He was a transplanted Cajun from Ascension Parish, but not overly attuned to his cultural roots. She watched as he tried to remember.

"I think it means 'too late,' " he said. "Could be wrong. It's been a while since I been with folks who still speak *Cadien*."

Too late.

"Hey . . . Dulcie, you're white as a sheet." Lucille's voice seemed to come from far away. "What's wrong?"

"Nothing," Dulcie managed to get out, in a

voice that surprised her with its calmness. Both Lucille and Adam watched her, concern on their faces. "I'm as fine as I can be under the circumstances."

Lucille threw her a look, half a grimace of exasperation, half a moue of sympathy, then looped an arm through Adam's and dragged him off.

Left alone, Dulcie told herself she was being paranoid. *Too late*, Julien had said—but it could have applied to Marcel's death, or a dozen different things besides their growing relationship. Or so she hoped.

She wouldn't believe it was the *adios, sayonara*, so-long-it's-been-good-to-know-you sort of too late.

Or worse.

She rubbed her hands along her bare arms, chilled by the rising winds. She glanced at the sky. What had started out as a pretty day was showing signs of rain. New Orleans lived up to its dubious honor as the wettest city in the United States.

A movement in the door of the cabin caught her attention, then she saw a familiar blond head, blessedly intact. She hoped she would find Julien as undamaged.

"Guess that about wraps up things here," Bobby said to her. "I'll be working late at the station for the next couple of nights so if you need anything, anything at all, you give me a call. You can page me, too. I don't care what time of the night it is. Got that?"

"Yessir." She gave a mock salute.

"Behave," he grumbled. "I mean it. See you on Saturday."

As he began to walk past, Dulcie impulsively reached out and grasped his arm. She regretted the wary look in his eyes, but the small smile playing about the corners of his mouth took away a little of the guilty sting. "Hey. Thanks, buddy." She leaned over and kissed his cheek. "And see to it *you* behave yourself."

He shook his head, a rueful expression on his face, and gave a wave to Les and Lucille. The sound of growls and huffing caught his attention, and he sent a brief, perplexed look at the small fur ball intent on devouring fifty feet of rope. "Whose dog?"

"Julien's," Dulcie answered.

Bobby snorted, then reached down and wiggled a finger against the furry head. He surveyed the pile of rope again and grinned. "Either this is the most ambitious dog I ever met, or one of the dumbest."

"The general consensus is dumb," Dulcie admitted, smiling back. "Dumb and cute, my favorite kind of male animal."

The puppy startled at Bobby's loud laugh. "Damn. I almost feel sorry for Langlois. He'll regret he didn't jump ship when he had the chance. I'm gonna enjoy watching you make mincemeat outta that man."

"She can go ahead an' have a crack at it," came Julien's dry voice from behind her. Dulcie turned, and her smile widened as he slipped his hands casually, possessively, around her waist. "But the tougher they come, the harder they are to mince.''

Bobby shook his head again, a reluctant gleam of humor in his eyes. He called to Adam, ''Okay. Let's head out. We're done here.''

Dulcie stood at the deck rail, Julien behind her, and watched the unmarked car pull away, bouncing along the rutted dirt path that passed for a road. Lucille drifted back to Mike's cabin for a quick snooze, and Les and Del settled down in a deck chair on the pier for a little bit of fishing.

''I'm still starved,'' Dulcie murmured.

Julien grunted. ''Me, too. C'mon.''

He took her hand in his and led her back into the cabin, past the bed—which made her mouth go dry with another and apparently unquenchable hunger—to the kitchenette. The dishes in the drying rack were the only evidence that Les and Lucille had helped themselves to food while she and Julien had been making love on the other side of the thin wall.

She blushed at the thought of what they might have heard. She and Julien hadn't exactly been restrained. ''Do you need any help?'' she asked as Julien began poking around inside the cupboards.

''Nope. Sit down. You look tired.''

So did he, Dulcie thought, curling up on a chair and yawning as lethargy settled in. She watched him move through the kitchen. From within the bowels of her cupboards and compact refrigerator, he created a snack of toast with jelly, fresh fruit, cheese, and cold beer. She sighed as he twisted the top off each bottle and the sharp, yeasty smell filled the room.

"Let's eat in my cabin," she suggested.

He shrugged his consent, and while he grabbed the plates she took the two bottles of beer. She quickly cleared a place on her workbench to set down the plates and bottles, and Julien turned the music louder.

"Leave the doors open," he said. "I like smellin' rain on the wind."

As she walked across the room, she heard him say behind her, "You have talent, Dulcie. Real talent."

She turned. He drew a careful finger down a doll's long braid and miniature pearl cap. Lifting the male doll, he asked, "Who are they?"

Dulcie met his gaze. "Romeo and Juliet."

A shadow crossed his face as he looked away and put Romeo down. He took a deep gulp of beer, then closed his eyes and leaned back against the workbench. "I'm tired," he whispered. "So goddamn tired."

An overwhelming urge to take care of him rushed over her. She wanted to mother him, smother him in love and affection, until all the darkness was washed away.

Not that he would let her. Not that she could. Too many emotions still swirled around them: awkwardness and awareness and wariness. Desire and distrust. Other, deeper and darker fears that troubled her yet.

Shakespeare would have understood this persistent, prickling unease of hers. Blood, death, and vengeance. All the ingredients needed for a tragedy.

But Dulcie wanted a happy ending. Unicorns and maidens. Flowers, fairy godmothers, and happily-ever-after. It might be too much to ask for—but she wanted it anyway.

Chapter 18

～

DULCIE OPENED HER eyes to the sound of distant thunder. She stretched against the warm length of body beside her, then smiled at Julien's sleeping face on the pillow. She almost reached out to brush his hair away from his eyes, but didn't. He might wake, and he'd been so tired.

Yawning, she looked down at the alarm clock on the floor. It was seven in the evening and they'd been napping, resting their exhausted bodies and overstrung nerves, for the better part of the past two hours.

Godamighty, she was hungry again—but she didn't want to move from the warmth of Julien's body. Finally, after a loud stomach growl, she decided to get up.

His deep, even breathing stirred her hair, some of which was trapped under his shoulders. It took her a good five minutes to free her hair, but he never so much as shifted a muscle.

Dulcie slipped from the bed and pulled the blanket over his chest. Her T-shirt didn't provide much protection from the cooler temperatures the storm had brought with it, and she hugged herself. A peek out the window revealed a weak light in Mike's place and Les sitting on the pier. Still fishing. She smiled. Slouched in the deck chair beneath an old rain slicker, he looked content and happy despite the steady drizzle. This assignment was probably the closest thing he'd had to a vacation in ages.

She checked on the puppy and found him sound asleep in his box, with one of her socks, tied in knots, as a play toy. He clutched it between his big, clumsy paws. Silly thing. She was hopelessly fond of Del already.

Very quietly, she made her way into the kitchenette. A pot of coffee sat on the warmer and she poured herself a big, steaming cup, grateful for the warmth. There was a box of donuts on the counter, probably brought by Bobby, and she helped herself to a powdered sugar one. The hot coffee had a bite to it, and washed away the sugar melting on her tongue. Her body was languorous and sleepy, still glowing from the day's lovemaking and the simple pleasure of waking up in Julien's arms.

She was happy. She even felt like singing. A sudden image of Julie Andrews, twirling around on a mountaintop to a swell of music, popped into her mind, and she almost chuckled. If she broke into arias, they'd pack her up and dump her in the nearest loony bin.

The coffee and donut perked her up some, enough to poke her head outside and wave at Les. He waved back, then jerked his thumb to the little cabin behind him. She assumed he meant Lucille was inside, which left her and Julien alone on the houseboat.

She grinned. The situation suited her just fine.

With the cup of coffee, she wandered back into her cabin and found her skirt, which had been tossed over Julien's gym bag. She pulled it on, then went to stand outside.

The rain was slow and gentle, the wind carrying droplets even beneath the flat, overhanging roof. The rain felt soothing on her skin, pattering against her face and slowly dampening her T-shirt and skirt.

She nursed the cup of coffee along, one sip at a time, and had almost finished it when she heard Julien's low, deep voice behind her.

"Here's a sight to greet a man when he wakes up."

He leaned against the door frame, wearing the fleece cutoffs and no shirt. His dark hair tumbled loose around his shoulders and his eyes were heavy with sleep or desire. Or both.

Dulcie glanced down. The damp T-shirt and gauze skirt were clinging to her skin, to the contours of breast and hip and thigh. If he hadn't already explored every inch of her body, she might have felt embarrassment. Instead, she experienced a comfortable pleasure at how his gaze freely roamed those places his fingers and lips had already been.

"Coffee?" she asked. "I was just going for a refill."

"I'd like that. What are you doin' out in the rain?"

"Enjoying the view." She stepped against him and tipped her face for a kiss.

He obliged, then murmured, "Cold out here."

"Put some clothes on."

"I'll settle for coffee." He gave her rear a possessive swat as she slipped past him, then neatly avoided her jabbing elbow.

"Hey! No cheap feels, Langlois."

The sound of his low chuckle followed her into the kitchenette. She heard him moving around in the cabin, but by the time she walked out of the kitchenette with their coffee he'd already left. She stepped back out to the deck and found him sitting cross-legged at the front of the boat, the harmonica by his side.

"Music?"

"Rainy day, warm coffee, a soft woman an' a little music. All I need out of life, *chère*."

Dulcie smiled down at him. He seemed genuinely relaxed and at ease; so different from the tense, hard-eyed man who'd stalked onto her boat. She handed the coffee to him. "Why, Julien Langlois—I do believe that under all that muscle and machismo lurks a romantic sort of guy."

Julien took a long sip of coffee, eyeing her with amusement. Then he said, "Come here."

She dropped down in the space between his crossed legs and then rearranged her damp skirt.

"Who's this Mike? Another jilted boyfriend?"

Dulcie settled back comfortably against his

chest. "A friend of my father's. A cop." She grinned when Julien made a rude noise.

"Mike's retired from the force, and his wife Arlene teaches at an elementary school. He keeps this place for a little peace of mind, where he can hunt and fish. He flew out to Atlanta to be with his oldest daughter, who's going through a difficult divorce. I have a standing invitation to come here whenever I want. It's quiet and peaceful, and I always leave feeling better than when I came. It's pretty."

"It sure is."

"What was it like, where you grew up?"

"Flat. Cattle country. I learned to ride a horse almost before I learned to walk. We once had a herd upwards of three hundred head. Pasturing got tight, so we sold off most of our stock. That's when my old man went to work on the oil rigs. Hardly saw him, when I was growin' up. He'd show up for a few weeks then leave again, an' there'd be another baby in the house before long."

"Must have been hard for your mother."

She felt Julien's shrug. "My *mère*, she never seemed to mind much. Used to it. She wasn't any different from other women on the neighboring farms. But long ago I decided that wasn't my idea of how it ought to be between a man and a woman."

The soft, mellow notes of the harmonica sounded behind her. Not a song, just a random testing of notes. "Was your family supportive of your interest in music?"

The music stopped. "Nope. Not a real job, see. A real job put food on the table every night and kept all the kids clothed and housed."

"Where did you learn to play like that?"

"Taught myself, mostly. Watched other musicians, listened to the masters. When I was about thirteen, there was an old man, out in Abbeville, who wanted to teach me fiddle. But my folks wouldn't let me go. Said it was a waste of time."

"I'm sorry."

"I went my own way in the end. Don' regret it, except for the trouble it caused with my family. Lately I've been wonderin' if maybe they were right all along."

He began to play the harmonica. Dulcie closed her eyes, letting the notes and chords wash over her. Peaceful, beautiful music, with the rain a perfect accompaniment. As the final notes of a song faded away, Dulcie opened her eyes. "That was lovely."

"Thought I'd gone an' put you to sleep."

"Not at all. You're very good."

"I've missed playin'," Julien admitted, and she heard the regret in his voice.

"Did you play in a real band?" she asked, sensing that music was the key to his innermost door. "Cut any records?"

He smiled a little. "I played in a real band. We even made some money at it, now and again. We did good, playing nights and weekends for the workin'man's crowd." His smile widened. "Honest music, for the kind of people who throw beer bottles at you if you play anythin' too tame. Even cut a record once, just for the hell of it. I played because I liked it," he added after a moment. "Not because of the money, which is damn good because I never made much at it."

The harmonica made a sound that was, she thought, almost rude. Then Julien finished with a rapid, blowzy flourish that had Dulcie tapping her toes against the deck.

He put the harmonica aside. "Gave up playin' this past year, with Marcel havin' so much trouble. Took a local job workin' construction, so I could be home nights. After he died I couldn't listen to music, much less make it."

Glad he was talking about Marcel, she turned and gently poked his hard biceps. "Construction? Guess these muscles are home-grown, then."

"Mostly," he said with a small smile. "Started goin' to a gym about a year and half ago, with Marcel. Wanted to get him focused on somethin' besides runnin' with those loser friends of his. Didn't work. He stuck with it for a few months, then left. I kept at it. Workin' out was relaxin'. I could escape there for an hour a day, an' didn't have to think."

Silence followed, then eventually more harmonica music. Julien preferred the more melancholy love songs. He *was* a romantic, she realized. A man of strong emotions in everything, from anger and grief to music and lovemaking.

She felt a sting of tears, but didn't think it was only the music that caused it. It was knowing she'd somehow helped him step back from that edge, in spite of her blundering. It was feeling that, together, they were good for each other.

"Hey," she said softly. "Wanna go fool around?"

He pulled the harmonica from his mouth and quirked a brow at her. "Nothin' shy about you, is there?"

"Mmmm, no. Not really."

Laughing, he pulled her close and wrapped his arms tightly around her body. "I don' know. After foolin' around with you I end up feelin' like I been hit by a truck."

"Really?" Dulcie asked, pleased. "Nobody's ever said that to me before. I mean," she added, as her skin warmed with a blush, "that is a compliment . . . isn't it?"

"Damn straight it is. Give me time to get back my energy, then we can fool around all you'd like. Now, don' go makin' that face at me—I'm probably up to some neckin' here."

She was still disappointed. "It'll do, I guess."

"Hey," Julien protested with faint indignation. "I do all right at it."

"So shut up and show me."

He turned her in his arms, positioning her so that she straddled his hips. His skin was chilled, but his mouth was hot. Hot and smooth, tasting of chicory. He did kiss nicely. His lips fit her just right, and he knew how to tease. From closemouthed kisses and feathery brushes of skin, to nibbles and thrusting, full-tongued invasions that made her squirm, flushed and aroused.

Suddenly Dulcie wondered if, under the cover of her full skirt, they could take these kisses to the next level. She itched to touch him through that thin fleece, and explore all his soft and hard places.

From what she could feel pressing against her thigh, he appeared to be recovering some of his energy. Yet she was in no rush to end their kissing, whether it was gentle, a little rough, or aggressively sensual.

"I like kissing you," she whispered, as his tongue traced the lower line of her lip. Julien cupped her bottom to hold her body in place against him. When he tightened his grip, Dulcie gave a low sigh. "Yesiree, I like it very much."

His mouth moved toward her ear, then he nipped at her lobe. It tickled, and she laughed. She was fond of the warm place just below the base of his jawbone, and he liked it when she teased him there with her tongue. His low, throaty groan told her so.

"Don' stop," he murmured as she pulled back. "I think my energy levels are gettin' back to normal."

Dulcie moved her hips against him. "If they get any more normal, you're going to scare me off."

"You can handle it, *chère*." His eyes crinkled. "You thinkin' what I'm thinkin'?"

"Oh, probably. Is mind reading another one of your talents?"

"Nope—I just know you."

"You think so, huh?" She twined her arms

around his neck, and tipped her head to one side. "Okay, mister, since you know me so well, tell me what kind of car I drive."

He kissed her nose, then arched a dark brow. "This a test?"

Dulcie laughed. "Just answer the question, Langlois."

He leaned back against the cabin wall, his hands lightly stroking her bottom. "I say you drive one of those sporty jobs, like an Eagle Talon. Stick shift. An' I bet you take your corners on two wheels."

"Ha! You're wrong."

"About what?"

She gave him a gentle poke against the side of his chin. "About the car. I do take my corners a bit fast," she admitted.

"So what do you drive?"

"A Jeep."

He shrugged. "That was gonna be my other guess."

Dulcie snorted. "Right."

"Your turn."

"For what?"

"Guessin' what kind of vehicle I drive."

Dulcie couldn't resist adding another kiss to the side of his mouth. She slid her hands down through his hair, then rubbed his jaw. "You need a shave. All right. You said 'vehicle,' so I take it that means you don't drive a car."

"An' she's smart, too," he murmured.

Dulcie grinned. "You look like a motorcycle kind of guy."

"Maybe the stripper would ride a motorcycle," he conceded, squeezing her behind until she squeaked. "But that's not what I drive."

With a look of reproach, Dulcie rubbed at her posterior. "You sure as heck don't drive something conservative. I can't picture you in one of those little puddle jumpers, and no way do you drive a minivan."

"So what's your guess?"

"A truck. A big, bad Chevy or Ford. And I bet you crank the music loud as you tear down the road with the windows wide open."

"Got me," he sighed. "God, woman, you fit in my hands just right. I'd like to take you in the front of my pickup, drive out to nowhere, and make love to you until we can't walk."

His low, fierce words had an immediate effect on her libido. "I'm here now," Dulcie whispered.

"You sure are."

He slipped his hands beneath her skirt, careful not to disturb the discreet cover it provided. She leaned closer, raising her hips slightly, and kissed him long and deep as his fingers fumbled with his shorts. She giggled when he cursed.

"Knot," Julien muttered. "Tied my damn drawstring too tight."

"Was that your way of telling me to keep my hands to myself?"

"Doubt it," he answered with feeling, then exhaled in satisfaction. "Much better."

She couldn't see what his hands were doing. But the result of all this undercover activity was a sensation of giddiness, forbidden and wanton, even though they were hardly engaged in anything more than heavy petting. Perhaps it was the possibility of Les or Lucille finding them in a compromising position, or Del sniffing around at an inopportune moment, that made her feel as giddy as a girl with her first boyfriend.

His hands kept up their business until something hot and smooth fell against her thigh. "Oh, my," she said, intrigued. "Now we're getting somewhere."

Julien grunted, shifting against the hard surface of the wooden deck. "We're tryin'." He began slipping her panties down, but she was straddling his hips and the elastic balked. When she smiled at his look of exasperation, Julien said, "Gimme a break. I'm makin' this up as I go along here."

"You have such a beautiful smile," Dulcie said with a sigh. She probably sounded like a lovesick teenager, which was how he made her feel. "And I love having your body around me—like a big, warm blanket. Comfortable and cozy. I want you wrapped all around me."

Julien gave her a look of mock offense. "A blanket? As in wet blanket?"

He hiked one side of her hip up, then the other, and her panties began to make progress down toward her knees. Dulcie started laughing, then gasped as his fingers found her.

"You're the only thing wet around here, *chère* . . .

and I want to be inside you. Right now.''

She wanted it, too, with a painful urgency.

More wiggling, undulations, and shifting followed until finally, without disturbing the cover of her skirt, her panties were off and then quickly stashed in her skirt pocket. Julien hoisted her hips and Dulcie braced her hands against his shoulders as he brought her down on top of him. Face-to-face, body-to-body, her legs around him and his around her, they couldn't have gotten any closer unless they shared the same skin. The position brought him very deep within her, and she caught her breath a little at the extent of the penetration.

''You okay?'' His voice was tight, short.

''Oh, yes,'' she whispered. ''Now what do we do?''

''Beats me. Whatever works . . . *prés à prés*.'' He kissed her hard. ''Close to each other. I like this . . . *si bon*.''

She was getting used to the Cajun French that rolled so easily off his tongue when he was caught up in passion and honest, blood-zinging lust. And, oh, it *was* good. She rocked her hips back and forth, adjusting the depth of his penetration. He made a low sound in his throat, almost inhuman, and then his hands were in her hair, coiling and twining, and his mouth over hers, a full thrust of his tongue, circling her mouth wetly.

An unexpected visitor would have found only a couple lost in an embrace, the woman sitting on the man's lap, with the wide circle of a rose skirt fanning out behind them. Only the sweat sheening their faces—and their erratic breathing, punctuated by gasps and breathless murmuring—would have told observers there was more going on than hugs and kisses.

But there were no intruders, or any inconvenient yips and barking; only Dulcie's soft laughter and Julien's sudden, low curse.

"No good. I can't move."

Dulcie rested her forehead against Julien's, her breathing controlled. "What are you going to do? I think I'm stuck," she complained, trying not to laugh again.

"Hold on now," he said. "We need to stand up . . . Wait, don' do that. I want you right where you are."

"That won't work. Not if we stand up."

"Sure it'll work. It's just a matter of logistics."

"Logistics?"

"Not so loud! Yes, logistics. I know a few big words. Think of it as an experiment."

"Experiment?"

"Your ears not workin'? Yeah, Dulcie, an experiment. A science experiment. Biology."

Dulcie laughed when he waggled his eyebrows, then quickly stifled the sound behind the hand not grasping his shoulder.

"See, if I hold you against me like this—" Julien yanked her close and his eyes suddenly glazed over. She gave a soft, muffled moan. After a moment, he took a deep breath and said, "Damn . . . where was I?"

"Logistics," Dulcie whispered, kissing the side of his chin.

"Oh, yeah. If I hold you close an' you keep your legs around my waist, I can ease up along this wall to my feet . . . all the while bein' right where I want to be."

"I'm too heavy!"

"Doubt it. All that bench pressin' ought to pay off 'bout now." Julien heaved himself upward and Dulcie had to close her eyes and catch her breath, or she would've cried out at the deep, shooting pleasure. She wrapped her legs tightly around his waist and dug her fingers into the muscles of his shoulders as he inched up along the outside wall. He was breathing like a bellows, and his skin felt damp and slick beneath her fingers, from sweat or misting rain—or both—she couldn't say.

"There," he panted. His hands supported her, and he was leaning heavily against the wall.

"I like your . . . experiments."

"Me too," he whispered back. "But we got us a problem here."

They were nose-to-nose. She rubbed her own against his, smiling. "What?"

"I can't move."

He was laughing silently, his chest shaking, but he was still hard within her, driving her crazy with wanting him. "Julien," she muttered in a threatening tone, then glanced down to see his fleece cutoffs on the deck. "That's no problem. All you have to do is walk real fast to my cabin."

He gave a shout of laughter. "Hell, no! I'm not

moving away from the wall. It's my bare ass here, not yours.''

''Is this modesty I'm hearing, from a man who takes his clothes off in front of countless women?'' He actually flushed, and Dulcie felt a sudden rush of love, fierce and powerful. Something she'd never known with any man before Julien.

She tightened her legs around his waist until he groaned. ''C'mon, Julien . . . get us inside without letting me go. You can do it.'' She arched against him, making his eyes go unfocused again. ''I have faith in your biological abilities.''

''Damn,'' he swore, but it sounded more like an endearment than a curse. He scooted his bare feet along the deck, moving carefully.

''Go the other way,'' Dulcie gasped. ''The pier's on that side, and Les is out there fishing!''

Julien stopped short, then moved in the other direction. He kept his back against the wall and at one point stopped abruptly, his eyes squeezed shut. Through her own warm, liquid daze of pleasure, Dulcie watched his lips moving and realized, with surprise, that he was counting. By the time he reached twenty-five, he'd opened his eyes again. He licked his lips. ''How close are we?''

''Real close.''

''Good,'' he muttered.

A few torturous moments later Dulcie said, ''Wait. Let me make sure there's nobody on this side. Lean over a bit.'' He did as she asked, and Dulcie peered around the corner, feeling like a guilty kid.

The side deck was empty, and since both Mike's cabin and the pier were on the opposite side of the boat, she said, "Coast is clear. Hurry!"

Julien held her tightly against him, and his harsh, heavy breathing warmed the skin of her neck. She closed her teeth over his shoulder to keep from laughing or crying out. Finally they were through her cabin door, and Dulcie reached over his shoulder to lock it. A few more steps brought them to the bed, and he eased himself down, bringing her to lie across his chest.

"Success," she whispered.

"Yeah." Silence, then, "Here we are again. In bed."

"Guess we better do something about that."

"Guess so."

She kissed Julien. Her Julien; emerging from the layers of lies and deceptions, from the depths of grief and anger. A generous, loving man. Hers, *hers*. She hoped fiercely for a baby. No regrets, no doubts. No fear for the risk she might be taking. Only the love and the need.

The rest of the night passed in a gentle flow of hours, full of laughter and kisses. Julien made a pot of rice pudding in a communal effort with Les, Lucille, and even Del underfoot, occasionally giving Dulcie's hand a light rap when she "tested" the results a little too frequently. Later, they all played *bourré* in the rain and the dark, with only a kerosene lantern for light and using pecans in place of money. After the rain had let up and they'd dined on the results of Les's triumphant fishing efforts, they cranked up the volume on Dulcie's tape player and danced on the pier to honky-tonk music.

Once, watching Julien twirl Lucille around, Dulcie's worries managed to break through the barriers she'd put firmly in place.

Two days. Two days.

The words whispered within, insidious. But she quelled the rising panic, laughing loudly as Les swung her around vigorously in a Cajun two-step she just couldn't get right.

She wouldn't think of Saturday, of Julien leaving. Each moment, each second of the here and now was precious and vibrant. She would horde the memories so that one day, if she had nothing else, she could keep them close to her heart.

Much later, when only croaking frogs and buzzing insects broke the silence of night, Julien and Dulcie collapsed into the bed, fitting warmly together in each other's arms, and fell asleep.

To Dulcie, it seemed she'd just closed her eyes when a voice, hoarse and incoherent, broke across her deep slumber. She sat up, and it took a moment for the grogginess to clear before she realized it was Julien who'd awakened her.

He moved restlessly in his sleep, one arm raising and lowering, as if warding off something. He spoke again, this time more loudly. "Don' want to look . . . Put it back!"

She reached over to flick on the dim lamp, then shook his shoulder gently. His skin was cool and damp with sweat. "Julien?"

In an unconscious reflex, he knocked her hand aside. Hard. Her arm tingled from the force of the blow.

"Don' want to look!"

"Julien, wake up."

She gave his shoulder another careful shake, this time breaking through the dream's hold over him.

He shot up. In the low light he blinked his eyes, and she saw his confused gaze, the expression of panic on his face.

Slowly, his eyes focused and the fear faded. Then, turning away, he swung his legs over the side of the bed, rested his elbows on his knees, and buried his face in his hands.

Alarmed, Dulcie rested a hand on his back. "Are you all right?"

After a long silence, he whispered, "I can't forget . . . I can't."

She rubbed her hand along his back. There was no need to ask what he wanted to forget. "I have dreams like that sometimes, too."

"Don' want to remember him that way."

His voice broke, and in that moment all the laughter of the previous hours faded. The darkness in him would always be there; it could not be vanquished. No matter how much she loved him, no matter how much of her strength she gave to him, it wasn't enough to take away this pain or anger.

"It doesn't do much good to fight it," she murmured, still stroking the warm, bare skin of his back, hoping some part of her comfort reached him. She understood, remembering all too clearly a call she'd responded to years ago. She even remembered the date. July 12. A two-year-old had been shot in the head. Up close. She still had nightmares about that little girl.

He was shaking. "What's wrong with me?"

His whisper sounded so raw that Dulcie couldn't speak for a moment. Her throat was too tight, too dry. "Nothing, Julien. Nothing at all. You're only hurting. It will fade someday, but I'm afraid it's something you'll never be able to forget."

In silence, she continued to make wide, gentle circles along his back. Each breath he took was slow and careful.

"I should've gone after Marcel when he called."

Nothing she could say would take away his guilt, or that dagger edge of anger he'd turned inward upon himself. She could only hold him, and listen.

"I had him, Dulcie. I had the Dragon."

She slipped her arms around his chest and tightened them. He still hadn't raised his head from his hands.

"But I didn't pull the trigger."

At his quiet, almost inaudible admission, she went still. She'd always assumed his plans at the Cracker had gone wrong before he'd had a chance to kill Jacob Mitsumi. Never had she imagined that he'd let the chance slip him by.

"Why," Julien whispered. "Why didn't I?"

Dulcie couldn't answer. She couldn't even be sure what he was questioning: why he hadn't gone after Marcel, or why he hadn't killed the Red Dragon when he'd had the chance.

She understood the one, but was afraid to consider the other—because with each passing day, she grew more convinced that Julien hadn't given up on killing Jacob Mitsumi.

Chapter 19

~~

Friday

THE WEATHER BETRAYED her, that last day in Bayou Terre aux Boeufs. It should have rained, but the sun was bright and shining in a clear blue sky, with only the gentlest of breezes to dance with the Spanish moss and ripple the still, dark waters.

From where she stood by the cabin window, Dulcie watched Julien as he slept; a magnificent sprawl of bare skin, black hair, and baby-blue sheets. The rising sun cast its mellow light through the window, touching his face with an aureate glow. He looked like Apollo himself, god of the sun and beauty, lord of the lyre and music.

But he wasn't a god. Or immortal, either.

A chill crept over her as she stood in the sunlight's warmth. This might be their last full day together. When she returned the houseboat tomorrow to Lake Pontchartrain, he might leave and never come back. Either by his own choice, or because that choice would be taken from him.

She refused to think about that. Instead, she

watched the steady rise and fall of his chest, how he turned his face from the dawn's invading light. He had the most beautiful lashes. Long, thick, and curling.

He needed a shave. She liked to watch him shave. He was so endearing, standing in front of a mirror in his underwear with all that white, puffy soap over his face and his tongue moving around like a marble inside one cheek in accompaniment to the razor along the other.

The door to the kitchenette opened, followed by the sound of heavy footsteps. Les, no doubt. He started banging pans around, whistling a vaguely familiar tune. Before she could go tell him to be quiet, Julien stirred, shifting against the pillows, muscles bunching and stretching.

His eyes opened. "Mornin'," he said, looking to where she stood watching him. His voice was raspy with sleep.

Earlier, Dulcie had determined to say nothing about his nightmare. Not for a while, at least, and she'd also decided not to press him for details on what he would do tomorrow when they got back to New Orleans. It took only a small effort to find a smile for him. "Morning. Les is making breakfast."

"Thought maybe we had a whole percussion section movin' in."

"Les isn't married. He pretty much does what he wants when he wants. I doubt it even occurred to him that banging around early in the morning sends some people into homicidal frenzies."

Julien arched, with a massive, muscle-shaking stretch that rattled the bed. Dulcie was impressed. "That must've been about an eight on the Richter scale."

He eyed her. "What?"

"That little shake, rattle, and roll you just did there."

"Ah. Thought you meant what you an' me were doin' most of all day yesterday."

She felt her skin warm. "*Cher*, what you and I do is clear off any scale at all." At her low, husky words, a look of complete surprise crossed Julien's face. It was all she could do not to rush over and kiss him silly.

As she walked toward the bed, Dulcie saw his gaze drop, moving down her body and then up again. Julien didn't know it yet, but she was wearing a hot-pink bra and matching panties beneath her well-worn jeans and shirt. He'd focused his interest on her shirt, which pleased her. She'd chosen it because it was tight, but also because tiny hooks and eyes fastened it closed. At least twenty of them, from neckline to hem. A challenge he wasn't likely to pass by.

"Get your bones out of bed. And shave. I think I lost the top layer of my epidermis last night," she added, rubbing at the still-tender skin of her cheeks.

He eased himself free of the sheets. "You complainin'? Don' women pay big bucks for fancy skin treatments like that?"

She waited hopefully for the sheet to fall a bit to the right. When it didn't, she looked back into his amused face. "Abrasion by beard? It's an interesting thought. Sex with scruffy men results in healthy skin that can make you look ten years younger," she intoned in her best TV advertisement voice. "I'll go ring up the *National Enquirer* right now."

He stood then, absently rubbing the knuckles of one hand against his chest. "Sex cures headaches. PMS. Hangnails." As she stared, his cheeks grooved and his eyes crinkled. "Does wonders for increasin' tax deductions, too." The smile vanished, replaced by a mock scowl. "An' I'm not scruffy."

Dulcie poked his flat belly. "Yes, you are. But I like you scruffy, so don't give me that hangdog look." She planted a quick kiss on his cheek. "You in the shower first, or me?"

"Why not both?"

"Because I'm sore," Dulcie admitted. "You always this ready and willing, or has it just been a while?"

He blinked. She had clearly veered off safe territory once again. But instead of ignoring her question, as she expected, he only shrugged and said, "Been a while."

Intrigued, she watched as he began pulling clothes out of his gym bag. "Really? With the sort of lifestyle you were involved in, there must have been plenty of opportunity."

"There was. I wasn't interested."

"Why?"

"We're havin' another early mornin' grillin'?"

She sighed. "I'm sorry. I come on much too strong sometimes . . . I want to understand you, Julien, that's all. You have a great passion for life, a wealth of charm, and you're good-looking. Just wondering why you didn't take advantage of all that."

"I did. I married her, remember? Then divorced her."

Dulcie suddenly wondered how long 'a while' was. "Hasn't there been anyone special for you?"

He tossed the clothes on the bed, his expression somewhat grumpy, then sat down. "Bein' attractive to women doesn't mean I have to sleep with all of them. Some men might think with their cock, but I'm not one of them. Casual sex don' do much for me. My last girlfriend moved out after Marcel moved in, an' my brother needed me more than I needed a woman. I wasn't lookin' for a lover."

"When did Marcel move in with you?"

Julien leaned over, elbows on his knees, and returned her look. "He'd been with me, on an' off, since he was ten. Moved in three years ago because my folks couldn't control him. And no," he said, forestalling her question before she asked it. "I haven't gone that long without sex, an' no, I didn't go to bed with you because I was hard up."

She'd expected this subject to come up sooner or later, and found herself wishing she could've had a strong cup of coffee first. "I think we both know why you went to bed with me."

"Do we?"

Dulcie nodded, but she couldn't meet his gaze.

She looked away, to where the sleepy puppy was peering over the top of his box. He yawned, showing sharp teeth and a curling tongue.

"An' why did I make love to you, Dulcie?"

She couldn't quite read the emotion in his voice. "Because I wanted you to. Because I let you."

"An' you hadn't been yankin' my chain at all?"

She reached down and picked up Del. He licked her chin and whined. "You were playing a stupid game of truth or dare, and I decided to play back. I used sex to get through to you. I'm not proud of what I did, but . . . at the time, it seemed the only way to make you listen."

"Why? Why did it matter to you at all?"

Del was warm and wiggling, and his nose was wet. Dulcie looked back at Julien. "At first, you made me mad. After I found out about Marcel, I felt sorry for you." His face went still and his lashes—those damned lashes—dropped lower. "You had the power to put the Dragon in prison, and I wanted it. I wanted to help you. I wanted to sleep with you . . . Oh, hell, Julien, I don't know why I did what I did. Does it matter so much now?"

"Where do we go from here?"

Del started squirming in earnest, so she put him down. He immediately trundled off toward Julien, who absently reached down between his knees to pat the dog's head.

"That's up to you," Dulcie said.

Oblique attacks on major obstacles gave her a headache. She wanted to come right out and tell him she didn't want him to leave. She even considered getting down on her knees and begging him to stay. Except that it wouldn't work. Where Marcel was concerned, Julien had developed a formidable set of blinders.

Julien suddenly yelped, leaping upward from the bed and startling Dulcie from her morose thoughts. He cupped his hands in front of his penis and glared at the puppy. Aware he'd done wrong, Del whined and scratched a paw against the floor.

"That ain't no toy!"

Dulcie forced back her laughter. She arched a brow, lips still twitching, and said dryly, "Some things are better left not dangling around, big guy."

Julien turned, scowling, and grabbed his underwear. "Damn dog," he muttered. As she began to speak, he jabbed his finger at her. "You keep that pretty mouth of yours shut an' don' say it."

Dulcie pressed her lips closed, faintly resentful that he'd just put a kabosh on her clever quip about dogs chewing on bones. And, thanks to Del's playful near-miss, the serious mood of the previous moment had vanished. Dulcie didn't have the heart to drag it all out again.

Julien finished dressing in silence. After he tucked his shirt into his shorts, he said, "You go on an' take a shower first. Just leave enough warm water for me."

Dulcie nodded, playing with one of the hooks on her shirt. She looked up when she realized Julien stood before her. It was so comfortable, so easy, to tip her face upwards for his kiss. So comfortable and easy, to lean against him as he took her in his arms.

"God, I don' want to go," he muttered against her neck.

"Stay with me."

"I want to." The tone of his voice said it all, and Dulcie felt a familiar, seeping coldness. "But there's somethin' I need to do first."

"It doesn't have to do with Jacob Mitsumi, does it?" He didn't answer, but he didn't need to. She knew. "What we have together . . . isn't it enough, Julien?"

"I can't forget what happened. Don' you think I haven't tried? Dammit, give me a knife an' I'd cut it out of me if I could!" His voice was low, hoarse. After a moment the anger died away from his dark eyes, leaving them bleak. "But cut that outta me, an' I'm afraid there won't be much left."

She didn't want his bitter words to be true, but she'd realized already that a dark piece of him—the cold-eyed stripper, the angry man—would always be a part of her Julien, the Julien who made beautiful music, passionate love, and made her laugh and want to sing.

"Trust me, Dulcie." He kissed her. Again, then again. A gentle barrage of kisses, so that she couldn't answer. "I need to do this. For me. Not for you, not for Marcel. It's hard to let it go. I need time," he said, then put her away from him. "Go take a shower, then let's you an' me take that ol' rowboat on shore for a ride . . . in sight of Les and Lucy,'' he added. ''I'll even row.''

Julien watched Dulcie as she walked from the cabin toward the bathroom, pausing briefly to say good morning to Les. He gave her a cheery greeting in response, and then began whistling again. The same tune he'd been whistling for days: Marty Robbins' ''El Paso.'' Damn gloomy song.

At the brush of soft fur on his toes, Julien looked down. A smile tugged at his mouth. ''You sure are a sorry excuse for a dog. C'mon, let's take you outside for a walk.''

Housebreaking Del was progressing with the expected fits and starts. The puppy tried, sometimes forgot himself, and one stern word from Julien or Dulcie reduced him to contrite whines and much butt-wiggling.

Julien scooped the puppy up. ''Now, don' pee on me.''

Del launched a licking attack on Julien's elbow. Once Julien climbed over the rail to the pier, he put the puppy down and let it run its clumsy way toward Lucille, who was hanging out laundry on a clothesline strung between a tree trunk and Mike's cabin.

''Hey, little dude,'' Lucille said, bending to pat the puppy. ''And hey to you too, big dude. What's up?''

''Out for a walk. If I have to clean up one more puddle, I'm puttin' diapers on this mutt.''

''That's why God made babies and little creatures so cute. They can get away with the most disgusting behavior. Is Dulcie up?''

"Takin' a shower. Les is bangin' around in the kitchen makin' breakfast." Picking up a stick, he waggled it at the puppy, who attacked with growls of delight.

"So what's the plan for today?"

Julien glanced up. Lucille's uniform shirt, on the line beside Les', looked like it belonged on one of Dulcie's dolls. She was a small woman, but that was easy to overlook since she walked and talked bold as brass. "Thought I'd take out the rowboat for a while. I'll stay close, where you and Les can see me."

Lucille made a clucking sound as she pinned up a pair of socks. "It's not that we don't trust you. But we've got a job to do."

"I know."

"You really going back to New Orleans tomorrow?"

"I've got things to do."

"Hope it's not what I'm thinking. I'll be awfully disappointed in you, Julien Langlois, if you go do something stupid."

Del was discovering the doggy delights of digging. Julien looked up and met Lucille's shrewd black eyes. "I have to sort through this mess myself. Everything's happenin' so fast, I need time to get it all straight in my head."

Liar.

He looked her right in the eye, as he'd looked at Dulcie, and lied.

He didn't want to lie. He just didn't know how to get himself free of events he'd set in motion Monday night; didn't know how he could get himself free, and still finish what he'd started.

And he meant to finish Jacob Mitsumi.

"Now that's a relief to hear. Still, seems to me you could do some of that thinking right here."

"Suppose I could," he agreed. "But I don' want to. Got me a life, you know. Places to be, bills to pay."

"Halloran isn't happy about you going back."

"Nothin' about me makes Halloran happy."

Lucille grinned. "Not true. You're his prize witness. You'll be putting Jacob Mitsumi behind bars. He'd kiss your feet, if he had to."

"Now there's an ugly thought to start the day," Julien said, smiling back. The puppy wandered off, did his job against a rock, and came back, veering off course every few inches or so to investigate a wealth of new scents and interesting objects. Then he found a bug. A big, black beetle moving with ponderous, single-minded slowness across the grass.

Watching, Lucille said, "What are you going to do with the dog?"

"Take him home. Find a new place. Head out to the country, maybe. Dog needs a yard to run in."

"What about that nightlife of yours? Seems to me you were pretty much a part of the club scene."

"I'm not workin' strip clubs anymore."

"That's not what I meant. You liked to party,

judging from what friends and others said. We did quite a thorough background check on you.''

Julien nudged the escaping bug back toward Del. ''I'm givin' that up, too. Time to settle down. Do some growin' up. A man can't play his whole life long. Learned that the hard way.''

Lucille sighed. ''Tell that to a few guys I know. Sounds to me like you know what you've got to do. You must have a special angel looking out for you, because you were this close, baby,'' she said softly, pinching her fingers together. ''This close to losing it all.''

Julien looked up then, meeting her gaze, knowing she'd never see the truth he kept hidden. He could still slip on the lies, wear his smiles and charm like a mask. ''Maybe.''

''There's Dulcie. Were you heading for the shower?''

''Go on. I can wait to take mine.''

Lucille narrowed her eyes at a point just beyond Julien's shoulder. ''Aw, man . . . don't let him eat that bug.'' She made a face. ''Dumb dog.''

Julien looked around for Del, then reached behind him, flicked his finger, and sent the big black beetle into orbit. The puppy looked startled, then went off sniffing after his missing bit of sport. Julien watched as Lucille headed back to the pier, stopping to talk with Dulcie. And then Dulcie was walking toward him.

Every part of him went tight. Anticipation, colored with fear. Excitement, his heart banging away like a jackhammer. Even his palms were sweating.

Dieu, she had him acting like a kid with his first crush on a girl. Except she was no girl, he was no kid, and tomorrow night he had a date with a Dragon, not a beautiful woman who always smelled faintly of roses.

"Hey," she said. "Why are you sitting in the dirt?"

He shrugged. "Seemed as good a place as any. Keepin' Del from eatin' beetles."

Her lip curled. "Ugh . . . What's that he's got there?"

Julien craned his neck forwards, trying to see what the puppy was drubbing in the dirt. "Looks like a clothespin."

"Les said breakfast might be a while. Want to take the rowboat out now?"

"Sure." He whistled sharply between his teeth and Del looked up. "Here, Del. Time to go back in your box." He deposited the puppy in Dulcie's arms. "Bring him back, and I'll get the boat cleaned up. Make sure there's no spiders an' snakes." He smiled at her delicate shudder. "I know how much you hate snakes."

She blushed, and Julien felt a rush of warmth, sweetly sharp, in his blood. "You're beautiful, Dulcie," he murmured. "God . . . so beautiful. What'd I do to deserve you?"

She stood staring at him, the puppy held close against her breasts. Julien would have gladly traded places with the little mutt. Her hair was still damp, dark red and heavy-looking, tied in a simple pony-tail behind her. She had traded her jeans for shorts, revealing those long, lightly tanned legs of hers, and he itched to unfasten that shirt. One hook at a time.

He touched the side of her chin, then traced the shape of her mouth with a finger. "Lucy's right. There's surely some angel lookin' out for me," he said, then leaned forward and kissed her.

So this was what loving a woman felt like. A soft morning kiss. A pounding heart and a tingling in his groin. Feeling lucky, possessive. Scared as hell. He pulled back with reluctance. "Go bring Del in, an' I'll have the rowboat ready by the time you get back."

He watched her walk off, her hips swaying in that female way designed to drive men to distraction. Her ponytail was swinging from side to side like the clapper of a bell and when she disappeared onto the boat, he felt the most appalling sense of loss.

To chase it away, he kept himself busy with the old, weather-beaten rowboat. There were no snakes, but there were plenty of spiders, including some big enough to carry off Del. He wasn't too keen on spiders, and banged most of them out with the oar. The notion of squashing any of the big ones, with their swollen bellies, made him sick.

He shook his head at that. He'd thought himself capable of killing a man. Yet here he was, queasy over the idea of squashing a bug.

Some hero, him.

By the time Dulcie made her way back, carrying a tray, the boat was pretty well clear of spiders and webs. He dusted dirt off the narrow wooden seats as she came to stand beside him.

"You sure that thing is safe?"

"Looks okay to me. Checked for holes." Julien glanced up at her, then quickly away again. Those legs of hers were too close for comfort, and he had a strong urge to lick her, from her ankle to the curve of her thigh. He cleared his throat. "How deep is the water? Just in case."

"No more than five or six feet, I think. But Mike didn't like us swimming out there. Alligators."

"Who was 'us'?"

"Me and my brother, Sean. We used to come here with my folks when we were kids. I told you Mike was an old friend of my dad's."

Julien stood, then dragged the rowboat toward the water's edge. "Your old man still alive?"

"Yes. Both my parents are. They live in Baton Rouge, like Sean."

"You and your father close?" He was up to his calves in water. Cool, swirling dark water, his bare feet sinking into the soft, mucky bottom.

"Yes. I was the classic daddy's little girl." She hesitated, then said, "I miss my dad. And Mom and Sean, too."

Julien envied her easy, loving relationship with her father. He and his old man had never managed to get close. "So what made you stay in La Ville?"

"Always loved New Orleans. Even when I was a kid."

He looked back. She was standing ankle-deep in water, still holding the tray with napkin-covered plates. At his questioning look, Dulcie glanced down at the plates and shrugged. "Les said it's breakfast to go. Fried egg sandwiches."

"Damn."

She grinned, coming up beside him. "He said that if we row on over, the coffee he made just might walk off the plank and hop into the boat with us."

"No wonder he ain't married." Julien lifted the top of one napkin. Flattened toast filled with fried eggs, all looking a little too brown at the edges. "Guess we'll have to make do." He held out his hand. "Your barge awaits, *ma chèrie*."

The hand closing over his was warm, strong. Julien remembered the feel of her hands on his skin as she touched him, stroked him. How she'd held him last night, after the nightmare. He'd been able to fall back asleep as she played with the strands of his hair, massaged his tight muscles. He'd never been able to fall asleep before—he'd just lie in bed, sweating and nauseated, until morning came and he had to get out of bed and face the day.

Peace of mind. She'd given him something he thought he'd lost forever . . . and so much more.

The chance to take back his life, after he'd come damn close to messing it up for good.

Julien helped Dulcie settle in the rocking boat, then climbed in after her. Taking both oars in hand, he gave a half dozen long, sure pulls and the rowboat shot out toward the inlet.

"Hey, Captain, do you think we can keep this at sub-light speed?"

The morning sun was sharp and brilliant, and her hair glowed around her face. Julien eased back on the oars.

"I was hoping for a lazy sort of ride. You know, where I recline in your lap and you feed me—" She broke off, gingerly lifting one of the napkins. "Butter-saturated toast and burnt eggs. Guess you won't be peeling me any grapes today, O galley slave."

Her joking chased away his heavier mood, and he smiled. "Some imagination you got, *chère*."

"Mmmm, you have no idea. I'm entertaining thoughts of loincloths and studded leather belts. I think I've watched too many reruns of *Spartacus*."

"Sounds like you've watched a few floor shows at one of my clubs." He pulled at the oars again, steering them away from the houseboat toward the far end of the small inlet.

She frowned, and her gaze moved over his T-shirt, shorts, and bare feet. "How did you ever bring yourself to go through with that?"

"The dancin'?" Dulcie nodded, and after a moment Julien shrugged. "Didn't think about it much. I'd blank my mind, slap a big ol' lady-killer grin on my face, then count my way to the end of the show. One-two-three bump. Four-five-six grind. Seven-eight-nine flex."

She looked perplexed. "You *count*?"

Julien concentrated on turning the rowboat, one oar still in the water, the other slowly paddling. The boat began drifting around. "It kept my mind busy."

"You were counting yesterday."

He remembered yesterday. He smiled again. "Yeah. Helps me keep control. Been doin' a lot of countin' with you, Dulcie Quinn."

She shook her head, as if still puzzled by something. "But didn't you find it . . . well, demeaning to dance on a stage half-naked while a bunch of women watched?"

"Demeaning," he repeated. "No. For me, it was a means to an end. To some of the guys, like a few bodybuilders I knew, it's just a job. You spend all that time workin' to make somethin' special of your body, you may as well get paid for showin' it off. Some guys, they just like women. Others get to do the exhibitionist thing without gettin' thrown in jail."

He shrugged again, trying to gauge her reaction. But she only watched him, her expression now faintly curious. "For the women, it's a chance to do a little safe fantasizin'. Housewives forget about cryin' kids, dirty dishes, or that her man spends more time with his drinkin' buddies than with her. Workin' women forget about deadlines an' stupid bosses. Older widow women have a chance to do somethin' wild for the first time in their life. Some women just like to look at men. Nobody forces them to be there."

"Do you enjoy it?"

Julien hesitated. Now here was a trick question if there ever was one. He wouldn't admit that it sometimes felt a little like making love to a hundred women at once, and somehow everybody came away satisfied. "It was just a means to an end," he repeated. "An' bein' on a stage is nothin' new to me. Never was the shy sort."

She smiled, but it didn't quite reach her eyes. "I love it here. It's so wild, yet I feel safe and at peace."

Julien suspected her good humor was an act for his sake, and while he wondered at the abrupt change in subject, he played along. "Even at night?"

"Especially at night." She smiled again, and this time he was certain it was forced. "Why shouldn't I feel safe at night?"

His darker mood stole back, on cold, clawed feet. "Ah, you never heard of the *feu follet*."

"Of course I have. I've lived in New Orleans long enough to pick up on local folklore. Pixies or something, aren't they?"

"Nope. *Feu follet* are evil spirits who chase folk into the swamps and bayous. Make them lose their way."

He fell silent, remembering. Always remembering. What he wouldn't give to forget. "My *grand-père*, he used to tease us kids. Try an' scare us with stories. I never believed him. Didn't believe in evil spirits until I went to New Orleans. *Feu follet* moved to the big-city swamps, see, makin' people lose their way. That's where they went. Easy pickings, there."

A bird sang as it dipped and glided on outspread wings. Julien watched its graceful flight until it disappeared into the distance. Eyes still focused on the sky, he said, "I told Halloran I wouldn't give him any trouble about testifyin' against Mitsumi."

Dulcie put the tray down, her motions deliberate and slow, then leaned back against on the side of the boat. "I wasn't going to ask you this . . . but what the hell, right?"

He went still, waiting for the question he knew was coming, letting the rowboat drift aimlessly.

She looked down at her toes. "What are you going to do tomorrow night? You have something planned. You didn't agree to stick around for five days just for the heck of it. What are you up to, Julien?"

For a brief moment, he considered telling her the truth. Considered sharing his fears and explaining the tangle he'd made for himself, and what he meant to do about it.

But he said nothing.

Partly out of fear: fear she wouldn't understand, or that she'd tell Halloran and take away his last chance to make up for failing Marcel. He wanted to finish Mitsumi, and he wanted Dulcie. If he kept his mouth shut for a while longer yet, he just might get it all.

"I need to think," he said. This much was the truth. "I told you that."

"Think about what?"

Damn, she could slice through his lies to the heart of him. "About my future."

Again, it was the truth, if not the whole truth. If the plan taking shape in his mind went wrong, his future might not extend any further than tomorrow night, so it was best she didn't know. But a small part of him knew better than to believe she'd be so naive as to swallow his explanation.

"Where are you going?"

"Home."

Dulcie nodded, then shifted on the seat, closing her eyes. A long silence followed and she trailed a finger in the water as he rowed, directionless, in the lagoon.

No woman like her. Something squeezed him inside, hard. He took a deep breath and watched her lazing quietly in the sun.

Fear.

Fear compressed his lungs, coiled his gut. He might never hold her again, and the possibility was more than he could bear to consider. "Dulcie—"

"I think you should sleep somewhere else tonight," she said, interrupting him. She didn't open her eyes. "It'll be easier for me . . . I'm going to need some distance."

Whatever he'd planned on saying, wanted to explain, died away. Julien wished she'd open her eyes. He wanted to see if her eyes were as cool as her voice. "Okay," he replied, after a moment.

She was punishing him. It made him angry, but he knew he deserved it. He was acting like a first-class bastard, and it was better all around that they put a distance between them. He'd hurt her enough. She'd given him so much, and he kept on taking and taking . . . It was time he gave something in return, even if it was nothing more than a little of the peace of mind she'd given him.

"Maybe we should head back," Dulcie said. In the stronger sunlight, he could see a dusting of freckles beneath the peachy tan of her skin. He wanted to kiss her so bad he hurt. But he could already feel the distance, the coolness, and he wouldn't even try.

"Okay," Julien said again, and turned the boat around.

She continued to talk to him, to smile and sometimes touch him, but for the remainder of the day Julien was well aware of the wall Dulcie had erected between them. When he got too close, she turned away and tended the puppy, or pretended she was busy with something else. When he tried to get her alone—to talk, just to talk—she made excuses. After lunch, she promised to meet him in her cabin. After waiting nearly forty minutes, he realized she didn't intend to see him at all.

He'd been furious at first, that she could push him away, as if his feelings meant nothing. Then the guilt settled in, whispering doubts and recriminations: why should she concern herself with his feelings, when he hadn't shown consideration for hers?

By late afternoon, all the anger and the guilt had gone, replaced by a pervasive, smothering sadness. A deadening of his emotions that he was all too familiar with.

Silence came with the sadness. Silence in the houseboat and even the swamp itself, it seemed to Julien. Aware of the volatile undercurrent of emotion, Les and Lucille kept apart and they all moved about as if the others didn't exist.

Julien hated it. He could have stopped it. At any time, he could have stood up and said, *Mitsumi hasn't left New Orleans. I challenged him Monday night to meet me on Saturday at my club. To finish the game.*

Julien wouldn't change his plans. He had no intention of getting himself killed; he was sick and tired of lying; and he wouldn't let anybody else get hurt. But he still wanted revenge—what little there was left to take.

It wasn't too much to ask for, and a growing, uneasy part of him needed to know he wasn't capable of killing a man after all. Julien wanted to prove to himself that he was the decent, hardworking man he'd always thought he was, despite the many mistakes he'd made in his life. And he wanted to prove to himself—and to Dulcie—that he was no longer the man who'd first walked onto her boat.

He'd have his revenge, give Marcel his justice—but he wanted to be able to look Jacob Mitsumi in the eye and show him he was the better man. That he was the winner, no matter what.

By nightfall, after Les and Lucille had returned to the little hunting cabin, Julien was almost thankful for the descending darkness. Less cause to be wary, to keep hiding. He didn't have to sit and pretend to smile, pretend he didn't care. Or that he wasn't spending every second thinking about Dulcie, and how much it hurt to be outside the circle of her trust and love.

After all he'd been through, he didn't think it could be so hard, but it took all his strength to go into her cabin for a blanket and keep up a nonchalant appearance.

He shut the door behind him, and saw Dulcie sitting at the workbench, sewing. She looked up when he walked in.

He gave a brief, one-sided shrug of his shoulders. "Came for a blanket. For the sofa."

She nodded, then turned away from him.

Julien never realized how loud silence could be. He moved toward the bed, then stopped. "Dulcie—"

"Don't. Just take the blanket and go."

He looked away from the unyielding, ramrod-straight line of her back. The only blankets he saw were on the bed and he didn't want to take those. In the cupboard above would be her things. Her clothes. Her pretty underwear, all smelling of roses.

Julien turned and walked away, his arms empty, his jaw set in determination. He'd damn well freeze before asking her to unbend that stiff back of hers on his behalf.

"Julien!"

His hand was on the door when she called his name. He didn't turn. He should just walk out, but big fool that he was, all she had to do was say his name and he'd do whatever she asked. Almost.

"What?"

"I thought you wanted a blanket?"

"Forget it," he said, his voice as cold as hers.

"This isn't easy for me either, you know."

He turned then, staring. "You do a damn convincin' job of showin' me otherwise, *chère*." He took a few steps back into the cabin and folded his arms over his chest. "You know I want to be with you so bad I can hardly think straight. Be mad at me. Holler an' scream. Go ahead an' hit me, but don' play no more games with me. We're done with that."

"Are we?" She stood from the table and walked toward him.

"You an' me, yeah."

"Why is it I don't believe you?"

"Because you only believe what you want. Listen to me. I'm not lyin' to you when I say I have to get my head straight. An' I'm not lyin' when I say I'll come back to you, Dulcie; I—"

"Promise?" she snapped.

At his hesitation, her eyes narrowed. He made a brief, frustrated gesture with his hands. "I'll be back."

They stared at each other across the small room, as the boat rocked on the water. "You want to be with me so bad you can't think," she repeated his words, in a voice tight with an anger he could only guess at. "When it comes to sex—"

"Why do women always assume that if a man wants to be with her, it's only because of sex?" It was all he could do not to lunge across the room, grab her by the shoulders, and shake her until her teeth rattled.

"Isn't it?"

"No, dammit!" He was going to hit something. His fists clenched. He unclenched them, after counting to ten.

"You can honestly stand there and tell me you don't want to go to bed with me?"

"No, I can't, but you're not listenin' to what I'm sayin'. A man can want to be with a woman for no other reason than he likes the way she laughs. Or because he likes the way she makes him feel, to just be with her." He could still see the hostility in her eyes, the hurt and the anger. Then his temper faded; ebbed to a cold fear. "Don' shut me out, Dulcie. Please."

Her face paled, and she turned away again. "I can't do this," she whispered.

It was over, then. Numb, he backed toward the door.

"I can't . . . Julien, stay with me."

A second or two passed before he understood she'd asked him not to leave. She hadn't turned around, and he couldn't seem to move. Couldn't go to her, couldn't go away; just standing frozen like some poor dumb animal before the yawning jaws of a predator.

"Right now, I want to hit you over the head with a two-by-four. It's what you need, somebody to knock some sense into that thick skull of yours. But . . . what you need most of all is not to be alone anymore." She turned then. "And what I need right now is for you to hold me."

By the time her voice broke on the last word,

he'd already crossed the room. Her fingers hurt, digging into his flesh. But he didn't care.

"I don't want to be alone anymore, either. Don't leave me, Julien."

"Never," he whispered into the silken warmth of her hair, eyes closing as he held her tight. "Never."

He didn't know how much time passed as they stood wrapped in each other. He wasn't sure who took the first step toward the bed, but it didn't matter. They were together. That was all that mattered.

"Would you play the harmonica for me?"

Her request surprised him and he hesitated before answering. "I'd like that."

He'd like nothing better, except maybe to get naked with Dulcie Quinn and make love again. Both made him feel alive and happy, and he wondered if she understood that; if it was the reason she'd asked him to play for her.

After he found the instrument in his gym bag, Dulcie turned off the workbench light, plunging the cabin into a darkness relieved only by silvery moonlight.

They settled down on the bed again, back to back. Dulcie's head rested against his shoulder. Julien raised his knees, bracing his heels on the mattress, and took her weight against his back. Then he raised the harmonica to his mouth.

Julien didn't need the light to play. He found the music inside him. It had always been there, ever since childhood. People had misunderstood, trivialized, or celebrated his affinity for music, but it

had been there regardless—even when he had ignored it and refused its release. If he never made
a dime off the music, he would still play. Because
not to do so was not to live, not to be himself.

So he made music. For himself, for Dulcie. A
lullaby he'd played for his younger brothers and
sisters. Songs he knew by heart, others that came
from only his heart. The tones of a harmonica were
like the threads of life itself, high and low and
somewhere in between. Twining together, sliding
from one to another, it was color and sound and
life.

He stopped after a while, when he began to feel
light-headed. Dulcie shifted behind him, but didn't
move her head from his shoulder. He could feel the
bones of her spine against his.

"I have never heard anything so beautiful," she
whispered.

Julien tipped his head back, closer to her face.
"I'll have to play fiddle for you next time."

"You like the fiddle best?"

"*Mais* yeah, Dulcie," he said softly, putting the
harmonica aside. "Always did."

"Why?"

He thought a moment, trying to find the words
to make her understand this thing he could only
feel, not explain. "It talks to me," he answered
quietly. "Has a voice like nothin' else I've ever
heard. It weeps an' laughs. A fiddle can be angry,
sexy. Playful. It can fly."

He turned around, wanting her in his arms again,
her body close against his own. "It feels good in

my hands. Warm wood, that shines. It has a nice shape. Round on top, narrow in the middle, then round again,'' he whispered, sliding his hands down her sides, from round breasts to waist to curving hips. ''All curves, smooth and warm. When I touch it, one string at a time, it sings for me, an' then I'm flyin' with the music too.''

Dulcie kissed him, her mouth warm and soft, and he kissed her back.

When he made love to her that night, he let his body speak to her. Lips, fingers, and hands, his whole body, spoke of his love. Slowly and gently, not rushed or frantic. He wasn't saying good-bye. He was giving her a promise he couldn't yet say out loud.

Chapter 20

Saturday

JACOB MITSUMI MET the solid wall of his body-guard's chest as he exited the warehouse's back door. Greg had the car waiting, but it didn't take a genius to read the look on the man's broad, homely face.

"Give me the keys," Mitsumi ordered, seeing that Greg was going to be difficult about this.

"Sure you won't change your mind, sir? You should let me come along. I don't think—"

"I don't pay you to think," Mitsumi snapped, holding his hand out. "I pay you to obey me. If this becomes too difficult for you to manage, I can arrange for the termination of your employment."

The man paled, then handed over the keys to the gleaming black Lincoln Continental. "No, Mr. Mitsumi. It's not too difficult."

"I don't want to be followed, either. This is my problem. Understand that, Greg. I will be angry if you or any of the others take it upon yourselves to interfere with my plans for Langlois."

"We won't, Mr. Mitsumi."

Greg's face had gone gray and damp, and Mitsumi was satisfied at last. "Good. Now make certain my sister doesn't go out tonight. I don't care what you have to do. Tie her to the bed if you must, but she is not to go to any bar or club tonight."

Greg nodded. "Yes, sir. I'll see to it myself that Chloe stays out of trouble."

"Make sure she understands how displeased I will be if she disobeys me." He took the .357 automatic out of the pocket of his black leather jacket and slammed the clip into place. It made a cold, satisfying click.

"You sure Langlois will be at the club?"

"More than sure. I know this man, Greg. I know how he thinks. He hates, and hate is something I understand. I feed upon it."

Mitsumi opened the door, then slid into the plush leather interior. He turned the ignition key, and the engine purred like a beast well fed and content. "The Dragon is hungry tonight," he said in a soft voice. He smiled at the uncomprehending face of his bodyguard. After a moment, he began to laugh. "Say '*Bon appétit*,' Greg."

Greg shuffled, and then stepped back from the car. "*Bon appétit*, sir."

Mitsumi slammed the door, roared the engine, and shot out into the street in a squeal of tires.

The Dragon was not only hungry, he was invincible. Tonight, the bastard who had caused him such inconvenience, and who had used his sister, would die.

Nobody tarnished his treasures, just as nobody challenged the Dragon's power. And if, by some chance, he did not walk away from this night's duel, then he would take Langlois down with him.

Either way, he'd win, his honor pure and undimmed.

Chapter 21

~

IT WAS ALMOST seven o'clock in the evening by the time Dulcie steered her houseboat back into Lake Pontchartrain, and nearly another hour before she approached the familiar line of piers she'd called home for the past two years.

It was a bleak and empty place; never more so than now. Being with Julien this past week had forced her to admit she hadn't been making a new life for herself here. She'd just been hiding from life.

She only hoped this little bit of self-knowledge hadn't come too late.

Dulcie turned to Julien, standing beside her with his hands in the pockets of his jeans. "Well, here we are," she said. "And there's Bobby."

"You said he'd be late."

"He would be punctual the one time I wanted him to be late."

Julien had stayed at her side throughout the day. She was grateful, although she'd sometimes sensed a distance in him, as if his mind was far away. She hadn't pretended to be happy about his determi-

305

nation to leave, or pretended not to suspect he was up to something. But still, now that the moment had finally arrived, her hands had begun to tremble.

"You sure you don' mind watchin' Del for me?" Julien asked, as Bobby, Adam, and the familiar, bulky figures of the Bruiser Boys made their way toward the boat. Les and Lucille were busy securing the houseboat to its pier.

She'd folded, in the end, on the matter of the puppy. "No, I don't mind."

"I'll call you. Later tonight."

Dulcie nodded. Bobby's cowboy boots were thudding loudly, coming closer. She wanted to say something more, then decided against it. No goodbyes. He'd said he would come back to her. She believed him, and right now that belief was the only thing keeping her strong and calm.

"Halloran," Julien said evenly, as Bobby swung himself up onto the deck.

"Langlois." Bobby gave Dulcie a brief, searching look. Then he focused his attention on his witness. "You ready to go?"

"Ready as I'll ever be, *mon ami*."

"Don't call me that," Bobby snapped. Adam, standing behind, looked acutely uncomfortable. "I ain't your friend. Grab your things and let's get the hell out of here. I'll take you wherever you want to go. Les, Lucille—you two go with Adam. Is there anything you need, Dulcie?"

Everything and nothing. There was no answer for his question and they both knew it. She glanced at Julien. "No."

"Then say your good-byes. I don't want to stick around here too long. Just remember, I'll be working late for the next couple nights. You need me, you call."

Lucille gave her a quick hug as she left, and Les murmured something about bucking up.

It was time. Bobby, bless him, wasn't going to allow any lengthy, difficult partings. She turned to Julien. "Take care of yourself."

Julien picked up his gym bag, slung it over the shoulder of his black drover coat, then leaned forward and kissed her firmly on the lips. "An' you take care of y'self, *chère*. I'll see you later."

He walked away from her, but at the rail he stopped and looked back over his shoulder. His gaze held hers for what seemed an eternity before he said quietly, "I promise."

Dulcie didn't move, or look away from Julien's dark, broad-shouldered figure as he walked down the pier toward the parked cars.

I promise.

After fighting them back all day, tears finally sprang to her eyes. They welled, distorting her vision, but didn't spill over onto her cheeks. She watched the others pile into the cars and listened to doors slamming, engines revving, and tires crunching on the loose gravel as the cars pulled away.

The last of the headlights disappeared. Alone in the darkness, she stood for a long time by the rail. It was as if her body had simply shut down, to allow her to adjust to what was happening.

A small yip finally broke through her numbness. The puppy needed her. Food. Attention. Something.

She turned, scrubbed the palms of her hands across her eyes, and walked back into the cabin.

It was so empty and bleak. Dulcie sank to the floor, holding the puppy close against her chest, and cried into his fur as he licked her face and whined.

"I wish you'd think this through," Halloran said, without taking his eyes from the busy traffic of Chef Menteur highway, which followed Lake Pontchartrain back toward the French Quarter of New Orleans.

Julien, sitting in the backseat of the unmarked squad car, focused his own attention on the headlights whizzing past. "I did."

More silence followed, broken only by the low hum of the engine, an occasional crackle of static, or the deep, scratchy voice of the radio dispatcher. He wasn't in any mood for talking, but apparently Halloran was.

"You want us to send a squad by your place?"

"You mean you don' already have a cop over there? To make sure I don' go Dragon-huntin' no more?"

Halloran sent a chilly glance over his shoulder. "You got a smart mouth, Langlois."

Julien didn't bother to answer. Halloran probably did have someone at his apartment. He didn't doubt they'd watch his every move.

The rest of the ride progressed in silence as Halloran weaved his Ford Crown Victoria back and forth between lanes, his speed never dropping below sixty-five. The man was in a hurry, which suited Julien fine, as he was in a hurry himself.

Halloran parked the car before Julien's lower Quarter apartment, an elegant red brick two-story with tall, shuttered windows and decorative grillwork along the balconies and front entryway. Two huge clay urns, overflowing with colorful azaleas, framed the white door. Since Halloran had never asked for directions, Julien knew his earlier suspicions were on target. Halloran had been here sometime this past week, and one of his officers would be sitting close by right now, watching.

As Julien swung the car door open, Halloran turned and rested his arm along the back of the seat. "One more time, Langlois. Think about it. You can't testify with a bullet hole in your head."

"For the last time," Julien replied, one boot out of the car already, "I thought about it. I'll testify. There won't be any holes in my head. But thanks, *mon ami*," he added, and watched Halloran grimace.

"No tricks, Langlois."

Julien slammed the car door shut and smiled through the open window at Halloran's scowling face. He made a big 'X' across his chest. "No tricks."

"Damn fool," Halloran muttered, as the automatic window whined shut. With a squeal of tires, he drove off. Julien watched the red taillights of the car until they disappeared around a corner. He glanced along the street at the cars parked along either side. Then he fished his keys from his pocket, unlocked the door, and trudged up the stairs to his apartment on the second floor.

Only a week since he'd last been home, but it felt longer than that. He ran his finger along the side of the door, checking for any signs of a forced entry before he slid the key into the lock, opened the door and walked in. He stood for a moment in the entrance before he turned on the lights.

Nothing had changed. He saw a large living room, comfortable and well lived in. Overstuffed chairs, pillows, and a big futon dominated the room, along with bookshelves, a wealth of expensive stereo equipment, magazines, and a few clothes he'd left around. The carnations and roses in the vase on the table were dead, and their darkened, dry petals lay scattered over the hardwood floor and table.

He shut the door and locked it, dropping the gym bag where he stood. He stripped off the drover coat, then tossed it over the nearest chair.

After a quick check through the rest of the apartment—kitchen, bathroom, studio, his bedroom, and Marcel's old bedroom—he walked into the kitchen, grabbed a cold Dixie beer from the refrigerator, and leaned back against the counter.

It didn't look like any of Mitsumi's goons had even tried to get in, but maybe they'd figured it was too hot and stayed away. He hoped his truck was similarly untampered with.

He took another long drink, then walked to the kitchen window overlooking a side street. A few parked cars. People walking the sidewalks. A group of teenagers gathered on a corner by a muffuletta shop. Same old, same old. Nothing ever changed. Life just went on. He let the curtain fall from his fingers.

Stopping by the hall desk, he saw there were sixteen messages on the answering machine and a pile of old bills he should've already paid, along with another letter from his sister Grace. He hadn't opened it, just like he hadn't opened any of the others she'd sent these past six months. On a sudden impulse, he put the beer bottle down on the desk and slit the envelope wide. Inside was a brief, two-page letter. Leave it to Gracie. Short and to the point, that girl.

The first line almost made him put it aside.

What the hell's the matter with you?

A few terse paragraphs followed, updating him on the family. His *mère* was doing better since Marcel's death, but the old man had been having trouble with chest pains. Julien frowned, reading on.

The baby will be born in early March, and I want you home to see your new nephew.

Dieu, Gracie was pregnant again. He found himself hoping it was a girl this time around. Before he got to the end of the letter, he put it down and drained the beer left in the bottle. He got another one from the kitchen, then made his way to Marcel's room.

It had never looked this neat when Marcel was alive. He'd been a slob, like most kids his age. Clothes on the floor, shoes and socks, pizza boxes, cigarettes, CDs, haphazard piles of homework. Basketballs, several skateboards. An occasional girlie magazine. The usual rebellious teenager things.

Now, the bed was neatly made and all the clothes and shoes were packed away in boxes, along with all the books, sports equipment, and his brother's other belongings. Posters of rock groups and busty models still adorned the walls, but the fish aquarium, Marcel's pride and joy, was drained.

Julien eased himself down on the bed, his gaze resting on the one thing he hadn't boxed up, because he hadn't the heart to do so. Marcel's old stuffed dog, Blue.

Marcel and Blue had been constant companions for the first five years of the kid's life. Blue was actually dark brown, but mostly denuded of fur, and his plastic eyes were scratched and gouged. Multicolored stitches showed where Julien, or one of his brothers or sisters, had repaired the toy many times over the years.

Julien closed his eyes. This was real. Marcel wasn't coming back. Ever. There was nothing left of the little brother he'd raised except bittersweet memories, guilt, and this old stuffed dog. *Dieu*, how easy it would be to slip back into the blind violence.

He opened his eyes again and murmured, ''What you say, Blue? Lonely in here by y'self?'' He touched the much-hugged, kissed, and abused fur. "Me, too."

Julien settled the toy back against the pillow, then heaved himself up off the bed. In the doorway, he turned and looked one last time at the empty, quiet room. He didn't wipe away the tear rolling down his cheek. "*Adieu*."

Dulcie sat eating ice cream in the kitchenette, watching the sky darken. Del whined and batted her with his paw. Knowing what he was begging for, she dipped her finger into the cold, creamy vanilla and then let him lick it off her finger with his raspy, eager tongue.

"Mmmm, good stuff," she said softly. Del's rear end waggled, then he whuffed. "No more. If you eat too much you'll get a bellyache and throw up all over my floor. Besides, I've had enough too."

She put the lid on the carton, then shoved it back into the small freezer compartment. She was plugged into the shore generators once again, and everything hummed. A man's loud laughter carried across the water to her, along with a woman's querulous tones. Somebody was having a row, sounded like.

God, she worried about Julien. What she wouldn't give right now to have a row, too, then kiss and make up.

He hadn't called yet so she never went far from the phone. She paced the deck. Paced the cabin. Binged on ice cream. Cried a lot.

She couldn't keep on like this, or she'd go crazy. Dulcie turned back to the cabin, toward the workbench. The dolls had kept her sane before; maybe they'd keep her that way for a few more hours.

Del protested when she dumped him in his box, whining and barking before he finally settled down and slept. She went to work on her Southern belle. This was a larger doll, standing over two feet tall when completed. She fixed the eyes in place, then carefully glued each eyelash in place. The minutes marched by as she forced herself to concentrate on creating a lifelike portrait from porcelain, paint and glass.

When the eyes were in place and the glue was drying, Dulcie turned to the wig box for hair. She decided this one looked like a brunette. She wanted her belle to have dark hair, dark as Julien's.

It wasn't until she reached for the wig box itself that she saw something was wrong.

The box had been moved—and she hadn't done it.

The Colt!

She stepped back, bumped against the workbench, and whispered, "Oh, God."

Her hands wouldn't move; refused to lift the lid of the box and verify what she suspected. She stared at it, feeling the palms of her hands go damp. Then, with a low curse, she grabbed the box, knocked off its lid, and stared inside.

The gun was gone.

*   *   *

Julien finished dressing. Today, he'd be himself for the first time in six months. No fancy clothes, no silk or punky leather. Just an old, worn pair of jeans, a plain T-shirt that had once been navy but was now a faded, dark pewter color, and his favorite boots.

His bedroom, like the rest of his place, was orderly but lived in. He could find what he needed in the piles of folded clothes. He'd bought the waterbed after he'd married Alana, and often considered getting rid of the thing. But he'd never gotten around to it.

Not much warmth to the room, nothing that made him think of it as home. Wholly a man's room. A man who lived alone. No frilly things. No woman's shoes. No makeup in his bathroom. Right now, he wouldn't have minded seeing a plum-purple bra dangling over his headboard, or picking out three-feet-long auburn hairs from his sink.

Soon as he could, he was dumping the place. All of it. The furniture, even Marcel's things. He'd take a few clothes and mementos, but nothing else.

Except, of course, the fiddle.

It lay on his bedspread beside the gym bag. He unsnapped its battered case, then unwrapped the instrument with reverent hands. It was an Ortego, a work of art in contrasting wood grains and colors. Black gum and cherry wood, with fingerboards and pegs of African ebony, and a genuine Brazilian bow hanked with horse's hair. It had cost him a small fortune.

Julien sat down on the bed, his fingers tracing

the gleaming, polished wood and taut silver strings. He brushed away a speck of lint, then raised the fiddle and settled it beneath his chin.

Like riding a bike. You just never forgot how to make the music.

He closed his eyes, then drew the bow across the strings, listening to the pitch. Not bad for having been ignored in the back of a closet for over a year. He tuned it automatically, tightening the pegs until he was satisfied.

Julien moved his fingers over the frets, easing the bow along the strings until he coaxed a sweet, melancholy march of notes from the instrument. Then he made it sing: first a flirtatious love song, followed by a frenetic piece that would've had an audience stomping their feet, clapping their hands, and howling into their beer.

The music died away, but left behind a small flicker of warmth inside him. It had been too long since he'd held this little beauty; too long since he'd set the music free. He wrapped the fiddle back in its protective covering and repacked it in the case, then unzipped the gym bag. Inside were his clothes, wallet, keys, and Dulcie's gun.

He'd almost left the gun behind, but changed his mind at the last moment. If something went wrong with his plans, he was going to need it.

He lifted the heavy gun. She'd taken good care of it; kept it well-oiled and polished, in perfect working order. No doubt this gun could take care of Jacob Mitsumi, once and for all.

Julien held the gun, running a finger over its cool

metal smoothness. He stared at its lethal beauty, and the memory hammered at him again.

Fury flared anew, red-black and hot. The hatred he hoped he'd conquered rushed forward like a hungry beast. Julien watched the gun waver as his hand began to shake. He wasn't as in control as he'd thought. He could pull the trigger yet. If he came face-to-face with Jacob Mitsumi, he wasn't so sure he could do what was right.

The realization scared the hell out of him.

He was a hair trigger away from letting Mitsumi drag him down into the black pit of hissing, soulless snakes.

Julien closed his eyes. He could never forget Marcel, but he remembered Dulcie's face, her sassy mouth. The scent of her hair and feel of her skin; the pleasures exploding between them when they made love. He remembered the flights of music, and beat the fury back where it belonged.

He was a lot of things—not all of them something he could be proud of—but he wasn't a killer. Never, never that.

Opening his eyes again, Julien returned the gun to the bag, along with the fiddle and Blue. The last two to give him strength to see this thing through to the end, the other to make sure no one else would be hurt because of it.

A quick glance at the bedroom alarm clock told him it was time to go. He had a show in fifty minutes. He stood, then pulled on a worn black leather bomber jacket. Shouldering the gym bag, he locked the door behind him and walked out the front door of the building toward his truck, which was parked down the street.

Some cop in an unmarked car was watching, he was sure of it. Didn't matter. Nothing they could do to stop him now.

Only once, in the last two years, had Dulcie visted the 8th District police station where she'd worked. It had been an awkward experience, leaving her depressed for days afterwards. Because of it, she had sworn never to step foot in a police station again.

But now she didn't have a choice.

She brought her Jeep to a jolting halt at the curb outside the main doors, yanked the keys from the ignition and ran. The 8th District station, an elegant old building located in the heart of the Quarter, was open twenty-four hours a day to assist the city's constant flood of tourists—and she was relieved to see the desk sergeant on duty was someone she knew.

She shoved past a hefty, middle-aged tourist couple and said, "Jim, I need to talk to Bobby Halloran. This is an emergency."

"I'll phone him for you," the sergeant said, over the woman's huffy grumbling, and immediately did so.

A few moments later, she saw Bobby coming toward her. "What's wrong?" he demanded.

"Not here," Dulcie said, glancing at the staring tourists.

"Fine. In my office. Come on."

Bobby shared his office—a handsome old-fashioned room with high ceilings and decorative, white-painted moldings on its light blue walls—with several other detectives. Tonight it was quiet, with only one other person plink-plinking away on an old IBM typewriter. No buzz of conversation, no phones ringing, no arguing voices.

Still, it was comfortably familiar, even the ugly office chair that Bobby rolled out for her, its casters clattering like castanets. It even smelled familiar: musty office air tinged with the scents of sweat, stale coffee, and old paper.

"What's wrong?" Bobby asked again.

"Julien took my gun."

Bobby sat down on his chair, which creaked in protest. "You didn't tell me you had a gun on your boat!"

"You didn't ask," she retorted.

"Oh, for—" He broke off, then ran a hand through his hair. "You're sure he took it?"

"The gun was there last week. I didn't move it."

"Was it loaded?" At the look she gave him, he sighed. "Damn." He reached for his phone and punched in the numbers. "Gil? Halloran. Langlois has a gun. You go in and get that boy and bring him back—" He stopped, listening. "He left? When? You were supposed to call me if he made a move! Oh . . . Yeah, I left my desk for a minute or two. Are you on him? No, no . . . don't pull him over yet. I want to know where he's going. Stay on him and keep me posted. And get yourself some backup, Gil. Now."

He slammed the receiver back down, and swore quietly. "Not a homebody, my witness. He's on the move." His eyes on her were sharp, not entirely pleased. A little suspicious. Sometimes she forgot she wasn't part of the good-guy patrol anymore, until moments like these.

"I don't know what he's up to." Dulcie glanced away, her gaze settling on the disorganized pile of paperwork and files on his desk.

Bobby quickly dialed another number. "Adam. Halloran. Hate to bother you at home, but I need you. Things may get lively tonight. I'll fill you in on the details when you get here. Yeah. Bye."

Dulcie continued to stare at the mess on Bobby's desk. Oh, God, what was Julien doing? Why had he taken her gun?

"You could've just called me about this," Bobby commented, after a few moments had passed. Whenever the typewriter stopped, she heard the clock on the wall, ticking the seconds away.

"Guess I wanted to be here to make sure you didn't send out the National Guard, the FBI, or any bounty hunters."

"You know me better than that." He leaned back in his chair. It creaked in protest. "Coffee?"

Dulcie wrinkled her nose. "I remember that swill. No thanks." She rubbed her palms up and down her jeans. Anything to keep her hands busy. "Now what?"

"We wait."

Wait. She'd never been very good at waiting, and her nerves were already frayed beyond hope.

"Maybe I'll take some of that coffee, after all."

"I'll get it. You sit tight."

As Bobby stood, the phone rang. He snatched it up before it could ring again. "Halloran."

Dulcie saw his eyes narrow. Her hands stopped their nervous rubbing and balled into fists so tight that her nails gouged the skin of her palms.

"Aw, Christ," Bobby swore quietly, as he grabbed a pencil and scribbled quickly on a notepad. Dulcie couldn't see what he wrote. "Has your backup . . . I *know* we already got an officer watching the place, but you call for backup anyway. No, don't go in after him. Not yet. I've called Adam. Hang on for a few minutes more and we'll be right down."

She waited until he'd hung up the phone and sat back down. "Where is he?"

"He's gone to work." The tone of his voice was one of disbelief. Then his fist slammed against his desk, splashing cold coffee onto a pile of yellow phone messages. The typewriter stopped its plink-plinking.

"Work? You mean he's gone to a club?"

Bobby didn't answer. He was looking at her, but his gaze wasn't focused. She could almost see the wheels turning inside his head. "What the hell is he thinking? Why would he risk going out on stage?"

Dulcie knew. She had known all along, but hadn't wanted to admit it. The moment Bobby made the connection, she saw his gaze suddenly focus, sharp and furious.

"Because he isn't going Dragon-hunting," he snarled. "He's made himself Dragon bait!"

Julien pushed open the back door of *Le Homme*, the elegant ladies' club in New Orleans which featured nightly floor shows of male dancers, along with a full bar and a pricey dinner menu to complement the expensive, coldly hi-tech atmosphere. Saturday night was his night. He was the Ragin' Cajun, the club's major draw and the dancer most requested.

The club would be full tonight. Already the parking lot looked packed.

"Where the hell have you been? I've been calling you for the past three days!"

The deep female voice belonged to the club's owner, Rochelle Paine. She was short and plump, with her iron-gray hair cut stylishly, and turned out in her usual suit and sensible pumps. Julien stopped just inside the door, and waited as her heels click-clacked across the floor to his side.

"Been busy," he said.

Rochelle was in her mid-forties and an attractive woman. Hard-edged and shrewd, but fair. Right now, he saw suspicion in her dark eyes. "You look like shit, Julien. You're not on anything, are you? You know my rules—"

"An' you know me better than that. I'm tired, is all."

She still didn't look pleased. "Whatever the problem is, deal with it. My customers pay to see beautiful men, not one who looks like he's half-dead. Make sure you put on enough makeup to cover those circles under your eyes. And get dressed! You're on in a half hour.'' She gave him a stern glare. ''One of these days, Julien, you'll push me too far and I'm going to fire you.''

Julien liked Rochelle, and didn't have the heart to tell her he was going to quit long before she fired him. If he didn't get killed first. He donned his most charming smile. ''You tell me that at least twice a week, Shelly.''

Used to dealing with young men who were often as irresponsible as they were good-looking, her lips twitched. ''I don't understand your appeal, Julien, but it packs my club. Must be all that restrained sexuality of yours. Look but don't touch. That air of danger you seem to carry around with you. You're good, you gorgeous oaf, and you know it. Now get dressed!''

He listened to the retreating click-clack of her heels as he made his way to the communal dressing room, just to the back of the main stage.

Half hour. Not much time.

Two other dancers were in the room when he came in: Ricky, an acrobatic young black dancer who went by the stage name of Ali Baba, and Kurt Horowitz, a dark and brooding bodybuilder with muscles that looked pumped full of air.

''Hey, Jul,'' said Ricky. ''Our ladies are hot, hot tonight.'' He'd just come off a show, and was busy totaling the many bills the women had placed beneath the band of his red Spandex G-string. He grinned, then tipped his head in the direction of the scowling Horowitz. "Kurt and Tookie had a fight. She kicked him out. Again."

"Shut up," Horowitz growled.

"She'll come around," Julien said, as he always did when this happened. And the beaming, busty blonde would come back, all sniffles and big, blue, beseeching eyes.

He moved quickly toward the wardrobe racks. Rochelle gave her performers free rein in their choice of dance routines and costumes, so long as they were titillating yet tasteful. No full nudity at her club. No table dancing, no mingling with the customers. Rochelle traded in handsome men, good drinks and food, and knowing how to play into her female clientele's secret fantasies.

Julien grinned to himself humorlessly. Le Homme was still a strip club, but a classy one. He'd sure danced in worse, in his quest to catch Chloe Mitsumi's attention.

He'd do the Desperado routine tonight, since it was the only way he could slip a real gun past Rochelle and the bouncers. He peeled off his clothes and boots, and began dressing in his costume. The G-string first, basic black Spandex, followed by a pair of black snakeskin boots and modified black jeans, with zippers running the length of each outside seam. The black Western-style shirt had pearlized snaps instead of buttons.

Easy on, easy off.

Ricky's shrill whistle brought Julien's head up, and he saw the younger man staring and grinning.

"What?" Julien asked, not at all in the mood for any of Ricky's stupid cracks.

Waving his hand in the general direction of Julien's chest, Ricky said, "She must've been something, Jul. Never seen a scratch or hickey on you before. Wondered if you'd ever unfreeze enough to let any woman close. Rochelle said you were probably shacked up with some chick. Shit, I hate it when she's right about these things. Now I owe her twenty bucks."

Julien ignored Ricky's smug, leering face. He touched a faint scratch on his chest, then finished snapping the shirt closed. Damn if he didn't feel branded, and damn if he didn't like the thought of it.

His fingers fumbled as he tied a red bandanna around his neck, and the buckle on the holster gave his unsteady fingers trouble as well. Then he turned his back on his two fellow dancers, tossed the toy gun inside his bag, and replaced it with the real one. He grimaced. If anyone looked too closely, he was in trouble.

But there was nothing he could do about it now. He tied his hair back, settled a black Stetson on his head, then finished off the costume by pulling on a black duster and black gloves.

Good-bye Julien Langlois, hello Ragin' Cajun.

He listened to the muted sounds of the audience, and frowned.

That was the one unforgivable mistake in this plan of his. When he'd shouted his challenge to the Red Dragon nearly a week ago, he hadn't been thinking too clearly. Innocent lives were at risk here, if Jacob Mitsumi came gunning for him.

If. Maybe Halloran was right, and he'd slipped out of New Orleans for safer places. Julien wanted to believe it, but he knew a whole lot more about Jacob Mitsumi than Halloran did, and had good cause to doubt the scum had bailed.

Chloe had talked freely to him of the brother she both loved and hated. Mitsumi was clever, but arrogant. Damnedest part of it all, the man believed in personal honor. When his personal honor was challenged, he retaliated.

Julien had certainly challenged the Dragon's personal honor; witnessing Hernandez's murder was just the final straw. Mitsumi would come for him, bold and sure in his power. A week ago, it had made perfect sense to arrange a showdown in this club. Tonight, listening to the feminine voices and tinkling laughter from the audience, Julien saw it for the giant mistake it was, a result of his hate and heedless rage.

But he hadn't left himself any way out. If he'd called the cops earlier, they'd have come with sirens blaring and guns drawn, and Mitsumi, who could smell a setup like a bloodhound, would slip away. Then Julien would really need to go into hiding. He didn't want to spend the rest of his life afraid of dark corners and shadows, because he had a future planned—and that future included Dulcie Quinn.

He knew what he had to do. He'd planned this, all day during that long ride from Bayou Terre aux

Boeufs. He wanted to go eye-to-eye with the Dragon. He wanted the man to know who was taking him down. He was cutting it close, maybe, but this way he'd finish Mitsumi. Legally. Completely. For good.

Providing the *chien* showed up at all.

Julien walked to the far end of the dressing room to the phone, and tossed a battered business card on the table beside it. Keeping his back to the other two men in the room, he picked up the phone and, with one black-leather-clad finger, punched in Halloran's number.

Dulcie sat with a Styrofoam cup of thick, cooling coffee and watched Bobby in action. She was too tense, too angry and worried, to regret that she was no longer a part of these adrenaline-pumping moments. A storm of activity whirled around her, and she sat in the center of it, quiet. Waiting.

"All the doors to the club are secure," Adam Guidreau was saying, balancing his fists on Bobby's desk. He looked tired and excited. "From here on out, nobody's going in or out that we won't see."

"We got all our people here?" Bobby stood on tiptoe, counting the eight people milling about in the room. "We're ready to ride. A few last-minute instructions: now listen up here, people! Hey, listen—"

The phone rang. Again. It had been ringing almost nonstop for the past fifteen minutes. Dulcie stared at it. At the third ring, Bobby snatched up the headset and snapped, "Halloran."

At once, he stiffened. She knew who it was on the phone, even before Bobby made a violent chopping motion with his hand to quiet the din in the room.

"Langlois! Dammit, man, you'd better talk and talk fast, because right now I ain't happy!" He jabbed his finger at the phone on the next desk and Adam picked it up, listening in.

Then Bobby's gaze swung to her and he didn't look away. "Christ, Langlois, are you outta your mind? You—"

In the short silence that followed, Dulcie watched Bobby's mouth thin with fury. "You're sure about this?"

Adam, his hand over the phone's mouthpiece, cursed quietly.

"And when did you tell him that?" Bobby demanded, breaking eye contact with Dulcie to glance at Adam, who was shaking his head, the expression on his face stunned. "You stay put. Don't do a damn thing. We're on our way ... Yeah, I hear you."

He slammed the phone back on its cradle, ripped the page off the notepad he'd written on earlier, then turned to Dulcie. "I don't have time to explain. You stay here. Jud!" he shouted, twisting around. One of the younger cops came running. "Stay with Ms. Quinn. Make sure she's comfortable and give her anything she wants." He hesitated, then added, "Anything within reason, that is."

Dulcie came to her feet. "Take me with you."

"You know I can't do that," Bobby retorted, as he pulled on his coat. "I'll call as soon as possible. I'm sorry, but that's all I can do. Adam, let's roll. The rest of you, follow me. We got us a situation, boys and girls, and it ain't good!"

In less than a minute the office had emptied, and she was left alone with a wide-eyed young cop who looked like he'd just graduated from training.

The only thing Dulcie knew for certain was that Julien was in trouble. Probably of his own devising, judging from that phone conversation. She was terrified for him, but anger kept her calm. When she got her hands on him, she was going to peel his handsome hide right off his bones.

He'd lied to her!

She glanced at the notepad on Bobby's desk, then back at her Styrofoam cup clutched in her hands. She'd all but crushed it.

"Hey," she said, looking up at the young cop. Squeaky-clean, polished and pressed. Poor kid. He didn't stand a chance. "My coffee's gone cold. Would you mind getting me a refill? I think it's going to be a long night."

"Yes, ma'am," the kid said, scrambling forward. He took the misshapen cup from her hand. "I'll be just a minute."

"Oh, no hurry," Dulcie said with a bright smile, as the young man dashed off. Once he was out of sight, she moved to Bobby's desk. Grabbing a pencil, she lightly rubbed its lead over the notepad, revealing bit by bit what Bobby had written earlier.

"Life shouldn't make it this easy to be bad," she muttered to herself.

Le Homme. Bourbon.

Dulcie frowned, then tore off the page and stuffed it in the pocket of her jeans just as the young cop came back with a steaming cup of black coffee.

"Thank you . . . What was your name again?"

"Officer Judson Kirkpatrick, ma'am."

"Now isn't that a mouthful," she said, smiling sweetly. "Mind if I just call you Jud?"

The kid reddened. "Not at all, ma'am."

Dulcie took a sip of coffee. "You know, I've already had a few cups of this stuff. I'm going to need to find the ladies' room. Do you know where it is?"

She knew where the bathrooms were; she'd worked in this building for over six years. But poor Officer Kirkpatrick didn't know that.

"Just around the corner, ma'am." As Dulcie came to her feet, the kid helpfully pointed out the door. She gave him another smile.

"Thanks. I'll be right back. If Detective Halloran calls, you make sure and tell him I'll be right back. I don't want to miss his call."

"No problem, ma'am."

Dulcie put down the cup, then walked from the office. By the time the kid figured out she hadn't gone to the bathroom, she'd be halfway to Le Homme on Bourbon Street.

Chapter 22

~~~

JULIEN WAS LEANING against the dressing room wall when Halloran, Guidreau, and the goons came in through the club's back door. He didn't bother to move away from the wall, but made sure the duster covered the Colt, which protruded a little too far out of the holster for his comfort.

"Look here, boys." Halloran's drawl was thick. "If it ain't the Midnight Cowboy himself. I take it you're the Ragin' Cajun they're advertising at the front door? Not too original."

Julien shrugged. "Nobody claims it's great art."

Halloran glared, then snapped at the staring Ricky and gape-mouthed Horowitz. "You two stay put—and I mean it. Adam, take the gun off our Ragin' Cajun here."

Julien stiffened as Guidreau moved toward him. If Halloran knew he had a gun, then Dulcie . . .

Damn, damn, damn!

Guidreau shoved Julien back against the wall, none too gently, and plucked the Colt from the holster. Without a word, he handed it over to Halloran and stepped back. Ricky whistled, low and impressed.

"You are in a heap of trouble, mister," Halloran said in a voice full of restrained fury. He hoisted the gun. "Theft. Concealed weapons. Obstruction of justice."

"I know."

His admission had the effect of quieting Halloran. But not for long. "I understand what you're doing here, Langlois, but innocent lives are at risk."

Julien pushed himself away from the wall. "I made a mistake. I'm doin' what I can to correct it now."

"Why the hell didn't you tell me earlier? We could have formulated a plan, we could—"

"Would you have let me be part of it?" Julien demanded quietly. Halloran's silence was his answer. "Mitsumi won't come without me bein' here. You need me to bag the Dragon, an' I wanted to be the one to take him down. I'm doin' it your way, Halloran, but on my terms." There was a brief moment of silence, and then came the sound of music. Pounding rock, heavy on the drums and electric guitar. "That's my cue. I'm on in five minutes. You got a plan?"

"Not much of one," Halloran admitted. "We didn't have a chance to search the place, but your boss hasn't seen anyone fitting Mitsumi's description. Though that doesn't mean a thing. I have four plainclothes policewomen in the audience, including our friend Lucille. I'll be on stage with you, behind the curtains. Guidreau's going to the bar, where he's got a pretty clear view of the entire club. O'Donnell here," he said, motioning to one of the linebacker duo, "will take the front door. Martindale goes to the back. Your boss, by the way, says you're fired."

Julien managed a smile. "I was gonna quit anyway."

"Dulcie'll be glad to hear it, if she don't kill you first. When she showed up at the station she was spitting nails, man."

The smile faded from Julien's face. "Dulcie knows I'm here?"

"Not exactly," Halloran muttered, yanking at the knot of his silk tie. "If I'd told her, she'd be here. Got one of my kids baby-sitting her back at the station." He glared at Julien. "We're never gonna pull this off."

"I want to know what the f—" Horowitz began.

"Shut up," Halloran interrupted, without turning.

"Never say never," Julien said. "Cheer up, *mon ami*. He might not even show."

Before Halloran could reply, the sound system began playing a heavy rock song—his signature song—blaring out a pounding drumbeat at a decibel that vibrated clear through muscle and bone and shook the floor. Soon, wine in glasses would be quivering, silverware thumping on tablecloths. Soon, women would be calling his name.

Halloran looked up. Julien squared his shoulders, then walked out the dressing room doorway and up a short flight of stairs to the curtained stage entrance. The primal, beating drum thrummed right through him, like an electrical current, and he took a deep breath.

"Later," he mouthed to Halloran behind him. To himself, he muttered, *"Arriver à la fin."*

We've come to the end.

Then he parted the curtains and moved onto the stage.

It was something, walking out on a dim, smoke-swirled stage to the cheers, whistles, and shouts of a hundred women. He hadn't tried to explain this to Dulcie, because he wasn't sure he could make her understand that deep-gut thrill he felt every time he pumped a room full of women to a pitch of excitement.

Some part of him enjoyed all this, although he wouldn't miss it when it was gone.

Julien sauntered to the end of the stage, a seductive half-smile on his face, and he scanned the crowd gathered in the dark club. Only the stage itself was lit, with low runner lights, a few spots shining hotly down from above, and the ever-present strobes.

Lucille stood close to the stage and, in spite of his tension, Julien suppressed a smile. She was issuing a series of shrill wolf whistles, but she was also constantly scanning the room, keeping an eye out for the elusive criminal the entire NOPD had been trying to nail for a week.

Julien listened to his music cues, all the while moving around the stage in a slow, tantalizing strut, keeping the brim of the Stetson low. Women loved the fantasy of a mysterious, dangerous man in black. One platinum blonde with impressive cleavage almost snagged his coat hem, but he managed to move back quickly enough.

On cue, he snapped the duster open and gyrated his hips. The women in the audience grew more vocal, more animated. They knew the show was about to begin in earnest. The duster came off, slinking down one shoulder at a time, then he whipped it back toward the curtain. He had a brief glimpse of Halloran, just out of sight of the audience.

His gun was drawn.

The music accelerated; the beat became more frenzied, louder. Pounding. He began easing the shirttails free of his jeans, with slow and sinuous movements that set the women to whistling and shouting his name, swearing their love for him.

He knew what their love was worth.

With the shirttails out, he rocked his hips to the throbbing bass beat and ripped the snaps wide, baring his chest, sending his audience to a fever pitch of raucous anticipation. The shirt slid down his arms into his waiting fingers. He stared at the hands reaching out toward him, where he stood just out of reach. Hands opening and closing, beckoning.

He knew what they really wanted.

Julien whipped the shirt above his head, sending it sailing into the audience amid more screams and squeals and whistles. He scanned the crowd, what little he could see through the strobe lights and fake smoke. No sign of Mitsumi. Just the women.

Now for the holster, without even its fake gun,

easing it out from the belt loops, slowly drawing it out in front of him in a sly, suggestive motion. He discarded the belt and holster, spending a few beats flexing his biceps and chest muscles, which always got the ladies smiling and clapping in appreciation.

New music cue, waiting for the beat to change. He shot a quick glance toward the bar. Nothing.

Moving slow again, hands framing his crotch. The women liked that. Their shouts nearly drowned out the pounding drums of the music. He tossed the Stetson aside and shook his hair free. Moving to the music. Never stop moving.

Where the hell was Mitsumi?

Next music cue. He snapped open the waistband button, ran his hand down over the zipper. Lingering, teasing.

He saw Lucille clapping enthusiastically, even while her eyes darted from him to the crowd, watching. Waiting.

He eased down in a split and the women hollered and clapped. One grandmotherly woman with bright red lipstick banged her hands on the stage and mouthed, "Oh, baby, baby!"

Julien tossed back his hair. Then, through the swirling, artificial smoke, he saw a man walking toward the stage from the kitchen doors. A man he'd know anywhere, anytime.

The Red Dragon. Winding his way through the mostly female crowd with an arrogant, easy grace. Black hair tied back, wearing a black leather jacket, white T-shirt, and blue jeans. Looking like a Hollywood street tough; either ignoring or unaware of the cops who couldn't shoot in the crowd, who couldn't seem to move fast enough.

Julien froze.

Music pounded and his heart thudded to its beat. Time slowed.

Mitsumi walked closer, reaching inside his jacket.

Julien pushed himself to his knees at the sight of the gun, just as Halloran hit the stage at a run.

Women were still screaming, but now their screams were those of terror as female cops with drawn guns pushed them under tables or to the floor, shouting at them to stay down. Drinks toppled. Glasses silently shattered against the floor, their breaking drowned out by the music.

Mitsumi pointed his gun at Julien's chest.

Julien knew he couldn't move in time. He was going to die, like Hernandez. Like Marcel.

The force of the blow slammed him backwards. He rolled over, groping for the wound, but found nothing. He realized he'd been knocked aside as he saw Halloran fall hard, the gun spinning out of his hand.

Julien didn't think. He lunged for the gun. The metal was cool and smooth in his hand as he brought the barrel to bear on Mitsumi.

Point-blank. One last time.

Over the gun barrels, their eyes met and locked.

"Go on," murmured Jacob Mitsumi in the sudden, appalling silence. Someone had killed the sound. Mitsumi's gun remained steady, pointed at Julien's belly, despite the fact that a half dozen cops had him in their sights and would shoot him if he so much as twitched. "Pull the trigger."

"Nothin' I'd like better." Julien didn't blink, didn't even glance down at Halloran, who lay still, dark red blood seeping from the wound in his shoulder.

The memory rolled over him again, dragging him back toward the darkness. Marcel, Marcel . . .

Julien's hand tightened on the gun handle, on the trigger.

"Go on," Mitsumi urged. His black eyes glittered.

"Hold your fire!" Guidreau shouted from somewhere to Julien's right. "Langlois, we've got him— put the gun down and back away. Now!"

His gun unwavering, Julien stared into Mitsumi's eyes, seeing nothing but the cold gaze of a conscienceless creature. So close again.

So close.

Mitsumi's smile widened. "Finish it."

Julien's focus remained locked on Mitsumi, and he wondered why the cops hadn't moved or opened fire the moment Halloran went down.

"Julien," came Dulcie's soft voice. "It's over. Every gun in this room is on him . . . and on you, too."

He'd never seen her enter the club. She must have walked through the shadows and smoke of the dark room while the attention of every single person in Le Homme, sobbing customers or flint-eyed cops, was on the two men standing gun-to-gun with each other.

She was behind Jacob Mitsumi and walking closer. Right into the line of fire!

Guidreau sent a quick, desperate glance at Dulcie, then another at Julien. "Drop the gun," he repeated, frustration making his voice rough. "Dammit, Langlois, drop it!"

"I'll get out," Mitsumi said in a conversational tone, dragging Julien's attention back to him. "I'll find you. And your family." Then Mitsumi glanced over his shoulder at Dulcie and a sudden, shrewd light shone in his eyes. "The pretty lady, too."

Dulcie. The bastard meant Dulcie! Julien held his gun steady, pointed straight at Mitsumi's heart. Or where his heart should have been.

He couldn't let Mitsumi leave the club; he'd just get out of prison. Nothing but a bullet would stop the Dragon. He'd always known that. Always known this moment would come.

"Langlois!" Guidreau, again. Vaguely, Julien was aware that several of the police officers had turned their guns on him.

Losing Dulcie would send him back to that living death he'd known ever since Marcel's murder. Mitsumi knew it.

"Julien, *cher*," Dulcie whispered. "Please!"

No. No more.

"Go to hell," he muttered to Mitsumi, then pulled the trigger.

The explosion of the retort echoed through the tense silence of the club. Several women screamed, high-pitched and hysterical, as the bullet exploded a spotlight in the ceiling above. In the split second of silence that followed, Julien whispered an inward plea for forgiveness. Wherever his baby brother was now, Julien hoped he'd understand.

Then Martindale and O'Donnell dragged Mitsumi to the floor, wrestling his gun free, and Guidreau had Julien's arm in a painful, crushing grip, ripping Halloran's gun from his fingers. They dragged him back from Halloran's body.

Julien went cold. Halloran wasn't moving, but he refused to believe the detective was dead.

Dulcie was trying to get up on the stage. Julien reached down with his black-leather-clad hand and pulled her up. She was in his arms again, all long red hair and soft, warm body.

Chaos, all around them. Noise and churning movement. Julien, still holding Dulcie, was momentarily forgotten. He watched the Bruiser Boys and two other officers drag away the handcuffed Mitsumi. They'd stripped off his leather jacket, and a fire-red dragon tattoo peeked out beneath the sleeveless T-shirt.

Mitsumi glanced back over his shoulder and his gaze found Julien. Before the cops yanked him along again, a sly, arrogant smile crossed his face. A smile that said, *I'm not through with you yet*.

Julien looked away, then back toward Halloran. Lucille and Guidreau were all over the downed cop, trying to stem the flow of blood.

"Where's that ambulance?" Lucille shouted. She pulled off her short jacket and pressed it hard over the bleeding wound. "We've got an officer down!"

There was blood everywhere. Bright red, flowing, glistening in the dim stage lighting.

"I have to go to him," Dulcie whispered.

Even though he wanted to hold her close, Julien let her go. He was cold. So cold. He shivered, watching her sink to her knees beside her friend. Beside the man who'd taken a bullet meant for him.

"Dulcie, hold his head up," Lucille ordered. "I want to keep his air passages clear. His breathing doesn't sound too good."

Julien took a step forward, then another and another. He faltered once, when he got close enough to get a good look at the raw, bleeding wound and torn flesh. He closed his eyes, swallowing, and forced himself to remember this wasn't his brother. This man wasn't dead.

Yet. There was a damn awful lot of blood.

"Christ, Halloran, hold on," Julien muttered as the wounded man stirred, then moaned. "Don' you go an' die on me before I get the chance to punch out y'lights for takin' that bullet."

Halloran's eyes fluttered open. Dull with pain, shock. Unfocused. "Mitsumi?"

Julien hunkered down at Dulcie's side and laid his hand over hers, which was holding Halloran's. "Bagged him. You did it," he said quietly.

"With . . . you."

Julien didn't answer, and Halloran clamped his teeth tight as Lucille pressed down on his wound. The blood continued to seep through her fingers. Christ, had the bullet hit an artery? Why hadn't the pressure stopped the bleeding? Julien met Dulcie's worried gaze. Then, in the distance, came the wail of sirens. But Halloran's eyes had closed again.

"Hey," Julien said quietly, and the blue eyes fluttered open. "You looked pretty good on stage, Halloran. Hear the ladies screamin' for you? Give it a try, man. They usually don' shoot you on stage, just grab any body part within reachin' distance."

"Sounds like . . . the life. Pity you got . . . to give it all up."

"Thought I'd do private shows from now on."

Halloran smiled, or tried to, but was too weak now. His eyes were drooping, although he tried to stay conscious, as if he knew that if he slipped away he might never come back. "Dulcie'll . . . like that," Halloran whispered.

The crowd parted, admitting running paramedics and a gurney. "Thanks, *mon ami*," Julien whispered into Bobby's ear. This time, he meant the words. "Paramedics are here. You go bleed on them now, an' keep your eyes open. Dammit, Halloran, I'm not losin' anyone else to a bullet, y'hear? Don' you die. Dulcie'll never forgive me."

Dieu, he'd never forgive himself, either.

"Won't . . . die," Bobby muttered, as the paramedics closed around him and jostled Julien and Dulcie back. "Gonna dance at . . . your wedding, Cajun."

It was after three in the morning before the police allowed them to leave the scene, and there were a few bad moments when Dulcie was afraid they meant to arrest Julien. Finally a weary, irritated, and elated Adam Guidreau told them to get the hell out of the club and go home.

Home.

Dulcie wondered where that was going to be. She was still angry with Julien, but the worst of it had been burned away by the night's violence and fear. Right now, all she wanted was for him to wrap her in his arms. She couldn't even feel any triumph or vindication that Mitsumi was finally locked away. Julien didn't look like he was feeling too triumphant, either.

In silence, they walked down the street. Police lights twirled like red and blue strobe lights against the street and buildings, and a constant hum of voices filled the night. Several news teams had arrived, and light bulbs flashed, blinding white.

"Where to now?" she asked, waiting until they'd moved beyond the general throng. They threaded their way through a gradually thinning crowd of curious onlookers. Julien had one hand shoved deep in the pocket of his jeans, while the other held his gym bag—and what looked like a violin case. He'd insisted she wear his bomber jacket.

"That's up to you, Dulcie," he answered.

She took several steps before realizing he'd stopped, leaning back against a black Ford pickup truck. She sent him a questioning look.

"My truck. You want a ride?"

"I'm parked down tne next block."

"I can walk you there." When she didn't budge, he didn't move either. After a moment, he produced a self-conscious shrug. "I'd like to come back with you. If you're not too mad at me."

"Oh, I'm mad all right," Dulcie said. "But after everything that happened tonight, I'm too tired to fight about it. You could have been killed." Her voice caught, and he watched her, his gaze searching, measuring. Waiting.

"He'll be okay," Julien said, after a moment.

When she could trust herself to speak again, Dulcie said, "He's going to drive everybody in the hospital crazy." She smiled a little. "He can't sit still at all. And he'll have the nurses eating out of his hand in no time."

"I'm sorry, Dulcie. I'm sorry he was hurt. It was my fault; I should've—"

"Yes, you *should* have told Bobby that you were playing chicken with Jacob Mitsumi!" Her belly gave a strange little twist at the flash of pain on his face, before he dropped his gaze to his boots. "But Bobby will be all right, Mitsumi's in jail, and your testimony will help keep him there. His shooting a cop will keep him there even longer. What you did was wrong, but it's over. Over," she repeated fiercely. "Now, let's go home."

Dulcie waited, but Julien didn't move. A few moments passed. Frowning, she laid her hand on his chest in a gentle caress. "It's okay. Come on. You can drive. I'll pick up my Jeep tomorrow."

He straightened, then fished his keys out from his pocket. They clinked and rattled together. He raised his hand, watching the violent tremors, then sank back against the side of his truck. "I can't drive."

Dulcie gathered his hands in her own, understanding what was wrong, and took the keys from him. "It happens like this, sometimes. You'll be okay in a little while."

The shaking had progressed beyond his hands to encompass his whole body. Without a word she helped him into the truck, where he collapsed back against the seat, his eyes closed and arms pulled tightly against himself in an attempt to control his shakes. He wasn't even capable of buckling his seat belt, so she did it for him. Then she walked to the other side of the truck and climbed in.

She drove fast through the quiet, empty streets, occasionally sending a quick look at Julien to make sure he was holding up. He still had his eyes closed, but the tremors seemed to have eased. Then a sudden thought came to her.

"You want me to put on some music?" She'd noticed the tape player, and the collection of cassettes in the rack just under the dashboard.

He nodded, but said nothing. Splitting her attention between the road and the tapes, she pulled out a few. She settled on a group she recognized, one famous for their haunting ballads and a capella melodies. Music to soothe that beast dying away inside him.

By the time she pulled onto the gravel road that led to her Lake Pontchartrain pier, Julien had straightened in the seat and had even exchanged a word or two with her. When she parked the truck, he was able to get out without her help, although she noticed his hands were still trembling.

Silently, she slipped her arm around his waist. After a moment, he did the same, pulling her close as they crossed the pier to her houseboat. Dulcie suspected he held her close for physical support as much as the need to be near her. Still, they probably looked more like lovers who'd just come home from a late-night movie rather than a shoot-out in a strip club.

The remainder of the night passed in a strange state of quietude and peace, while Julien stayed awake and laid the last of his ghosts—and his dragons—to rest.

Unable to sleep herself, Dulcie simply sat in a deck chair and waited for him. It wasn't until dawn began to color the sky in streaks of orange and purple that he came to her and took her hand in his.

"Let's go on in to bed," he said quietly. "It's gonna be a long day."

"Probably," she agreed.

Then, in a low whisper, "Dulcie Quinn, I love you."

"I know."

"I'll never stop lovin' you."

"Promise?" she whispered, twining her fingers in his.

"Promise."

Chapter 23

〜

"THIS IS SUSAN Carson at the Parish of Orleans Criminal District Court, bringing you live coverage of what people are calling the year's biggest trial. Three months ago, New Orleans police arrested Jacob Mitsumi, the alleged drug dealer known as the Red Dragon. Prosecutors hope to convict Mitsumi on charges of illegal drug trafficking and twelve other counts of criminal conduct, including the shooting death of Juan Hernandez and the assault on Detective Robert Halloran.

"Today, the jury expects to hear testimony once again from the prosecution's most controversial witness—Julien Langlois, the former male exotic dancer who himself is accused by the defendant of attempted murder. Despite this rather bizarre and unexpected twist, trial experts are predicting a quick conviction against Jacob Mitsumi. Tonight, perhaps, the citizens of New Orleans can go to sleep and know that tomorrow, when they wake, the streets will be a little safer for all our children. Again, this is Susan Carson, reporting live from the Criminal District Court for *KJUN News*."

Dulcie, walking past the camera crew, paused to listen to the newswoman. As she moved on, pushing through the crowd gathered at the front of the courthouse, she murmured to herself, "Amen to that, lady."

The trial had been in progress for a week, and already the media had turned it into a circus. The defendant was photogenic, clever, and fascinating, and his defense attorney a consummate showman. The prosecution's difficult witness—her Julien— was also photogenic, fascinating, and appealing, as was the handsome detective who'd been shot in the line of duty. Dark and light, Julien and Bobby. The reformed Bad Boy and the Hero Cop. The media ate it right up, and were playing merry hell with her and Julien's personal life.

She'd made it halfway up the steps before a reporter recognized her. She wore sunglasses, but there wasn't much she could do about her height and long auburn hair.

"Ms. Quinn! A moment, please! What are your feelings about your fiancé going on the witness stand again today?"

"What do you have to say about the recent allegations that the police department mismanaged the Hernandez case?"

She said, as she always did, "No comment."

"Aw, c'mon, Dulcie, give us a little something to work with here. We're just doin' our job!"

She recognized that cajoling drawl. She glared at the young man over the top of her glasses and repeated, icily, "No comment. Go away, Johnson."

She was rescued by Adam Guidreau, who managed to whisk her off just as Bobby Halloran got out of a car at the curb. Like a horde of insects, reporters swarmed toward him. Dulcie grinned at his grimace of annoyance. When he looked up and caught her gaze, she waved gaily.

"How're you holding up?" Adam asked, keeping his arm protectively around her—not that she needed it, but she thought it endearing nonetheless—as he ushered her through the milling crowds to the courtroom.

"I'll be glad when it's all over and Julien and I can get back to some sort of normal life."

"I hear you," he said, smiling at her. "Halloran's been a pain in the ass to work with lately, and I don't believe him anymore when he says it's just his shoulder that's making him so damn touchy."

"If you had cameras poked in your face every time you went to the grocery store, you'd understand. Or," she added, lowering her voice, "women propositioning your fiancé in restaurants."

Guidreau laughed as they entered the courtroom, which was already full. "What do you do when that happens?"

"Show my fangs. They run pretty quick. Julien thinks it's funny. 'Course, he would."

"Set the big date yet?" Adam asked, as he helped her to her seat. He sat down beside her.

"We've been talking mid-June, but I think it may need to be a little sooner than that."

"Oh?" He gave her an inquisitive look. His grin slowly widened as understanding dawned. "So when is the baby due?"

"August." She couldn't help grinning back. She was so excited by news of the baby that it took a physical effort not to shout it out to everyone. To the whole world. But so far, she and Julien had only told a few people.

"Bobby know?"

"We told him last night. He and Julien spent so much time beaming at each other you'd think *they* were pregnant and going to give birth!" She sighed, still unable to chase away the grin on her face, which she knew must look silly and loopy. "Men."

Adam leaned over and gave her a quick buss on her cheek. "Congratulations, sweetheart. I'm glad it's all worked out for you. Is Julien here?"

"Not yet. He left before I did, but said he had to make a stop before coming downtown."

Adam glanced at his watch. "Trial's set to begin in a half hour. Bobby'll crucify him if he's late."

"He'll be here," Dulcie answered comfortably, then settled back to wait, a hand resting on her stomach.

The place looked a whole lot different in the day than it did at night. In the day, the small cemetery was peaceful. Almost pretty. Maybe it had always been that way, and he was the one who'd brought the ugliness to it.

Julien stared at the gray headstone, and the neatly chiseled name of his brother. After a moment, he reached out and touched the stone, as he always did when he came here. For some reason, it comforted him. So cool. Smooth, like polished glass.

"Hey," he whispered, as his hand dropped away again. "Today's my big day. Gonna put the Dragon in prison for good. Won't be because of what he did to you, but I'm learnin' to live with that."

And he was. An imperfect justice, as Dulcie had once said, but it was still better than none at all.

"Talked to Gracie on the phone again last week. She says the family may come down for the trial. Haven't seen them yet. Not sure if I want them there at all."

The sunlight shone against the polished stone, bright and gleaming. It hurt his eyes. "But it'd be nice to see everyone again . . . See how much Joe's grown, an' Gracie's new baby is comin' soon."

It was a beautiful day. All blue sky and brilliant white sun. Julien took a deep breath. He listened to the birds chirping in the trees and the distant hum of traffic. He wasn't alone. An elderly couple stood by a small grave marker not far from him; maybe visiting a baby they'd buried some forty, fifty years ago.

Dulcie had been right about that, too. The pain never went away, but it was getting easier to bear.

Hunkering down, Julien straightened the small wreath of silk flowers at the foot of the headstone. "Hey, I'm gettin' married soon myself. Gonna take that ol' plunge again. You'd like her. She's got a smart mouth, just like you did. An' we're havin' a baby at the end of this summer. Kinda hopin' for a girl, but wouldn't mind at all if it's a boy.

"Gotta go now." He stood up, his hands once again deep in the pockets of the long coat he wore over his suit. "Love you . . . an' miss you, kid. *Adieu.*"

Whether by fate or by choice, Julien and Bobby walked into the courtroom together. In the past three months the two of them had worked around to a grudging acceptance, and finally to a genuine friendship. While Dulcie was pleased by it, she still couldn't have imagined a stranger friendship than that between Bobby Halloran, so quirky and intense, and Julien Langlois, who could spend hours lost in a piece of music that caught his fancy.

Right now, seeing them together brought a smile to her face. Julien was dressed in an expensive, conservative gray suit, with a white oxford shirt and a simple striped tie in yellow and gray. Bobby, in contrast, wore a dark teal suit with a pale yellow silk shirt and a paisley tie that, even kindly, could only be described as loud.

"Well, if it isn't Mutt and Jeff," she murmured and Adam, still sitting beside her, chuckled. Julien winked as he walked past her, and Bobby flashed his wide smile. She watched them move up the aisle toward the front of the courtroom, where their seats were waiting.

Walking behind Julien, Bobby slowed as he approached a petite woman in a simple black dress. Dulcie had noticed her earlier. The woman wore a black straw hat with a wide, rolled brim that hid most of her face, except for her small nose and generous red lips.

She leaned closer to Adam and nudged him. "Is that who I think it is?"

Adam, following the line of her gaze, nodded. "I believe so. Hard to recognize her outside of her usual leather and lace."

Chloe Mitsumi. A hothouse orchid, exotic and potent even in plain, unrelieved black.

Julien either hadn't noticed the woman he'd once used as a pawn, or he simply didn't wish to cause a scene.

Dulcie watched as Bobby stopped by Chloe and bent low. The exchange was brief. Fascinated and intrigued, Dulcie leaned forward as the woman's shielded face turned toward Bobby. Though Chloe said nothing to Bobby's quiet words, she nodded once. When he moved away, Chloe's head turned and she watched him take his seat.

"What do you make of that?" Dulcie asked.

"I have no idea," Adam answered. It looked as if he meant to say more, but at that moment the judge walked into the courtroom and the time for talking was done.

After the usual introductory proceedings, the prosecutor, Elena Sinclair, got right down to business, and her strong voice cut across the low murmuring of the courtroom.

"The prosecution would like to call Julien Langlois to the stand."

It had begun.

Doing his best to live down the playboy image the media had tagged him with, Julien had made a conscious effort to look as conservative as possible. But even without meaning to, he drew every eye in the courtroom. There was no disguising the long hair, tied back though it was, or the powerful build in the suit. The whispers following his progress up to the witness stand told Dulcie he hadn't lost his showman's touch, even three months after swearing off the lifestyle that had made him—at least until the next scandal—a household name in New Orleans.

She hoped to God this was one performance he would pull off without a hitch. He glanced her way and she smiled, giving him a discreet thumbs-up signal.

He raised his right hand, swore the oath of truth, and as he turned to sit, hesitated for a moment. It lasted only a fraction of a second, that hesitation. Not long enough for anyone else to notice, perhaps, but Dulcie did.

Once he was seated and Elena Sinclair began asking her carefully prepared questions, Dulcie turned to look behind her. At the back of the courtroom, looking both nervous and uncomfortable, she saw an older, plainly dressed couple and a group of younger adults, including a young woman who was quite pregnant.

Oh, God . . . Julien's family. That tall, angular man with the weather-worn brown skin must be Joseph Langlois; the short, round woman in the old-fashioned print dress, Cecille. The pregnant woman would be his sister, Grace, and the others the older Langlois siblings.

Tears, unexpected and hot, stung the back of her eyes. Marcel should have been standing there, too.

Marcel, who'd wanted to live the *bon vivant* like his big brother, but instead lost himself to drugs before dying in an act of random violence that tore apart his family and nearly destroyed his brother.

Dulcie turned and stared at Jacob Mitsumi, so cool and distinguished in his three-piece suit, looking more like a Fortune 500 company executive than a criminal.

As if he felt her stare, Mitsumi turned and met her gaze. Cold dark eyes, a thin mouth turned up slightly in a handsome smile. As if he still thought all this merely an inconvenience, and he'd be off the hook after doing a few years of hard time.

No way.

Get him, Julien, she said to herself, her lips moving although she didn't speak the words out loud. *Go get him.* Then she leaned close to Adam and whispered, "Julien's family is here. I want to make sure they get a place to sit."

What those poor, ill at ease people thought of the tall woman making straight for them, she couldn't imagine. But she did her best to present a friendly, smiling face.

Julien's mother was pale, and Dulcie's heart went out to her at once. But it was the pregnant woman she spoke to first, since she knew it was largely Gracie's doing that Julien's family was here in the first place.

"Grace?" she said, softly. "Are you Grace LeMieux?" When the pretty, dark-haired woman nodded, Dulcie smiled again and extended her hand. "I'm Dulcie Quinn. Julien's fiancée. He told me you might be at the courthouse today."

Grace had a beautiful smile, much like her older brother's. "Oh, Dulcie. I am so pleased to finally meet you. This is my mother and father, Cecille and Joseph. This is my husband, Ed, and everyone else are brothers or sisters."

Dulcie would have to put Alex, Elise, Anton, Tom, and Paulette's names to the right faces later. "Let me talk with one of the bailiffs and see if I can get you a place to sit so you don't have to stand," she said, with a last look at Gracie's big belly. Dear God, in a few months she'd be as big herself! She could hardly wait. "It's going to be a long day, I think."

Surprisingly, the trial itself was over by noon. The defense attorney had done his best to discredit Julien's testimony in the murder of Juan Hernandez, but Elena Sinclair, while not dramatic, was sharp and shrewd—and could probably argue the devil's part to God himself.

Not that it hadn't been ugly. Dulcie had felt

slightly ill, being forced to listen to sordid insinu-
ations on everything from Julien's sexual practices
to suggestions that he was a psychopathic killer.
But Julien never once lost his composure, always
presenting a facade of quiet, respectful dignity.

If she'd found the whole smear attack distasteful,
she couldn't imagine what it was like for his
mother and father to hear such slander aimed
against their child, even one who had certainly
caused his share of troubles around the family
hearth. Joe Langlois' austere, lined face never dis-
played an emotion she could identify, but his round
little wife spent a great deal of time wiping her eyes
with a sodden embroidered handkerchief. The
brothers and sisters wore changing expressions of
anger, dismay, and hurt.

In the end, as everyone expected, it was the
shooting of Bobby Halloran that buried Mitsumi.
Nobody, but nobody, countenanced a cop-killer.
Even if the cop in question hadn't been killed, or
even disabled by his injury, the judicial system
came down hard on criminals who shot those who
were paid to uphold the law.

After just an hour and a half of deliberations, the
jury came back with its verdict.

Guilty.

Dulcie found herself holding Gracie's damp,
warm hand as the verdict was read out loud, then
searched for Julien in the front of the courtroom.
He sat still and straight, but when the sentence of
life imprisonment without parole was handed down
upon the man indirectly responsible for his

brother's murder, Julien seemed to close in upon himself. He hunched over, shoulders slumped, and Dulcie felt tears welling in her eyes.

The tears spilled over when Bobby leaned over and gave Julien a fierce, exultant embrace, complete with much shoulder thumping.

"Is it over?"

Wiping away her tears, Dulcie looked over at Julien's red-faced, puffy-eyed mother. "Oh, yes," she said. "It's over."

"This Mitsumi, he goes to jail, him?"

Dulcie smiled. "He certainly does. For life." She glanced at Jacob Mitsumi, nearly lost in the swirl of his defense team. He wasn't wearing any sort of smile now.

She quickly scanned the crowd for Chloe Mitsumi, but the woman had disappeared. No diminutive figure in a black dress and deeply brimmed black hat. Like a ghost, she seemed to have simply vanished.

Then Dulcie realized that the trial wasn't over yet for Julien. Right here, in a crowded courtroom with no privacy, he would come face-to-face with his family for the first time since Marcel's death.

Dulcie saw Julien trying to wade through the press of people, but it was like swimming against a tide.

Gracie twisted her hands together as the rest of the family closed in on itself in a tight knot, their expressions anxious and nervous.

"Oh, God," Gracie said. "Here comes Julien."

Bobby, perhaps understanding what was happening, had managed to redirect attention to himself, allowing Julien to make his escape.

"Just stay calm," Dulcie ordered, and hurried toward him.

Julien was pale, his face lined with fatigue, and she didn't think he looked anywhere near being able to manage this meeting. But he didn't have a choice, and if she'd learned nothing else from those five, intense days on her houseboat, it was that Julien Langlois had to face his troubles head-on.

But she needn't have worried. Julien's mother pushed past her, arms held wide in a welcoming gesture no child, young or old, could mistake. Then Julien had his arms around his mother, lifting her small, plump body at least a foot off the ground. Even when he put her back down, Cecille didn't let her son go.

"Julien, *tu s'en retournez . . . tu s'en retournez*, Julien."

Dulcie had lived in New Orleans long enough to pick up a smattering of French, and since Cecille repeated the same words over and over, Dulcie finally made sense of it: *Come home, Julien. Come home.*

It was if her words released the others from some magic spell, and they all came forward at once. Except for Joe Langlois, who walked toward his son with careful, measured steps.

His other children made way for him. Gracie wiped the tears from her eyes and both the older brothers backed away. Dulcie found herself holding her breath.

"You heard your *mère*, Julien," said Joe Langlois. He had a deep baritone voice, startling in a man so spare and wiry. "You come home, boy. We need you home."

Father and son stared at each other, and Cecille let her son go, with a gentle pat on his back.

"Been thinkin' about it," Julien said.

He had? Dulcie blinked. It was news to her. She'd discuss this with him later. Right now, she wanted to take Joe Langlois by the back of his old suit coat and shove him into his son's arms. Wanted to shout at the old man, tell him to give his son a chance.

"Come here," Joe Langlois said gruffly. "Let me look at you in those clothes . . . Such the fancy man, son."

Julien, still silent, came several steps closer to his father. The old man lifted his hands, sunbrowned and gnarled by years of physical labor, and clasped his son hard by the shoulders. Then somehow they managed an awkward embrace, brief yet intense, and Dulcie wasn't the only one who let out a pent-up sigh of relief.

"Oooh," Dulcie groaned, crawling into the bed beside Julien. "I didn't think this day was ever going to end, and I didn't think we were ever going to get back to this boat."

He moved over, so she had room enough to settle against him. She felt warm and smooth, all bare skin and silky hair. Instead of answering or opening his eyes, he made a low, noncommittal sound.

He felt drained. Dragged down, like he had lead in his veins instead of blood.

With a soft sigh, she wiggled against him. Her hand settled at his groin. *Dieu*, he hoped she didn't want to make love. At the moment, neither the flesh nor spirit were willing or able.

"Tired?" she whispered.

" 'Fraid so, *chère*."

"That's okay."

Despite her words, her hands had moved lower, caressing him with gentle, light strokes of her fingers. Julien was surprised to feel his body respond. Not quickly, not with instant, rigid eagerness, but responding. Maybe it wasn't lead in his veins after all.

"That sure feels nice," he admitted with a low sigh. "But I don' think I can manage anythin' more than touchin' tonight, Dulcie."

"That's okay," she repeated. "I want to touch you and kiss you. Don't do anything at all. Just lie there." He chuckled, and she nudged him with her elbow. "Indulge me."

That finally prompted him to open one eye. "I indulge you plenty," he said, and moved his hand to her belly, brushing his fingers against the flesh that was warm, still flat, but nestling his child within. Their child.

A baby. Every now and then, the reality of it all scared the bejesus out of him. But he didn't say much about it, since she was more frightened than he was, still haunted by those fears—however unfounded—that she couldn't carry a baby to full term.

He'd insisted she visit the best gynecologists in New Orleans, and each doctor had stressed the same thing: there was nothing wrong with her; nothing to interfere with carrying a baby to full term or giving birth vaginally. They cautioned that her bad back might require her to spend the last few months of the pregnancy on bed rest, just to ease the discomfort, but a few months in bed was a small price to pay to welcome a new child into the world.

A twinge of pleasure brought him from his reverie. He opened both eyes. Damn, she had the cleverest hands! And a wicked mouth. Wicked, sinful, luscious. Heaven. Her teeth and tongue were teasing his nipple, and somewhere along the line she'd shoved the sheet aside. Cool air brushed against his bare skin. She settled between his legs, her hands busy with their gentle stroking and featherlight touches.

"You always get your way," Julien said as he brought a hand to her hair, pressing her mouth closer, not wanting her to stop. Not really.

"Yeah, and you protest so hard," she whispered, looking up from his chest to grin mischievously. Her fingers were growing a little bolder, and so was he, Julien realized. More than growing a little— growing a lot. "So hard," she repeated breathlessly.

"I love it when you talk trashy." Those wicked, luscious lips were moving lower. She was going to kill him with kindness, drive him mad with lust. Damned if he wasn't going to make love to her all night long and sleep until two the next afternoon.

Sometimes, a man just had to know when to give in.

Her hot mouth closed over him, and her tongue played hell with every nerve end in his body.

"All right," he muttered in a voice somewhere between a growl and a groan, arching upwards. "You win."

Sometime later, after a lazy bout of lovemaking, they lay quietly in each other's arms. Julien discovered his weariness had gone. He wasn't exactly up to running a marathon, but his mind was refusing to shut down for the night. He knew Dulcie hadn't fallen asleep either.

"I've been doin' a little thinkin'," he said into the silence, tightening his arms around her warm body.

"Me, too."

Her thumb was brushing lightly against his ribs, almost but not quite tickling. It felt just right. "We should head downtown and get a marriage license soon. Unless you've changed your mind about tryin' for a church weddin'?"

"No. Not with you being Catholic—lapsed or otherwise. It would be too difficult, with the old divorce. I'm perfectly happy with a civil ceremony. Your parents will have to adjust to the notion, but they want to see you happy. They'll get over it if we don't have a church wedding."

"What I said earlier, about goin' back home. I meant it."

"I figured you did. You've been thinking this over for quite some time, haven't you?"

"I don' want to raise a family on houseboat, Dulcie. An' Del is gettin' too big for this place," he added, as she laughed. "He near took out the screen door last week."

"Miserable mutt," she said, but the tone of her voice belied her words. "Leave it to you to pick the only dog in the world that somehow manages to function on one-quarter brain juice."

Julien chuckled. "He's got character." Del surely wasn't the brightest creature, but the dog had a sweet temperament and was fiercely loyal. After a moment, he turned the conversation back. "It'd be different if I was a company man, but you know how it's been for me. Never had that kind of job, never wanted one. Livin' off my own skills is what I do best. I've got enough money saved for a down payment on a bit of property and a small place. If you don' mind."

She leaned closer and kissed his chin. "No, I don't mind. I'm tired of this old boat. I don't need to hide away here anymore, and I can make dolls and black-eyed Cajun babies on a farm in Acadiana as easily as anywhere else."

He smiled at that. Black-eyed Cajun babies. Maybe he was up to giving Gracie a run for her money, after all. "There's somethin' else."

He felt her hesitation, then the relaxation of the muscles in her body again. "Out with it."

"If we get a farm, I'd like to hire on kids who've had it rough. Let 'em work hard, show 'em what it means to take pride in yourself an' to believe in yourself. Not kids who've been in serious trouble, but the ones who don' have anyone to care what happens to them," he added hastily, as Dulcie raised herself on her elbows. When she still didn't say anything, Julien sighed. "It was just a thought."

"How long have you been considering this?" Dulcie asked quietly.

"Just this week, during the trial. Been doin' a lot of thinkin' about Marcel . . . about what you said to me once. That what I'd wanted to do was a poor monument to my love for him. Maybe this is a better one."

"I think it's beautiful," Dulcie said, and kissed him. "Why don't we look into it, once we get settled? Find out what's involved."

"Already had one lady call today an' ask me to come speak to a group of high school kids."

Dulcie rolled over onto her belly, chin cupped in her hands as she watched him. He stretched out, then brought his hands in back of his head. "She seems to think these kids would listen to me better than another adult. Guess bein' a reformed bad boy has a few advantages."

"You're a hero, Julien Langlois. To a lot of people."

"Ruinin' my reputation." The long curve of her back was just too tempting. He rolled over to his side, propping his head on one hand as he trailed a finger down her spine. Over the warm, smooth skin. Over the puckered white scar and the even, little white dots where the stitches and staples had been.

His woman. Mother of his child, soon to be his wife.

He smiled, doodling against that smooth, fair skin he never seemed to get enough of.

Dulcie peered at him across her shoulder. "What are you doing?"

"Nothin'."

"Doesn't feel like nothin' . . . Are you writing mushy stuff on my back?" she demanded with a grin.

"Nope." He brushed across her back with his hand, as if it were an eraser, and started writing again.

" 'M,' " Dulcie said. He drew another imaginary letter in her skin. " 'I.' " She frowned, concentrating, as he drew the last two. Then she laughed. " 'N' . . . 'E.' M-I-N-E. You wrote 'MINE' on my back? Aren't you territorial today."

She gave a muffled yelp as he flipped her to her back and surged over her body. He delivered a hard, firm kiss on her mouth and growled, "Damn straight."

"Mmmm, this goes both ways." She shoved at him, until he lifted his chest high enough for her to draw, in clear strokes with her fingernail, the letters Y-E-S.

Julien frowned, then rubbed at the faint red lines

her nail had left. "You branded me, Dulce. Is that a 'Yes, I'm yours' sort of 'yes'?"

Dulcie shrugged, watching him.

"I don' get it, *chère*."

She laughed again, a low laugh. A woman's laugh.

Julien's lips curved upwards. "Nothin' shy about you," he murmured, the tone of his voice admiring. "Dulcie Quinn, you wanna fool around again?"

Dulcie sighed, tightening her arms hard around his neck. "*Mais* yeah."

Epilogue

SAMUEL MARCEL LANGLOIS made his arrival two
weeks early, on a humid, rainy afternoon in August. He was placed first in the capable hands of
his father, screaming with all the power in his diminutive lungs, and then into his mother's eager
arms.

Sammy was a great favorite in the nursery—but
then, so was Sammy's daddy. Dulcie didn't mind
if the nurses fussed extra over Sammy whenever
Julien was around. She floated on a cloud of pure
elation, not caring that the lower half of her body
felt as if it had been turned inside out following
delivery, that her stitches itched, or her breasts—
and, oh, did she have breasts—ached like the dick-
ens.

She had the most wonderful husband on the
planet, and the most beautiful baby in the universe.

Sammy was perfect. She thought him a near replica of his father. His small head was covered with a shocking thatch of black hair. He had ten perfect fingers and toes, and the sweetest little bowlegs. His nose was tiny and precious, and his greedy lips tugging at her nipple as he nursed made her feel all shaky inside. It was hard to believe that something so small could have captured her heart in such a short time.

The sight of Julien holding his son simply melted her. The first time Julien raised the baby and kissed his soft skin, she burst into tears and didn't even worry about how silly she must seem.

A year ago she had been lonely, afraid of all the changes shaping her life. Now, she couldn't imagine a life without Julien or Sammy.

Or the whole Langlois family, for that matter.

Sitting up in her hospital bed, with the warm bundle of her son sleeping in her arms, Dulcie glanced around the chaos of her room and smiled. How Sammy managed to sleep through it all, she didn't know. But she was thankful that she'd been blessed with a placid, easygoing baby.

There were, at the moment, eleven people having a celebration in her room. Whenever a nurse came by with a frown, Julien and Bobby cranked up their good ol' boy charm to Full Ooze and the poor woman went away dazed, with only a mild admonition that the new mother needed her rest.

The new mother, however, was tired of being in bed—having spent the last two months of her pregnancy on her back—and in spite of Julien's teasing that he had her right where he wanted her.

No, a room full of people made her happy. There were Julien's parents and several of his brothers and sisters, including the younger ones. She'd finally got them all straight.

Standing in front of the TV with Julien was the eldest brother, Tom, who still lived on the family farm with his own wife and kids, and helped his parents with the work. Anton, who had his own farm and had married his high school sweetheart, was lounging by the door. His wife, Christine, stood beside him with her hand casually in the back pocket of his jeans. Pretty Paulette, who'd eloped a month ago with a cowboy her parents barely tolerated, was perched on the only chair in the room. Wisely, she'd left her husband at home. Young Annie had just graduated from high school, and the baby of the family, Joe, was eleven.

Joe, as Dulcie had quickly learned, was a handful.

Missing were Alex, who'd gotten married two years ago and was living in Houston, and Elise, the only Langlois of marriageable age not married. She was an army sergeant and was still trying to negotiate a short leave. Gracie, her husband Ed, and their growing brood lived in Lafayette and would probably be down to visit soon.

There was also Nonc George, Cecille's garrulous brother. Dulcie's own family, including her brother Sean, had visited that morning, but this afternoon the only non-Langlois in the room was Bobby, who was deep in conversation with Nonc George about the New Orleans Saints. Annie was exhibiting serious signs of having a crush on Bobby.

Dulcie felt a tug on the sleeve of her robe and looked over to the thin, less-than-clean face of the youngest Langlois brother. Nonetheless, with his liquid dark eyes and classic features, he was going to grow up to be a heartbreaker.

"What's up, Joe?" she asked, shifting the sleeping lump of her son in her arms. Eight pounds sometimes felt like quite a lot.

"Brought him a tree frog. Big one."

Dulcie gulped, looking down at a small cardboard box with a tiny hole cut in it. A bulbous froggy eye blinked out at her. "That's very sweet, Joe, but I don't think Sammy's interested in frogs just yet. Maybe you could take care of the frog for him until he's a little older?"

Joe shambled closer and poked a dirty-nailed finger at his infant cousin. "He sleeps too much, him."

"He's supposed to," Julien said, keeping a sharp eye on his youngest brother, new son, and the disgruntled tree frog in a box, all the while trying to participate in three conversations at once. "Gimme that box, T-Joe."

A brief wrestling match followed, which Julien won, and in the course of it Bobby escaped Nonc George to sit down at the foot of Dulcie's bed.

"So small," he said, touching Sammy's face with a gentle finger, and she wondered at the almost wistful tone of his voice.

"He won't stay that way for long," she sighed. "Want to hold him?"

"I was wondering when you'd ask. I didn't want to fight with the family, but even that grubby brat Joe got to hold him before me."

Dulcie grinned, carefully placing Sammy in Bobby's arms. "Hey, you look good holding a kid. You should think about having one or two of your own."

He glanced up briefly, then focused his attention on stroking Sammy's wild mop of hair. Dulcie still found it awkward talking this way with Bobby. She didn't think he still seriously carried a torch for her, but it felt strange all the same.

"May think about it, darlin'," Bobby answered softly. "But only if I can find a woman as fine as you."

"There's a gazillion women out there, Bobby. You'll find the perfect girl someday soon. Hopefully, one who won't let you walk out the front door looking like that."

He grinned, dispelling the faint awkwardness, and jiggled Sammy against his neon orange T-shirt. "My personal style. I won't change for anyone."

"A pity," Dulcie said with a laugh. "You're just going to have to find a woman as tacky as you are."

"Hey!" Bobby protested loudly. "Julien, your wife just called me tacky."

"Don' worry," Julien said, hoisting his son from Bobby's hands. "We'll put up with you just the way you are."

Dulcie felt her tears brimming as Julien cradled Sammy in the crook of his arm. "Damn," she muttered. "I'm going to start blubbering again."

Bobby leaned back on her bed. "Go for it. We don't mind. You've been crying ever since you got married."

She smiled, remembering. She and Julien had gotten married in a quiet civil ceremony, but the reception that followed at the Langlois farm had been anything but quiet.

She'd never seen so much food, never imagined that so many people crammed into such a small space could have so much fun. The band was made up of local Cajun musicians, and Julien himself had joined in. Every time he'd played his fiddle, she'd cried. Bobby was right about that much; he just didn't understand why.

Nor did Bobby know she'd sniffled at every wedding Julien had played at since—all twelve of them.

"Brides always cry at their weddings," she said.

"I bet you cried all the way to the bank, afterward. How much money did you have pinned on that veil of yours, anyway?"

Dulcie laughed and watched as Sammy was passed to yet another pair of arms, this time to Grandpa Joe. Going with an old Cajun bridal custom, she'd worn a long white veil and male guests had 'bought' a dance with her by pinning a dollar— or sometimes a larger bill, depending on how much whiskey he'd had—to the veil. "That's one Cajun custom I like," she admitted.

"I bet," Bobby drawled. "You being six feet tall and all, I reckon a long veil must've been a real advantage. You'd bring in a lot more than some little five-foot bride.''

"At least thirty dollars of it was yours," she retorted with good humor. "That last time, you pinned a twenty on me, then walked all over my toes. You were boshed, Bobby Halloran."

"Nonc George's fault. That mash should be illegal."

"It probably is. Glad you didn't tell him you were a cop."

"Glad there are times I can forget I am one. Those looks Julien's giving me mean that I'd better get off your bed." Bobby grinned as he came to his feet, then carefully eluded Annie and joined Alex and Nonc George in their hot debate over local politicians.

Julien, having appropriated his son once again, placed the sleeping baby in Dulcie's arms. She sighed as he sat down on the bed beside her. "This is one laid-back kid."

"In this family, he'll need to be." Julien swung his legs up on the bed, boots and all, and settled beside her. "Wouldn't mind a nap myself. Nobody told me you'd be in labor for thirty hours."

"Poor Julien," she murmured. "How do you think I felt?"

He laughed. "I know how you felt. You told me often enough."

A blush warmed her face. "Women in labor say all sorts of things they don't really mean."

"Thank God. You were pretty graphic 'bout certain parts of my body."

"You look real scared, Julien."

He kissed her, as if they were all alone. A passionate, full-tongued, possessive kiss. Somebody whooped, somebody else clapped. Dulcie ducked her head, embarrassed.

"Welcome to our crazy life," she whispered against Sammy's soft skin. "You'll love it, *cher*. Let Mommy tell you a little secret: I wouldn't have it any other way."

She met Julien's dark eyes over the top of their son's head.

"Damn straight," he said softly.

Dear Reader,

Next month, there are so many exciting books coming from Avon romance that I wish I had two or three pages to talk about them all! But I only get one page, so I'll get right to it.

October's Avon Romantic Treasure is *A Rake's Vow*, the next in Stephanie Laurens' scintillating series about the wickedly handsome Cynster family. Vane Cynster has vowed to never marry, no matter that his cousin Devil has just tied the knot. But once he meets the very tempting, delectable Patience Debbington he decides that some vows are meant to be broken.

Kathleen Harrington's *Enchanted by You* is for anyone—like me—who loves a sexy Scottish hero! When dashing Lyon MacLyon is saved by Julie Elkheart he can't help but tell her how much he wants her—in Gaelic. But pretty Julie understands every scandalous word of love that this sexy lord says...

What if you could shed your past and take another's identity? In Linda O'Brien's *Promised to a Stranger* Maddie Beecher does just that, and discovers she's "engaged" to a man she's never met. Trouble is, she falls hard...for her "fiancé's" brother—enigmatic Blaine Knight. And when Maddie's past catches up with her, she must decide if she should tell Blaine the whole truth.

And if you're looking for a sexy hero to sweep you off your feet—and fix your life—then don't miss Elizabeth Bevarly's delicious Contemporary romance *My Man Pendleton*. When a madcap heiress runs off to Florida, her rich father sends Pendleton after her...but he never thinks his wayward daughter will fall in love.

Until next month, enjoy!

Lucia Macro

Lucia Macro

Senior Editor

AEL 0998